GHOSTLY LIGHT

GHOSTLY LIGHT

BRENDA HURLEY

Copyright © 2023 Brenda Hurley

The moral right of the author has been asserted.

Apart from any fair dealing for the purposes of research or private study, or criticism or review, as permitted under the Copyright, Designs and Patents Act 1988, this publication may only be reproduced, stored or transmitted, in any form or by any means, with the prior permission in writing of the publishers, or in the case of reprographic reproduction in accordance with the terms of licences issued by the Copyright Licensing Agency. Enquiries concerning reproduction outside those terms should be sent to the publishers.

This is a work of fiction. Names, characters, businesses, places, events and incidents are either the products of the author's imagination or used in a fictitious manner. Any resemblance to actual persons, living or dead, or actual events is purely coincidental.

Troubador Publishing Ltd
Unit E2 Airfield Business Park,
Harrison Road, Market Harborough,
Leicestershire LE16 7UL
Tel: 0116 279 2299
Email: books@troubador.co.uk
Web: www.troubador.co.uk/matador

ISBN 978 1 80514 172 3

British Library Cataloguing in Publication Data.
A catalogue record for this book is available from the British Library.

Printed and bound in Great Britain by 4edge Limited
Typeset in 12pt Adobe Jenson Pro by Troubador Publishing Ltd, Leicester, UK

Matador is an imprint of Troubador Publishing Ltd

This book is dedicated to my family.

1

SEPTEMBER 1973

Debs felt her blood run cold that Sunday, when she read about Mike and Katie dying in such strange circumstances in North Yorkshire. The feeling she might have expected at the news of Mike's death had not materialised. She had wished it many times over, but instead of revenge and triumph, she felt a sense of loss. A coldness that was heavy, brutal even, lay in her breast.

Wearily, she trudged back to her bedsit, memories whirling, swimming up from the depths where she had hidden them from herself for the last year. Now, she had nowhere to hide. Mike, perhaps, had deserved his comeuppance, but Katie…?

The key grated as she turned it in the lock. It needed oiling; it needed a little bit of TLC like the rest of the house. She opened the door to a dingy porch and the stairs that led to her shabby bedsit.

The magnolia paint had turned yellow with age and there were ugly black marks where the vacuum cleaner had knocked up against the paintwork. She sighed unhappily; so much needed smartening up, but Mrs Green wasn't for spending her rent revenue. Lord, how Debs hated these thirteen steps and the carpet with the clips holding down this threadbare runner.

The radio was on in her landlady's room. She heard it playing softly as she slipped past the doorway, trying to avoid getting engaged in conversation. Conversations with her landlady were generally composed of nosy questions. She counted the steps one by one, until on the top landing, she faced her door, dreading to unlock it and greet the emptiness within. With no choice, she turned the key and pushed it open to the memories she was now carrying. The clothes horse, with her 'smalls' as her mother would have said, was erected near the electric fire. Not that she needed the fire on. It had been a peculiar kind of day, warm and sunny, but the afternoon had become muggy and threatening. Too warm for September and that was a fact.

She imagined his jacket, and her black dress drying on the clothes horse in front of the fire. She looked over to her bed, and imagined herself sitting there, tending to her weeping heels, the night Mike had abused her. Her new shoes had bitten into her flesh, and the blisters had burst. She remembered the pain. Physical pain was only part of the memory; the emotional pain he caused her had been far, far worse.

Her stomach twisted now at the thought of how much she had wanted him. He had been her secret love, and, in her desire, she had allowed herself to become a plaything, an object to him. She had been something he could use and discard.

The power of the hatred that she felt in the aftermath of his attack had fed her to tell anyone who would listen what sort of a man he was. Now, she had to admit that she hadn't been a hundred percent truthful in her account. She had given herself freely to him in the bedroom in Katie's home, and the promise of more lovemaking had been an unspoken understanding between them when they had left to go to her bedsit. Any sensitivities he had displayed earlier in the evening had dissolved with his intake of drink and his demand for sexual favours became unreasonable. She still felt anger at his act of pinging her bra while she was tending her heels. He had no sensitivity for her vulnerability and that had been especially hurtful, as she tried to protect her bare breasts from him.

Now, a lone tear ran down her face. Angrily, she pushed it away with the back of her hand. The memory stung her heart.

Mike had deserved to get the sack for shattering her dreams. She swallowed away the lump in her throat. She had wanted to hurt him. The sound of her hands clapping when he left work in disgrace had reverberated in the silence. The rest of the staff had stood like statues, witnessing his walk of shame.

That should have been the end of it, but she hadn't been able to let it rest. Katie had not thrown Mike out like she had expected, but had allowed him to stay as her lodger. It wasn't right. Debs had wanted Katie to punish him, as well.

Every day that Katie came into work, Debs felt let down. Katie was a constant reminder of how Mike had betrayed her trust, and that hurt niggled, like woodworm burying itself into a beautiful piece of furniture, damaging it beyond repair. As the weeks went on, Debs felt less confident in herself. The full force of her hurt and anger turned on Katie. If she was going to be plagued by that fateful night, then Katie should be too. That was the way she had seen it, but now...

A new image presented itself. It was of herself and Mike creeping down the stairs from his bedroom. They had disturbed Katie with the noise of their love-making. How they had giggled; it had all seemed such fun. Katie had been in the kitchen and the radio was on full volume as they left. Katie had probably never heard them leave. Up to that point, the evening had been very special; she had been wined and dined and made love to. She had not wanted it to end, but once out in the night, even nature seemed against her. The starlight and moon had been hidden behind a body of clouds, and there was that feeling of damp in the air which threatened imminent rain. Despite that, Mike had insisted on calling at the off licence to buy whiskey.

The promise of a taxi had disappeared like the stars. He had said they were only a couple of streets away from her flat and the walk would do them good. When the drizzle started, it dampened her spirit, and with it her happiness was washed away.

She remembered her coat being wet to the lining, and her beautiful new shoes – shoes that were meant to be seen rather than walked in – had bruised and blistered her feet.

With the memory, another tear slid down her face.

She had shouted at him to get out, waking Mrs Green, who was a light sleeper. She had come to her door to see what the noise was all about, and had interrupted his unwanted advances. Mike had left literally under a cloud and in the rain.

Debs blushed at the thought of the fight with Katie the day she left the Echo. She had painted a picture of herself as an abused victim, but Katie had been forthright, telling the office that she had heard Mike and Debs having sex that Friday night and that it had been consensual.

She shook her head at the memory. Another tear escaped.

Over the last year, the sympathy she had had at the Echo had waned; people had their own problems to deal with, and her scandal was yesterday's news. She really needed to move on, but she had no idea where to go.

Her family didn't want her or, rather, her mother didn't. She had never felt totally loved. She wondered if her mother could love at all? She had often wondered why her father had left when she was fourteen. According to her mother, he had gone abroad to work, but she had never seen him again and she had missed him dreadfully.

When she had met Carl at fifteen, he had fulfilled every longing. He was seemingly so right to love, but that was another hurt, another rejection she had to face. And with it, came the greatest loss of all. She could still feel her baby girl's hand holding tightly onto her little finger, and the deep blue eyes that were not ready to see her mother's face yet. The discovery of a deep maternal feeling overcame her as she held her newborn child in the mother and baby home. One minute she was in her arms. Then she was gone. Debs had been a child, but a mother, nevertheless.

A deep void seemed to grow in her chest. She would never get over it, Annie would be all grown up now: eighteen, a woman. She hoped her daughter hadn't made the same mistakes that she had, loved too soon, had her trust betrayed. Wistfully, she thought if she could only go back in time, she would not allow herself to be bullied by her mother or the

Church. What in hell's name did they know about love? A baby at fifteen was a disgrace but Annie was her mother's grandchild. Her mother had abandoned them both.

Tears came freely as they always did when she was hurting. The past came hurling back to haunt her. She sobbed as she tried to push that chapter of her life away. When the tears stopped, feeling even more drained than she had been, she tidied the kitchen and made a cup of tea. She had read the article twice already but now, deep in thought, she reached for the newspaper once again, unable to put the awfulness of the news to one side. Katie and Mike had died together in a graveyard; their new start had ended in their deaths. She had seen a news clip on the television. The church where it happened had been the backdrop for the presenter and the snippet had caught her imagination. The church looked old; she could see that. The building was solid, rooted to the town's history. A faint smile hinted at her mouth. 'Safe, and old fashioned'. A yearning passed through her. She wanted to feel safe, to find somewhere she could root down in, get away from her past.

She had no real reason to stay around here. She was unhappy at work, and she positively hated living in this dreadful room. Who was it that had said it was much cheaper working and living in the North? She remembered that it was Janet, Katie's friend, who had moved to Leeds to work at another paper. How she envied her. Janet had shown the courage Debs wanted to find in herself, to start a new life away from here and shed her bad memories. Her money would go further there on rent and food. She suddenly had a fancy to take a trip to the North. She had her annual holiday still to come and she hadn't booked anywhere because she had nowhere to go. Now, perhaps, she had.

She came back to the moment, hearing the radio playing downstairs the same tune as the one that was playing when she and Mike let themselves out of Katie's home. She looked at the old, tired wallpaper on the walls and the threadbare carpet. It made her feel old, too; tired, and unhappy.

It was time to rethink her life and take charge of it. It couldn't be worse than this and it would possibly be a lot better.

She moved to the clothes horse, testing her clothes to see if they were dry.

As she gathered and folded her smalls, another thought struck her. It was strange he was called Louis Parker, and she wondered if he had changed his name because of her.

Had he, too, needed to close the past down? Perhaps she could do with a new name… the idea was left hanging in the air.

When she woke on Monday morning, although she didn't have the details, she knew she was ready for a new direction in her life. Instead of getting up and fearing the day, she found herself humming her favourite tune as she made her breakfast. The radio was on below; the news seeped into her room through the thin soundproofing of her floor. Mrs Green would have a new tenant to wake with that noise instead of her, soon. Debs' heart leaped with joy.

She pushed the door open to the office with new zest and reached her desk with a spring in her step. Settling down to work, it was her intention to use her lunch hour to find out exactly where Ravensend was, and if the National Bus Company had a station near it. A train journey was too expensive.

She telephoned the Yorkshire Tourist Board. (It was against the company rules, but what the heck? You only live once, and she had no phone at her bedsit.) A very nice man said he would send her details of B&Bs in the area and a bus timetable to her home address. As she put the receiver on the cradle, a feeling of satisfaction flooded through her body. She had made a start to realise her new dream. She would use her holiday time to look at North Yorkshire.

Time for a coffee. She made her way to the bay. She remembered that this was where Mike had invited her out, over a year ago now. Her mood changed at the thought. He had been just another man that had cheated her, abused her trust. Now he was dead.

'Are you alright?'

The question was so sudden, it nearly made her jump out of her skin. Charlotte was standing behind her with a concerned look on her face.

'Oh! I didn't hear you come up. I was miles away, thinking about Mike and Katie.' Debs' voice dropped to a whisper; her voice throbbed with emotion. 'They're dead! Did you know?'

A flash of distress crossed Charlotte's face.

'Yes.' She nodded over her shoulder to Mac, who was at his desk. 'We saw it on the telly. I can't quite believe it. We saw them just before they moved; they were so happy.'

Charlotte looked sheepish. 'Sorry, Debs. I know things didn't work out for you.' Then she said, almost to herself, 'I wonder if Janet knows?'

'It was in all the Sunday papers; she's bound to know,' Debs observed.

'I ought to write to her. She'll be devastated.' There was a hint of distress in Charlotte's voice.

The emotion passed from woman to woman, and it overtook them. Before they realised it, they were comforting each other with a hug.

Mac, who happened to look over at that moment, was astounded at what he saw. They had never got on, Charlotte didn't even like the woman, not after the way Debs had treated Katie. And that went for him too.

Debs dropped her voice again. 'When do you think the funeral will be?' She paused, 'And where?'

'You can't be planning to go?'

'Well, no. But someone ought to go from the Echo, don't you think?'

'To Katie's certainly, but where will Mike's be? Or should I say Louis'?'

'Yes. Do you know why he had changed his name in the north?'

'I can't say I did, but I have to say he was a changed man the last time we saw them. Mike wasn't the Mike we knew here. He was so different that even Mac noticed. He actually helped to make the tea. Can you imagine Mike willingly working in a kitchen?' Charlotte waited for a response. None came.

'Perhaps he just stopped drinking and his true personality came out. And perhaps with a new name, he felt a new man.'

'Well,' agreed Debs, 'that's one explanation and maybe it's true.'

The clock on the wall, read one o'clock. Lunchtime was over. Time to get back to work, but before Debs made her way to her desk, she called into the accounts office to book her overdue two-week holiday. She had until April next year to take her break and March seemed good: the end of winter and the start of spring. And besides, money was always a little short; March would give her time to put a few more pounds together so she didn't need to scrimp.

Back at her desk, she crossed out the last two weeks of March 1974 on her work schedule, and a smile lit up her face. Spring was a new season, a signal perhaps of a new start, it was her first step to look outside the narrow world in which she found herself.

2

The smell of bacon woke Louis from his daydreams. He lay in the shadows, under the tree of life. Since entering his sanctuary, he hadn't thought once about the outside world. But now the aroma had called him back into the world beyond his and the cooking of food for breakfast. In his world, he had no need for food, but the aroma of bacon stirred his memory, and his stomach rumbled.

Since coming home to his kingdom on the other side of the headboard, he had not heard a sound, not a whisper, from the mortal side.

Now, he assumed, his cottage had new tenants.

He sat up, patting his dog who lay at his side. Champ yawned, opening one eye to acknowledge him, before settling back down when his master hadn't moved.

Louis was curious for the first time since being catapulted back to his paradise beyond the bed.

It wouldn't hurt to take a peek.

Ordering Champ to stay, he pushed himself up from the grassy bank and walked towards the other world beyond the wooden veil.

Pressing his spiritual body against the invisible doorway, he listened. No sound came from beyond his world. He moved slowly, pushing his face through the carving, to see into the room. It would be a shock if someone on that side had second sight and saw him.

What he saw had him scratching his head in surprise. Some of his carved pieces were here together in this back bedroom that he knew so well. But he wasn't in his bedroom at the cottage; his bed had been moved to this room at The Royal Oak. This was the room that Katie and he had slept in after they had moved out of the Avondale Hotel.

Time had passed, but how much he wondered? His kingdom held no calendars, and there were no such things as clocks; none were needed. Time in the nether world was irrelevant.

And now he was here in the Royal Oak again, an uninvited guest, with Katie behind the veil of wood in their nether world. He gave a grateful sigh for every moment he had spent with Katie. She was his soulmate, willing as she had been to come north and start a new life for him. She had even refused passing over into the heavenly light, so she could be with him in spirit.

Doris, the landlady of the Royal Oak, must have bought the bed. She had a love of exceptional carving, and she had admired the bed from the moment she laid eyes on it, the day he had moved into the cottage at Ravensend.

Her sharp eyes had recognised the craftmanship when the bed was being unpacked and stacked against the wall of his cottage bedroom, back in place, finally; back to where it had first stood in 1820. Now, it would seem that his bed had moved again, and he approved.

Doris had remarked to him, 'the same hand might have worked the rocking chair and carved box.' She was, of course, right. But she had never suspected that his were the clever hands that had fashioned them.

She had been the keeper of the carved toolbox that held his original tools, wrapped in sacking. She had used it as a coffee table in her snug; that, and the rocking chair he had made for his father, were her special pieces, her heirlooms. They had been bought by her ancestors from his workshop, back in the nineteenth century. Now the three pieces were together again. It pleased him to know that Doris, his good friend, a warm-hearted and determined lady, owned them. They would be well looked after by her.

He closed his eyes again, letting the smell of bacon melt with memories in his past and recent history.

Doris must be downstairs; seeing to breakfasts for her guests, he supposed. A smile crossed his face while he drifted in old dreams.

Everything that surrounded him was in balance again; his works of art were all together. It was time to retreat into his world, back to the peace and quiet that ruled the sanctuary.

The partly hidden cottage that lay nestling under the hills was where he and Katie lodged. Their sanctuary in the meadow was well away from the opening to the mortal world.

Katie was quite surprised when Louis told her that their bed was now installed in Doris' small hotel.

'She always did have an eye for quality. How do you feel about different guests sleeping in our bed?'

'Katie, my darling girl, as long as you are here with me, I care not a jot. As long as we have the kingdom, we don't need the bed. Let Doris put into it whom she pleases.' Judging by the love in his eyes, as he said those words, she knew he meant it. She put her arms around him and, stretching up on tip toe, kissed him. He was the kindest man she had ever known; death hadn't separated them or their love. Now that they both were in spirit, they were as solid as mortals.

The sun was warm on her face. The dappled light pushed through the branches of the tree of life, filtering through leaves that rustled over her head. Louis was holding her as though he never wanted to let her go. She half expected Champ to push his way between them, as he often did, to share the affection. He had wandered off towards the stream, bounding along, chasing dragonflies and birds.

She hoped they would keep him busy for a little time; she was enjoying those little thrills that were racing down her spine. Louis' lips were caressing her neck and her whole body was responding to his touch. She shut her eyes and allowed herself to float on her emotions.

Louis lifted Katie off her feet and laid her gently on the ground. Like a cushion might, the mossy grass took their weight. It was soft and smelled of clover and fresh grass. As he lay beside her, he had her head in the crook of his arm. Katie gazed back up into his face. She could see he wanted her as much as she needed him.

'I love you, my darling girl. How did we get so lucky as to find each other? Was it ordained by the angels? Massie always believed…'

Katie reached up and, holding his face close to hers, said, 'Stop talking. Kiss me.'

Later, much later, Champ joined them, wet-nosed, wet-furred, and muddy-footed.

'He's been the stream again,' moaned Louis, when Champ, on cue, decided to shake himself dry. The spray of water gave the couple a good wetting.

'Get away, you mad animal.'

In total obedience, Champ moved away and flopped to the ground, his head between his paws, his large eyes pleading innocence and his pink tongue wiping his whiskers dry.

'Look how he loves you,' laughed Katie.

'He's got a funny way of showing it,' retorted a smiling Louis, wiping the moisture off his face with the bottom edge of his shirt before he tucked it back where it belonged.

He lay back. The trunk of the tree supported him and, as he pulled Katie towards him, he whispered, 'His timing was about right' – he squeezed her – 'don't you think?' and with a twinkle in his eye, said, 'Thank you.'

Dog, man and girl closed their eyes and drifted in tune with the kingdom.

Louis was disturbed by the tiny yelps coming from Champ, who had somehow, as he dozed, managed to crawl up beside him. Champ's body twitched in between the small barks.

'Chasing birds, are you? Or is it dragonflies? So, it's alright for you to dream, is it?' – Louis chuckled and winked at Katie – 'But not us.'

Champ cocked an ear at Louis' voice. Louis tugged gently on it, and a large brown eye opened in response.

'You'll never catch them, you know.'

Champ was on his feet, his tail wagging twenty to the dozen, his wet tongue sliding up Louis' face and his body pressing its weight against his master.

'Okay, okay, that's enough.'

Content with the greeting he had given Louis, the dog then tried to get in between the couple, trying to push Katie to one side, but she pushed back.

'Come on then, you silly mutt.' She allowed him just enough space, without being separated from Louis.

Louis sat forward, his knees bent to his chest and his arms resting on them. His eyes searched the horizon, admiring the vista. He sometimes forgot just how lovely it was. His hills seemed greener today, though how they could be was beyond his reason. Perhaps he was more receptive to beauty after making love to Katie?

A small dark speck in the sky caught his eye. He watched as it grew, until a large bird appeared with a huge wingspan.

'Louis,' cried Katie, grabbing his arm and pointing at the bird, excitement in her voice. 'It's a red kite.'

The bird made lazy circles in the blue sky, as if performing a dance, gliding lightly on the thermals. It was majestic in the air.

'I've never seen one of those here,' she said, looking at Louis, waiting for him to respond. He looked puzzled, shrugging his shoulders as though to confirm her words; he too wondered where it had come from. He had never carved birds on the headboard. Katie had brought them with her imagination.

Katie sat beside him. 'Did you call it to your kingdom?'

He had to be honest and say, 'No.'

How had it appeared in his sky if she had not thought of it?

He stood up, shielding his eyes from the sun. It was magnificent; he could almost feel the strength in its wings as it came nearer. It glided until it was overhead. The bird swooped low, taking a closer view of the grasses that were moving gently in the breeze. It came three times, searching with the bright beads of its eyes before turning tail and flying back up into the blue. Obviously disappointed at the failure to find food, it circled once more, before moving off to where it came from. Once again, it was only a dark speck in the sky and it disappeared over the hills and was lost from view. The couple looked at each other. Louis raised an eyebrow.

It had been a day of surprises.

One he could explain, but the bird…

The only explanation Louis could come up with was that Sophia, his previous wife, must have brought it in when she broke into their kingdom. But her interests had been planting and growing flowers, especially roses. He had never known her to have an interest in birds. Sophia, with her jealous heart, had haunted as a ghost from one century to the next, but now was gone.

'Do you think that Sophia had visitors when she came here?'

Katie didn't answer, but the look on her face confirmed his worry.

It was only half a question; he had had visitors by connecting to their souls. He could see no reason why Sophia could not have had the same power, but whom would she have connected to?

He shuddered. Could evil have rested here? Surely not. He shook off the cold shiver that slipped down his back, and hoped it was only his anxiety.

Reaching out, he took Katie's hand; he was suddenly worried about this place, his sanctuary.

3

By the time Debs had reached the bus station, she was wondering if she had made the right decision.

She had had to get up early to get a train into London. She was carrying a heavy case, filled with what she considered to be her winter clothes. She was, after all, going north, and it was March. But now she wondered if she had packed too much. She could have made fewer clothes last the holiday.

More than that, she was worried. The impulse to go north… that had been so strong. It had been, in part, a need to convince herself that she wasn't in any way to blame for the deaths of her colleagues. However illogical it was, she had come to believe they had gone north because she had had them sacked from the Echo. She feared that the one night when she thought love had come calling had been a catalyst for all that had happened. Nevertheless, she was also curious to see where they had gone to live, and that too needed to be satisfied in her, though she had no idea why.

There were a dozen single decker coaches, some with their engines idling. Their drivers stood around, taking a few minutes break to chat and share a smoke before settling in the cabs.

The bus station was a noisy place, smelling of petrol and diesel. Oil spills on the concrete, marked the bays. Some still looked sticky; she must avoid them. She lumbered along the pavement, dragging her case that had taken on a leaden weight, her eyes taking in the destinations on the front of the coaches above the driver's cab, until one announced 'York' at the front. This was hers.

She dropped her burden with relief. York was where she had to change, before reaching her final destination, but for now, it was one step at a time. She turned to a man who stood by the doorway. At her smile, he came up to her.

'Are you going to York, love? Can I see your ticket, please?' It was all in order. Tearing off his part, he handed hers back before he placed her suitcase in the hold, in the belly of the vehicle. Smiling, he invited her to the three steps that led up to her seat and the start of her holiday adventure.

She had thought the bus station was noisy but was taken aback by the loud chatter coming from a cluster of women in the middle of the coach. She walked up the narrow aisle, her eyes scanning the seat numbers. There was only one seat empty, it was by the window and right in the middle of the throng of the lively group, who all seemed to know each other.

'Excuse me,'

'Why, what you done?' came back from a young blonde with a northern accent. It would seem the comment was funny, judging by the chorus of laughter from the group.

'Never mind them, love,' said the woman who was blocking her passage to the window seat. She struggled to get up from the seat, but once on her feet she pushed her friends down the bus to let Debs through. 'You settle yourself down, love; we'll be off as soon as Carl has his last fag.'

'Carl?'

That was a name that brought back memories. A frown crossed her face.

'The driver, love, he brought us down for our weekend outing. We got to know him quite well.' Then she giggled. 'We've had a bit of a knees-up, left the old men at home. Sal's getting married in three weeks.' She nodded to the blonde. 'Her last fling.' She winked at Debs.

The giggles and hugging were interspersed with choruses from *Joseph*, the new Lloyd Webber musical.

Happiness and good humour spilled over and most of the other passengers had smiles on their faces and tapped in time with the singing.

At the precise minute on the timetable, Carl climbed aboard and closed the door; the coach pulled away from its bay and headed out. The bus was comfortable, but the going was rather slow as it tried to navigate the urban sprawl. The shops they passed all looked rather glamorous to Debs, with bright colours and patterns on the frocks that the mannequins wore. They were so unlike her own clothes, purchased from the mail order catalogue. She couldn't see the prices but knew just by looking they were out of her league.

The ladies were still reliving their Saturday night on this Sunday morning. The woman who sat next to Debs was going home to Leeds. She worked with the others as machinists in a small factory. She introduced herself as Pat, and for the first hour she never stopped talking. She still lived with her mother. They had a couple of poodles that were important to her. Pat talked about them as though they were her children. At one point, she grabbed her handbag from her feet, and after a search, found a wallet from where she pulled out a whole bunch of photos of her 'babies': Tom and Jerry. She laughed – they were just as funny as the cartoon; it was her joke. The photos were well worn, ear-marked and a little grubby from her loving fingers.

She told Debs about *Joseph*.

'Eee, he were a grand young man and a good singer' – she nudged Debs lightly on the arm – 'the one that played Joseph, like. And the pharaoh, who looked like 'Elvis'; he was a bit of a dish, too.'

The memory of it glowed on her face and Debs felt rather envious. She had never been to a London theatre. How was it, when you lived near to local entertainment, you never found time or the money to visit them?

Debs half appreciated the friendly manner from Pat but without really understanding it; she felt the cultural difference of north and south. Pat didn't understand personal space. Debs would have kept herself to herself, whereas this woman, she felt, could lay everything in her life bare, from personal things to politics.

Was she meant to reciprocate or just listen?

Soon they had left the city behind and once they were on the M1, Debs was happy gazing out of the window at the countryside she had never seen before. The motion of the bus was hypnotic, and miles were being eaten away. The troupe of women had gradually fallen silent, along with Debs' neighbour. Her eyes were closed; she was nodding.

Last night had finally caught up with them, Debs supposed.

She felt she might do the same; her eyelids felt heavy. The morning had been frantic – she had been up since six am – but she was here now, traveling towards...

Panic knotted in her stomach. Suddenly the excitement of the day before, when she had finally closed the lid of her case, locked it, and put the key safely in her purse pocket, was waning. Her thoughts tumbled. That internal torment she knew so well was starting to niggle again. Would it never let her go free?

Carl. The name had made her heart jump. With it came shame and it took her back in time. She felt ridiculous, like a child again. Eighteen years had passed since she bore the hurt that nearly killed her. She never wanted to feel that way again. Only, she couldn't hide it from herself. The stain was always there. The stain of her stupidity, her naivete, her broken heart. It was there to haunt her.

When she joined the Echo at twenty, she had locked away her previous life. If anyone asked about her background, she shut them down, closed them out. She didn't trust men, while secretly she longed to find a man she could love.

Mike was the man the women in the company called a piece of beefcake, an Americanism. He looked like an athlete, a man's man, very handsome with his Irish/Italian blood mix.

He flirted with them all but he had never really seemed to notice her. And then, out of the blue, he had invited her out. She had let her guard down and look where that had got her. He had been no better than Carl.

She couldn't doze now. She was irritated with herself for all the feelings she couldn't control. Carl. Her eyes filled with tears and distorted the view of the landscape through the window. She wiped them away quickly in case Pat saw them. Some things you couldn't share with anyone.

Bitterness was pumping through her veins. Why was she thinking of him? He had abandoned her, destroyed her relationship with her family and had never even seen Annie, their daughter.

Control, she had to get back her control.

4

The sighting of the red kite wouldn't leave his mind. He and Katie had watched its magnificent flight over the meadow, effortlessly gliding toward the distant hills. His hills. Hills that he had never sought to visit, simply because when he had carved the headboard, his kingdom ended with those hills. To his mind, there had been nothing beyond them, nothing to see and now that had all changed. The bird had disappeared. Louis couldn't pretend to understand where it had travelled to, but he knew he would have to go and seek the puzzle out.

He felt, in his soul, that Sophia had influenced his kingdom while she had lived in it. He had no idea how long she had used his world, but felt in his heart of hearts, that she had tainted his world with the evil intentions that she had towards Katie and himself. He was settled on walking into the hills alone. He had no intention of putting Katie in harm's way, not knowing what he would find at the end of his quest. The image of Sophia being devoured by a demon that she called for came rushing back to him.

The memory of it brought another image. Next to Katie, the body of Mike was sprawled out, having released Louis' spirit from it. After more than a year of enjoying a mortal life with his darling girl, he was a ghost again. He would never forget the pain of seeing Katie dead, with roses around her head. She had brought the flowers to put on his father's grave, but instead, they surrounded her. He shuddered at the thought, but then smiled, his wonderful girl had been waiting for him in spirit, in his own blessed kingdom. They were together again, joined by their love.

It was time for him to seize the day and go for what might be a very long walk. There was no time like the present. Katie was nowhere about. He wouldn't bother her by searching for her; it would be better to go initially by himself.

She was probably down by the stream. It was her custom to visit it each day; she said the water played like music to her. His world was beautiful, restful, but the only sounds the kingdom heard was that of their voices – and Champ, of course. Movement and sound were stimulation; Katie understood that.

Champ had been curled up, asleep at Louis' feet, but when his master stood up and moved up the track, he was beside him, matching his four legs with the stride of two.

'There's no show without Punch, is there, boy? Okay, you win, come along.'

The track was flat, if a little stony. Walking it with purpose was strange to him. He had only used it to walk to the cottage; now, he barely noticed his meadow and the movement of the grasses that whispered as he passed. His eyes were on the horizon, and the unknown that he was going to meet. The white cottage stood like a sentry: solid, erect. It was the place that he had regarded as almost at the end of his world, but now he knew better. He followed the water course. The stream was his guide now. It came down from the hills and he walked up towards them. He followed the twists and the curves, liking the sounds of the stream, as it made its running over the pebbles and rushing against the rocks. It was like listening to fairy music: a lullaby of nature, the tinkling of its notes of love, kissing the air.

For the first time, Louis wondered where the source of the stream began. It had been in the plan of his vision when he carved the bed. He had accepted it as his, but not now. What he had thought was an empty kingdom, he now knew had never been empty. Nature had been all around him. In his grief and loneliness and his feeling of entrapment in his nether world, he hadn't looked beyond his nose. That was all in the past, but as he strode out up that stony track, he couldn't believe how poor his judgement had been. He was starting to feel excitement at this adventure, in a nervy sort of way. What would he find?

Louis walked to meet the tree line. All those different trees that made his life complete were growing there. Each had its own distinguishing shape and individual leaves, and the barks were so different. Why had he not come this way before? He had no answer. He had tools, and he had the time. The wood spoke to him; he felt he was with friends, surrounded by a wealth of natural beauty. Spirits in the wood were waiting for him to release them. He would come back soon and take his pick, but they would have wait until he found out what was beyond the horizon. He touched the bark of the nearest tree and his hands connected to its soul; he could feel the heartbeat of the tree speaking to him, and it raised his spirit.

'Thank you,' he mouthed, before moving back up the track.

Champ was no longer at Louis' side; the trees were a great distraction for him. Dashing around the trees, sensing and being led by scent on the ground, playing games that only a dog could play. A roe buck suddenly dashed across the track, surprising Louis, and stopping him mid stride. Not so Champ who was following hard on the animal's heels. They were out of sight before Louis drew breath, having registered what had happened. Puzzled Louis had to decide: did he march on or try to find the path that Champ taken? And what was a roebuck doing in his hills?

It was a gut feeling that made him leave the track, moving as speedily as he could among the trees, calling Champ as he went. A distant yap was the only clue that told him he was going the right way.

The ground was rough under his feet. Tree roots and tufts of wiry grass seemed to be waiting booby-traps, ready to catch his feet and unearth him. Regardless, he moved quickly towards the distant sound he could hear ahead. The trees were tightly packed together, and the land rose sharply, so much so that he was labouring as he climbed up the slope.

At last, he broke free from the trees and was surprised to see a bleak moorland stretching out to a golden glow horizon. Two worlds touched each other, with a large wide sky of pale blue. In the sky, not one, but three red kites circled, making patterns as they rested on the thermals. It was breath-taking. The land looked wild, rough and untamed. Louis could see that the deer, looking no more than a tiny dot in the distance, was darting across the moor alone. There was no sign of Champ.

Surprise. Shock. A mystery engulfed him. What was this all about? It was a space he had never envisaged. The birds and the roebuck were visitors, but from who or where? Questions rotated in his mind; he needed some answers.

Louis started to move towards the vast space in front of him, but his feet felt like weighted lead and were fixed to the spot. He could go backwards but not forwards. He tried again, and again. Each time he attempted to move in the deer's direction, his upper body became unbalanced and awkward. He must have looked like a clown in a circus as he floundered on the spot. The land he had discovered flowed into a golden glow on the horizon, but it appeared he was banned from it. He felt that he was standing on the top of the world, but there was an invisible barrier that wasn't going to let him enter into it. The animals and birds had got into his kingdom, so he assumed there must be an opening somewhere. At that moment, he resolved to find it.

Now he had to find Champ. He turned back. Travelling downhill was almost as hazardous as going up, and there was still no sign of his naughty friend. He soon sighted the track that had led him here and heard the gurgle of the stream. He reminded himself he still had to find the source of the stream, and maybe the opening to the moorland was at its source. The red kite had found a way in and out; he must be able to find it. He was looking through the trees and into the distance. There was a lot of land to search, but not now. He picked up the pace to return to his meadow and hoped that Champ would find him on the way. As Louis walked past the cottage he could hear Katie was calling him. He had been gone some time and she must have missed him.

'Katie, I'm here.' He waved at her, and she responded by waving back.

He could see her under the tree, and, not quite believing his eyes, he saw that Champ was at her side.

How that rascal had got past him he didn't know. A few strides later, the three of them were united and relaxing in their familiar place together. Louis sat with Katie resting her head on his shoulder.

'Where have you been?'

'I walked up into the hills. I was curious to see where the red kite had come from.'

'What did you find?'

'To be truthful, I'm not sure. I saw three kite. All I can tell you is that there is a moorland beyond ours, and there's a little mystery going on. When I have the answer, I'll tell you.'

'A mystery?'

'Yes. Patience, Katie. Let's just say, I saw more than my own kingdom, but I'm not sure what I saw.'

Katie settled back onto the grasses. She trusted Louis. Patience was a not a new concept to her. She reached out for his hand and closed her eyes.

The leaves rustled overhead as a breeze wove itself through the branches over Katie's head. She had felt fidgety for some time now; she couldn't explain it and hadn't told Louis how she felt. She loved him, and this place was his own delightful design, though some of the ideas that had been brought to it had been hers. The sunlight that peeked through and dazzled her eyes reminded her of twinkling starlight, of black-blue night sky, filled with a variety of pinpricks of dazzling, reflected light. She was shocked as a powerful feeling of loss pushed through her like an ocean wave crashing against a sandy headland. She stretched out her arm in an upward movement to the light, as though she was trying to reach the sparkle and catch it in her hand.

Her empty hand reached out again, but this time to touch Louis who lay beside her. His eyes were closed to the dappled light. He looked asleep and contented and was being used as a pillow by Champ, his head on his master's thigh now he had been scolded and forgiven.

Katie sat up.

At her touch, Louis' eyes opened.

'What is it?'

'It's a silly thing, really, but as I lay there and looked through the leaves, I suddenly missed seeing the night sky and the stars. It's wonderful here; of course it is. But it's daylight all the time. I don't know why, but I miss the night.'

Louis frowned. What had brought this on? Champ stretched out, yawning as he did, then, as though he knew something was not quite right, went and sat next to Katie and offered a paw.

'Champ, you're wonderful,' she said, patting him, before he sprawled out and lay his head on her foot, his soulful eyes looking directly into hers.

'What does he know that I don't?' asked Louis, ruefully.

'Don't you ever feel sad?'

Louis cast his mind back to when he had first become a spirit in limbo. Anger and sadness had consumed him. He had been guilty of haunting, terrifying the mortals who had bought his bed, vowing that no one would sleep in it but himself. He had forgotten how trapped he had felt. It had never occurred it him that Katie could be less than happy here with him.

'You know, Katie, it's an easy problem to fix. All we have to do is to check if it's night on the other side of the veil. We can visit the Royal Oak in our favourite room, and you can see the stars at your leisure.'

Katie was delighted. She looked deeply into Louis' eyes; such love lay in them. He kissed his own fingertip and touched her lip with it, smiling.

'I love you, my darling girl.' His eyes were moist with emotion. He took her in his arms, nuzzling her hair, his arms growing tighter around her slim body, squeezing her with a growing passion.

'You, my love, are my star, the brightest there will ever be in my kingdom.'

'And you, Louis, are my whole. Without you, my soul would be destroyed. I would be in hell.'

5

Apart from a sad-looking ham sandwich which she had grabbed from a café at the bus station in York, Debs hadn't eaten for hours.

By the time the single-decker bus had dropped her at the town square in Ravensend, she had been traveling all day. She was weary and wanted nothing more than to settle in one spot.

The Royal Oak was in sight, and her spirit rose as she purposefully moved across the cobbled square toward the building where she would be staying for the next few days.

It was late afternoon. The weather had stayed fine, although she did feel a nip in the air; it was definitely colder here. She was pleased that she had foreseen the difference in the temperature and that her case was filled with warm clothes, even if it did weigh a ton.

The door opened on to the bar. It looked very old, with dark wood carrying a marble counter edged with brass, and a canopy where the glasses were stored, along with a few tankards that also looked old. A few regulars stopped talking and gave her an inquisitive glance as she came through the door. Not recognising this newcomer, they quickly returned to talking and drinking with their mates.

Fortunately, a large notice graced the bar with a pointer directing visitors to the lounge, restaurant, and reception. She put the weighty case down for a minute while she collected herself and took in her new surroundings. A balding man behind the bar greeted her.

'I'll get that case for you and take you through.'

His voice was nice, as was his smile. He showed her through a passage before it opened up into a small hall, from which a number of doors led off to various parts of the inn.

A small, dark-haired woman was stationed behind a desk in an alcove; she acknowledged the new arrival with a smile.

'Thank you, Barry. Can you pop back in a few minutes?'

He nodded, leaving the young woman and her property with his boss. Another sign over the desk indicated the lounge, restaurant and bedrooms.

Among the many smells that lingered in that space was the aroma of cooked chicken. Debs' tummy rumbled; hunger was starting to nag her. That ham sandwich for lunch had been eaten a long time ago.

'Can I help you?' invited Doris, smiling.

Putting her hunger to one side, Debs smiled and introduced herself.

'I've booked a few days here; my name is Deborah White.'

'Yes! Here you are,' said Doris, shifting some papers on the desk, finding the booking-in diary beneath them. 'Eight days, bed and breakfast?' She waited for confirmation.

Debs felt a little awkward; money having always been a bit tight she had decided not to commit to the evening meal. She planned to find a Co-op and buy a few bits to have in her room, but she couldn't tell that to this woman.

'That's right.'

'Lovely. My name is Doris. If there's anything we can do to make your stay with us better, just let me, Barry or Julia, my general help, know. If you decide to eat with us, we serve from seven pm in the restaurant and in the bar from six pm. It's a slightly reduced menu there, but home-cooked and delicious. Even I eat here.' She laughed at her own joke. 'Right, let's get you up to your room. I've put you in a pretty single that's at the back of the hotel; it's nice and quiet, well away from the bar. Breakfast is from seven am until ten am in the dining room.' She pointed towards the restaurant that was through the lounge.

Doris pinged the brass bell on her desk. It called Barry back from the bar. Doris gave him the key and he picked up Debs' case.

'Let me show you up.'

Obediently, she followed the nice Geordie up the staircase, listening to his lyrical voice as they climbed. He was telling her about some of the local places she might like to visit, but all she could see was the red carpet. It was thick, and she sank into the pile. It was new, by the looks of it, and the paintwork up the stairs was clean and smart, so different from those familiar steps up to her bedsit. It seemed to confirm to her that her life could be different, and she was going to enjoy being here.

As they left, Doris watched the two walk to the stairs. She sensed that all was not well with that young woman, but, dismissing the thought, turned back to continue her duties.

Debs' room at the Royal Oak was not only comfortable and bright, it was all the things that her own bedsit wasn't.

'I'll put your case on the small chest, shall I? You can unpack at your leisure, and if you have a mind for it, we serve tea in the lounge until four thirty.'

Barry didn't wait for an answer, but her gave her a genuine smile as he closed the door.

Debs felt disconcerted for the second time that day. She was wondering why she had really come north? At the same time, the thought of ever going back to Mrs Green's house and her bedsit filled her with dread.

Suddenly the thought of opening the door on her return to the Echo made her downcast; the people there were only acquaintances. Her colleagues had enjoyed the gossip and painful drama of her brief encounter with Mike. What she needed was a good friend.

Her stomach clenched with tension.

'Mike! Katie! Both dead.' The words had escaped from her mouth into this lovely room, and she shivered.

Why was she feeling guilty? She was innocent, wasn't she? And then she came back to the mystery. Why had he changed his name? Had she driven them away, only for them to die here? She pushed away the negative thoughts; she was tired, it had been a long day. The light from the sky that pulsed though the window was dimming. The day was nearly over.

She would have to dine in the hotel that evening. She cheered up a little. Homecooked, Doris had said. The thought of a good meal was something she could look forward to. Her stomach grumbled in agreement. She might even see that nice Geordie again. A small smile graced her face.

After a delicious dinner, which was just as Doris had described, she decided on an early night. She hadn't seen Barry and she was surprised to find she had been quite disappointed.

A young red-headed woman was just leaving the bedroom as Debs arrived back. A badge on her blouse named her as Julia; this was the face that belonged to the name Doris had given her.

'Leave the door, thanks, I'm going to retire.'

'Thank you, Miss. I've just turned down your bed and left a chocolate on your pillow.' She moved to allow Debs to enter. 'Sleep well,' she said with a friendly smile before moving off.

When Debs finally tucked herself up in bed, she was bothered by intrusive thoughts and doubts. They crept in as she closed her eyes, suggesting that having seen where Katie and Mike had lived, she would have done what she came here to do, and that once she had done that, there was no reason to stay.

She hadn't thought it through. That was one of her flaws: acting on impulse, then regretting her actions. She pushed the idea aside. She snuggled down – wrapped in warmth, in a comfortable room, full of good food, exhausted – and she waited for sleep.

A faint smell of tobacco seemed to waft in from under the door. Someone must be having a crafty smoke but Doris had said all the rooms were non-smoking. Debs yawned and turned over and let sleep overtake her.

6

Doris was in her snug. Mouser, her ginger cat, had crawled up and was being petted on her knee. Who was comforting who? That was the question Doris asked, smiling, enjoying the warmth and love the cat was giving her. It was good to take the weight off her feet.

The extension and the new restaurant had been a success. Harry Ramshaw, a gentleman farmer and her business partner, had been surprised how quickly the restaurant had taken off. Their two full time chefs had brought in new clients. Maurice's reputation from the Harrogate restaurant had followed him and the new menus had been well received locally; Nick, her second chef, had worked for her for years.

She had been worried about Nick's nose being put out when she hired Maurice as head of the kitchen, but surprisingly he had accepted Maurice well. There had even been articles in the local newspapers about the culinary success at the Royal Oak. Doris felt rather smug. They had taken trade away from the five-star Avondale Hotel, which was her main competitor; such a snooty lot. She knew she could never match their accommodation or position, but she had certainly outmatched their fine dining reputation.

She frowned a little. The success had become a bit of a problem.

After the winter season, January and early February were slow and normally they would have laid off staff, but this year it hadn't been necessary. Two of her girls had left one after the other; the only reason they gave was they didn't like the hours.

Now, she was in a bit of a pickle. Easter and the new season were looming; March was busier than usual, and she had a fully booked diary for April and May. Everyone in hospitality, like herself, would be looking for new staff, and find some she must. The clients must be kept happy to build the business. And then on top of that, she had a memorial to go to midweek.

A lump caught in her throat. Louis and Katie. She had liked them so much and so had all the people that knew them. It was only right that the staff of the Royal Oak paid their respects, as none of them had been able to attend the funerals. The service would be on Wednesday, at St Mary's; the irony was that that was where the couple had been found dead. The printed service would be delivered the next day, Monday.

She reminded herself she must put a notice out on the desk and bar in the morning, saying that lunch would not be served on Wednesday, and also that the lounge would be closed that afternoon in order to hold the wake.

Six months had passed, and she still hadn't got used to the idea they were dead. But, of course, the reality of it was there upstairs; their bed now dominated the back room. It fit so well with the toolbox and rocking chair that had been handed down to her. The bed could have been carved by the man who had made her items; she had never known his name, only his mark. A butterfly identified his work. Legend had it that he had died by his wife's hand at the turn of the 1800s. Jealousy, it seemed, had come between them, and the wife had been hanged for it. The same hands that had made the shutters up at the Hall had made the chair and toolbox, but that could not be true of the bed; she was there when it was delivered from Hertfordshire, one year ago. Her eyes filled with tears.

It was almost the end of the day, and Doris was ready to close shop. Her business partner, Harry, usually called in at the end of the day when the bustle had died down. She got up, chasing the cat away. 'Go catch a mouse.'

Barry, her trusted barman had already brought a bottle of wine into her room. A corkscrew had been thoughtfully left with two glasses on her desk, next to the pile of papers that never seemed to get smaller. She sighed at what was waiting for her there; those would have to wait until tomorrow.

A slight tap on the door announced Harry's arrival.
'Come in, then,' she said loudly, looking towards the door.
Harry pushed it open and popped his head around it. 'Are you decent?'
'Cheeky beggar,' she said, laughing. 'Come on in and shut it behind you.'
'Busy day?'
'Isn't it every day? Pull up a chair and have a glass.' She nodded towards the bottle sitting there waiting. He uncorked it and poured them a glass each.
'I missed you,' he said, giving her the wine. His voice was soft, and his eyes showed he meant every word.
'Did you?' Her tone had changed. The boss and business partner had disappeared; the woman that was left was vulnerable and looked a little lost.
'Yes, I did.' He went over and kissed her lightly on the cheek.
'Can't you do better than that?' The tone was a little gruff; the Doris he knew was back, the real woman he knew. That was the one he admired and the one he had learned to love.
'Come here, woman, and I'll show you.'
She smiled coyly. Now he was seated on her two-seater sofa, she joined him. The wine was put aside, and his arms locked around her. The one kiss stirred their emotions, leading to more passionate kisses. Emotions were raw and very needy. When they came up for air, there was just one question.
'Will you stay on tonight?'
'Do I need to answer that?' Harry pulled her towards him again; she didn't resist.

Making love would have to wait until she had locked up, dismissed the staff, and seen that the Royal was ready for business tomorrow. Thank God, Harry was a businessman and understood.
Doris smoothed down her hair; the promise of an evening of love had been spoken, and she needed him rather badly.

The bed in the back bedroom called to her. It had been strange that she had not once in six months let out that room to a guest. The bed somehow still belonged to Katie and Louis, but tonight she would take Harry there. It would be their secret, like the affair that had been hidden from her staff. It wasn't any of their business after all. She and Harry were both were over twenty-one and single, so what was she worried about? But that old saying kept popping into her head: 'Don't mix business with pleasure.'

Still her heart belonged to Harry. Their involvement happened by chance after Katie and Louis died. They had come together in grief one night after work. She hadn't been able to keep the tears at bay. She was sobbing in her little snug when he arrived to discuss something or other, Harry had taken her in his arms, cradling her as the pain flooded out of her. It must have triggered his own pain, for when she pulled away, his eyes were damp with tears. Somehow the comfort they gave to each other bonded them. They became more affectionate when they met, a stroke on the arm, a kiss on the cheek, and the caring between them became love.

'Back in a few minutes, enjoy the wine,' she whispered, looking into his eyes. She patted his cheek, before finding a tissue to remove the lipstick she had left behind when she kissed him.

He watched her leave the room and heard the five-minute bell sound out through the Royal, announcing drinking up time before it closed. It would be at least half an hour before she was back. He settled himself down, his had been a long day too.

It was a good wine and with three quarters of a bottle still to drink, he thought to take it up to bed with them. She deserved something to unwind; she worked so hard and, apart from himself, she couldn't share much with her employees.

Forty minutes later, they climbed the stairs together, but instead of turning down the passage to Doris' room, she led him to the room he knew. This was her special room, a room that had become something of a shrine.

'Really?'

'Yes, really, it's time to acknowledge they are gone. And they knew how much I loved them and the carving. Perhaps using it will honour them better.'

To that, he had no answer.

When she opened the door, Harry could have sworn there was a faint smell of pipe tobacco.

This time it was pipe tobacco that filtered through the veil to where Louis was whittling a piece of wood. Champ was fussing around his knee, trying to get in on the action, pushing his nose close to where the knife was busy.

Massie, his father, must be visiting his rocking chair in the bedroom. It had been some time since he visited. In fact, when Louis thought on it, he had only seen him once since coming back to Ravensend to live as a mortal, and that was well over a year ago. But this was marvellous; he would go and meet him.

The old man sat rocking slowly, whilst staring out of the window into the darkness of the night. Illuminated only by the moon, Louis could see the white of his clay pipe settled in his mouth. As Massie pulled on it, a small red glow lived for a short moment in the bowl before it died away, and the smell of tobacco was left behind.

As Louis emerged fully, Massie turned to see his son.

'There you are, lad. I'd hoped I'd see you. I hope one day you will be able to come and join me and your mam.'

Louis filled up. It had been a long time since he had thought about his mother. A picture of her face came to him. She had died when he was a young man and learning his trade away from home. Now he remembered her singing to him, in bed before he fell asleep.

'Can you bring her here?'

'Nay lad. She's content where she is, but I like to visit the old place. The chair calls me from time to time. I was fond of the world I had to leave. The angels told me what you and that lass went through. Evil is never far away; darkness is attracted by light. Watch out, son.' His head nodded slowly as he spoke. 'There's the beginning of it right here in this building. Let's hope it's not fed and grows.'

'What do you mean by that, Dad?'

'Just what I say.'

Massie was starting to lose his substance; Moonlight was shining through his faint outline, but before he left, he spoke with some urgency.

'Take care on your journey.'

'Journey?'

'That's what they do say.'

'Who say? And how can I journey anywhere?'

But Massie had disappeared, leaving Louis full of confusion.

As he turned towards the veil, he heard footsteps coming towards the bedroom door. It was time for him also to disappear and he evaporated through his carved headboard back to his own world.

It was really happening; he was going to stay the night. On the occasions they had had made love, Harry had always left so not to be there the following morning – partly because he had his own businesses to run and in part so as not to embarrass her.

She was glad her staff would at last see the two of them as a couple. It was time.

She felt like a schoolgirl sneaking out of her parents' house to meet a boy. That forbidden thing that made you very excited. And she did feel excited, giddy almost, and that was even before she touched the wine that Harry held in his hand.

The door shut behind them. No one would look for her here, though why anyone would need to at this time of the night was in real doubt. She dismissed the thought; she was nervous.

The room had a chill to it, and she noticeably shivered.

'It's cold in here.'

'Come here,' said Harry, pulling her into his arms. 'I'll warm you up.'

She shivered again, but she wasn't sure whether that was the chill or the thrill of expectation.

The wine and glasses were forgotten, and a sense of relief flooded through them. They always seemed to be waiting for the right time to join in love. They were the sort of people for whom business came first. At last, those demands were pushed to one side, put in a box until tomorrow.

Undressing slowly, they enjoyed the adventure of touching and pleasing each other. A little time passed before they crawled in between the white crisp sheets to lie in contented nakedness and make love, knowing that the night didn't have a time limit on it.

Sleep came after the tensions of the day were overcome. And entwined together, they slept under the watchful eyes of Adam and Eve.

It was the middle of the night when Louis and Katie came through the veil to see the stars. Their dear friends were cuddled up the carved bed that had been their own.

'Isn't it wonderful?' said Katie. 'They have found each other. I always hoped they would.' Louis nodded in approval; he loved them both too.

7

Morning came creeping into her room. She was warm under the blankets and for the first time in a long time she had been able to sleep and wake up naturally. She could hear people moving about and wondered how long she had slept. Still half-asleep, she peered at her wristwatch and almost jumped out of her skin, realising it was eight thirty and breakfast finished at ten.

She threw back the blankets and moved quickly to the bathroom. Twenty-five minutes later, showered and dressed, she closed the bedroom door, just as a well-dressed man was entering the room opposite. He bade her good morning, and she made her way down to the dining room.

The doors were open wide, but it was almost empty when she walked in. Was she the last to arrive for breakfast? An elderly couple looked as though they were finishing off their last pieces of toast; mini jars of jam were open, and empty packs of butter were discarded by their plates. They were busy in conversation and didn't notice her standing there.

'Did you sleep well?' inquired Barry. She liked his Geordie accent. He was wearing a welcoming smile, standing at a desk just inside the door, pen in hand, possibly waiting to cross her off the list that he was holding.

'Yes, thank you.'

He ushered her towards a small table on the other side of the room. She remembered he had been serving behind the bar the afternoon she had arrived.

'That's good. And what would Madam be wanting, this fine morning?'

Madam? Who did Barry think he was talking to? But it was rather nice to be treated like someone special. Madam made her sound important, when most of the time in her life she felt invisible. Also, it was good to see to a friendly face.

'You were working yesterday as well, weren't you?'

'We all work as a team here, as and when, as and when. We are a little short-staffed but, believe me, you won't notice. We fit in where a space needs filling.'

'You make it sound as though you are a family.'

'You could say that. Doris is a good sort, one of the best to work for. Here we are.' He pulled out the chair and invited her to sit down.

She felt quite the lady, tucking her skirts under her as she sat. He pushed her chair up to the table, which was draped in white linen and graced by a single red rose in a simple glass vase. It was so stylish. She was impressed.

Barry handed her the menu that had been slotted between the condiments.

'What can I get you?'

She didn't need to look. 'I'd love a full breakfast.'

'Right away. Tea or coffee and toast, white or brown?

'Tea and brown, thank you.'

She looked directly into his eyes. They were kind. Something passed between them in that moment. He was no longer a stranger, just someone she didn't know.

While she waited in the silence of the room, she scanned it. Scenes of moorlands, painted in soft natural colours, looked down at her from the walls.

She wondered if they were local landscapes, and then she caught sight of an angel carved in wood, seemingly in mid-flight. The angel looked as though she was carrying a key, and was that a dormouse? It was beautiful; it had an ethereal quality, delicate and sensitive. She had a pressing urge to go and touch it, but she resisted.

'It's lovely, isn't it?'

Debs hadn't heard Doris come up beside her.

'Yes, it is,' responded Debs. 'But, what's it about, what is it trying to say?' The words were out, but it was almost to herself.

'What indeed? Louis was a very talented man.'

'Louis?' Debs shivered with curiosity. 'Louis?'

'Yes, a dear friend who died quite recently with his wife. Such a tragedy. We are holding a memorial for them on Wednesday, so lunch will not be served that day. Funnily enough, they came from your part of the country, although his roots were here.'

Debs was at a loss. If Louis was the man she knew as Mike, how could that be right? Mike, she believed, had been brought up in Hertfordshire. But, she had to admit, she didn't know where he had been born. She had come to solve a mystery only to find more to solve. It all felt wrong.

'I hope you slept well? Is everything okay?'

Debs nodded. 'Better than okay. Thank you.'

That pleased Doris; she loved a happy guest.

Nick had been looking through the window in the serving door that led into the dining room. Just one more guest, then he would be off duty for an hour or so. He was getting hungry himself and he wanted to be away so he could eat.

He had seen the exchange between Barry and the young woman. 'Lucky beggar,' he thought.

'You're in there!' exclaimed Nick, as Barry came into the kitchen through the swing door, giving him a nudge as he passed by. 'Judging by the way she's looking at you, you're on a promise.'

'What's wrong with you? Have you no respect?'

'Touched a nerve, have I? When did you last get your leg over?' Nick smirked. 'Look, mate, if you can't see she's just asking for it, that's your loss.'

'Man, oh man. Is your mind always in the gutter?'

Barry held his clenched fists down by his thighs. It would be so easy to punch him.

Barry ordered the full breakfast for the guest and then went over to make the tea and toast and set the tray. He was seething.

He wouldn't pay this guy in washers if he was in charge; if he was in charge, he would be gone. Doris didn't realise she was being conned. She only saw what Nick wanted her to see, and not the Nick the staff saw.

For example, the way Nick treated Julia. The poor girl was hopelessly in love with him. It seemed like every day she was in tears, or at least red-eyed. How many times had Barry advised her to give the ring back and break it off before Nick destroyed her love? But she never heard. Nick didn't understand love at all.

There were plenty of men out there who would love Julia for her good nature. She was a bonny lass and modest.

Barry couldn't prove it, but he suspected that the reason that the last two girls that had been employed here left was because of something connected to Nick.

A bell rang behind him. Nick, still smirking, held the full breakfast on a dinner plate, ready for Barry to serve.

Doris was ready to walk away when Barry came hurrying out of the kitchen, carrying Debs' breakfast with a white serving cloth. 'Sorry for the wait.'

'That's okay,' came the reply.

'Tea to come. Just give me a minute.'

Under the watchful eye of Doris, he placed the breakfast in front of Debs.

Barry turned to the kitchen. Seconds later he was back, bringing tea and toast on a tray with small jars of jams that he settled on her table. Barry looked at Doris. She smiled and for the second time in two days she wondered how she would cope if she ever lost her special Geordie, her loyal barman who always stepped up when the job needed him.

8

Debs had had two wonderful days. Her first trip, on Monday, took her to Darlington, just over the River Skerne. The landscape was rich in farming, green and lovely. Not a mill in sight.

Darlington was very old and the largest market town in County Durham, according to the leaflet she'd picked up. The bus had dropped her off at the open market. She joined the bustle of shoppers; the voices around her were loud and cheerful, and she heard the endearment 'pet' being widely used by everyone.

These stalls' and shops' prices were more in keeping with her pocket. A further building with large warehouse doors pinned back led her into the covered market. Row after row of permanent stalls delighted her eyes. The smell of breads and cheeses, cakes and fruits filled the air, and as she pushed further into the throng, fabrics and clothes were on display. Dresses on metal hangers were hung in glorious colours, row after row; flared skirts and gathered sleeves, necklines with wide collars, all were inviting her to buy. She had wanted to buy a new dress to bring on this holiday but had thought better of it. However, these she could afford. The red bodice with a black skirt seemed to have her name on it. As she hovered, a voice spoke behind her.

'Nice isn't it, what size are you, pet?' The small woman was taking it off the rack. 'Size 12, right? I can always tell.'

Before Debs could say a word, she was being shown into a tiny, curtained area at the back of the stall, complete with a long thin mirror.

'Take your time.'

Now she was sorely tempted.

With her bag gripped tight, her purchase inside, Debs left the market. She saw a steeple. It towered above the houses around the market, and she made her way towards it.

The imposing church was clothed in blackened stone, the dirt from some industrial period still clinging to it.

St Cuthbert's had been on the site since 1183, according to the notice. She wasn't sure why she had come to visit it; she didn't have the best history with the Church and religion. Once inside, she walked around and looked at all the religious pictures and stained-glass windows. They were quite fine, she thought, and they told the story of a special love for humanity.

The vaulted ceiling was shaped like the bottom of a boat and had saints and cherubs carved on the boss rose where the columns met and supported it. She sat in a wooden pew, alone but not feeling so. The huge space was filled with a tranquility and a peacefulness that she really enjoyed. It was the first time she had been in church on her own for a very long time.

But the peace didn't last. As always, the memories came back to haunt her.

She felt indignant that when she had needed help, as a teenager, the Church had shown no sympathy. Worse than that, her church had turned their back on her and Annie. Where was the love they preached?

Hadn't her child been part of that plan for humanity?

The pain of loss never really went away, although it buried itself for a bit.

Despite all of that, the faith of her childhood was deep. She frowned. She argued with herself. God hadn't heard her then, so, why, sitting here in His house, should she expect Him to see her now? But she couldn't dismiss the peace she felt, and she hoped she *was* being seen. She was wrong to think that God was like the clergy who had betrayed her, she reflected. She had loved badly and was deceived. A lot like Christ.

On her way out, she saw some leaflets on local interests and museums. She picked up two, deciding to go to the museum to learn more about this town.

'Are you new here?' The woman coming towards her was carrying flowers in one hand and a vase in the other. 'I'm just doing the flowers for the altar. The name's Judy. You're looking a little lost – can I help?'

'I'm on holiday.' Why did she say that? Debs rounded on herself.

'That's nice. What brings you here?'

'That's something I've just been asking myself.'

'Well, we're always open if you have a mind to come and you're welcome. By the sounds of you, you're not from round here, are you, pet?'

'No, I had friends who moved north, and I thought I'd like to see what the north was like.'

'And do you like what you've seen?'

'Frankly, yes I do.'

'Well, that's good, but don't tell everyone or they'll all want to come. You have a good holiday, mind. God bless.'

Picking up her vase with a smile, Judy moved off, leaving Debs with the blessing, and the rest of the day to explore.

She walked to the museum called a 'Head of Steam,' and learned that Darlington was famous for wool and linen. Then, in the early 1800s, two Quaker families, the Peases and the Backhouses, had taken an interest in the collection and delivery of coal. Pack horses and horse-and-carts had been the transporters, until the invention of the railway. George Stephenson was the mastermind behind the design. The Quakers spearheaded the railway that changed Britain in 1825. The first steam locomotive ran from the collieries at Shilden through Darlington and onto the port of Stockton-on-Tees. Black gold, or coal, was transported to where industry needed it. That certainly explained the fine Market Hall and clock tower, and Darlington's solid buildings. Debs had had no idea she was interested in history until that day. It came as something of a surprise.

The bus back to Ravensend was a godsend for her poor feet.

Mike and her blisters flooded memories back to her, but that was then, and this was now, and her feet were not damaged. It was just she would not normally have been on them all day; her job required her to sit. She realised then that not only was she unhappy at work, but that her job was boring.

She didn't go down for dinner that night; she had bought a few bits from the market to have in her room. What she needed was to get her feet up and rest, because tomorrow she had planned a day in Helmsley.

Debs was blessed with a fine day of crystal crisp light and an azure blue sky. The journey to Helmsley took over an hour and half, but Debs was happy. The route was winding and hilly, cutting through hamlets and villages that reminded her of chocolate box covers. The north was not so different from the south with its picture-perfect villages. The landscape was stunning: pastoral England; open land with sheep and cattle. Trees – a little twisted with the winds, she thought – and stone walls stood sturdy in their greyness. The walls had stood for centuries.

Down a hill and across the bridge over the River Rye, the bus was passing small shops that she was eager to explore. It stopped in a square rather like the cobbled square in Ravensend, but much larger. A few cars were parked here and there, and benches were dotted around, providing rest for the shoppers.

Debs stepped down. The sun was warm and bright on the buildings. It seemed she had arrived in a Grimm's Fairy Tale town. All around the skyline, the red and grey roofs were higgledy-piggledy: tall and small, some dwarfing their neighbours; a cottage joined to a three-storey house; a large inn squashed in between the terraced houses. The red tiles against grey granite or redbrick gave the town an enchanted look.

Debs walked towards a pagoda-style memorial, which was raised and had a statue enclosed in it. The Feversham Monument seemed to be the highest point in the square.

Three large public houses and a town hall were facing onto the square. Another Royal Oak caught her eye. Such a popular name, it would seem.

She might well go to the Royal Oak for lunch, but that was not fixed. Looking around, she saw she was spoiled for choice. A tearoom also faced the square and by the smell of fish and chips lingering the air, there was yet another option she still had to find.

She looked at her watch. It was eleven. Perhaps a cup of coffee would be a good start to her day. At the door she suddenly stopped in her tracks; she felt that eyes were burning into her back. Puzzled, she turned to look at the square. It was only the face of the statue that was staring at her. She almost laughed at her foolishness, but it did look familiar. How odd that she hadn't noticed it earlier. But who did it remind her of?

Shock went through her body. The face seemed come alive. She could have sworn for a moment that it was Mike staring back at her. It took her breath away. She blinked and looked again and saw it was nothing more than a stone portrait with no life in it. What had she just seen? Her stomach was filled with butterflies. Was her guilt playing on her nerves?

The coffee did the trick. Fortified, she decided to walk to the castle. From the hill on which it stood, she supposed she would be able to see the whole of the town.

An old-fashioned sweet shop was tucked away behind the square. The window was filled with jar upon jar of humbugs, licorice, sherbet lemons, and round dark balls called black bullets. Intrigued by this quaint shop, Debs called in and learned from the shopkeeper that they were made from black treacle and mint.

'So, you've never seen them before, have you?' He offered the jar for her to pick one. 'There you are, bonny lass, you enjoy it.' She popped one in her mouth. It was smooth on her tongue, and the flavour was like a childhood memory, sweet and comforting. His accent was the same as Barry's.

'I have some weighed out here.' He pointed to a basket on the counter. 'Ten pence a bag.'

She was happy to buy a bag.

'Thank you, pet.'

There it was again, that common endearment that was used so readily. She liked it; it made her feel welcome.

The castle was only part ruin and stood tall on the high ground overlooking the town. It was a bit of a pull up to it, but the view was worth every step. The gardens that ran out from it had high walls with chimneys. She had never seen that before. The walls kept the crop of fruits free from the frosts during the coldest months; she even saw the cavities where the fires were lit by the gardeners. Greenhouses were being prepared for the next growing season. The countryside was so exciting, compared to living in a town.

A small tearoom was tucked away by the wall. If she hadn't gone to the castle, she would have missed it. Homemade parsnip soup was Soup of the Day. Homemade: they did a lot of that here. The thoughts of her suppers of canned tomato soup, when her money was running out, depressed her. If she had a garden, she could grow vegetables… but that was only a pipe dream. With her job, what time did she have for a garden? A cold draught caught her on her neck and legs as she sat to eat. March could be quite blustery, she thought, as she pulled up her collar.

The last bus dropped Debs off in Ravensend. She walked with sore toes to the Royal Oak.

'Nice day, Madam?' Barry met her with a huge smile as she passed through the doors feeling exhausted.

'Oh, please don't call me Madam. My name is Debs.'

'I'm sorry Miss, I can't do that. Doris wouldn't like me to be familiar with our guests.'

Her face fell with disappointment. It was as though she had personally been rebuffed.

'How about I call you Miss Debs? That should satisfy Doris.' His voice dropped and he looked directly into her eyes, hopefully, for a response. 'And I hope you too.' It had the desired effect.

A small smile touched her lips. 'Thank you. Yes.'

'If I'm to call you Miss Debs, you must call me Barry.'

'I know your name,' she admitted, rather self-consciously. 'I heard Doris call you it when I first came here, and there was a nice young redhead too.'

'That would be Julia. She's a hard worker and a good girl. We think a lot of her.' A cloud seemed to pass over his face. Debs noticed it but made no comment, but she knew that look. Something was bothering him.

'Did you have a nice day?'

'Helmsley is so lovely. I think I have fallen in love with Yorkshire.'

She laughed at the end of her sentence, a nervous look on her face.

Barry indicated a bar stool. 'Why don't you sit and tell me all about it before I get busy?'

Her feet were aching; it would be good to get off them. This was an invitation she wouldn't refuse. Normally, she had no one to talk to and share. And she liked him.

She found the seat and settled.

They were soon chatting like old friends. He was patient and listened as she went through her past two days in detail with him.

'You have the memorial tomorrow,' she said. 'Are you all ready for it?'

'That's kind of you to ask. Yes and no, if I'm honest. We are a bit short staffed, but we'll manage. I feel rather sad though. They were a grand couple.'

'Yes, I've heard so. What happened?'

'We'll never really know. For a week before they died, they seemed out of sorts. I can't think why; they were so suited to one another. They loved working, Katie had plans for this place and Louis had a real gift with wood and carving. Did you see that piece in the dining room? He was a real old-fashioned gentleman, so caring.'

Debs smouldered; she couldn't believe that this Louis was her Mike.

'Did he have no bad habits?'

'Perhaps working too hard. He forgot himself when he was carving, according to Katie.'

'It was funny seeing names in the papers; he was using a new one.'

It was out before she could stop herself, but Barry didn't seem to notice. Almost talking to himself, he confirmed that all the staff had been puzzled with the newspaper's report.

'We wondered about it, but hey, it's none of our business. If a man wants to use other names, that's up to him. He was well liked here. It was a hell of a shock when we were told they were dead. And in that churchyard. We couldn't explain why they were there.' A large sigh signalled he was at the end of his story. 'Tomorrow we say goodbye and thanks for knowing them. We move on.'

'Yes.' It was time she did the same. Let that part of her life go and start a new one.

9

Katie had become unsettled, and it affected Louis. He had been contented, up to her saying that she missed the seeing the stars. He recognised, and well remembered, that feeling of restriction, like the one he had felt so long ago. It was back.

If his father could move from domain to domain so freely, thought Louis, why couldn't he? At their last meeting, his father had told him he was to go on a journey. Had the angels given permission to release him from the life's blood curse he was trapped in? If the angels had ordained it, perhaps he should test it. There were places he would like to see again.

The last time he had lived as a mortal, Louis had worked for Harry Ramshaw, Doris' business partner, who owned property around the district: property that Louis had maintained for him as a carpenter. Harry had been much more than a boss; he had been Louis' friend. Louis had worked in many of the local towns. One, in particular, he enjoyed on each visit was Helmsley, to the east of Ravensend. He thought now how much he would like to visit the castle again and see the River Rye, walk in the square and sit and watch the pigeons. His roots were deep in this place.

He was thinking about the square and the memorial when he suddenly became part of it. He was encased in sandstone and looking out through the eyes of William Feversham, the stone effigy.

This was thrilling! A mere thought had brought him here; he couldn't wait to tell Katie. He looked out on the cobbles. It was such a familiar scene, visitors milling about. One woman, standing in front of the tearoom, caught his eye. She looked very familiar. He took a second look, but it couldn't be; she couldn't be here.

10

When Doris opened her eyes that Wednesday morning, it was to a cold and misty day. Winter had gone but it was a reminder that it was still only March and spring hadn't quite arrived.

Doris had hoped for a blue-skied day, for the memorial service later that morning. Nevertheless, she didn't doubt that there would be a good turnout by the good neighbours of Ravensend, hot, cold or rain.

She could hear the distant sounds of voices in the kitchen; Nick must be already preparing for the wake, before his duty of cooking breakfasts for the guests. She ought to get down there to help. She slid out of bed to a coldish bedroom and dragged herself into the bathroom. She would have to put up with a wash down this morning.

Harry hadn't been able to stay overnight, but she would see him later at the church. The thought brought a smile to her face, and she remembered Monday evening and the love they shared in the carved bed. Perhaps she would switch bedrooms and they could make a habit of it. That thought pleased her even more.

The smell of baking met her as she strode down the stairs. That would be the sausage rolls, pasties and the corned beef and potato bakes. Nick was a good lad. He had said he would see to it.

She wasn't disappointed when she pushed open the door of the kitchen: the counters were covered with cooling food. Nick and Julia were working as a team, though the kitchen wasn't part of Julia's duties.

Nick beamed at Doris, as she came through the door. Julia smiled but looked a little embarrassed.

'You came in early today, Nick; it's much appreciated,'

'Just for you, Doris.' And he gave her a wink.

Cheeky beggar, thought Doris, and then it occurred to her that Nick must have come in very early to have got so far forward this morning.

She looked over at Julia. 'Did you sleep well, love?' Julia didn't speak, just nodded, her face flushing up bright red.

So, he'd stayed the night, had he? It was against the rules, but they were engaged; maybe she should turn a blind eye. Nick still lived at home with his parents and Julia lived in. Her room was twin bedded, and at the moment she had it all to herself. They didn't have a lot of time to spend together. Doris was sympathetic. 'We all need love, after all,' she thought, but she was in a quandary. Should she scold them or let it be? She looked at the baking… She would let it go this time. Another time? She didn't think so.

The day was still cold, but it had cleared up. Once the mist had burned off, a weak sun revealed itself in the pale blue March sky. The church looked like a painting in the light as Doris walked down the path to meet Harry. He was giving out the order of service to the mourners who had turned up to pay their respects.

In the church, the soft light from the sun gave a warm glow to the stained glass windows. It had been some time since Doris had visited a church. She and God didn't see eye-to-eye on a great many subjects, but this was different. If there was a heaven, Doris would wish her friends to be there. And this service was for them and all the people who knew them.

Both she and Harry were able to say a few words after the priest had finished, and they gave Louis and Katie real character references. It was a pity he had not known them. But he meant well.

By the end of the service, Doris was full of sadness, but at the same time she felt thankful that they had been part of her life for a little while. She remembered them moving into the cottage and seeing their bed as it was being unwrapped. A smile lit up her face. She was pleased she had a piece of them in the Royal: their bed that had become hers and Harry's on Monday. If the bed could speak, it would speak of love.

'You are all welcome to come back to the Royal and join us in a wake to celebrate their lives. They will be missed.' The smile was gone and a tear, that might have been mistaken as nothing more than an impatient gesture on Doris' part, was dashed away from her eye before anyone could see.

11

The Beautiful Angel, coiled and in his most comfortable form, felt a flutter of discontent in the kingdom. He recognised the signs from when he was grooming Sophia. She had been delicious, both to convert and devour.

He was languishing in a crevice, his snakelike form curled up, and his head resting on his coil. His brown and orange reptilian eyes opened, suddenly alert. He was alone and in his own claustrophobic silence. His army of chaos was busy elsewhere, helping a war lord or a dictator to grow in strength and power. His army would corrupt them utterly until they were totally his.

Once they were completely bloated with their own sense of infallibility and evil, he would reel them in and devour them. The more evil they were, the stronger he became. It was so easy to find a gullible, greedy human. Even one that started out with morals and a sense of fairness only needed the right conditions to change all that. A pretty face, a man in a high position, and money. Yes, that was usually the key.

There were two sorts of people on the earthly plane, and they both held their arms out wide. One to stop others getting in front of them; one to freely give their love. He favoured the former.

A new feminine potency was filtering into his dark and craggy plane of existence. This female was young and fresh. He sniffed the air with his forked tongue. The scent told him that this was just the beginning of her dissatisfaction. He should go and help her to grow it.

Uncoiling himself, he put on his best disguise. It was amazing how humanity mistook beauty for a good soul and trustworthiness.

He stood addressing himself; his eyes were now a liquid blue, and his handsome, squared-jawed face was bronzed. Dark, wavy hair framed his face, and his body was muscular. His legs were, in fact, rather short. Below the knee they became furry stumps, ending with cloven feet. That he couldn't change. Powers that were stronger than he had decreed it so. But no matter; once a victim looked into his eyes, they forgot about the rest of his anatomy.

This female, he was sensing wasn't exactly calling him – but delay, and he might lose the moment. He was ready for another victim.

Katie was in her favourite place under the tree, lying flat on her back, looking up at the different patterns the light made among the branches and leaves. She still felt a disconnect with the kingdom without knowing why. The night sky had settled her a little, for she loved the stars, but there was something else she sensed she needed to do. She had no idea what it could be.

An odd-shaped leaf caught her attention: so different from the others. Cautiously, she got up to inspect it.

Once she was up close, she realised that it wasn't a leaf at all. She touched it tentatively. It seemed to be stuck to the branch. It mildly tingled her fingers rather like touching a stinging nettle. Shocked, she withdrew her hand.

It had felt like skin under her fingers, but it was iridescent, with the colours of green and gold shimmering in the sunlight. Puzzled, she saw it was snakeskin, such as she had seen in reptile houses in the zoo. However, Katie had never seen a snake in their kingdom. It was as odd as the red kite that they had sighted recently. She felt an urgent need to show Louis the strange object. Despite the warning tingle, she reached up to snatch it from its lodging.

Once in her hand, the tingling was stronger. It grew and spread through her body, and she became unsteady and lightheaded. Her vision was blurred, and the shape of a man suddenly appeared from the tree and stood beside her.

She felt hands grasping hers. She didn't have a choice but to hang on to him or she might fall. A wind sucked at her heels and then her body. The man was close. His hands had released hers and instead he had wrapped his arms around her.

One second, she was in the kingdom; the next she was back at the place where she had died, standing next to a man who glowed with confidence. He was a handsome soul. His black hair shone, curling and waving down into the nape of his neck. His eyes were looking intensely into hers. When he spoke, his voice had a honeyed tone to it.

'You called me?'

'No. Who are you?'

'I'm your angel. I've come to remind you why you died. That's why I've brought you here.' He smiled, showing even teeth and a pink tongue.

The gravestone had not been moved from where it had fallen on that fateful day when she had died. Katie shuddered. She remembered little of her final breath, but she did remember seeing her bloodied body, with roses strewn around her head next to the headstone of Massie, when her soul was released.

'Why have you brought me here?'

'This is where you lost your future because of Louis.'

'Louis? No. No. He had nothing to do with it. I was trapped in a tornado, spun by evil. The dirt was stinging my skin and it separated me from Louis. I tried to reach out to him but couldn't. And then she came, clawing at me. Sophia used me and killed me.'

Katie's torment at Sophia's hands came flooding back. She had been unable to escape from the bitter and malicious ghost. It was as fresh in her mind as when it had happened.

The sunlight was full on the angel's face, and for a moment she thought she saw an iridescent layer under his skin. Scales. A gold and green pattern shimmered under his tan for a second and then it was gone.

That honeyed tone was back in his voice, persuading, soothing.

'You died too soon. Don't you remember your ambitions? And your parents, do you remember them? They lost you.'

Katie thought for a moment. He was right. A sadness passed through her spirit. She had loved them so much. Was that the reason for her forlornness? Her mum and dad, whom she would never see again. They would go into the light when they died; they would go to a different place. She had given that up to be with Louis. Her soul felt heavy, as if the universe was lying on her breast. What had she done?

Watching her closely, the angel licked his lip with the tip of his tongue.

This was good. His pink tongue played on his lips continually. He could feel her pain; it was a start.

'Come with me. Follow me to my world. Meet my army of souls who have been betrayed like you. You belong with me.'

She was shocked. What did he mean by the word betrayed? Love could never be wrong – foolish perhaps – but unconditional love was what everyone needed in their lives. Louis had never betrayed her; she could feel his love even now.

That word 'betrayed' somehow hurt her and brought her back to her senses.

What was she doing here? She hadn't come willingly; she had been kidnapped. Her soul mate was still in their kingdom, and she wanted to go back to him.

The demon was disappointed; even with all his charm, he knew she wasn't for him. However, he was not too discouraged. When he had come to her in the kingdom, he had tasted the air and he had felt a small hint of immoral sinfulness in it. It came from a man. He would find this new soul and procure it.

He let her go.

For a few millionths of a second, when she was no longer distracted by the angel, she reassessed her bearings, looking around towards the church. She was confused when she saw Doris walking down the path towards the open door of the porch. As she looked further, the man in a grey suit who looked like Harry, was standing waiting for her. What were they doing here in the place where she and Louis had died?

The speed at which she was carried back to the kingdom made her feel giddy. It was almost as though she had dreamed the visit from the angel and to St Mary's Church, except she knew she hadn't; she could still the feel the texture of the small green and gold scale that she was still clutching in her hand.

She must tell Louis.

12

Debs decided to stay in the hotel and rest on Wednesday. Her bus trips, and spending on food had been a drain on her pocket money. It was time to have a break from trekking about the countryside and besides, she was tired.

There was an empty silence in the Royal Oak's lounge. It was almost midday and she sat in a winged chair with a book. Barry hadn't appeared to serve her that morning at breakfast; instead, it had been the young redhead she had met on the first night outside her bedroom. Julia was very attentive and looked after Debs with a large smile; she was a pretty girl. Nothing was too much trouble for her, but Debs thought she looked rather tired.

The breakfast room hadn't been particularly busy that morning. She had seen some guests checking out on the Tuesday morning, as she left to catch her bus to Helmsley. It made her think that Wednesday, being midweek was probably always the quietest day, especially in the winter months.

Debs had had a late breakfast, which meant she wouldn't need another meal until suppertime. It was just as well, as the hotel wasn't serving lunch today. It was the day of the memorial; the notice was still on the desk in the hall. Not that she needed a prompt. She hadn't slept particularly well, what with her sore feet and memories that invaded her mind whether she was awake or asleep.

The staff and friends would be at the service, along with her Geordie barman Barry. She warmed at the thought of him and his kind eyes that led her to believe he was a caring man. A voice whispered a warning in her head. 'You've been here before, remember?'

With a shake of her head, she dismissed it. She didn't need to think too much about it. She would be traveling home in a few days, and she would never see him again. That warm glow faded, and she felt bereft.

Debs' mind was all over the place and not on the book she had picked up in Helmsley. She settled back in her chair, staring at the book cover, though she had no enthusiasm to open it up. A ginger cat walked into the lounge, yawning, and it stretched out before sidling up to Debs and brushing up against her legs. She leaned forward to stroke its back.

'Are you feeling lonely, too?' she asked.

In her wide, winged chair, hidden from the bar and reception, she had finally started reading and was on the second chapter when a chorus of laughter broke into her silence. The cat, who was curled up at her feet asleep, lifted its head. Springing up, it stretched out again, before it strode towards the kitchen. The chorus had come from the public bar: men behaving badly! If they could only hear themselves, she thought. They would be shocked at what they sounded like.

Who was serving behind the bar? A man's voice was interacting with the locals. Debs tried to ignore the noise and the inappropriate language. The men's jokes were getting bolder and smuttier as the minutes passed.

The noise must have reached the kitchens or the breakfast room because Debs heard the voice of that nice young woman, Julia?

'Nick, you better keep it down. If the guests hear –'

Julia was stopped mid-sentence.

'Leave us alone, woman, there's no one around. We're enjoying a bit of men's time here. Take yourself back to the kitchen where you belong.' He laughed as though he'd told a joke.

'Nick. Please.'

'Away with you, woman.'

She heard a thin line of laughter and approval from the men, but the level of noise dropped considerably.

Nick's voice however would not be stilled. 'Why do women have small feet?' There was silence, while he waited for an answer. 'I'll tell yer then. So, they can get closer to the kitchen sink.' He laughed out loud. And another round of laughter went up from the locals.

Debs didn't think she liked this Nick person much. He seemed to have humiliated Julia on purpose. The poor girl. Debs saw her quickly retreat to the kitchen.

About thirty minutes later Julia approached Debs.

'I'm very sorry, Miss, but I must cordon off this room for the wake. They'll be back from the church soon, and I must put the food out and get the drinks ready. I hope you don't you mind?'

'You look a little flustered. Are you okay?'

'We are a little behind today. And Doris will be back soon.'

There was a hint of panic in the girl's voice.

'Look, I'm not doing anything. Could I help?'

'Oh, Miss, that wouldn't be allowed.'

'Well, we don't have to tell anyone, do we? Tell me what needs doing and we can do it together. You'll be in charge.'

They worked together as a team for the next hour, moving tables together, laying white cloths and napkins on them, making sure there were enough chairs for the throng. Crates of water, wine and orange juice were carried up from the cellars. The food that was covered with wraps was carried out just as the main door opened and Doris and Harry walked in.

'Oh, my goodness,' cried Julia wide-eyed, caught with a hotel guest laying pasties and pies on the pristine cloths on the table.

'What the Dickens is going on here, Julia?' asked Doris, hands on her hips and red-faced. She stood looking at the girl and waited for an answer with Harry at her side.

Debs jumped in before Julia answered, facing Doris squarely on, ignoring the man in a grey suit who had a wry look on his face, his head half-cocked waiting for a response.

'Sorry. It's my fault, Doris. I wasn't doing anything today and wanted to help.'

'You wanted to help?' Doris' voice was raised but not shouting. She looked as though she had swallowed a wasp, her lips pursed as though holding back what she wanted to say.

Julia was hovering with a plate of sausage rolls still in her hand.

'Oh! Put the plate down,' stuttered Doris, exasperated, still waiting for an answer from her young help.

'Sorry, Doris, Nick was behind the bar, and I was on my own. I got behind. When she offered…' Julia's voice trailed off, a very uncomfortable look on her face.

Doris turned to her guest. 'I could get into trouble for this, Miss,' Doris said, choosing her words.

'Not if I was one of your staff. I heard you were short staffed and I'm looking for a change. You could hire me. This could be a sort of trial; something like that.'

Doris was taken aback.

'Well, you're got it all worked out, haven't you, Miss?'

'I'm sorry if I've overstepped the mark. It's as I said: I need a new job and I've fallen in love with North Yorkshire.'

'Have you indeed?' Doris raised her eyebrows. 'Well, perhaps you better come and have a chat with me later in my snug?'

'Really?'

'Really. We'll call it a trial, shall we? Help Julia with the serving and drinks. It seems I could be paying you, instead of you paying me, come the end of the week. Shall we say four thirty? I'm behind the bar. Julia will show you where.'

The draught from the door, and the noise of guests piling in, brought the four of them to turn their heads. Barry was leading the way into the lounge. The throng surged forward to the drink table, where he assumed his normal role as bartender. He frowned a little and had a bemused look on his face when he saw Debs was helping people serving food with Julia. But he said nothing.

'Well, perhaps you can explain yourself?' Doris was sitting on her two-seater sofa drinking a cup of tea. Debs stood in front of her like a wayward child might, feeling awkward with her hands clasped tightly behind her, her knuckles turning white with tension.

'I like a girl with a bit of a personality, and you had a bit to say out there, didn't you? Are you free to join us or are you employed back home?'

There was an uncomfortable silence.

'Well?'

Debs was smiling with a kind of excitement.

'Doris, I've wanted a new start for some time now. I can put my notice in at the office by phone. That leaves me able to help you out for the next few days. On Tuesday, I go home, work my notice out and come back.' Her voice dropped and a frown creased her brow. 'I'll have to find somewhere to rent.' Her smile faded. Damn, she'd done it again. Reacted on impulse, it could be months before she found somewhere to live.

'I'll give you a six-month contract and you can live in.'

'Live in?'

'Aye, you can share with Julia until you find a place. She has a large twin-bedded room in the attic. It's warm and comfortable. Only temporary, mind. You'll get on with her, she's a good girl.' Doris gave an inner sigh of relief; that would put paid to Nick's overnight visits, good and proper, for a while at least.

'You'll stay where you are, for the time being, in the single, and we'll show you some of the duties you'll be expected to do at the end of the week. Be a guest until Friday. Work for me Friday and the weekend. Monday is your own. Do we have a deal?'

'I believe we do,' said Debs, beaming. 'Thank you.'

'Good. I'll put you on the books. That way I'll not be in trouble.'

A prayer it seemed had been answered that day for both of them. Perhaps going to church had opened a new dialogue with God again. Doris shrugged; wishful thinking, perhaps.

It was a strange position to be in, part guest and part employed, and that was a fact, but Debs couldn't believe her luck. She had surprised herself. That old Debs she had known as a young teenager had resurfaced; the woman she knew she was had been enabled again. She wouldn't let herself down this time, or ever again. When Debs pulled the cover over her in bed that night, she was the happiest she had been in years.

Barry's heart had quickened when Debs had returned from her trip to

Helmsley. She seemed so full of life as she bustled through the doors carrying a small bag of shopping: young and vulnerable, and so eager to talk to someone to share the adventures of her day.

It had been a pleasure to welcome her back and sit at the bar with her and let her talk. She was lonely, that wasn't hard to guess. As a barman, he had read these signs many times over the years. And before coming here, he knew that feeling personally. He smiled when he pictured her face when he had called her 'Miss Debs'; that he would keep close to his heart. If only he had been younger, if only the bar hadn't separated them at that moment, he could have kissed her.

She had been a guest up to yesterday when everything changed.

How strange it had been, to come back from the memorial service and find her working with Julia. That in itself was astonishing. He pictured her in the lounge and smiled to himself. She had stood up to Doris and defended Julia; he liked that. Nick should have been helping with the wake, but as usual had left the work to Julia. Then later that day Debs had walked from Doris' snug as a new employee.

There had been a change about Debs; her face was shining, and he had thought she looked even prettier.

It seemed she would be one of them, working under the same roof and become part of their family. Could he dare to believe they might become more than friends? Probably not. He shook his head; she wouldn't be interested in a middle-aged man; he was at least ten years older than her. If he had to settle for friendship, then so be it. Half a loaf was better than none. And – who knew? – then perhaps a close friend. Love happens sometimes when you least expect it. A warmth surged through his body. If she could only see beyond the balding head and see the person within.

Wistfully, he thought that Debs would be gone in a few days, and he would like her to know he had feelings for her before she went. In a month's time she would be back. Spring would be in the air, lighter nights and blossom on the trees, lambs would be playing in the farmers' fields, and the feeling of newness and rebirth would be all around. A time for new love? He pulled himself up. He was making plans without taking the first steps. How was he to tell her?

13

Katie was in the meadow, walking with Champ when Louis caught up with them.

'I was looking for you. Were you down by the stream? Where were you hiding? I need to talk to you.' He heard a throb in her voice and saw an accusation on her face. This wasn't like Katie.

'I'd taken myself off into the hills.' He ushered her back up the track, back to the grassy knoll under the tree.

As they sat next to each other, Champ fussed about them, coming to one side of them and then to the other, as if imploring the words to start, so the tension between them might cease. Louis caught hold of him, commanded him to sit; then, taking hold of Katie's hand, said. 'Well, I'm listening.'

Katie opened her hand slowly, as though the object was a precious stone. The snakeskin of emerald and gold touched by the sun shimmered in the light.

'What is it?'

'It came from our tree. It was hiding among the leaves. When I picked it, I think it called an angel to our world. When the angel touched me, I was transported to where I died, next to Massie's grave. I could see myself, a red halo of blood around my head and the roses. You remember the roses?' A tear slid down her face; her eyes were wide, beseeching him to understand.

'He told me I was discontent because I missed my parents, and I do. But he said it was your fault that I had died. I told him that wasn't true. You were always kind, and I loved you. He released me then, and I was suddenly back here. It was like a dream. But I couldn't find you.'

She slumped against him, and he held her. His memory retraced the history of his release from Mike's body, when Sophia in her madness tried to push him out from the living shroud in which he had been trapped. It had been an act driven by jealousy and desperation, as she wanted to live as Louis had done. But the stress had been too much for the body and the heart gave out.

Things had started to happen when they saw the red kite. The bird seemed to herald change, and now Katie talked of an strange angel.

A chill careered down into the small of his back, and he shuddered. Sophia had called on her beautiful angel in the last throes of the killing. He had seen it. The handsome face of the man changed once in the embrace with Sophia. Transformed, his forked tongue and worm-infested hair announced a demon. Evolving, the snake-like creature had devoured his ghost wife and all the evil that she had become. He and Katie were free of her, but they had paid the price in losing their lives.

Louis had been privy to the sight of Katie's corpse, minutes after she was killed. If he had not already been dead, it would have certainly killed him there and then from distress. He had thought he would never see her again. It was all too terrible. Her voice brought him back to the present.

'I saw Doris and Harry at the graveyard, did I tell you? I was at Massie's grave, those roses, that red. Do you know, I never got to say goodbye? It all happened too fast.'

Louis realised she was in shock, and pulled her close. Despite the sun in his kingdom, she was shivering. This couldn't be happening. This was their haven.

'You'll be alright, my darling, I have you. Rest on me.' He kissed her hair. She was shaking, and he tightened his arms around her.

'I couldn't go with him because I love you. But my parents… I hadn't thought about them until today. I was content, Louis. Now' – she gripped his hands – 'My head's spinning in circles. Help me.'

Champ was whimpering and pawing her knee. Her sadness had reached him too.

'The angel was very beautiful, but something wasn't quite right. I'll remember in a minute. What was it?'

Louis kissed her head and stroked her hair, promising that everything would be alright soon.

'Promise.'

'Promise.'

A weak smile appeared on her lips. Relieved, she sank further into his arms.

'I think it's time to sleep and dream, my darling girl. When you're feeling stronger, we will talk.'

He was ready to tell her of his visit to Helmsley. It would be a surprise.

If the bed had released them both, it might allow them to visit places they were connected to. They would be able to roam the different planes as Massie did. That would be a great gift. But Louis wanted to let her rest now.

Katie had woken with a start at the sound of a voice and a door closing in the world beyond hers. The bedroom that joined them was occupied. Louis was moving too, rubbing his eyes, as Champ in playful mood leaped on him to lick him awake.

'Down, you disgraceful animal.' He pushed his faithful hound to one side, wiping his face with his sleeve. And then he remembered why they had slept.

'Katie, darling, how are you?'

'It felt like a dream, but I still have the scale.' But when she opened her hand, only dust was left in her palm. She allowed it to fall onto the ground and the dust flew off in the breeze. 'How long have we slept?'

'Does it matter, my darling girl? All that matters is you feel better.'

'I feel better.'

14

Those last few days in March were the longest days in some ways; long because when Barry wasn't working, he was yearning to see her. Time moved at a snail's pace. In a few days she would be gone, and he hadn't had the courage to tell her how he felt.

It was Sunday before he found a few quiet minutes to talk to her freely.

'I hope you're going to be happy here. You are sure you have made the right decision? Moving north is a big move.'

'Oh, I will, Barry. You have no idea how much I'm looking forward to being part of the family at the Royal. I like Doris very much and Julia seems a sweet girl. I hope I don't cramp her style and she doesn't resent me sharing.'

'She's a good girl, naturally good and sensitive. I personally think she will be glad of a woman's company. She's quite vulnerable, being an orphan. She's had to look out for herself, and that's been hard. No, you'll get on fine; she's a kind girl and no mistake.'

'She's an orphan? I didn't know.'

'Well, strictly speaking, I shouldn't have told you. Pretend I haven't, and look surprised if she tells you, will you?'

'Of course, it's our secret, Barry. I know you are fond of her.'

'I am. She needs someone to watch over her and that's a fact.' Barry shrugged. 'I guess I've made myself an adopted uncle to her. Everyone should have someone. The girl only has us at the Royal.'

'Barry, I can tell you there is more affection here than most get from their own families.'

Barry looked into her eyes but didn't comment. The way Debs had expressed her thought filled him with compassion. A flash of sadness had moved across her face; her smile was back, but Barry knew what he had seen. Perhaps one day, when they had become good friends, she would share with him, and he would be there for her.

Two days later she was on her way home, to settle things so she could return and make a life here.

Not that the others would have noticed, but there was an emptiness in the place for Barry; he kept busy. There was plenty to do and he went through the motions, but she was never far from his mind. He had never thought he would fall in love, not at forty-five. He had no idea what fate had in store for him. He clung on to hope.

It was with a wonderful feeling of freedom that Debs got on the bus to take her back to the north.

It hadn't been at all hard to say goodbye to her job at the Echo. In truth it had been a relief. Everyone had been lavish with their best wishes, but Debs knew no-one would miss her, at least not for the right reasons. It wasn't that she was disliked, not exactly, but ever since Katie had left the Echo, the atmosphere had been heavy, as though there was an elephant in the room. No-one directly blamed her, except, of course, herself.

Mrs Green had been dreadfully put out, when Debs had told her she was leaving, but what the hell? It was no tragedy to leave behind that shabby room that hadn't had any love spent on it. Never a lick of paint or new curtains in all the ten years she had rented it. Mrs Green had hardly been a great landlady and she would never have to see her again.

Settling down for the journey, she was reminded of her last trip when she had met the group of friends who all knew how to enjoy life. Debs had never had that sort of friendship, at least not like them. She had envied them. Now, she was going to new friends and giving of herself. Now, she understood.

Spring was in the air; the greens of the fields they passed were of light emerald, and the trees displayed young shoots of in a variety of green hues. It was as though Debs was seeing the world with new eyes. It was a good feeling, traveling the road.

Barry's face popped into her head, and she smiled rather wistfully at a memory. Actually, she had thought about him often over the month. She wondered if he had thought about her. She snuggled down in the seat, watching the countryside pass. It reminded her of her life. The fleeting sighting of bits of land she thought might be glimpses of happiness; they were out of sight before she could grasp them, but she would not let go of life this time. Full of hope, she reflected that she did like Barry, and his eyes told her he liked her, too. But he wasn't the reason she was moving. She was determined to make a go of it in Ravensend.

It was late afternoon when she got off the bus and walked across the cobbled square to her new life. She had barely opened the door of the Royal Oak before she was greeted.

'Welcome back, bonny lass.' Barry's smile was a mile wide.

15

Hidden from the mortal world, the demon had sought to find sadness, misery, anything that would feed him. A tiny morsel of anguish would be a welcome titbit. His forked tongue had done its job, as it always did. It had found feelings, tiny particles hanging in the air, coming from beyond his world through the thin partition from the mortal world. These particles, however, were not coming from that kingdom behind the wooded veil. These hints of pain were coming from within the mortal's walls.

He had visited the place for travellers before. The frequent passage of men brought mixed readings to him, but this was different. He knew this from an earlier visit. This hurt belonged to a resident.

He was ready to seek her out. It was a woman; he was sure of it.

The demon blended with the shadows. He watched from them and used them to move in their darkness.

Now, he was ready to visit her world. The crack in the bedroom wall was wide enough for a shadow to filter through. He slid along the floor, ignoring the couple who were in the bed. He was under the door and out into the passage in half a second, using his senses to pull him in the right direction. Instinct drew him down the stairs, and, keeping to the old part of the Royal, he went through the lounge and into the kitchen.

A short, heavily built man was putting on an apron, muttering to himself. He was reaching up to take down a large stainless steel pan that hung on a hook over the counter.

Yes, there was discontentment here. This man was prickling with suppressed anger. The demon moved from the shadows and his dark, snake-like shape sidled up to the man's shoes. A shadow crawled up the leg and blended with the balding man.

Maurice stiffened as a chill ran through up his spine. His legs and arms suddenly felt heavy, so heavy that, as he reached for the pan, he fumbled with it and it fell on the counter, catching the end of his small finger. Maurice swore loudly, just before plunging his whole finger in his mouth, to soothe it.

Sampling the man's self-absorption and pride, the demon believed he should help those thoughts along,

A voice in Maurice's head whispered *I shouldn't be here*, which Maurice repeated out loud. 'I shouldn't be here.' The words rattled around the empty kitchen, echoing as they bounced around in the large space. Maurice's mutterings were given a life.

Delighted, the demon continued with *I'm being used…* 'I'm being used.'

I'm not a servant… 'I'm not a servant.'

I'm too good for this place… 'I'm too good for this place.'

The demon continued his game until the man was consumed with anger.

It tasted good and the demon's waist was suddenly bulging. That would keep him going.

He was about to leave, realising he had not found the woman he had come for, when his senses were suddenly in a quiver. He heard and felt a new soul striding towards the kitchen. This was not just an ordinary soul. The newcomer had the gift of sight, and right here and now he didn't want to be seen. Leaving the man quickly, he sought to find the shadows on the ceiling to cover himself before finding a crack to slip through. He was just in time. As he slid into an upstairs room, he heard a young voice greet Maurice.

'Good morning, Maurice, are you well?'

He didn't wait to hear the answer.

She wasn't on this floor; she was somewhere above him. He crawled up the walls and there, in between the coving and the ceiling, he found the scent of her. Following it, he went into the attic. His smile was broad when he found the woman asleep; here was his victim.

The easiest way of finding out about her was to blend with her. Her subconscious wouldn't fight him; he would be part of her dreams.

He kept to the darkness usually, unless it was necessary to charm a soul, then he resorted to being beautiful and shining with an unholy light. This was such a time. The dark shadow changed shape, discarding the serpent's image, his form becoming clearer, and the beautiful angel with all its deceit stood by the bed.

Her memories were a jumble. There were layers to this woman, with, it seemed, a tender heart. His senses were working hard. He saw her working in an office, sitting at a typewriter; the work was boring, but it was better than living at home. He approached her, smiling his most confident smile.

'Who are you?' she asked, looking up at him.

'A friend, come to help. You can call me Malkira.'

'A friend? I don't have many friends.'

'Well, you have one now.' He moved out of the dream line, allowing her to refocus. There was more. Debs was trying to hide something. He needed time to peel back that layer, but for now, he concentrated on the office and the story that was playing out.

There were many faces, but he couldn't see them clearly, except one. Another woman was comforting Debs; her face became clearer as Debs allowed him in. He knew that face. Debs' dream was quite vivid, although the emotions were confused. It was as though Debs was trying to correct a memory; that this was what should have happened, but didn't.

The woman's face was that of the spirit of Sophia. What was she doing in Debs' dream?

Then, unexpectedly, he saw a baby, a girl. And lots of tears and pain.

His smile widened; this was more than a snack. This was an opportunity. If he could peel away into that place, she might even be ripe for his army of chaos. The scene was whisked away, and the picture of the babe was changed, hidden under more scenes of the office, and the woman with the chestnut-coloured hair was hugging Debs.

She was fighting him, trying to shut him out, pushing against the hurt and bringing hope back into her dream.

Malkira's senses suddenly tingled in warning. There was a disturbance on the mortal plane. Another soul was making an appearance, not mortal but spirit, and a spirit would be able to see him. It was time to retreat and find the shadows. The shape shifted, and the serpent found his way back to his lair.

16

Louis had had that sighting in Helmsley of Debs. He had believed she couldn't be here in Ravensend, but now he wasn't so sure.

When he had told Katie what he had seen, she had been speechless – it was so improbable– but, nevertheless, she had encouraged him to look around the Royal. It was an hotel after all. Why Debs would want to come north was beyond her imaginings, but strange things were becoming normal around here.

They had rested. The shock of the demon's visit and the graveyard was behind her, except that it transpired that there had been a memorial service for Louis and her. That was why Doris and Harry had been at the church. It was rather pleasing, that they had been so highly thought of by their friends.

When Louis announced that he was off for a look around the old place, he meant it. The Royal Oak had been his local at the turn of the 19th century. Now, he was here to haunt it, in the friendliest way possible.

The bedroom was occupied, not that they could see him when he slipped in through the veil. Doris and Harry were in deep discussion, sitting in bed like an old married couple. It soon became clear that the subject was not love, but business.

'Do you think we are over the worst, Harry?'

'I hope so, love. The three-day week and inflation has been crippling for so many businesses. We are all affected by it. The government needs to understand the real problems in the country. Do they ever think about the people beyond London?' Harry was shaking his head; he put his arm around Doris, and pulled her close.

'There is a global oil crisis coming. The miners don't trust the government and the government doesn't trust the unions. Inflation is a curse. I don't know where it's going to end.'

'Forget about the world and politics. Let's concentrate on us. We'll get by; you see if we don't.'

Doris snuggled into Harry's arms. 'Of course, we will, we always do. God, it's got cold in here. I'd better check the radiator.'

Half-naked, Doris got out of bed, pulling a dressing gown around her, almost walking through Louis, as she made her way to the pipes.

For decorum's sake, Louis made a retreat through the door into the passageway and down the stairs.

There was a clatter of pans coming from the kitchen, it signalled people and Louis followed the clanging. The vain little round man was giving a tongue lashing to Julia, who, Louis assumed, was assisting the head chef preparing breakfasts. For a moment, she seemed to look straight at Louis.

Maurice was at the counter, and his face was the colour of thunder. Julia was starting to get out the provisions from the pantry. She jumped, as he declared in a loud voice.

'Good morning, is it? Well, no, it's not.' He removed his small finger from his mouth as he carried on talking; righted a pan on the counter as he did. 'I'm an artist, not a short-order cook. This is not what I came here for.'

'Doris knows that, Chef; it's just for a little while. Nick will be in to do the lunches and you can go home. We are short-staffed, you know that.'

'I didn't train all these years to cook scrambled eggs.' Banging a pan down on the wooden top, he glared at Julia with beady eyes, as though it was all her fault that he had had to come in early that morning. His hair, that he had been combing over his balding crown, had flopped out of place, and now hung in a long length, touching his collar. He shook his head at her. His ruddy face was becoming purple.

'I would be obliged if you would keep your opinions to yourself, girl. That woman will get a piece of my mind when she has the grace to join us.'

Another pan was brutally banged on the countertop.

'Doris has always treated us well, Chef. We're a family here. We look after each other.'

Maurice flung the pan at Julia. 'Your family, not mine.' He followed in the pan's direction, whether it was to retrieve it or not, Julia didn't know, but she took no chances. She turned tail, and shut herself in the pantry.

Doris arrived just as Maurice was trying to pull open the pantry door, shouting, 'Come out, you silly girl.'

'What the Dickens is going on here? I could hear your voice halfway up the stairs. Think of the guests. What are you up to?'

'So! You have decided to join us, have you?' He turned his anger on Doris.

'I'm listening.' Doris stood her ground, facing him.

'I made your restaurant the best around here, and what do you do? Belittle me. Make me a short-order cook. Breakfasts, for God's sake. Well! I won't do it. I quit. I'm going back to Harrogate.' Maurice pulled off his apron, deposited it on the counter with great flourish and walked out.

Doris watched him go. She didn't try to stop him. He had huffed and puffed for months, now; in fact, it had been obvious from the start that he thought he was too good for her place. He had never fitted in. But his going would leave her with a problem.

The pantry door inched open, and Julia's face peered through the crack.

'Is he gone?'

'Yes, he's gone. Though how we are going to manage, I don't know. Still, first things first, get me an apron; there's breakfast to prepare. Our guests will be down shortly.'

The door to the kitchen swung open, and Barbara walked in, pointing to the door behind her, as she joined them.

'Morning. I've just passed Maurice going the other way. Is everything all right?'

'Not right at all. Maurice has just walked out. I need a new chef. It looks as though Nick will have to take his place in the short-term, and I'll join him to run the kitchen. He'll get a pay rise, of course'

Julia emerged with cartons of eggs, looking as pleased as punch.

'Really, Doris?'

'Really, and if he proves himself, who knows?'

Both Julia and Barbara looked pleased. Once the eggs were safely placed on the counter, the girls hugged each other.

'Come on, ladies, let's get to it. The guests will be up soon. Is Barry in?'

Barbara nodded. 'Yes, he followed me in.'

'Thank goodness, we'll manage,' Doris said, with a sigh of relief.

Louis never did like the man. He was far too big for his boots. A popinjay if ever there was one. He remembered the way Maurice had strutted about, the very first time he had met him.

'It's a good thing Debs has joined us. We are going to need all hands-on-deck in the next few months.' Doris was speaking, but more to herself than the girls.

Louis hung on her words. Was it a coincidence, that name, or was that Debs, the one from the Echo? The girl whom he had seen in Helmsley. But how could she be working here with Doris?

'Shall I go and get her up, Doris? She was on the late shift last night.'

'No, Julia, not yet. We can manage for another hour. Then go and give her a shake.'

So, this Debs was asleep upstairs. It was time to go have a peek in the bedrooms. He seemed to remember that Julia slept in the attic. He would look there first.

Louis carried a chill through the Royal, with his ghostly body.

Small sounds of movements were coming from behind the doors; guests were getting up. He moved through the door of the attic and stood in a comfortable twin bedroom. A figure was under the covers with just the top of her head free from the blankets. Her face was partly hidden, concealed by a white cotton sheet. The unmade empty bed next to the sleeping figure seemed the best place to sit and wait for the woman to wake. She was uneasy in her sleep; he had seen nightmares do this before. Instinctively, he touched her forehead and was drawn into her dream. He recognised the office and saw his own darling girl with Debs.

'Who are you? You remind me of someone.' Debs' unconscious soul was staring at him.

'I'm Louis.'

'Where's the other one gone?'

'The other one?'

'The one that said he was my friend. The handsome one, called Malkira.'

Louis knew that name. The Angel of Iniquity.

It was sometime later when someone knocked on the door before it opened, revealing Barbara.

'Debs, are you awake?'

A muffled noise came from under the sheet. An arm flung itself out into the air, before a head peeked over the bedding.

'What time is it?' The voice had a husky tone to it. 'I was on late rota last night.'

'I know, but Maurice walked out this morning. Doris has taken his place in the kitchen, but we need you out in front of house. The guests are due anytime soon for breakfast. You'll be on with Barry.'

'Maurice has quit? I'm on with Barry? Give me a minute to come round and I'll be downstairs.'

Barbara nodded and closed the door, just as Louis left Debs' body.

The bedclothes were flung back, and the woman sat up.

Settling in with Julia had been much easier than Debs had anticipated. In fact, she had felt at home as soon as she was met by Barry on her return.

Six months had flown, and she had grown fond of Julia, learning about her sensitivity, kindness and, like Barry, Debs wondered what the attraction was to Nick, but she knew better than most how blind love could be.

They had mostly got to know each other, in between shifts or talking into the night when sleep didn't come, or when Julia had been upset with Nick over something, which was often.

Now she was trying to wake herself up. Her fingers went through her hair before she stretched out and flung the bedclothes back, her feet pushing into a pair of well-worn slippers.

'Brrr, it's cold in here,' she said to herself.

17

Barbara had woken Debs before she was ready to wake, and it had left her with vivid flashes of memories of her dream. The two men didn't fit in the office. What had they been doing there?

It was just a silly dream, but something niggled at her memory. One man was quite beautiful and glowed in a surreal way; the other was also handsome, and familiar somehow, but he didn't belong in her dream either.

She shivered. She was still a little groggy as she looked around the room. Her clothes were where she had left them, piled on the bedside chair. Barbara's face had disappeared. But her voice hung in the air as she left. 'See you downstairs.'

With her arms full of her clothes, Debs followed Barbara's footsteps down to the next level before veering off to the staff bathroom. It was bliss standing under the shower. She enjoyed the warmth of the hot water flowing over her body, refreshing her. Her mind was running as fast as the water streaming down on her. Her thoughts summoned up the chef. He had never been her favourite person; in fact, he had made her skin crawl.

Maurice was an obnoxious sod. He used to eye her up and down quite openly as though she was something to purchase. He treated her as though she should be pleased with his attentions. He obviously fancied her and his chances and couldn't keep his hands to himself when she was around. She would avoid getting too close to him; he would use any excuse to touch her. He'd pat her arm or back as he passed her; once he had patted her bum, at which she had turned on him and told him to keep his hands to himself. The arrogant man had smiled and pretended it was an accident. How many times had he hidden behind that smile to conceal a leer? He was almost as bad as Nick for his unabashed lusting after the female staff but, she had had to be careful; she was the new girl. She had come north to start a new life, not to get sacked. She was part of the 'family' now and it was a good feeling.

'How?' she thought. 'How could he conjure up such wonderful food and be such an awful man? Thank God, Doris kept him in the kitchens, out of the way of the guests. What would they have made of him?'

So, Maurice had gone. Good riddance to the dirty old man. A sense of relief flowed through her body with the last ripple of water as she turned off the shower.

As she stepped out into the bathroom, she yawned. She had been up late last night, laying tables for the morning's breakfast. She had had to wait until the last guest had left the dining room.

Back in the attic, Debs folded her nightwear and popped it under her pillow. She made her own bed before she decided she would make Julia's as well. That girl needed looking after. Feeling fresh and awake, Debs was ready to get down to kitchen to help.

She was looking forward to it, now she knew she would be on with Barry. She felt so comfortable when she was with him; she didn't have to hide or be something she was not. Ever since the time when she had come back from Helmsley last March and he had invited her to talk, there had been an ease between them, as they chatted for hours. He called her lass, or bonny lass, or just plain Debs. It was the way he spoke to her that mattered. She smiled at the thought. He had made her feel visible and that had given her confidence. The time spent with him had been the start of her turning her life around.

The smell of bacon cooking met her halfway down the stairs to the kitchen. It was an aroma she never tired of. It was symbolic of the comfort and homeliness that she associated with the Royal.

Her mind was elsewhere as she pushed open the swing door to the kitchen, so much so that she almost bumped into Barry.

'Morning, lass.' His wide smile and friendly manner flowing around him.

'Morning, Barry, I understand we are on front-of-house this morning.' In a low tone, she continued, 'Did you hear that Maurice has left?'

'I did. Julia just told me.'

Another voice joined their conversation. 'Well, are you two going to blether all day? Barry, see to the guests waiting and seat them. Debs, take the orders. We're ready to go.'

They turned to see Doris, cooking; she was looking hot, holding a spatula in one hand and a teacloth in the other. Fresh bacon was sizzling on a flat hob, waiting to be turned. Her two helpers were also busy; Julia was putting tea bags in teapots and Barbara was putting plates into a warming drawer.

Debs nodded and donned her apron, while Barry was already opening the door to the dining room; six guests were waiting.

Three hours later, the breakfast shift was over. Maurice had not been missed. Doris was feeling especially pleased with herself. She had been a short order cook when she first started out in the leisure industry and although that was years ago, it was a skill that she had never lost. The part-timers would be in soon; the bedrooms needed servicing. Then there was the preparation of the food for lunch and dinner, and she would have to think about replacing Maurice. Having fed her guests, it was time to cook for her staff. The five of them had breakfast together. It had been an early start and it would be a long day.

Barry was putting on his coat when he stopped Debs as she tried to pass him.

'Can I buy you a cup of coffee if you're not busy?'

Debs was surprised and stuttered her reply.

'We've just had breakfast.'

'Okay, how about a walk? The sun's out. If we get off now, we could catch the bus to Helmsley. I know you like it there.'

She almost floated upstairs to get her jacket.

Helmsley didn't disappoint her. It had been spring when she had last been in the small town. Now with Barry, she was seeing it in a different light: through his eyes, so to speak. He knew the place well, and to her surprise seemed to know many of the shopkeepers. He was easy to be with and she assumed his natural friendliness rubbed off on people.

He invited her to link arms as they walked the castle walls together, and when they stopped for afternoon tea, he treated her to the northern treat of Singin' Hinnies. They were served warm, with butter and jam, and strong tea.

Barry explained that these griddle cakes were a delicacy from Northumberland, his part of the north, and one of the best areas of the country for its beauty and the friendliness of the people. It somehow proved these little cakes were much loved by the common people, the miners, and farmers alike.

'That didn't mean that the people were all perfect, mind.' He laughed when he added, 'Just me.'

'The name for the cakes came from when they were cooking on the griddle. The butter in them melted and sizzled and so they sang.' Barry looked into her eyes. His hand found hers on the dazzling white tablecloth. 'Hinnies is a term of endearment,' he whispered over the table and winked at her. 'A bit like honey, or love.' And he squeezed her hand. She could feel herself blushing, was he flirting?

The afternoon sped by, but before they returned to the Royal, Barry took her down a side street to the sweet shop she knew. The bell chimed a greeting to them as they pushed open the door. Rows and rows of glass jars sat proudly on white shelves, and through the glass, they revealed their succulent wares. The shopkeeper was serving a mother with a small boy, who was reaching up to collect a paper bag from the man.

'Jelly babies are my favourites too,' said the shopkeeper.

'He likes the black ones,' the boy's mother was saying.

'And the red ones too, Mam.' She laughed with the boy.

'And the red ones too,' she repeated, guiding her son out of the shop.

A look of surprise and friendship crossed the man's face when he saw Barry. The hand of friendship was eagerly sought when Barry extended his towards the shopkeeper.

'Tommy, how are you doing, mate? How's the missus and the bairns?'

Tommy answered, in the sing-song voice of the north east.

'Everything's canny. Mind, I've not seen you, Barry, for an age. Where have you been keeping yourself?'

'Busy at the Royal. It's been manic since the new extension was completed and the new chef, Maurice, joined the team. You know Doris.' Barry shrugged his shoulders. Tommy nodded. 'But let me introduce this little lady who's come to work for us, all the way from near London. Debs, this is Tommy, my good friend that I went to school with a million years ago.'

'Give it a rest, man. I'm not that old, you speak for yourself.' He turned to Debs. 'Hello. I hope he is showing you the best of Helmsley, pet.'

Debs nodded, and Barry agreed. 'That's why we are here, Tommy. Can we have a quarter of Black Bullets. Sweets for the sweet.'

'Oh, I bought some the last time I was here.' She smiled and told the story to Barry, and reminded Tommy of when she had visited the town.

'We get so many visitors. Sorry, pet, I didn't remember you, but never fear – I won't forget you now.'

They talked a little but were mindful of the time. As they walked back to the bus stop, Barry was plunged in nostalgia.

'I miss the old county sometimes, especially when I meet old friends. You remember the good times, the stunning beauty of the land and the windswept dunes of the coast. God, there's a wind that comes off the sea that could cut you in two. Well, it certainly could take your breath away.' Barry chortled at a thought. 'You'd come away with a red nose and cheeks and your lugs would tingle with the cold.'

'What's a lug?'

'What's a lug? Can a sophisticated girl from the south not know that?'

He was smiling at her. 'Ears, what else?'

'It sounds rather uncomfortable.'

'But it's bracing, girl, it makes you feel alive.'

He was silent for a moment as he relived a sad memory.

'As with everywhere in the north, there are pockets of poverty. I shouldn't forget that.'

'Don't you find Yorkshire beautiful?'

'Yes, I do. Or I wouldn't be here, but I especially like it when a little more beauty comes to live in it.'

Debs looked quizzically at Barry, but he was not looking her way. She wondered what he meant.

The Royal was waiting, calling them back. On the bus, Debs, with the white paper bag full of black treacle sweets deep in her pocket, patted the bulge affectionately. She had had the perfect day, with a perfect man.

Barry couldn't quite believe it. To fall in love at his time in life was so unexpected. Seeing Debs almost every day had put a skip in his step. There were times, when he actually felt like a teenager again, and, at his age, it wasn't becoming. But tell that to his heart. He knew his heart wouldn't listen.

Those emotions kept on bubbling up, bringing the longings and dreams he had left behind in his dim and distant past. He'd had his share of girlfriends but not one relationship that he felt would have matured into a lasting love match.

He kept telling himself he had no chance with Debs, he was years older than she was. What would she see in him, beyond friendship? Yet, it was true that it was himself that he was trying to convince; he was afraid of being rejected and losing the friendship they had. If he didn't say anything, and not rock the boat, then their closeness would continue, and he liked that thought, while wishing for more.

The weeks had flown since April, when Debs joined the staff at the Royal. She had brought an energy and enthusiasm with her, and, to her credit, she was building up a friendship with Julia. There were times when the two ladies carried sadness with them. He had noticed it once or twice, usually when things were quiet in between shifts and they were on their own and trapped in their own thoughts. He knew that Julia carried the trauma of growing up alone in the orphanage. With no family anywhere, the institution had looked after her, fed her and clothed her, but she had never known love. That was why Barry felt for her, and acted the way he did. Someone had to.

Family had been central in his young life, so important that the loss of it had hurt him badly. The war had claimed his father when Barry was eleven. He remembered, with great clarity, his mam crying even before opening the telegram, clutching the envelope to her breast, as she implored God for it not to be what it was.

What good were the medals that the army had sent them? They already knew Da was a man of honour?

So many men died. In their street alone, eight of Da's mates had been killed in the same battle. They had all joined up together in the regiment, been squaddies together, shipped out together, and died together.

It was just him and his mother after that. Barry had become the man of the house, his mother used to tell him. They were better off than most, him being the only child. His mam worked for them both until he was fifteen, when he left school and got an apprenticeship at the local barbers. He often laughed at the sight of himself in the mirror these days. His locks were long gone, and, anyway, he preferred what he was doing now.

He couldn't have just upped and left his mam, even if he had wanted to. After his mother died of cancer ten years ago, though, he took work away from his roots and his memories. He came to the Royal without a family.

Doris, with all her bluster, had a heart as big as the moon. She had seen his grief and helped him through the worst of it.

Even with the pain of his loss, he was grateful that he had known an unconditional love, that stretched over the boundaries of death. Many a time when he was low, he could feel his mother with him. Love never really dies.

With the inheritance money from the sale of his mam's house, he had bought a two-bedroom home in grey solid stone: a terraced house, just two streets away from the inn. He had a small, squarish yard that was flagged, with two raised borders, one that held roses, and the other bulbs and shrubs and spring flowers. It was good to see the seasons in his tiny garden.

Sitting in his living room, he wondered if Debs would come and have a meal some time. He patted his leatherette Chesterfield. It might not be genuine leather but in its racing green, it looked good. His slippered feet pushed against the Axminster carpet. The diamond pattern, in greens, emerald and gold, went well with his settee. The carpet had cost a packet, but it would last him out. 'Buy cheap. Buy twice,' his mam used to say. It echoed in his mind and he smiled, as a warm feeling touched his heart. She was with him again.

It was so good to have a warm floor covering, so unlike the stained wooden floorboards and the clippie homemade rugs that most people had had when he was growing up. He remembered his mother cutting up old woollen garments and making the rugs, usually during the winter, sitting in front of the coal fire.

His eyes strayed to the Victorian fold-down table that had been hers, so cherished and polished until it shone with love. It sat under his window and his mother's favourite vase graced it in the centre. It was catching the sunlight through the glass; the crystal reflected a rainbow image onto his cream wall.

Two chairs stood empty, waiting on either side of it. Wouldn't it be wonderful to have Debs sitting on one across the table from himself? He should ask her to tea if he could find the courage. He had not felt alone in his home until now.

18

When Louis returned to his kingdom, he told Katie about the dream and that Debs had told him about another handsome visitor, called Malkira.

Louis was sure Malkira was the spirit that had taken Katie to the place where she had died. To have a malcontent spirit, a demon, roaming the Royal was worrying.

'But what is she doing there?' asked Katie for the third time.

'I wish I could answer that. In her dream, I was astonished to see that you and she were close friends in it. Imagine that!'

'Dreams can be tricky things; the poor old brain spends its time trying to sort things out. Mostly trying to right the wrongs and mending the broken, but sometimes just reflecting one's own insecurities.'

'I suppose so, but that's not answering your question, is it?'

Louis took Katie's hand and kissed it, looking squarely into her eyes as he tried to reassure her.

'I've helped people by joining them in their dreams. You remember I came to you, my darling, through yours? I could join with Debs to find out why she's here. From what I saw in the earlier dream, I would say that woman from the Echo doesn't exist anymore.'

'Do you think so?'

Louis nodded. 'I'll be very gentle with her.'

'You're a kind man, of course you will. When will you visit?'

'Tonight. No time like the present. What shall we do for the rest of the day? I've got no plans. A walk, maybe? I would be very glad to share an odd hour or so in your arms. What do you think?'

'Well sir, since you asked so nicely, let's find our favourite spot.'

And they headed for the tree of life and the grassy knoll that was theirs.

The moon was high in the sky, when Louis ventured out of his kingdom into the world of mortal men.

His curiosity regarding Debs living in Ravensend was an itch he couldn't scratch; the question he couldn't answer unless he blended with her. It must have been midnight in the Royal Oak. Apart from the settling of the building, letting out creaks as though it was complaining, all was quiet. He passed along the landing. The guests were in bed and the staff would be sleeping now. He became aware of the faint odour of sulphur. Louis knew what that meant. His recollection of years ago, when he had fought an evil spirit, revisited him. Was history going to repeat itself? The smell was fresh and sharp, which meant that some evil had moved along the hall landing not long ago.

Louis moved a little more quickly, aware that the smell was more pungent the nearer he got to the attic stairs. In the darkness, the mouth of the upward passage looked like a black hole, one that if he entered might not be friendly.

Why was that? Normally, it was not especially bothering, but that smell was sending signals to him. As he stepped into the void, he looked up. Two reptilian eyes stared down at him from the ceiling at the top of the climb. They stopped him in his tracks. He watched as the eyes changed from orange and black as a layer of blue overlaid the discs, until they were the colour of forget-me-not blue in a male, bronzed face that was looking down at Louis.

The demon was back. Louis shivered.

Malkira disappeared through the walls. Louis must be quick to get to Debs' side before the demon connected with her.

He was too late; the demon was out of sight, but his signature was still wafting in the air.

Only one of the beds was occupied, though it looked as though Julia had used her bed. The bedclothes were crumpled and laid back, but he hadn't seen her on the landings.

Debs was asleep, laid on her back, muttering some indistinguishable words. Whatever the dream she was having, she was not comfortable in it.

Louis laid his hand on her forehead, and he was transported to a shop of some sort. Groceries were displayed on the shelves and tins of biscuits with glass lids were stacked out in front of the counter. A door was open to the right of it. Louis could hear a male voice coming from the next floor; he knew he must go up to see what was going on.

It was something of a shock to find Debs, distressed and prone on a bed, while a young man was using her for his pleasure.

Her face told a story. She was biting her lips, and her eyes were tightly closed, as though she could shut out what was happening to her. Her hands were gripping the sheets; it seemed to reveal her agony.

If that was not bad enough, Malkira was taking pleasure from the spectacle as he hovered from the ceiling, above the bed. Pain and suffering were like hot buttered toast for him; they fed his hunger. His beauty was dissolved by the bloated belly he was displaying, and by the dispassion in his now icy blue eyes. True to his name, Malkira was the Angel of Iniquity.

Louis was disgusted – appalled – by the scene in front of him. He tried to force the man off Debs, forgetting that this was a dream, and that these were shadows of a lost reality, shadows that danced across the mind and were only silhouettes of no substance. There was nothing for his hands to purchase on, though, and they cut through the moving figure without stopping the motion of the man, or disturbing the dream.

Louis cast a pitying look at Debs. He was further downcast when he saw a much younger version of Debs lying there. Not the woman she was now. Here she appeared to be no more than a child.

Laughter came from above the scene; the demon was enjoying the spectacle; his distended stomach held in his hands was huge.

The laughter ricocheted into Louis like a bullet. This creature from hell should not be here, and he lunged towards the demon, but the spirit saw the movement and reacted.

Louis was too late. As he reached the ceiling, the demon withdrew through it and out of the dream.

Louis turned back for a second to look at Debs before following Malkira. The picture was different, the dream had changed, and the image of the bed and the young man were gone. They were replaced by another scene of a young Debs, sitting alone in a shabby room, surrounded by a heavy silence of sadness. A deep sob escaped from her into the gloom. She was holding a photo close to her breast, rocking backwards and forwards in a motion of despair. Louis could see her eyes were wet with tears; another sob escaped, and she crumpled into a tight ball on the settee.

Full of compassion, he was by her side in an instant. What he was going to say, he wasn't sure, not after seeing what he had seen. He touched her shoulder, forgetting for the moment that she was a dream, his hand passing through that shadow of the past.

There was something different happening here. In the past, he had been able to connect to dreams. He could only assume that Malkira's influence was stopping the connection. At least he should be able to talk to her, and was about to do so, when he noticed a door was partially open in the corner of the dark room.

Movement came from behind it. As it opened wider, a middle-aged woman came through. There was a feeling of annoyance carried by the woman as she walked into the sadness. She was frowning as she moved towards the weeping figure of the girl hugging the photo. The girl sat up hastily and a look of fear slid across her face. The dark-haired woman exchanged the frown for a scowl and snatched the photograph from the child's hands.

'Give it back.'

The girl tried to reach up and take it, but the woman turned her back and ignored the plea.

'You'll get over it.' The woman's voice was husky and hard, not a jot of sympathy in it. 'You'll go back to school, and everything will be back to normal.' She then turned back to face the girl and, without hesitation, tore the photograph into several pieces. 'You won't need this.'

The squeal of anguish from the young Debs was pitiful to Louis' ears. Who was this woman?

Between the sobs he heard, 'I hate you, Mother.'

Debs was reliving a part of her life, but whether this was a true version or twisted shadows, he couldn't know. What he sensed was this wasn't the time to invade this dream. Who or what was in the photograph? He couldn't intervene; it was too intrusive. He had learned something, however. There was a lot of pain hidden in Debs' past.

19

Debs had turned over heavily in bed, throwing herself to one side, so that her body was hanging over the edge of the mattress. Her subconscious was in fight-or-flight mode and recognised the danger of falling to the floor. She woke up with a start and in a sweat. The dream had been too real.

Her eyes flew open in a kind of panic. Distress was tight in her chest, and she realised that she was at the edge of tears. The attic was dark, but she knew from the familiar black and grey shapes and the smell that she was safe in the Royal Oak. Relief overcame her as she gulped back her tears.

The nightmares she had woken from were shadows of her past and they couldn't hurt her now; at least, not like the excruciating pain she had known back then. She shivered at the cold of the night as it encroached on her.

The past was past. The year 1956 should have been long gone, except, like a bad penny, it kept coming back to remind her. She shivered again. The nightmare had been strange. Those two men had been in her dream again and they didn't belong.

In her dream, she had felt the weight of Carl on her and grimaced.

She remembered the laughter above her as she lay on that bed. Another self was seeing the drama in that room, and her younger self pinned down on the bed, and she saw the bloated image of the beautiful man, Malkira, floating on the ceiling, enjoying the drama centred around her. Then she saw the other man, Louis, looking shocked and disgusted at the sight of Carl straddling her. He had tried to help and had chased the floating man out of the scene.

The image of her mother flitted into her headspace. She shuddered. Her heart was heavy. Her eyes filled with tears. There was no love there. She could never remember being hugged. She pushed the image away; it didn't help

She had escaped from all that now and had found a new family here at the Royal. Relief swept through her. She pulled up the covers, determined to get warm – the chill was quite intense. She closed her eyes to sleep again, but with the cold and the dreams, sleep was a long way away. Just as she was thinking of getting up, the bedroom door started to open.

Julia was tiptoeing into the room by the light from the landing. A look of surprise crossed her face when she saw Debs reaching over to the lamp and triggering the light while she struggled to sit up.

Debs recognised at once that look of 'God, she knows,' written all over Julia's face. Debs had worn that face many times herself as a teenager; she could still hear her mother's voice in her head, chastising her.

Julia's ruffled red hair and the love bite on her neck confirmed Debs' suspicion of some assignation.

'Where have you been?' Debs didn't mean to sound like a mother; it just came out. Disapproval hung in the air between them.

'You won't tell Doris, will you? I've locked up, now I've seen him out,' she blustered, blushing. Of course, thought Debs: Nick.

'You won't need to tell her anything with that love bite on your neck.'

Julia looked horrified as her hands flew up to hide the tell-tale mark that revealed that moment of passion.

'Oh God! She'll know that Nick stayed after work.' There was real panic on her face and distress in her voice. 'She'll sack us, for sure.'

Debs felt for her. Julia was a young, naïve girl who didn't see trouble coming. There was irony there, Debs thought. Wasn't she guilty of that, too?

'He must have got carried away.' Julia was biting her bottom lip, but said it as innocently as if she hadn't been there.

Debs wondered if the cocky young sod had done it deliberately, marking Julia as his, like a brand. Perhaps he hadn't thought beyond his own vanity and his prowess as a lover. Did Nick really think Doris would miss that blood mark on Julia's neck?. Only if she were blind.

He obviously hadn't thought at all. Doris missed nothing.

Debs was getting out of bed and moving towards Julia, who was looking decidedly uncomfortable. She put her arm around the girl's shoulder, and encouraged her to sit together with her on her bed.

'Don't panic, Julia. I'll lend you some foundation cream. A couple of layers of that and no one will see it. Just make sure you put it on for a few days until it's gone. But, looking ahead, you must warn your headstrong man not to do it again.'

'It's the not seeing him regularly that drives him mad.' In a dropped voice, she confessed, 'Me too.'

'It's none of my business, but I hope you do know what you're doing? Don't you?'

'We love each other,' Julia said defensively. 'I can't go to his and he can't come up here. What are we meant to do? We need some special time together, the same as everybody. What's wrong in that?'

For the life of her, Debs couldn't think of one reason, except the danger of pregnancy.

'Forget it, it's none of my business. But you are taking precautions, aren't you?'

'As a matter of fact, yes. Nick's not ready to be a father yet, and besides, his mother would kill him.'

'Good, that's a relief.' Strangely, it was. 'I'm going down to make a cocoa. I've just had an awful nightmare and I won't sleep for a while until my mind settles. Do you want one? I could bring a tray up?'

It was much nearer two in the morning when the pair of them finally settled to sleep. They had talked for over an hour, over the hot cocoa, and a bond had formed between them. They had been working colleagues until now, but now they had become firm friends.

They had revealed parts of their lives that had not been talked about before. They discovered that they both were running away from the past and were searching for a meaningful new life. They talked about making mistakes without being specific. It was clear that there was a lot of regret.

They both wanted to belong, and to find unconditional love. They were, it seemed, not so different.

Debs was honoured that Julia had trusted her with her life story of being in an orphanage, and how she had hated it: never belonging to anyone, like her friends at school did. How she had envied the children who were met at the school gate by their parents. She had been lonely for years and years. Being on her own was normal. It was sad.

It pained Debs, thinking that her own baby might have experienced something similar. Had it not been for the promise from the maternity home that Annie would be adopted and loved by a family who couldn't have children, the pain might have killed her. That promise had been Debs' one comfort through the years.

Under the blankets, Julia was thinking about the more intimate moments she had shared with Nick that night. It wasn't easy to be romantic in the kitchen at the Royal, but it was the one place that wasn't visited by staff after eleven pm. It wasn't comfortable, even with a couple of coats on the floor, but when the passion overcame them, it didn't matter. That urge to be so close that they became one drove them in the madness of love. It made her feel secure. She felt strongly about him, loved him, even when she didn't always like him. He was handsome, at least to her. Nick was her cheeky chappie, who often poked fun at her and made her laugh at herself. He said she was too serious and needed to relax more. Perhaps he was right. She had never had someone say they loved her until Nick. Her heart still leapt at the memory.

Was it really two years ago when he proposed to her? Her thoughts took her back to that afternoon in March, sitting in the lounge with him, between their shifts. They were enjoying a drink together when two things happened. First, she remembered when the gift had come to her. She was part way through answering Nick when she was suddenly overcome by a voice speaking for her. It was quite eerie, and she had felt ice move through her veins. The conversation didn't seem to come from her; she wasn't in control of her own voice or thoughts. When Nick confessed to cheating on her, she had been distraught with the betrayal but he promised he would never stray again. That was when he proposed.

She remembered he had asked while the fisherman talked of fish and Doris was sitting over a radiator in the lounge. It was cold. Even Nick was shivering when he asked her. It was the coming of her gift and it had affected them all. She heard and saw things now that she never had. Whispering voices came from nowhere; they came and went. She wasn't always sure what she heard, and she wasn't sure that the messages were for her at first but, over the past two years, transparent shapes were becoming more distinct, and the words were clearer. She assumed the voices were of the departed, and they posed no problem; they were souls that were just visiting. This inn was very old and many generations of Ravensend folk had touched it, passed through it. The images had become stronger as her gift grew.

Now, she could see the spirits; they were wearing old-fashioned clothes and hairstyles. It was comforting in a way: that proof that life existed beyond death. She had tried to tell Nick about the ghosts in the bar, and not forgetting the old man upstairs sucking on his clay pipe in the back bedroom. But he didn't respond well to her revelation.

'Bats in the belfry, if you ask me. Are you going nuts or something?'

Julia had been a little offended with the cutting remarks, but she understood that not everyone had an open mind about the afterlife. She, however, had always talked silently to her guardian angel when she was in the orphanage, and she believed in a universal love that came from beyond this world. It was a different kind of love she had with Nick, but that was the only kind of love that Nick understood.

Their kind of love made her breathless: a physical passion that took control of her emotions. It was a kind of madness that she never wanted to stop when she was in his arms.

Tonight had been special because she hadn't seen much of him outside work recently. It occurred to her that he was making excuses not to see her, and fear of rejection had been tearing her apart, but tonight her fears had dissolved. He had been her cheeky chappie again and all was well with the world.

Julia nestled down. In four and a half hours she would have to be up. She heard Debs turn over and was happy to have a friend near her. She was greatly comforted by the thought, and she was glad Debs was part of the Royal family.

20

His white markings were the only sign of him: his ginger fur blended in with the shadows. His back was arched and his tail stiff as though it was wired upright. His nose was in the air and the hairs on his neck were standing on end.

Mouser was on the prowl. The cellars had been inspected and were mice-free. The rest of the building was ready to be checked and he climbed the stairs. His senses heightened.

Something had passed him at speed in the shadows and it was neither man nor mouse. He was on high alert. Was it time to fight or flee? The few seconds he stood in the pool of darkness were enough to assess that the danger had passed. He remembered that odour. He had smelled it once or twice before but not as strongly as it was now.

He stretched out a paw into the dimness of the passage. His ear twitched. Something else was coming towards him. His nose sniffed the air, and his whiskers trembled with the shake of his head, right and left. His eyes turned: where was the presence coming from? It was different; whatever, whoever it was, Mouser wasn't afraid of it. In fact, there was something strangely familiar about it.

Louis was making his way towards the back bedroom. Mouser crept across his path, meowing a greeting, only once, as though recognising him.

Silly old cat. Animals were sensitive to the spirit world; the fabric between the animal and spirit worlds was extra thin. Louis knew Mouser could sense him and probably see him.

'It's me, Louis,' he said, stopping and bending, offering his hand to scratch Mouser's head, but the cat was not persuaded to be that friendly. He didn't run nor spit; curious, he stood on the spot. It took intense concentration on Louis' behalf to scratch the cat's ears, but there was no response.

'Have it your own way,' Louis chuckled, as the cat suddenly decided to rub up against his leg, only to pass through it. Almost in a huff, the cat turned tail and was down the stairs and out of sight in seconds.

Louis continued to the back bedroom. Passing through the door, he was aware of the faint smell of sulphur. Although the room was in darkness, a sliver of orange and gold light was shining through a thin ribbon of a crack in the wall near the window. The split was the full depth of the wall, and a bubbling yellow substance was escaping from the base of it.

Louis felt a presence other than the couple who were asleep in his bed. The reptilian eyes he had seen in the attic appeared and disappeared in a flash in the wall by the split. There was no mistaking it. This was the portal to the underworld of the demon's hell: Malkira's doorway to the mortal world and to his own kingdom.

Amazed, Louis watched as the crack started to close, slowly at first, like a zip fastening a case. It moved from bottom to the top, sealing itself until no evidence was left that there had ever been an opening. All the odour of sulphur disappeared with it, but Louis knew that this wasn't the last he would see of the angel and his wickedness. Warning bells were sounding in his head and the prickling on his neck confirmed it was just a matter of time.

It was with some relief that Louis walked up the path to his Tree of Life. Here in his kingdom, goodness still existed: Katie was still here; love was still here. These were the real things of value and he had to protect them. The fabric that separated the spiritual kingdom and the mortal world varied in its strength and thickness. It must be very thin in the bedroom, to allow that sort of doorway from hell.

Somehow, he had to seal that opening in the adjoining bedroom, though he hadn't a clue how it could be done. His father, who, when he visited that room, left no trace except perhaps the smell of tobacco behind him, might have an idea of what to do. His father had been on the heavenly plane for many mortal years and must have some knowledge about the underworld. Louis must try to summon him. To have the devil's lair on the other side of his wooden veil was disturbing, and Louis also realised how easy it must have been for Malkira to access his kingdom and take Katie to the churchyard. There must be no more visits. His darling girl must be protected, no matter what.

Here she was, playing with Champ. What a pity his dog hadn't been with her that day Malkira targeted her. Louis was sure Champ would have protected her.

Life went on, on both sides of the veil. The split in the bedroom wall had stayed joined. It was a relief. The whole house seemed to settle, and life was back to normal for now.

Louis found himself a new routine, checking out the Royal most days. If he wasn't doing that, he walked in the hills, where he was still looking for that opening to the moors where he had seen the stag and the red kite. He had found several tracks that led there, but an invisible barrier kept him on his own side. Even Champ with his trusty nose was defeated. He had yet to find a way through.

Louis was about to start out on his journey to the hills with Champ when a whiff of pipe tobacco snuck through the veil, and hit him.

'Dad! You're just the man I wanted to see.'

'Well, that's why I'm here. The angels had heard mutterings.'

'Mutterings?'

'Aye, they are always watching.'

Champ was fussing around Massie as though he knew him.

'Excitable, you were always excitable,' said Massie, patting the dog on his head.

Louis was puzzled. 'Dad, you can't know Champ. I carved him on the headboard.'

'Then, how come he's here in the mortal space? Tell me that. No, I'll tell you. Do you remember Pip, one of the farm dogs that took to you?'

'I do. It hurt to leave him behind when I went off to my apprenticeship, but that's life.'

'Aye, right enough. But you see lad, the love you had survived. The angels allowed his soul to enter your carving as you were moulding him. Didn't you feel something touching the wood? Well, never mind. Champ is your Pip, or Pip is your Champ. That's another gift from the angels. Love doesn't die. He was given to you so you could take him on your journey.'

Louis was astounded. It was true: he remembered finding the right spot on the headboard and being lost in his work. And now, the dog had been able to venture from the kingdom. It hadn't struck him before that only living souls could move from one world to the next. And it was also true that there was a tight bond between them, and now he knew why. It was a good feeling. Champ seemed to know too and pressed his nose into Louis' hand. The dog's dark eyes connected with his own. There was no doubt: love was there.

'So! What do I call you now?'

'Don't fret yourself, lad. It's not the name that matters. It's the way you use it.'

Louis nodded at the wisdom of those words.

'That brings me on to my next question, Dad. I was able to visit Helmsley. I just thought about the place, and I was there. I was taken by surprise by it but it made me think: suppose Katie and I wanted to visit other places we knew, that were hundreds of miles away. Can it be done?'

'Lad, you've been in spirit for over a century, and you are still a novice in the spirit world. You've always had the ability to transport yourself. It was you that tied yourself to the bed. Your insecurity. So, it held you. Trust yourself; the power of the spirit can take you anywhere.'

It was a day of revelations. However, the next question must be asked.

'Dad, what can you tell me about the underworld and Malkira?'

Massie stopped rocking. Slipping his pipe from his mouth, he leaned forward, using its stem as a pointer. Pointing it at Louis, he said, 'He's a bad lot, even for a fallen angel. He's a feeder: eats up pain and misery, loves a good war. He'll come and go, just when you think you're free of him, he'll pop up again. He has the world to roam, and he destroys what he can, as he travels. He has an army of lost souls, all seeking victims to feed from. One thing I do know, he can't stand goodness. Oh, and light.'

'What shall I do? He came and took Katie, took her to where she had died, and pretended to be her friend. He blamed me for her death, but she dismissed his claim of friendship. She saw through him and he let her go.'

'So, it's true he's been here, testing the ground. The angels will help if they can, but he answers to no one, except the devil. And the devil approves of him. I hope you can protect the place. You'll know when he's back; he brings the odour of Hell with him.'

Massie was fading. The visit was over.

Louis was perplexed. What could he do against such an adversary?

'Trust your guide,' was the last thing he heard his father say.

21

Something was going on between Barbara and Nick; Barry was sure of it.

It was the little things that he noticed.

Barbara seemed to spend more time in the kitchen than she needed to lately. Nick was full of good humour and smiles when she appeared. Barry had seen those long moments of eye contact, as though they had forgotten that they were not alone. And if they hadn't taken that forbidden step yet, in Barry's opinion, they were thinking about it.

He couldn't tell Julia; he couldn't destroy her dreams, and yet, they would be destroyed, whether it was today, tomorrow or in a month. Her world would come tumbling down. It was usually the best friend, and Barbara was her best friend. His heart was heavy, he loved young Julia and would protect her if he could. But how do you protect people from life?

How many times had he heard that the heart wants what the heart wants?

It was okay for the winners but what about the loser?

Harry Ramshaw had arrived to see Doris. There had been a change in the Royal. He and Doris were tucked away behind the bar in her office/living room. It was the room where they had found love. Doris had met him as he came through the door and spirited him away to give him some news: a story that Doris had heard from Maureen, an old school chum.

The tearoom on the High Street was a popular place for the locals. It was a watering hole for the weary shoppers or the ideal spot for ladies who lunch. It opened its doors at 7.30am and closed at 5.30pm. It was a dream realised for Roger, who had come from nothing. He hadn't done well at school and was a wayward teenager. The funny thing was, he didn't even know he could cook. Fate can be more mysterious than magic; his success was all because of Maureen: the most beautiful woman in the world and his. Good humour and care poured out of her. She made him feel wanted and safe; she was a harbour in the stormy sea of life. She, in short, had rescued him. They were an odd-looking match, like the children's poem 'Jack Spratt could eat no fat, his wife could eat no lean. And so between them both you see, they licked the platter clean.' He was thin and tall, quite scrawny, and she was what you would call ample: overweight but in all the right places. Her face carried youth in it, and she laughed easily. He often stood on his dignity. He smiled but not often; it was as though he had never learned how to.

Doris had been on the High Street a few weeks ago, when she saw a notice being put in the window by Maureen. 'Due to circumstances beyond our control. With regret…Your tearoom will close at the end of this month.' Doris couldn't believe it. She had known Maureen from school – and she admired the work ethic the couple had. They must have been on the High Street for over six years. How they had changed the dull snack bar, none too clean, and not well used, into a cosy, good eatery.

They were rivals in some ways, yet Doris understood all the work that went into building up a business. She found herself inside the tearoom talking to Maureen, with an offer to help. Maureen, who was always upbeat, was almost in tears when she related that the landlord wanted to double the rent. Roger had worked night and day to make this place their own; it was going to kill him to lose it. A single tear escaped down Maureen's cheek. That said it all. They were trying to find another shop in the town, Maureen said, but, in all probability, they would never find a perfect site again. Doris agreed. And with a lot of sympathy, she wished them well.

Two months had passed. Doris was looking for a new chef now that Maurice had quit. The Royal was fully booked at a time when much of the country was struggling. She had been out to place an advertisement in the local paper when she bumped into the couple.

'Well, now, how are you both? Did you find another shop?' She immediately wished she hadn't said anything. Roger looked daggers at her, as though she had insulted him. Maureen saw the exchange between them and wistfully told her, 'No.' Reaching out she took Roger's hand, like a mother might to give a child for security. 'No, not yet.'

'I'm looking for a new chef. I could perhaps take the two of you,' adding, more to herself than them, 'If Harry approves.' The words hung in the air, in a sort of disbelief.

Roger looked stunned, but Maureen had a look of sheer relief on her face.

'How about we have a trial period to see if we suit each other, should Harry agree?' Doris waited, not completely sure she was doing the right thing. But she had needs and they had needs. Hadn't she walked past the empty shop just days ago? It could be a win-win situation.

They had closed the shop and given up on their dreams. All the love they had bestowed on it had evaporated when they turned the key in the lock for the last time. The shop was up to let, but there had been no takers.

'Come and see me tomorrow morning. Talk it over and bring your answer.'

Maureen was suddenly animated: all smiles and nods.

'Thank you, Doris, we will. Would ten am suit you?'

'It would.' Doris smiled and went on her way, hoping that her empathy wasn't leading her into trouble. In her heart of hearts, she felt good about it, but what would Harry say?

Doris, in a moment of compassion had taken Roger and Maureen Potter on, and was telling Harry about the unfortunate couple without owning up to having hired them.

Harry Ramshaw, a landlord himself, couldn't understand the logic of what Doris told him. 'The man not only loses his tenants, but he also loses rent to boot until he finds new clients. Can you believe it?'

He was stopped in full flow, when Doris told him that Maurice had finally been replaced.

'Good news, love. That will take the load off you.'

Doris had been looking for some time now for the right person to join them. She had interviewed a few cooks and chefs. It seemed they couldn't settle in one job, and she didn't want to employ a chef that had a record of constantly moving. It was better not to buy into it.

Doris added, almost as an afterthought, that she had taken on the Potters.

'You what?'

'Well, Roger is a great cook. And Maureen, whom I've known forever, makes cakes that float, they are so light.' Doris had that look on her face that Harry knew well. She wouldn't be moved on this.

'Are you sure?'

'Positive. Even with our part-time staff, we are stretched at times. You know that.'

'I know, I know. I hope you told them that they are initially on trial.'

'Well, after employing Maurice and getting it wrong, of course I did. Except, I should add, I went to school with her. It will be fine. Trust me.'

'That's a coincidence. I was at school with him.' Harry shook his head. He loved her, but she still did things independently, even though they were business partners. She sometimes forgot to include him.

In fairness, his business interests were broad; he was a gentleman farmer and landlord of many properties. He sometimes wondered if he would drop one of the balls that he had up in the air, one day. But Doris was his only business partner, and he knew her judgements to be sound.

In their relationship, she had never put pressure on him. She was clever; she knew by giving him freedom, the time he spent with her was precious. She too liked her freedom.

He wondered if they would ever commit like other couples. Deep down he was beginning to miss not being with her daily. It had surprised him, the depth of his need. Looking at her now, self-assurance on her face, would she ever need him the way he needed her?

'Well, when am I going to meet my new staff?'

'I thought they might make dinner for us tonight. What do you think? A sort of test, just for you.'

'But you have hired them. Not a test, then?'

'Well, I did say that you have the last word, so yes, a test, and you'll see how well they cook.'

'Come here and persuade me,' he smiled. 'If you can.'

This time she was smiling; she always liked a challenge. She got up and closed the door of her private room.

Maureen Potter had always been a big girl. Her mother had told her she would lose her puppy fat as she grew, but she hadn't. Her size suited her, it didn't hinder her energy or enthusiasm for life. Roger had been attracted by her personality and he loved her. She was an ample woman with a sense of humour; not much dampened her zest for life. Five foot nothing in her stockinged feet, she rippled and shook when she laughed.

She was a good cook, but she specialised on the dessert side of the menus.

Her husband enjoyed cooking main meals, as he called them; 'meat and two veg', was his mantra. They were the perfect team in the workplace.

The Potters were making themselves at home in the kitchen at the Royal. They had spread themselves along the counters, with pots and pans and the many ingredients they needed to make Doris and Harry's evening meal.

Roger was preparing duck in an orange sauce. And Maureen was doing what she did best, and was busy making profiteroles served with chocolate toppings and double cream.

Nick was glowering on the other end of the counter. For the last month he had worked like a Trojan with Doris to keep the kitchen up and running. Even now he was preparing the food for the diners. Three large Yorkshire cheesecakes were cooling on the wire racks, and he was about to make a berry coulis, for the topping.

He had enjoyed the trust Doris had put in him, and with the casual help that came in, the kitchen had run like clockwork. He had thought that when they got more help in, it would be to assist him. He looked over at the couple who were working and chattering in harmony. Was he going to be pushed out? His nose was well and truly out of joint.

It wasn't like Doris to be disloyal; not like her at all. But why two extra persons, and who would be in overall charge of his kitchen?

He knew the Potters, but not well. He had taken Julia to the tea rooms once or twice by way of giving her a treat. More recently he had taken Barbara, and Maureen had been particularly friendly, he remembered. A small shudder went down his back. He whisked the berries rather harder than he intended, showering his face with flecks of raspberry juice.

He pulled the cloth towel from his belt, wiped his face clean, and looked over at Maureen. She was staring at him with a great grin on her face. God, she had seen him.

'Never mind, love, it happens to the best of us.'

She was waving a spoon that was dripping with chocolate, her voice was loud and it carried across the kitchen. The casuals stopped work, and stood looking at him. He felt like a fool, and, of course, he looked like one. Not to be outdone, he dipped his small finger into the mix, and tasted the contents.

'Delicious, even if I do say so myself.' The smile he returned to Maureen hid the anger that was raging inside him. It had not been her fault, yet he wanted pay-back for the humiliation she had brought to him in his kitchen. If they were to become staff, he would have plenty of time to sort out his revenge.

He smiled again, nodding to her, and the silly woman giggled.

22

Times were strange, some folks were tightening their belts, and had no money to spare. Others found it from somewhere and spent without thinking. Credit cards had made a huge difference to people's lives – spend now, and pay later – and the Royal had been busy since the spring.

With its ten guestrooms, it was still a small hotel, but a step up from the B&B it had been. They had cots and Zed-Beds to cater for families, but twenty guests was the average number of clientele. With that and the bar that the locals used, the business had done very well during the spring and summer. This year Doris was hoping for a good autumn; that way, no one would be laid off. Not that it was autumn yet, but the rate this year was passing, she felt she should have written her Christmas cards in January.

The Potters had settled in. And what a difference they had made. Roger had offered to tend the bar when and if he was needed. It made a change, he said, to see customers' faces instead of only feeding them. It was a suitable and fitting arrangement. The panic if anyone went off sick was no longer a worry. The rotas suited everyone. Doris was happy and if she was happy, so was Harry. Harmony filled the Royal.

Maureen was the glass-half-full type, always cheery, and hummed a lot as she worked. It was fortunate that she mainly worked the lunch and dinner shifts, because as the weeks went on, Nick was having difficulty being in the kitchen with her. He couldn't complain about her because she never put a foot wrong. Her food was delicious, and as Doris had said, Maureen had a lightness with her, when the kitchen could be as explosive as a volcano. Working in a crowded place, with people on top of you, and under pressure to get the customers served, caused a certain amount of tension and short tempers from the chefs. But not Maureen. Nothing seemed to bother her, not even when the soufflés dropped as they came out of the oven.

'Would you look at that?' A half-smile lingered on her face. 'I'd better get cracking those eggs again.' Shrugging her rounded shoulders and, humming a tune that Louis wasn't quite sure of – it could have been 'On Ilkley Moor Baht 'at' – she was back on the counter with a basin and beating yet more eggs, as she returned to her task.

Nick took a deep breath; Maureen had left the fallen dessert on the side table for the kitchen help to dispose of. Why didn't she clean up after herself? If he was in charge, he would see she did, but he wasn't, so he turned back to his work. He wasn't pleased at not being given the overall authority but as no one had, he saw the sense of it. Doris had somehow managed to make them all responsible for the kitchen, so that only she had the authority. He was steaming vegetables to go with the Barnsley Chop, that was finishing off nicely under the grill.

Barbara was waitressing and was in and out of the kitchen all the time, and that pleased him. She beautiful and was a bundle of fun. The attraction they had for each other they hid under the guise of friendship. As for his feelings about the girls, he was torn. Julia was faithful and he couldn't doubt her love for him, but she could be boring. Barbara made him tingle.

He sometimes wondered what had made him ask Julia to marry him. Was it the tears that she shed when he admitted he had been unfaithful, and why did he do that anyway? It must have been the guilt of sleeping with Barbara. With luck, Julia would never find out who he had slept with.

Nick struck the service bell to tell Barbara that the meal was ready. The pork chops were laid out on two white dinner plates, accompanied with chunky roast potatoes, rich gravy in a boat and a steaming dish of vegetables.

Barbara was dressed in an all-black uniform and looked stunning. Her fair hair was tied back with a black velvet ribbon, and the heavy fringe emphasised her large brown mascaraed eyes. Their eyes met, and a tingle went through his body.

'Table six.'

Louis took notice. Nick might as well have said 'I want you' for the words didn't matter, it was all in the tone.

Later, he saw Maureen leave with her husband. Roger had been working in the bar with Doris, but it had been a quiet night for it was wet and damp outside. Many of her local regulars had decided to stay at home. Doris had let Roger go early as Maureen was hovering.

'Get yourself off, we'll do no trade with the rain coming down like stair rods.' Maureen looked pleased. She had been in the kitchen since lunch.

Donning his jacket, Roger slipped his arm through hers, pulling up his collar against the inclement weather.

He said, jokingly, 'Let's see if we can't run in between the drops.' Maureen giggled. 'You are a daft sod. Come on, then let's go.' They leaped through the bar doors, with little more than newspaper for shelter held over their heads, as they set off for home. Doris smiled at Harry. She would be locking up soon and she wondered if he would stay for a nightcap. Harry had been waiting patiently, sitting on the bar stool to keep her company. Time had dragged that evening and Doris was waiting for the last customer to leave.

'I'll be getting off now, Doris.'

'Right you are, Ben, see you tomorrow.'

'Aye, if her indoors lets me.'

Doris laughed. "Course she'll let you, so she can have a bit of peace.'

Ben just winked. 'You know us too well.'

Harry watched Ben leave.

'I have to go too, Doris.'

'Will you not stop for a drink?'

'Not tonight. Sorry, love.'

'It's a pity you can't stay; I would have liked that.'

'I know, love, but business calls. I must get up to Middlesbrough for eight thirty tomorrow. People to meet.'

Doris gave him a cheeky smile. 'But baby, it's cold outside.'

Harry came beside her and pulled her close. In a low voice he whispered.

'Tomorrow night, I promise, neither flood nor fire will keep me away.'

'Promise?'

'Promise.'

And then he kissed her. And was gone.

Later that night, as Louis moved through the empty bar, making his way back to his kingdom, he heard a giggle coming from the kitchen.

The walls didn't stop him; he moved through them as though they weren't there and made his way towards the sound.

The kitchen was only partially lit, but even in the low light Louis could see it had been cleaned, ready for the next day. At the far end of the counter, away from an overhead light, a couple sat embracing each other on kitchen stools. Louis was taken aback, shocked to see Nick holding Barbara close. He was whispering words Louis couldn't hear, but whatever they were, they certainly amused her. Poor Julia. Julia was being betrayed and there was nothing Louis could do.

Louis left them to their deception. All he wanted now was to go back to his own darling girl, to hold her in his arms and love her. He knew the real meaning of love. The past had brought him the pain of deceit, the pain that Julia would feel soon. They would be found out; someone would see and tell. How could Nick do that to her?

As the weeks went on, Louis realised that the affair between Nick and Barbara was serious. It was strange that Julia had not picked up on the signs. Did she just not want to see what was going on? It was said love was blind.

23

Louis was on one of his night checks when he made the discovery.

The bar was, as usual, noisy and hazy with cigarette smoke. Heads huddled together over round tables that had seen better days. The polished wood was ring stained, where beer glasses had missed the cardboard mats and their wet bottoms had left their marks. The locals, mainly men, valued their friendships and their pints under the Royal's roof. There was a feeling of togetherness. It was a comfortable space, even for a ghost.

The banter that he could no longer join in with was not lost on him. He chuckled at the jokes and listened to the complaints about the families. It was usually about teenagers or the wife. Was it ever thus? He was in a good mood hanging around the regulars. Maybe that was why he was so shocked at what he saw.

It was late, the last order bell had gone, and the bar was emptying the locals onto the streets to find their way home. Louis was by the front door, watching the men he had known in life saying their goodbyes to each other. He would have loved to have touched them, said his goodbyes too. There were ghosts among those that left, as if they too were going home. How many spirits came to visit this old haunt, he wondered? He had been as they were when he met Katie. He wore his hair tied in a thong and breeches to below his knees. He smiled thinking about it; he had been quite fashionable in his time. Somewhere along the journey he had become a modern man, who had learned to live in this age.

Shadows were passing him. Some spirits seemed to stare, looking lost, as though they were searching, though for what, who could say? Once or twice, he thought he recognised someone from his past, but they moved on a different plane. He was still in his netherworld, and they didn't or couldn't communicate with him. The bar was emptying fast.

Barry put his coat on and called to Debs that he would see her tomorrow. She was looking as pretty as a picture. She hadn't been on duty that night and was dressed up to the nines. Barry's eyes were burning in desire for her. Louis could see it and he wondered if she could see it too. There was real happiness there and it was good to see them getting on so well. Barry was one of the good guys, and Debs needed one of those.

From where Louis stood, he could see Roger clearly behind the bar, holding a pot towel in his hand as he went to the till. Louis watched as Roger rang up the till, releasing the drawer and dropped a few coins into the tray. All normal, until he saw Roger use the towel to hide his other hand. Roger lifted what looked like a few pound notes from the tray, swiftly pushed the wadge deep into his pocket. He closed the drawer, using the towel to dust it and was busily polishing a glass when Doris came up behind him, making him jump.

She was there, as she was every night, to take the takings.

'Still here? You get yourself off; I'll lock up.'

'Right you are.' He carefully folded the cloth, and hung it over the beer taps.

'It's your day off tomorrow, have a good one.'

'Oh, I will.' He subconsciously patted his pocket.

'Going somewhere nice?'

'I'm taking the missus to Bridlington.'

'I hope it stays fine for you.'

The conversation was over, and Doris walked Roger to the door.

'Night, say hi to Maureen.'

'I will.'

Passing Louis on the way, Doris said, 'God, it's cold with that door open. Let's be having you and I'll lock up.'

Roger waved as he slid through the door and out into the night.

Stunned, Louis watched him leave. He could not get over the gall of the man. How was he to let Doris know what he had seen?

Louis was ever watchful as the weeks went by, getting more frustrated at not being able to alert his friends to this rogue, Roger.

Then Katie suggested that he blend with Harry the next time Harry stayed overnight, and in his dream state, show him or tell him what was happening.

Louis noticed that Roger only stole when he was on rota with Barry. He used the same method each time and was very careful always to put coins in the till before he took out the notes. Louis realised that Roger, if he was challenged, would genuinely say he was depositing cash into the till.

By chance, it was only a couple of nights later when Louis realised that Harry was staying overnight. He had made no attempt to leave when the five-minute bell was struck by Doris. And both of them had a certain look of anticipation with a glow on their faces.

The bed in the Eden Room was Doris' pride and joy. If the room was free, Harry and Doris used it. Tonight was such a night, and Louis waited patiently behind the veil, until the talking and the lovemaking was finally concluded.

Katie was beside Louis, encouraging him through the headboard. Roger had to be stopped.

Once out of the kingdom, they crept over and stood by the end of the bed. The couple were wrapped in each other's arms, and were sleeping soundly. They were completely unaware that behind the headboard the bed was occupied by Louis and Katie. The two spirits were smiling at the sight of the couple before them.

'They love each other,' confirmed Katie.

Louis smiled in agreement.

'Time to talk to Harry.' Louis just put a hand on his friend's brow and he was connected to Harry immediately. Harry was in a deep sleep that was dreamless: Louis had a blank canvas to work on. Louis wove a little magic and the bar appeared in the unconscious space of Harry's mind. Shadowy figures showed Harry the till, and the drawer that was void of any money except a five-pound note.

A man's figure came and stood over the open drawer. The five-pound note was in his hand and the till was empty. The man popped the note into his trouser pocket.

Louis related what he had seen, telling Harry he should check the daily receipts going back a while. Harry tossed himself over away from Doris. He was coming out of his deep slumber, coming up to the surface and reality.

Doris was being disturbed; the intrusion into Harry's sleep was waking her too. Louis withdrew his hand and backed away from his friend, hoping he had given him enough information to be suspicious, hoping he would remember it the next morning.

'I've done what I could,' he said to Katie. 'Let's see if it works. And I'll try again if it doesn't.'

Doris was muttering in her sleep. She had turned over and flung an arm out of the bed and was fumbling at the covers.

'Cold,' was all Louis heard. But he knew she was coming up from sleep.

'Time to disappear,' whispered Louis.

Together they floated back into their own kingdom and settled down to wait and see if Louis had done the trick.

What made Harry ask to examine the accounts the next morning he wasn't sure, but he had woken with a sense of urgency in him to do it.

Doris was surprised when he suggested they check the receipts and takings over the last month, especially when he couldn't explain why. But she was a great believer in following your gut instinct and agreed to get the information ready for them to look over that night.

24

Roger had had a great time in Bridlington with Maureen. The sun had been kind and the wind had been restrained; they had even managed a paddle in the cold North Sea. It had made Maureen shriek and dance, hopping from one leg to the other until it seemed less cold as her feet adjusted to the water's temperature. At that point she had decided to become playful, and she kicked with all her might at the incoming waves and caught Rodger at the water's edge, wetting his rolled-up trousers.

It had been a bit of a laugh and all the expenses paid for by Doris.

Roger chuckled to himself; it was so easy. God, how he had sweated the first time he had helped himself to the takings. What made him do it? He still didn't know.

He had been grateful at first for the job at the Royal. Maureen had settled in. She loved cooking wherever she was, but he had lost out. He was no longer the boss of his kitchen, and along with the guilt he felt resentment. He had worked hard; it hadn't been his fault that it hadn't worked out. His landlord had wrecked his life when he put the rent up. Hell, he still had a mortgage to pay, and he had had no money coming in.

No one could understand the pain he had felt losing his dream, when the door on his tearoom closed for the last time. For eight years he had worked morning and night, building up a clientele. Some came to his shop so regularly that they had become friends. Now, it was all gone. Even Maureen didn't understand his loss.

He was envious, Doris and Harry were doing more than well, considering the financial climate in the country. The resentment in his soul turned from envy to jealousy over the months. Why should they have so much when he had so little?

If only Doris had made him head of the kitchen, that at least would have given him some self-respect. He had been his own boss; now he was only an employee.

He did his job quietly and quickly, and he kept his head down. He didn't have the luxury of losing his job, and yet he couldn't help himself taking what was easy money.

His style of cooking food was plain fare. It couldn't be compared to Maurice's, but there were no complaints. Well-cooked food, in healthy proportions, was what people wanted, he believed: not food that had been messed about with. He nodded at that thought, agreeing with himself.

He had volunteered to work the odd night behind the bar, to help with his own finances. He had felt the pinch, having been without wages for two months when the café closed. The temptation came one night when he was working in the bar. He was putting change into the till, when it struck him how much money was staring back at him. A cluster of pound notes lay together. How many were there? he wondered. No-one would miss a couple. And so, it started.

He was careful not to take the money every time he worked at the bar, and he also made sure that Barry or Debs were on duty with him when he did. There was no pattern to his thieving and two or three suspects if the money was missed. Nobody would cotton on, would they?

Harry had gone through the accounts. He and Doris had worked into the night, checking and double checking but he couldn't find anything wrong with them. He compared day by day, week by week. Obviously, some days had fewer customers than others, so there were days when they showed a few pounds down here and there, but when comparing weeks, there was nothing to worry about. The balance was still healthy. What had troubled him so, he couldn't guess. He pushed it aside with a sense of relief, but over the days it kept coming back. He couldn't put it completely out of his mind.

One thing he had to concede was that the Potters had made a huge difference to the Royal, and Doris had been right to take them on. Because of them, they had not missed Maurice. It had ruffled Nick's feathers at first. You would have needed to be blind not to have noticed the scowl on his face in the kitchen. Harry had told Doris so, but she just said Nick would come around and once again she had been right.

It appeared that Maureen was a dab hand at all types of cooking. She had more talent than Maurice had, and Doris told her so. Maureen just preferred to cook desserts. Sweets for the sweet, she said.

Harry thought Roger was an odd cove. He didn't smile much, but, there again, fate had been unkind to him.

Now, because of their input, it meant Harry had more time to spend with Doris. She wasn't as tired all the time, holding all the strands of their business together, which pleased him. All in all, it was good.

25

In the depths of the underworld, Malkira opened a sleepy eye in the dim light of his cave. He lifted his head; he was still in human form, apart from his tongue,

His sense of smell was much stronger when his nose and forked tongue worked together, and his tongue was, even now, flicking in and out of his mouth. It filtered the air, rather like radio waves finding a signal. There were definitely possibilities on the mortal plane. And he would be ready to pursue that, once he had recovered from his trip to the war in the East.

He and his army had feasted for months on the pain and deaths that swept the countryside. The Viet Cong and the Americans were both losers. Only Malkira's tribe of evil were the winners. It was so fortunate that the humans never learned from the past. Both sides fought for peace; it was so superbly stupid of them, but it kept his kind fed. The war wouldn't last much longer, sadly.

This modern-day warfare was marvellously destructive. The weapons they thought they had invented came from him. Gifts. So many gifts. He was their inspiration, but they never guessed.

Six months more, perhaps, and it would end. He and his army would move on to fresh fields. He had gored himself with a feast of disaster and now he needed to sleep off his gluttony. Back in his favoured form, he coiled himself into a crevice. Laying his head on his body, he drifted off into his nightmarish memories and dreams of the wars to come. Africa and Afghanistan were earmarked for conflict soon: already his army was stirring hate. Odium had to have time to grow, but not yet. Sulphur clung in the air around him in his lair. He was back.

26

Things had not gone Maurice's way after his dramatic walk out on the Royal. At first, he wasn't worried, until he woke to the fact that Doris didn't miss him. It came as a terrible shock. She hadn't come knocking at his door, begging him to come back and save her business. He was confident he could walk quickly into another job, but when he showed his face in Harrogate again, it seemed there were no vacancies. Times were hard. Nothing happened the way he envisioned it, and he was devastated.

Still hoping that he would find a kitchen somewhere in the surrounding countryside, he applied at all the hotels, but after a month he had failed to get one interview. His hope and confidence dropped to zero. He decided he had no choice but to swallow his pride and try to get his job back.

Thinking it and doing it were not the same. How many times had he walked across the square to the front door of the Royal? Every time his courage failed him, and he hadn't been able to push the door open.

That door that had once been so welcoming now seemed more solid than a block of stone; too heavy to push open. He was ashamed of himself. He was embarrassed that he, a master of culinary skill, was being reduced to beg for work and, even more, that his courage failed him. It seemed the Royal Oak was a full yard too far for him to step up and go inside.

Another two weeks passed. He couldn't continue to hide out any longer in his rented home. Nervousness had prevented him going into the town, afraid he might meet the staff from the Royal, which would only further the humiliation of being jobless.

Denial was easy. He wasn't to blame. She – that woman, Doris – had derided him, worked him to the bone until he had had some sort of turn: A mental breakdown. He did remember feeling rather strange before she arrived in the kitchen. He had heard a voice so like his own, deep in his head. He had been overtired and had reacted to his emotions. That overpowering indignation which exploded from him was not exactly in character. He admitted he had a temper, but surely an artist such as himself was allowed a little licence?

Time had proved a huge learning curve for him and he finally faced the truth: a prima donna's temperament was only tolerated when you were at the top.

He looked in the mirror, combing his hair over his balding head. He sprayed it with non-perfumed hair lacquer; it wouldn't do to smell flowery.

He donned his jacket, straightened his back, took a deep breath.

This wasn't going to be easy. Several times he had gone to the front door, and he had tried to phone once, but at the sound of Doris' voice at the other end of the phone he had chickened out and hung up. Today he would go around the back. The door was often left open for fresh air. It was a warm summer day, with blue skies, and cottonwool clouds: a perfect day for the door to be wedged open.

The cobbles underfoot felt hard under his highly polished, black shoes: shoes that reflected his thoroughness, shoes in which he could almost see his face in the reflection, once he had cleaned them. One had to keep up appearances. That was important to him. He walked past the front door, following the wall down to the snicket and he disappeared up it. Head down, his eyes following his shoes, glancing up only once, he was relieved to see the door was indeed open.

A row of tightly lidded dustbins, lined up against the wall outside the kitchen, looked like soldiers on watch to guide him in. He stopped by them and listened.

Muffled voices were coming from the interior. A moment of panic flitted through his stomach, but he was here and the way was open and clear. He must see it through. Touching his head nervously to check on his hair – he must look tidy, he thought – he pushed his shoulders back and made his reluctant legs walk through the doorway. He got as far as the pantry and the door that led into the kitchen. It bustled with staff preparing lunch. A heavily built woman was working at his station, with a tallish man chopping vegetables beside her. Doris was nowhere to be seen. His gut twisted in raw panic. By the look of it, he had been permanently replaced. He was holding back his temper, but it was rising, Doris would be in her office and he knew the way.

'What, he came into the kitchen uninvited?'

'He did. Honestly, Harry, it was so awkward when he appeared at my door.'

In the soft lamplight in the Eden Room, Harry could see that his woman, who lay beside him, was still upset. The visit from their ex-chef had shaken her up. Doris was as tough as nails on the outside but as soft as marshmallow on the inside. She covered it up so well.

So much for romantic small talk. He looked in her face. 'Okay, let's be having it.' He pulled her closer in his arms, and kissed her hair; he knew she needed his reassurance, and he was the man to do it.

'I jumped out of my skin, Harry. It was no tap – he thumped the door and that's a fact. He was red faced and angry when he pushed his way into my snug.' She paused as the picture of him rose again in her memory. 'I ask you.' She paused. 'Then he demanded his job back.' She shivered. Harry detected a small sob, as though she had caught her breath.

'He was like a bull in a china shop. He told me he had put my restaurant on the map. He had made my business; it was his food that had made it a success. And that I owed him and owed a lot. I told him that he'd walked out on me – I hadn't sacked him – but he wasn't listening. Then he started threatening me, shouting in my face so close I felt the spittle erupting from his mouth as he spat out the words at me. God, it was frightening.'

'Doris, love.' He pulled her nearer. 'I hadn't realised.' Harry was stunned. The anxiety he could feel coming from Doris shocked him.

Doris gripped his hand and relived the moments when Maurice, still full of anger, shook his fist at her. 'You brought in the people from the tearoom to cook in my restaurant.' He had stopped mid-stream, gathering himself. 'A tearoom, for God's sake. I'll finish you.'

'I'm not often frightened, but I tell you, I was shaking. Thank God, Barry heard him from the bar and came to the rescue.' Her hand went to her mouth, and she was unable to speak for a moment. 'If he hadn't been there.' She shut her eyes tight. 'Anything could have happened. Oh, it was such a relief. He's a good friend.'

'My poor love. I should have been there for you.' And he meant it. Doris was his love, and should have been his responsibility. Doris shouldn't have been put in danger. There mustn't be a next time. There wouldn't be a next time, if he anything to do with it.

Maurice was beside himself with worry and anger.

Two weeks had passed since the angry exchange at the Royal. Barry had humiliated him still further by manhandling him and throwing him out. He could still feel himself being held by the scruff of his neck with one arm thrust up his back. He was bundled through the kitchen and pushed out into the alley, landing against the metal bins.

He almost choked on his shame, and felt a new depth of hate surge through him. Ideas of revenge flowed through his imagination. How to put them in practice was a problem, but he had promised Doris he would finish her, and that was what he intended to do.

It was just after dusk when Maurice slipped out of the house. He was only a ten minute walk from the Royal, and, under the cover of darkness, he felt confident he wouldn't be recognised by anyone.

He walked with his head down and had taken to wearing a dark jacket and an old flat cap that he had found in the hall closet in his rented house. A forgotten item from a past tenant, perhaps, it served its purpose that night. Dressed this way, the cap would hide his face as he walked under the glare of the street lighting.

His first act of vengeance was now in progress. He almost felt happy, now he was doing something to pay Doris back. He had decided to scatter rubbish from her bins on her nice 'clean' back doorstep. There was a mixture of excitement and anticipation pulsing through his veins as he quickened his pace up the High Street to the snicket. The darkness had closed in fast, with heavy grey clouds settling over the square, and the onset of light rain was excellent cover for him.

The few people that were about were scurrying by like bats out of hell, heads down, seeking a dry sanctuary. No one took any notice of him.

The light from the Royal across the square graced the pavement, bidding welcome to all those who sought warmth and shelter. Tonight, he was the only one walking toward it. He crossed the square quickly, hunched over, facing the rain, until he reached the alleyway and slid into it.

The dustbins were in their usual line. He sniggered. They would not be on guard tonight; by the time he left them, they would be more like drunks that had had one too many. They must be full to bursting, he thought, considering that bulging, black plastic bags were stacked on top of them. Two crates of empty milk bottles were also waiting to be collected, but they were not his target tonight.

Fate had been good; it was going to be so easy to knock the plastic bags off the bins. With a kind of joy and satisfaction, he pulled the first black container down, ripping it as he did. Eggshells, potato skins and carrot peelings fell out over the cobbled ground, together with coffee grounds, tea bags and all matter of waste. For good measure, as he was wearing wellingtons, he used his feet to grind the waste food into the cracks around the cobbles. Satisfied with his work, he decided to kick over one of the metal dustbins as a final touch. It rattled and clattered as it rocketed to the stone floor, and, with an extra kick, it rolled over the wet ground making a noise that could have woken the dead. He was enjoying himself, but, wary of the noise he had made, he decided enough was as good as a feast. The light rain had turned into a steady downpour. It was time to go. The cobbles were becoming slippery, and, mindful of his rubber wellingtons, Maurice made his getaway carefully.

He was almost giggling. He felt like a child again, running away on Mischief Night because of a prank. Knocking at doors and running away had been such fun. He remembered hiding just far enough away to see the door opening and the bewildered adult searching right and left for the missing visitor.

Those were the days. November 4th was not observed much these days – modern kids didn't know what they were missing. With a smile from ear to ear, he made it back to his home, shutting the stout wooden door behind him and resting against it. What he needed now was a drink. A small plum brandy would slide down a treat.

Phase one of his plan was complete. Tomorrow he would implement phase two, and report to the council that the kitchen at the Royal had mice droppings. He almost giggled again. Doris and Barry would get their just desserts. He would love to be a fly on the wall when the inspectors came in.

Barry was on the rota for the evening meal. He was in the kitchen when the sound of some sort of accident was heard. The noise had come from the back door, and had made the staff jump. He hoped it wasn't drunks fighting. He hurried to the door to see. He stuck his head out into the night, but hadn't expected what met his eyes. Rubbish was strewn everywhere and getting sodden with the deluge of rain that was falling. He looked up. The night sky was blackened with rainclouds; it was set for the next few hours.

'Oh, damn! A job for in the morning, I think?' The question was more for himself than anyone. Nature would just have to get on with it and do its worst. it was going to be a dirty job tomorrow. The rain was soaking his face. He wondered who or what had caused this. There was no sign of a cat around and certainly no people. In all the time he had worked at the Royal, this had never happened. He shut the door, sighing. He would have to come in early in the morning and deal with it.

'I think we probably had a couple of stray dogs round the bins last night. I can tell you, it was pretty disgusting the mess they made, what with the rain and all: soggy napkins and waste food lodged in the cobbles. Man, what a dirty job. I had to hose the alley down. Thank goodness it's bin collection day. We should get rid of all of it.'

Barry was telling Harry about the clean-up that he and Nick had tackled that morning.

Harry had popped in to have breakfast with Doris and caught Barry with his sleeves rolled up and wearing rubber gloves, his navy and white striped apron looking decidedly sad with grime and water.

'They would be after the scraps of meat, I expect?'

'No, it can't be that. We're very careful to wrap the scraps and they all go in one of the metal bins. But, on reflection, I suppose one of the casuals could have been a bit careless.'

'On another subject, and on the quiet,' Harry went on, 'Can you tell me what you think of Roger? He wasn't my favourite person at school, but people change.'

'He's a quiet one and that's a fact. Still waters run deep. He only really smiles at Maureen, but he does a good job in the kitchen. I have no complaints.'

'Thanks for that. I needed to know. I'll get out of your way and let you get on. I'm hoping to eat with Doris if she's free.'

'We'll make sure she is,' Barry confirmed with a nod. 'We don't want to upset the boss.' And then, as an afterthought, 'Either of them.'

27

Harry had known Roger as the bully of the playground: that noisy place, full of joy, laughter, shouting and skin-on-skin when the fights started. The hurly-burly of life, you could say, learning about the real world that existed outside school: the world they would join as adults in a very short time hence. It was a place acting like a garden nursery, where different plants grew: different shapes and coloured leaves, some plants tall, some small, some beautiful and some not so; incubated and shaped by the others around them and by the gardeners who had tended them.

Gangs seemed to form naturally among the boys, often with a bully as their leader. Harry had no idea what sort of background Roger came from, but, like all children, he assumed that all the other children lived a similar life to his own and had parents with the same values as his: rather strict and old fashioned.

Now, he knew differently. He supposed, from a teacher's point of view, that the children in his class must have brought all kinds of behaviour and personal problems with them, and, although, ideally, they should have been left at the school gate, they were not.

The playground proved that. Harry remembered poor old Four Eyes –Thomas, a skinny lad and small in stature too – being held in a head lock by Roger. A ring of boys surrounded the two of them. Thomas was trying to twist free and, in that minute, Roger grabbed his arm and held it up the boy's back, his movement pushing the boy forward so his spectacles fell from his face. There were cries from the crowd that brought a teacher to Thomas' rescue. The teacher had stopped the bullying, but Harry remembered there was no repentance in that word 'Sorry' that Roger was obliged to utter. If Harry hadn't inherited strength of character from his father, he wondered where he might have ended up. But didn't we all belong to one tribe or another?

Harry had not been a joiner. If he was honest with himself, he had been a bit of a loner. He got on with most of the lads, he had played sport well and was part of the school teams. He had enjoyed that; it gave him a sense of worth. He had been a bright pupil according to his father, and he knew good things were expected of him. But that was okay, he wanted good things for himself too, and, if he was truthful, he enjoyed learning.

He hated gangs, and Roger's comprised of several from their class. It was unfortunate that they picked on the smaller or younger boys, which made Harry angry. He had stepped into the fray a few times to stop a boy getting a thumping. Perhaps because he wasn't afraid of the gang, or Roger, they never went after him.

Harry realised, once he had become a man, just how lucky he had been growing up: so lucky, in fact, that he sometimes felt guilty about his comfortable beginnings. It had always been assumed that on leaving school he would work for his father on the land, in farming. He had never had a silver spoon upbringing; his father had seen to that. 'Never take anything for granted, lad,' was his father's mantra, and he believed it. When his father died, leaving him money, the farm and tenant cottages, he went about building up his own small empire, and he knew people like Roger never had that start.

Roger was the boy that had sat behind him in class, who flicked bits of chewed paper at him when Harry was working or kicked the back of Harry's chair when the teacher was speaking. Only once had Harry nearly retaliated, when his chair was pushed so violently that his dip pen had skidded over the page of work, leaving marks a spider might have made. His teacher had not been impressed and his work was marked down. Harry caught Roger in the cloakroom. He remembered the look on

Roger's face when he had backed him into a corner. 'You are never going to do that again, are you?'

Roger went red in the face. 'Say no, and that will be an end to it.' Harry had said it so calmly, without raising his voice, that Roger seemed to find it more intimidating than if Harry had threatened him. Roger nodded and said 'No,' very quietly. Harry had never needed to speak to him again. He hadn't snitched on Roger and had never hit him. What was the point of that sort of retaliation? Trouble at school would inevitably mean he would be in trouble with his father, who didn't take kindly to disruptive children. This had been a much better way, but he had never liked Roger since those so-called halcyon days.

As it happened, Harry had read in the local rag that Roger had married. Reading further into the article, he discovered they were both cooks and were setting up a tearoom on the High Street. He had been quite surprised at that, but at least the connection between them made sense.

The China Plate tearoom was a little oasis of calm and reflected the past more than the present. The cream and rose-pink walls were decorated with prints of garden flowers, with a small explanation of which flowers represented the sentiment that the Victorians loved so much. He had thought it must have been Maureen's idea. Harry couldn't imagine Roger choosing the flowers. A tulip meant love; a peony, happy marriage; gardenia, secret love. The walls were hung with prints of snapdragons, and daffodils, and lilies, not that he could remember all the sentiments that went with them, but together with the china crockery that didn't always match, the atmosphere was extremely comfortable.

Maureen was full of energy and warmth, and the breakfasts, lunches, and teas she served were exceptional. Her pastries melted on the tongue. Harry would visit from time to time. She treated her customers like friends. Roger's ample missis did the talking for both of them; he was more standoffish, but even he smiled, and in the back of Harry's mind, he saw him wave as customers left, with a refrain of 'Come back and see us again.' The tearoom was successful. It must have been a bitter blow that, through no fault of theirs, it closed.

Harry almost felt guilty that he could find so little charity in his heart for Roger, for, although he might not like him, Maureen was a good sort and the couple had worked hard to make the tearoom pay. What a blow, what terrible luck for them from a greedy landlord, who in his opinion had overplayed his hand. Harry had been lucky in life, and the bounty of his hard work was all around him. Cottages, businesses, and the farm. Harry was thoughtful in his dealing with staff, but there was something that he couldn't put his finger on when it came to Roger. There was that look of envy that he sometimes saw in the man's eyes.

Barry had told him what he already knew, but it was good to have it confirmed that Roger was working hard for the Royal Oak: an asset. It was time to let the playground go and see the adult Roger without the memories of the child Harry had disliked so.

28

It had been a long painful year: a slow-moving journey of grief, watching the days pass, with the regular monotony of living. The pain and void that Katie's death had left was still as large as ever in her parents' lives. Counselling hadn't helped and they were sick of hearing that time would heal them. The tears may have stopped, but the wound would stay open forever.

Days and months had passed. It was September and today was the anniversary of their daughter's death. They sat at the kitchen table, numb with emotion. In front of them sat bowls of untouched soup.

The couple had barely surfaced in the last twelve months. Once popular and outgoing, they had shut themselves off from their neighbours and friends. Their son and his wife had become their focus, afraid now of losing another child. They would be grandparents in three months, an event that they hoped would refill them and heal some of their desolation.

It was because of this new life, this coming blessing, that they had agreed, moments ago, to visit the place where Katie died with Louis. It was time to find closure, time to say goodbye, so they could move on. They hoped against hope that visiting Ravensend would have the desired effect.

In Ravensend, life was swimming along fairly normally until Doris got a letter, enquiring about a booking, from Joe and Lori Brown: the parents of Katie, her employee and friend, Doris was flummoxed.

Doris and Harry had been having breakfast in the dining room when Debs brought the post. A cream-coloured envelope with a Hertfordshire postmark was handed to Doris.

'What do you think of this?' She was holding the letter with her index finger and thumb. A puzzled look crossed her face, causing a frown at the written words. Doris passed the letter over to Harry. Moments later, he handed it back.

'Katie's parents!'

'Yes. Oh Lord, I feel for them. They want to come here, to where she worked' – she stopped mid-sentence and whispered – 'and died. I suppose I'd better confirm that we will expect them next week. Oh, Harry, I'm not happy about it. It's going to be difficult.'

Harry took her hand. 'Settle yourself, woman, we'll meet them together. I'll be around as long as you need me.'

'Thanks. I guess I'll manage, but I can see it being awkward.' She smiled. Harry had a heart of gold; she was lucky to have him.

Joe pushed open the heavy door that shut out the town from the Royal Oak and, holding it open, invited his wife through.

They had chosen to stay where Katie had worked. Lori wasn't sure it was a good thing, stirring up more memories, but Joe wanted to see where his girl had been so happy. Doris had confirmed the booking for a long weekend in her small hotel, and they had arrived.

A strong smell of beer that lingered in the bar met them. They looked around and saw the world they had stepped into was a mix of old and new. Doris had said that six more bedrooms had been built, but parts of the Royal felt as though they had travelled back in time.

The dark wood bar was almost black with age and marked from the many customers that leaned and drank at it. A brass footrest, lovingly cleaned, gleamed around its edge. A bar towel lay over the pumps; they were obviously not yet open to the public.

A sign pointing the way to the reception was displayed, and a short bright passage brought them to an area next to the lounge, where a desk held a dome-shaped polished brass bell. Beside it was an invitation to ring it if the desk was unattended.

Joe gratefully put the bags he was carrying down on a racing green coloured carpet and hit the dome with some relief.

On cue, a small woman appeared with a large welcoming smile from the lounge. Her dark hair framed her good-natured face as she said, 'Ah! Welcome,' looking at the couple and then the luggage. 'Would you be Mr and Mrs Brown?'

Doris already knew the answer. Wasn't the lady in front of her an older version of Katie?

Joe nodded. This woman, so deftly described by Katie, must be Doris, the boss she had been so fond of. He swallowed deeply, hearing his daughter's voice somewhere in his memories. He cleared his throat.

'Yes, that's right. You must be Doris?' He inclined his head, waiting, but he knew he was right. She gave the briefest of nods.

'Good, let's get you two a cup of tea. It is exhausting traveling, isn't it? Leave those bags there; I'll get Barry or Nick to take them to your room. Come this way.'

They followed her, already liking her easy manner. Their daughter had judged well.

'I've put you in the room that Katie and Louis stayed in. I hope I've done right? They were very comfortable there. I'm sure you will be too.'

Doris studied the couple's faces for confirmation that they were happy with her choice for them. Only a slight nod from the woman acknowledged her gesture of kindness. 'So, that's settled.'

There was an awkwardness about them, as they sat, grateful to be at their destination but not apparently ready to share their emotions. Doris made herself scarce but was back within minutes, carrying a tray of tea and a plate of shortbread.

Doris talked about the weather, the North Yorkshire landscape, and how much she liked the couple that she knew as Katie and Louis. She had thought him to be an open book, and she was a good judge of character. She edged around the different names Louis had used.

'They were a warm and loving couple. People liked them and trusted them. Which is at odds, when you come to think of it, with the fact that

Louis wasn't Louis Parker. Except he was to us. In his past he might have been called Mike, but he never used that here. Why he changed his name, I have no idea.'

Nothing came forth from the couple, but it was obvious that they too were searching for an explanation. They were unable to share anything with her. The mystery remained.

Joe was deep in thought. So! Doris, too, was looking for explanations. They didn't understand why Mike changed his name and pretended to be Louis when Katie and he had visited that Christmas?

Why had Katie not been honest with them and introduced him as Louis, and why did he allow that?

When she said Mike had left the Echo, it was as though she was talking about another person. It also niggled them that Louis' nature was kind and gentlemanlike. He could never be described as arrogant, threatening or a big drinker, like the man Katie had described as Mike.

And what happened that day they were killed in the graveyard? And why were they there? The big questions, the 'whys', were buzzing around in the back of his mind, giving him no peace.

On the second cup of tea, a well-dressed man joined them. He introduced himself as Harry. Joe and Lori looked at each other. This was another name they knew from Katie, and he had been described very well. Here was the man whose life force was woven with threads that bound him into Louis' and Katie's lives. He had given Louis employment only hours after Doris had recruited Katie. That generosity had secured them a place in Ravensend.

Harry wasn't quite sure what to say. The couple had a weariness about them. Well, what else could he expect? he admonished himself. Grief was a long journey, and the unknown depth of pain would make anyone anxious. What words can ever help when a parent loses a child? He had felt the loss of his friends deeply, so what these two poor souls were going through didn't escape him.

With a sincere smile and an outstretched hand, Harry greeted Joe with a strong handshake. 'Nice to see you got here safely. I hope you can join Doris and me this evening for dinner?'

Harry reminded Joe of Louis: direct, friendly, and strong.

Joe took Lori's hand. It was a way of trying to reassure her, while gauging whether she was up to a meal with strangers, albeit friendly ones.

When she squeezed back, looking into his eyes, he had his answer.

'I must let Lori have a rest, but yes, that's very kind of you. Shall we say seven?'

It was mid-afternoon. September had been kind. A short Indian summer had blessed them that week and the drive up to Ravensend had been pleasant.

The northern countryside looked its best in the dramatic light. The greens of the fields so richly clothed in emerald colours, and the other fields of golden stubble with tracks left behind by tractor tyres. Patterns of lines left after the crops had been gathered in. It gave an image of quintessential England. And not a mill in sight after Leeds. Nevertheless, it had been a long and tiring journey, and what with the undercurrent of sadness pulling at their heartstrings all the way, they both needed a rest.

'Will you have a cup of tea and sit down and join us?' Doris looked at Harry.

'I'd love to, Doris, but I haven't finished for the day yet. I just wanted to say hello and say how sorry I am…' His voice trailed off as did his smile.

Joe spoke up. 'It's alright; we are learning to live with the empty space that was once filled by my Katie.' Joe's voice was powerful. 'We were so proud of her. Still are. We have questions that you may be able to shed some light on. So, thank you, Harry. In your restaurant, Doris? Good; that's settled.'

It seemed the right time to show the Browns to the bedroom. Harry nodded a goodbye, and with a slight wave, slipped out of the room.

'Well now, I'll take you up. The room is in the original part of the old pub. Though we have added an en-suite,' she reassured them. 'I'm sure you'll love the room.'

Doris eyed the reception. The luggage had gone. Her Geordie barkeeper, waiter and friend, bless him, had read her mind. He was the best.

29

They climbed the stairs together, following their hostess. The oldest part of the building was decorated to suit its heritage, and the carpet, in a deep, rich red, looked new. Assured that their bags had gone up before them, they were looking forward to some privacy to catch their breath.

Doris was in full flow, chattering nineteen to the dozen, but they hardly took in a word. Glancing at each other, and reading each other's minds, they wanted to get away from this conversation. Doris was kind, but they were overwhelmed by the long journey and now finally standing in the place where their dear daughter had spent her working life.

The ghost of her voice was playing back to them like a whisper, reawakening memories that she had shared with them in conversation about the Royal a year past. It felt so real that she might even appear in front of them, if they were very quiet, but of course that couldn't happen.

At the end of the passage, a wooden door with a mortise lock was waiting for them. Doris held the old iron key. It turned easily and the door swung open on well-oiled hinges, to reveal a wonderful carved bed that faced them as they entered.

The bed was both stately and majestic; it filled the room with its presence. The strong sunlight from the window highlighted the drama in the scene of creation carved into the headboard. The feeling of peaceful tranquillity that stretched back, deep into another world, took Joe's breath away. The tree with its bounty of different fruits, standing in the sun and embraced by its rays, was powerful, and the lovers, Adam and Eve, were recognised immediately by Joe and Lori. They knew this bed.

It was Katie's. Its warmth seemed to wrap itself around the room and possess it, enclosing them with it. It was like being hugged by their daughter.

Doris broke into their absorption. 'The gold bedspread finishes it off, don't you think? Katie and Louis loved this room, what with the rocking chair being similar to their own bed. I brought my chest up here, too. The pieces seemed to fit together.' She pointed to what might have been a bedding box, except for the grandeur of the carving.

She smiled and backed out of the doorway. 'Fresh towels are in the bathroom. I'll be downstairs if you want anything.'

She left her guests standing in a room filled with treasures. In the sunlight that streamed through the large window, they seemed to be welcome by the Royal.

'Well, here we are.' Lori was still looking at the bed. Tears waited to be released, but stubbornly they wouldn't come. If they had, she might feel better. Her emotions felt like they were squashed up in a bottle, with the stopper glued on so tight she could burst. 'Have we done the right thing?'

'We have to come to terms with the past and say goodbye,' Joe said, kindly. 'We haven't been able to do that in Hertfordshire. That's why we are here. So, yes, I think so, and – like bookends – we will support each other.'

As an afterthought, he smiled and, putting his arm around her, said. 'Be brave.' Lori swallowed hard, knowing he was hurting too.

The sun drew Joe to the window. Absentmindedly, he pushed the rocking chair and watched it rock. The butterflies on the back of it seemed to fly towards him and back over the grasses that half hid the dormice. There was magic in the movement.

'This is quite special, Lori. This is so similar to the one that was sent to us by the house clearance people. It's just like the one Louis carved for Katie, isn't it?'

Lori agreed. 'Perhaps Louis got the idea from seeing this?'

Through the window, Joe saw a small courtyard with a raised garden bed and dahlias and gladioli still in bloom. The gardens here were a few weeks behind theirs at home; the blooms in his garden had come and gone. The day seemed to have kept its warmth and it looked peaceful and calm out there. Joe sat in the rocker, contemplating. Lori unpacked the few things they had bought and deposited them in the wardrobe and drawers.

'Why don't we go for a walk, stretch our legs? What do you think? I've stiffened up with that long drive. Are you up to it?'

'Good idea, love. I'm sure the fresh air will set us up. Let's enjoy the sun while we can.' The rocking stopped and Joe stood and stretched out his back. 'Let's find the cottage where they lived. It's light until after seven.'

Lori looked up from the open drawer. She wasn't sure she was ready for that just yet. But if not now, when?

Downstairs, Doris pointed the way for them, understanding that they would be back in time to wash and change for dinner.

Joe looked at his watch as he closed the door of the Royal. It was quarter to five already; they'd better snap to it.

Behind the wooden veil, in a different sunlight, Katie thought she heard a voice she knew. Her eyes opened to the sunlight dancing on her face. A ripple of uncertainty and a small frown showed on her brow.

'What is it?'

'Just as I woke' – she paused, unsure of herself – 'I thought I heard my father's voice.'

'You're missing him, my darling girl, of course you are. Your memory must be playing tricks on you. Part of a dream – but now you're fully awake you'll be all right; just see if you're not.'

Katie didn't argue, but the voice had sounded real to her, if a little muffled.

Champ came to join her, sliding his wet tongue on her cheek in greeting.

'You're a soppy dog, so you are. Time to stretch out and walk, I think. How about going to the stream? It's a long time since I had a paddle.'

Louis agreed, standing up and pulling Katie up too. They had time for long tender kiss, before Champ, who seemed to understand every word, was up and off, only stopping to check to see if the couple were following.

The kingdom was alive with bees and dragonflies that led the way to the water. Champ charged forward on the tails of the insects, snapping at them, hoping to catch one on the way. If he had caught one, Katie wondered what he would do?

Refreshed by the stream, she felt like a schoolgirl: so full of energy that she chased the dog down the path, making Louis break into a trot to keep up with them. All thoughts of the familiar voice were dismissed from her mind, which was overcome by a new excitement. Throwing down her shoes and lifting her skirt, she leaped into the ankle-deep water, following Champ. Her toes tingled as the cold bit into her; she looked as though she was dancing a merry jig, while splashing the dog to the accompaniment of its lively barking, all to the amusement of Louis, who was seriously wondering if he really wanted wet feet. His action spoke a million words, as he flopped on the bank to watch his family of two have fun.

Ravensend was a solid northern town, the old buildings sprinkled among the new. Louis and Katie's painted white cottage, at the end of a terrace, was up for rent.

There was little to see as Joe squinted through the window into the gloom of a deserted sitting room. He sighed; he didn't know why he had insisted that they walked up to see it. He had simply thought it might help to ease the heaviness of grief, but now he realised it only made the loss greater.

Dusk was on its way as they walked back to the Royal Oak, hand in hand.

'So that's it, is it?' Her voice was hushed and unsteady. 'What did you expect to find, Joe?'

He squeezed her hand.

'I don't know, love. I just thought we might find a little piece of her, left there. Crazy, I know. So sorry.'

'I know, love; I keep expecting to see her on the street. It's as though my soul won't accept what my brain knows to be true.'

At seven, they walked into the dining room. Doris and Harry were already there, waiting to greet them.

It was still early. The four of them were on their own, on a table under the carving of the angel. There was an awkwardness and an uncomfortable silence until Doris spoke.

'Did you find the cottage?' she inquired.

'The cottage, the cottage?' said Harry, one eyebrow raised.

'Yes, easily thanks, it was empty and up for rent. It's a nice little place for someone.'

'Someone, yes. It's my property, but I haven't been able to find a tenant since' – his voice trailed – 'they died. Plus, the connection to their deaths… people are sensitive,' confided Harry. 'Sorry.'

'If you can throw any light on their deaths, we would be grateful. Katie worked for you – and Louis for you, Harry – how were they before the accident?' Joe was leaning forward hoping for an answer. Doris and Harry looked flummoxed. There was silence until Doris spoke up.

'To be honest, they were a lovely couple, busy with life but happy. Very happy and in love.'

Debs was hovering with the menus, listening to the conversation. These people must be Katie's parents; Doris had been very open about them coming to stay. A spasm of anxiety stabbed at her stomach; she had hoped to avoid them. Thank goodness they didn't know her. Debs had not told anyone at the Royal Oak that she had worked with Katie and Louis at the Echo; it was her secret. If anyone found out, her new life here would be ruined.

'I'll be back in a few minutes. Take your time,' she said, as she handed out the menus to each of them.

'Thanks, Debs,' nodded Harry.

Joe registered that Debs' accent belonged in the south. He wondered casually what brought her here to the north, as he glanced at the menu.

He was hungry; they had had an early breakfast and had missed lunch. The tea and shortbread that Doris had provided was all they had eaten that day. It had put them on, so to speak, but now his hunger was starting to make indiscreet noises. It was rather embarrassing. The conversation had paused while they chose their food.

'It's all good, homemade, and Roger is the chef tonight,' explained Doris. 'He's a bit of a marvel at putting a meal together. Whatever you choose, you won't be disappointed.'

Harry smiled behind his menu. She was so proud of the establishment, and she had every right to be.

An hour later, after Debs came back and took the dirty plates away, Doris caught Lori looking at the angel on the wall.

'What do you think of it?'

'It has an ethereal quality to it, doesn't it? As though it's being caught in mid-flight going to heaven.'

'That's one by Louis. He had a real talent, you know.'

'Really, he carved that? We have the rocking chair he made for Katie, and a wall piece, but I didn't know he carved angels. It is rather good, isn't it?'

'I think he could have made anything he wanted, Lori. It's sad to lose that sort of talent in the world. They were a great couple together. The best.'

'That's what so peculiar. How could that work be created by Mike?'

Joe was shaking his head in a kind of disbelief. 'It's as though there were two of them. Twins or something.'

'Doppelgängers.'

'Look, we don't understand much of what went on here. We know Katie was happy; she seemed to fit right in.' Joe sighed as he recalled her old life in Hertfordshire. 'When she worked at the paper, she was, shall we say, very friendly with Mike. He lodged with her but as I understand it, he became troublesome. Drank too much, and was unreliable. According to Katie, he left the paper, and had moved on. Moreover, she told us she had met Louis in a store while looking for a bed. Why did she say that?'

Harry chipped in. 'I can't believe that Louis would ever do anything that was dishonourable. I knew him well. If he had a fault, it was he worked too hard, but he enjoyed what he did.'

Joe was shaking his head. 'The police said it was Mike, dental records and all, and for whatever reason he changed his name to live here. Was Mike the Louis we met? How do we explain that?' There was silence for a minute.

Doris put her hand over Lori's in a tender gesture.

'Lori. We only ever knew Louis, certainly not this Mike. Louis was a kind man, who was good with people and wood. An old-fashioned gentleman in many ways. He said he was born hereabouts, and from his soft accent we believed him. We never knew or saw a Mike.'

Lori gulped back a tear. The confusion and grief were back again.

Joe spoke up. 'Like I said, he can't have been Louis. Mike was a sports journalist, full of himself, according to Katie. A man's man, if you know what I mean.'

'Oh aye, we have a few of them round here.' Doris nodded knowingly.

'Anyway, Katie brought Louis for Christmas, before they moved. We liked him; they seemed the perfect match for each other. We were so happy for them.'

Debs was still within earshot of the conversation. She recalled what Charlotte had told her. How changed Mike was in comparison with the person she knew that had worked at the Echo.

Debs remembered that awful day when he came into the office. He was different somehow; only she had believed he was trying to discredit her story, bluffing her version to save face and his job. Perhaps she was wrong, and he had changed. Had something changed him? She could never ask him now.

Back at the table nothing had been solved. Joe was at least content to know that Katie and Louis had been loved by these two people he was sitting with.

He voiced his plans for the following day.

'Tomorrow, Lori and I will visit the graveyard to see where they died and say goodbye. We need to move on. Once we have done that, I'm hoping we can go home and restart our lives. It's going to be hard, but it helps knowing that my Katie spent the last year of her life working with people who cared about her, on so many different levels. I can only say thank you. I'm sorry that we still have a mystery: a mystery that I fear we will never get to the bottom of. But for now, goodnight. Until tomorrow, then.'

Harry and Doris watched as the couple walked arm in arm out of the restaurant.

'Debs,' called Doris. 'Be a good girl and bring us two large brandies.'

A sense of relief that dinner was over was followed by the frustration of not resolving the conundrum.

'Thanks, love, that's just the job to settle our nerves,' smiled Doris when the amber liquid was set down in front of them. 'It's all unreal isn't it? Two men or one? A mystery without a solution.'

30

It seemed the weather was reflecting their mood the next morning. The leaden sky looked set in; it was a dismal, wet day with gusts of wind wailing around the bedroom window.

Joe had been awake for hours. Somehow, what had seemed a logical idea – to come north to help the healing – hadn't worked. All he had done was to put Lori through more suffering. He knew she was bottling up all her anxieties; her silence at dinner the night before had spoken volumes to him. She had been restless during the night, tossing and turning and dreaming of their loss. She was calling out for Katie, and that was like dagger stabbing his heart. But he judged that they both needed this pain on this journey of grief to end. A trip to the church, to say goodbye, would give them closure; then tomorrow they would be on their way home. Just one more night here at the Royal, living in Katie's past. A frown crossed Joe's forehead; frustration and sadness gripped him. They must move on soon; their first grandchild, soon to be born, would need them. The thought instantly pained him. Katie would have been a good mother, if only.

Joe got up, leaving Lori sleeping. He sat in the rocker by the window and watched the trees move in the wind. A small moan from Lori brought his attention back to the bed and in the soft light he looked at the carving; the lovers carried a message to him. They reminded him of Louis and

Katie. It was hard to lose a child, but it eased him to know his lovely daughter had known a great deal of love in her life. His sadness was for himself; she had been happy.

Lori turned over; she was still restless. Thank goodness he had her in his life. Joe looked at his watch. It was almost seven, the sky was brightening as the sun broke through the clouds. He would let Lori sleep a little while longer. Neither of them had settled last night when they got to bed. He sighed; he would be glad of the sanctuary, when he opened his own red front door.

The smell of cooking was drifting up from the kitchens. He looked at his watch again: 7.15am. He would wake Lori in an hour. He lay back in the rocker and closed his eyes. Just for a moment or two, he told himself.

He woke with a start. Lori was tapping him on his shoulder. 'Come on, darling, wake up or we will miss breakfast.'

The dining room was almost empty when they arrived to eat. Debs greeted them and showed them to a table.

'How long have you been working here?' inquired Joe. 'You sound as though you come from our part of the country.'

Debs was coy, not really wanting to engage with him. How could she tell this couple that she used to work with Katie? The guilt she carried had become heavy again.

'I've been here a few months; I lived near Aylesbury. I came up for a holiday and loved it here and so decided to come here to live and work.'

'I see, from our neck of the woods then.'

Having put paid to more questions, she took out her order pad, and stood in anticipation. Once in receipt of their order, she walked away, relieved.

'Do we have to do this Joe? Go to the church, I mean.'

'I think we have to see where they died, love. We must come to terms with her death. Why else are we here?'

Breakfast passed in silence; the thought of their visit later that day hung over them like a dismal cloud, like the sky Joe had seen earlier that morning.

It was eleven thirty before Joe pulled up and the two of them got out of the car. With some trepidation, they walked through the lych gate onto hallowed ground. The sun had chased the grey rain clouds away and the wind had gone with it, but there was still a heaviness in the air.

Horrific stone faces stared down at the couple as they made their way towards the ancient oak doors. The gargoyles were overseeing the sacred place, guarding the building from evil, they supposed. A service was in progress, and the doors were slightly ajar as though someone was expecting latecomers. It allowed the music to drift out to them. The congregation was singing 'How Great Thou Art'.

Lori held her ground, holding her husband back.

'Oh! Joe, it's a funeral; we can't go in.'

'We don't need to Lori. We only need to find the grave of Massie Parker. According to Doris, that's where they were found. I've just connected the dots. Don't you see? Massie must have been a family member; that's why they were here. Probably retracing Louis' roots.' Lori nodded in agreement. Darn Louis, with all the name changes he had made; that must have confused them. Or perhaps it was grief. They should have caught on sooner.

They started their search from the church porch, working outwards the boundary walls, visiting the stones one by one. Many of the gravestones that they passed were weather worn, wearing white and green lacy patterns of lichen, proving their age and, in many cases, making the writing indistinguishable, and yet they had to find the one where their daughter had been killed with Louis.

Eventually, they found themselves at the opposite side of the church, away from the main entrance. They had been searching for almost an hour and were just yards away from the boundary wall, the farthest point from the building, when they came across a headstone leaning at a precarious angle.

It didn't look as though it would take much of a push to have it fall flat, thought Joe. Only part of the name was legible; the wind and rain, along with Father Time, had crumbled some of the stone face but it had spared the first name. Massie was visible under the lichen, and the first letter of his surname: P.

What they had expected to find, or feel, was abandoned as they stood in the September sun. They knew, from what the police told them, that roses had haloed Katie's head; her body had been found with Louis beside her, but now no presence resided here. If there had been something left from that tragedy, surely, they would feel it?

'We should have brought some flowers, in respect, Joe,' Lori exclaimed, with a throb in her voice.

'Out of respect, certainly; we should have thought of it. But, honestly, I have felt more of her presence in the Royal Oak than here. We can dismiss this place, Lori, say our goodbyes; we need never come back here.'

Joe watched Lori's face crumple, her hands covering her mouth until she let out a cry.

'She's lost forever.' Lori's well of tears broke through the dam. She sat on the trimmed grass, hugging her knees, her face hidden from sight. Her shoulders heaved as the grief poured out of her. Joe stood watching the wife he loved breaking her heart all over again. What had he done bringing her here?

She rocked, her arms wrapped around herself, no longer aware of where she was. The dark place she had entered was for her alone. Pain spun from her head to her toes, throbbing as it went. She wanted to die, to be with her lovely daughter. The question was always there. Why? Why? Why? Why Katie and Louis? They had their lives in front of them. Why not herself and Joe who had had a good life? She would have swapped if she could. She had no idea the stress she was causing Joe. She was in her own small hell.

A gargoyle opened its eyes and looked at the grieving couple. Behind its face, the beautiful angel sighed as he assessed them. His forked tongue flicked in and out, tasting the air; there was pain in it and his hopes were raised. The woman might come over to him at that very moment, but the man was honest and kind. That was the worst combination. The woman was so attached to the man that even if the angel invited her to join his army, her love for the man would stop her. As hungry as he was, it would be a fool's errand to try and tempt her, and he wasn't a fool. He closed his eyes and went back to his place of rest; they were not for him.

How Joe got Lori back to the hotel, he wasn't quite sure. She lay in the bed, still, but no longer sobbing. He wasn't sure if this was worse. She was curled up in a foetal position, her eyes staring but not seeing. She hadn't spoken a word for hours. He had hoped she would sleep, or at least nap, but he hadn't persuaded or reached her. He sat in the rocker, rocking and watching. If she didn't come around soon, he would have to get her to a doctor.

They hadn't eaten since breakfast, and he was conscious that they both needed food.

'Lori, love, it's getting dark. You need to eat something. Can you manage to come to the dining room with me?' He waited for an answer. It seemed to take minutes before he heard a whisper. 'You go, I'm not hungry.'

'Lori, that's no good, you need to eat. Come for a dish of soup, at least.'

'I can't, Joe. I have no energy. I can't get out of bed. You go. Perhaps you could have them send up some soup for me.'

He was relieved that she had responded to him and was willing to have some food.

'If you're sure. Perhaps soup with a sandwich?'

'Whatever you like.'

Joe left the room quietly, closing the door. He would speak to Doris and sort out some room service. Lori must manage something to sustain her for tomorrow's journey. He was convinced that once they were home, she would regain her strength and composure.

When he got back to the room, an empty soup dish was on the side table, but the sandwich was still on the plate, untouched. He sighed. Well, at least she had had something to eat, he thought with relief. She was breathing deeply and appeared to be sleeping soundly. The sleep would do her the world of good. Thankful, he decided to turn in himself. Cleaning his teeth, he saw a small residue of food in the toilet bowl. He was suddenly downcast, he wondered how much soup she had actually eaten. He hoped it was enough to give her strength, and maybe enough to help her to sleep through. He climbed into bed beside her. Her hair was hiding her face.

Gently he moved the locks from over her forehead and kissed her lightly.

'Sweet dreams, darling.' She looked so like his lovely Katie lying there. His stomach somersaulted, as he relived the day.

He hoped he would sleep tonight.

Louis wanted to attempt to travel two hundred miles to the south. He knew how much Lori and Joe meant to Katie. They had the connection, but would it be enough for them both to travel that far? He was hoping Massie would visit and he could get some advice on how to do it or if it was possible.

Katie was restless again; no matter how much Louis tried to divert her focus, her parents were on her mind. Tonight, she would look at the stars, the same stars that shone over her parents' home. Somehow that comforted her.

Louis reached out and pulled her close, kissing her under her ear. A shiver of delight went down her neck.

'How about we slip next door and look at the stars later?'

'Later?'

'Yes, later. I could eat you right now, if it were possible; instead, let's make love.'

Katie giggled, and kissed him back, then again, harder. The grass was springy under them and smelled fresh as they lay on it. Not that that was on their minds; it just helped the mood.

31

The lovers stole out of their dimension, into the dark bedroom, and emerged floating over a couple sleeping in the carved bed. The curtains were closed, hiding the sky that Katie wanted to see tonight. Moonlight showed, seeping from under the hem of the patterned drapes onto the carpet by the rocking chair.

It must be a full moon, thought Louis. Katie was going to love scanning the September sky, with the patterns of stars around the moon.

Focusing his mind, Louis' spirit reached out and purchased the curtain, pulling back the drapes to allow the moonlight to flood the room.

A man and woman lay in the bed. The woman stirred with the change of light on her face, but only for a moment. In her sleep, she turned over away from the beam. Louis breathed a sigh of relief. He didn't want to disturb them – not that they would see either ghostly spirit – but the cold he brought might upset them. The same thoughts must have been going through Katie's mind, as she looked at the illuminated dark sky with pinpricks of light looking like diamonds.

'We should get back to the kingdom, and not disturb these sleepers.' Turning back to the window, she added to the conversation.

'The stars are beautiful tonight, Louis. Do you know, those stars are the same stars that shine on my parents?'

'Darling, you're right.' Louis had his back to her and was gazing at the sleeping figures. 'Come over here, love. I think I have a surprise for you. In fact, I'm rather surprised myself.'

Intrigued, Katie moved over to the double bed and was stunned when she looked at the woman.

'Mother.'

Her parents were there in the bed that belonged to Louis, that held the wooden veil that separated the mortal world from the nether world. Would it be possible to meet with them in their kingdom?

'Louis, can we?' She paused. They were on the same wavelength, and Louis was already nodding.

'We have to connect with them and take them back with us. You take Lori, I'll take Joe. Place your hand on your mother's forehead. That will open a channel for you to slip into her dream. You can walk her to our tree. I'll see you there.'

The connection was painful. Katie hadn't expected that. The emotions in Lori were turbulent with grief; static electricity like prongs of pain shot out of her forehead and into Katie's hand. Katie jumped and whisked her hand away, not sure of what to do next.

'Louis, this is bad. Mum's in torment. It's because of us, isn't it?'

'I suppose so.' His voice faltered, deciding if he should share what he felt coming from Joe. 'I can feel the pain in Joe, too. I wonder what they are doing here? Why should they come to visit Ravensend? Look, try and connect again; I'll do the same. We'll meet under the tree.'

The dream that Katie found herself in was disturbing. It was focused on her old bedroom in her parents' home. Her mother was searching in the wardrobe.

'I can't find it.' There was tension in her voice.

'What can't you find, Mum?'

'I don't know. I just know that I've lost something, and can't find it.' Lori started to cry.

'Please don't cry, Mum. I'm here to help.'

'No, that's not right; you can't be. You went away,' she said accusingly. 'You went north, and you forgot to come back.'

'I'm here now.' Katie put her arms around her mother and hugged her. Doubt and a lack of trust showed in her mother's eyes.

'Come with me, Mum. I want to show you where I live now with Louis. Trust me.' Katie took Lori by her hand.

The dream seemed to shatter around them. Light was growing steadily, and the room dissolved into a single track, which widened until she saw the path that stretched into the kingdom. As they moved towards the brightness, Katie could see that Louis was already there with Joe. They were silhouetted against the sunlight, waiting under the tree.

The kingdom welcomed another guest to its bosom. Its sun was warm on their faces. They found spaces on the fresh grass to talk, under the shade of the tree's branches. The meadow sang with the insects' song of summer, and the blue hills shimmered in the heat. Peeking from its half-hidden position over the meadow, the white cottage looked back at them. Running water could be heard from a stream that was close, as was the sudden, happy yelp of an excited dog who bounded up to them, his pink wet tongue ready to greet these new souls. The place was perfect.

Joe and Lori felt the peace the kingdom gave, and they welcomed and patted the over-enthusiastic canine.

'Where are we?' asked Lori, of no-one in particular.

'This is my world,' answered Louis. 'Do you like it, Lori? This is our home now,' he said, looking at Katie.

'You see, mum, after our' – she paused – 'accident, we came here. We are happy and in love. We may have lost our bodies, but nothing has changed spiritually. We are as bonded to each other now as we were when we were flesh.'

Katie took Louis' hand, smiling with confidence at her mum, but Lori had a puzzled look on her face.

'Really, Katie? Are you sure? You haven't been very honest with us, have you?' Lori looked at Louis. 'Who are you? Where's Mike?'

'Mum, it's hard to explain, but let me try. I bought the bed when I was living with Janet. What I didn't know was that a ghost came with it. Louis was like a guardian angel. He watched over me and protected me before I accepted that he was a spirit who drew me into this kingdom to reveal himself to me. This is Louis. He blended with me just as I have blended with you, Mum, to bring you here.

'Mike came to live with me. I made a bad choice in asking him. He was not the man I thought he was. Louis protected me from Mike and his drunken advances. After a particularly bad event, I decided I couldn't live with him under my roof anymore. He came to the kitchen to discuss it, and while he was there, food lodged in his throat, and he started choking. In an attempt to save Mike, Louis blended with him, but he was too late: Mike had died. As Louis became part of Mike, Mike's spirit had left his body. When Louis tried to leave Mike's shell, the body refused to release him. Mike had passed, but there was no corpse, nothing to bury, and, trapped as he was, Louis had no choice but to pretend to be Mike. That was until we came here to Yorkshire. This is his home county. He was born here in Ravensend, over a century ago. I love him, Mum. I am happy with him. Be happy for us. Our love was stronger than death.' Katie took Lori's hand.

'Oh, Katie.' Lori took Katie in her arms and hugged her.

'You and Dad were good teachers; you taught me how to love. I'll always love you both, too.'

Joe, who had been silent, spoke up.

'I was right, Lori. I said he would look after her, didn't I?'

Joe smiled at Louis before shaking his hand with the same strength he had showed two Christmases ago.

Louis smiled back. 'Did anyone tell you that you have quite a grip, there, Mr Brown?' he said, rubbing his hand.

'One or two,' and they laughed.

'Dreams can be tricky things,' said Louis. 'In the morning, you may not believe you met us or believe our explanation. To prove that you were here in this sphere with us, I want you to look for my signature on the headboard I carved. A butterfly – my mark – is on an apple hanging from the tree of life. Look for it before you leave. In the morning, you will try to dismiss all of this as a dream. Remember a butterfly.'

For the first time in a while, Katie was happy with the sun, the light and warmth she enjoyed in the garden. The unhappiness that had been like a grey cloud over her head was gone. She had a long, emotional hug with her parents.

Lori clung to her. Katie had mixed emotions. As well as the happiness, she felt a shudder of sadness pass through her. When her parents died, they would go to the next world: the one that she and Louis had refused. Would she ever be reunited with them? She pushed the miserable thought to one side and soaked up the love. Their visit could only be for one night; once they started to surface from sleep, they would disappear from the kingdom and return to the bed.

Katie hoped that if they remembered anything of the dream, they might come back to Yorkshire and see them again. That was something worth holding on to.

It was like old times: a family sharing close moments, rather than four souls in a nether world whose time was limited to a few special hours.

Joe and Lori relaxed, eager to take part in exploring their daughter's kingdom. Together, the four walked through the fields, playing with Champ. They watched the dog dart into the stream, trying to catch the delicate dragonflies. In a world where time stood still, and the sun never set, all they felt was happiness. When it was time for Joe and Lori to go, both parties were content: sad that there would be separation again, but resigned. Louis had told Joe that if it were possible, they would visit, but not to tell Lori; he wouldn't want to disappoint her. If they managed it, he would leave a sign so Joe and Lori would know they had been.

'I'm sure I closed the curtains last night.' Joe had been woken by the morning sun shining on his face. He was feeling extraordinarily upbeat, which was odd, as he remembered climbing into bed the night before in quite the opposite mood. He turned over to Lori and touched her bare shoulder.

'How are you, my darling?'

'Hungry.'

It was music to his ears; he had been expecting to take her home to the doctor.

'Come on then, love. Let's go eat. You must be feeling better.'

'I can't understand it, I feel as though a weight has been lifted from my heart. I don't know why, or how, but I know Katie is alright. You were right, darling: coming here has made all the difference; we can move on now.'

'Funny, that's how I feel too.' He cuddled up to Lori, hugging her close.

'I see… feeling a bit frisky, are we? It's been a long time.' She reached up and kissed him. 'Welcome back.'

The morning had been well spent. They felt like new people. Breakfast had been terrific, and now they were packing to leave and saying goodbye to the Royal and Katie's bed.

'We must remember to thank Doris for her thoughtfulness in giving us this room and the bed that was theirs. And look at that headboard with the sun on it. It looks so much better in this light, don't you think? That tree of life and the lovers: what a story.'

Lori couldn't help but touch the warm wood, tracing her fingers over the surface, feeling all the groves where the carver had put energy and life into the solid oak.

'I like all the mixed fruit. Wouldn't it be wonderful if there was such a tree?'

'Wonderful, and extraordinary.' Joe went over to the carving, and he joined his wife in tracing his fingers over some fruit. In a split second, a memory flashed in his brain, and then was gone. What was it? Did he have something to remember?

'Lori, did you dream last night?'

'I did. It was a bit fanciful, but it helped my pain. I was in a beautiful place with Katie.'

'You were? Describe it.'

'It was the strangest dream; Katie took me there. There was a tree with all kinds of fruit on it, just like the carved one, but real in my dream. There was a meadow and a warm sun that stayed high in the sky. Funnily enough, I think it was midday. And don't think me silly, but I was with Katie and Louis, and they had a dog called Champ. It was a good dream.'

'You were taken there, to their world? Me too. Only I was taken by Louis.' Even as he said it, he was shaking his head. How could they have had the same dream – but then, grief can play tricks with the mind.

Lori explained how Louis had become Mike. 'It was something to do with a ghost and the bed. Katie's bed.'

Joe was staggered, they had dreamed the same dream that included a dog.

'We had the same dream, Lori,' Joe told her in disbelief.

It wasn't logical, and Joe was clearly trying to dismiss it as coincidence, though that didn't make sense either. Was it to appease their neediness and escape in some sort of fantasy, a made-up story in a made-up world? He had almost convinced himself of it, when he remembered the butterfly. He looked closely at an apple. There was no mark on it, nothing. Not giving up, he moved on to another branch with fruit. He ran his fingers all over the apples until he felt, rather than saw, an indentation on the underside. He pressed his finger hard on it, before viewing the imprint on his fingertip. A tiny creature with wings sat there. A butterfly.

32

The change of scene and employment had had a positive effect on Debs. From being a rather closed individual, she had blossomed, and she felt more secure now than she ever had done.

It was unusual for a southerner to come north; it was more common for people to move the other way. She had even learned that calling a spade a shovel was slang. In other words, people in these parts were straight talkers and were not always blessed with tact. And that was not necessarily a bad thing. Only a few were downright rude, and you got those kinds of people everywhere.

Julia hadn't resented her coming to share the bedroom with her. Debs wondered if she herself would have been so gracious about it. Certainly, she knew she would not have been so accommodating a year ago, but that was then. In the five months that Debs had worked at the Royal Oak, a whole new world had revealed itself. She was now part of the close-knit Royal Oak family.

Barry had become a good friend, and he seemed to watch over the place for Doris, without ever being asked.

Debs had seen Barry take an interest in Julia, rather like a father figure might. Debs found it pleased her, though she didn't know why, except it proved he was a kind man. If only someone like him had been around when she needed support. She had had no-one to go to, when she was in need at a young age.

Doris was satisfied that Debs had fitted in with the establishment and was eager to please. She went and did what was needed. It also delighted Doris that Debs got on well with Julia. Julia, Doris felt, was in need of a good girlfriend, and with the two of them sharing the twin bedroom in the attic what could be better? And although Doris had said Debs would have to find her own lodgings, it rather suited Doris to have someone keep an eye on the girl. In her opinion, Julia was far too much under the influence of young Nick. They were supposed to be engaged, but Doris doubted that the ring on Julia's finger would stop him from flirting. He was a likeable rogue, a one-off, but since she had taken on Julia's friend, Barbara, she had noticed that he paid Barbara a little too much attention for Doris' liking.

It was unfortunate that they had been so short-staffed in April. When Doris had advertised a position in the local rag, Barbara was the first to apply. At the time, Doris had thought it was a good thing – she knew Barbara was Julia's friend – but now, she wasn't sure. She had seen Nick and Barbara with their heads together, huddled up, so to speak, whispering and laughing. She didn't like whispering. It usually meant someone was up to something. Still, Julia was happy to have her friend working beside her: same age, same tastes, same everything. Thank the Lord the hem lines had dropped again, and the mini skirt was out of fashion; Nick would have thought all his Christmases had all come at once. She worried about the way he eyed the ladies. She had noticed Barry trying to keep him in place, but she was sure Nick was a good boy really.

Lori and Joe Brown were checking out.

'Thank you for making us so welcome, Doris. It's been an interesting two days.'

Doris was behind the desk in the small foyer.

'Thank you, and you're welcome. Harry sends his regards and hopes you have a safe journey home. May I ask how you are this morning, Lori?'

'Much better, thank you. It's been a strain. We are still learning how to live without Katie. It's not easy.'

'Believe me, we still miss her… and Louis. And, speaking of our artist, I have a gift to share with you.'

'A gift?'

'We – I mean Harry and I – thought you would like the carving of the angel. Katie told us it was the first piece he made after returning to Yorkshire. We think you should have it. Please.' Doris opened the desk drawer and brought out a wrapped parcel. Lori was overwhelmed when Doris handed it over.

'What can I say but thank you? It's a lovely piece. I remember Katie telling me how Louis forgot time and everything when he was carving. Katie said he only released what was trapped in the wood. Can you imagine being able to do that?'

'It's beyond me, but I admired the man.'

'Yes, we did too. Mike or Louis, what's in a name? It's the man that matters, and the man we knew was a good man.'

'Come back and see us sometime, won't you?'

Goodbyes were said quickly, and Doris watched them leave.

Almost as the door closed, it was opened again. Doris thought for a moment that the Browns must have forgotten something, but no. A well-dressed man, followed by a rather mousy woman, strode into the bar. His smile befitted a man of importance as he presented himself to Doris.

'Carl Greaves, and my wife.'

'Yes, of course. You are rather early. The room's not ready yet. Perhaps you could have coffee in the lounge until it's been cleaned? You booked the Eden Room, didn't you?'

An impatient look crossed Carl Greaves' face and the smile disappeared. He looked at his watch as though he wasn't aware he was early. Then the smile was back.

'We are a bit, aren't we? Not much traffic out there. We made good time.'

He looked rather pleased with himself, Doris thought.

'Yes, coffee would be appreciated.'

Debs was passing through the lounge when Doris called her. 'Can you get Mr and Mrs Greaves some coffee while they are waiting for their room? Oh, and tell Julia and Barbara to get a bustle on.'

Doris didn't seem to notice how pale Debs had become. She bowed her head and turned her face away from the couple, hurrying off to the kitchen to make the coffee.

33

Leaning against the door, Debs could hardly breathe, let alone speak. Panic bounced from her heart to her brain.

He can't be here. I can't be here if he is.

Nick was preparing food when she scuttled in.

'What's up with you? You look as though you've seen a ghost.'

Debs pulled herself together, giving him a rather feeble smile.

'Just came over a bit faint there; rushing, I expect. Coffee for two, please.'

'Well, sit down for a minute, while I make it.'

Still a little unsteady, she found a stool and did as she was bade.

'Have you seen Julia? I wondered if she could serve the coffee.'

'Upstairs, housekeeping.'

'Yes, of course, what am I thinking? I have a message from Doris for her. The Eden Room guests have arrived early. They're to clear that room first. I better go up.'

'Go steady then,' stressed Nick, as she left the kitchen.

Debs climbed the stairs two at a time not heeding his advice and reached the Eden Room, as Doris had named it, just as the two young women were making up the bed. Julia and Barbara worked well together, the redhead and brunette were very attractive girls.

'Doris sent word; the guests have arrived early, how long will you be?'

'Everything's done barring the bed and a quick dust down and I have to bring fresh towels,' Julia responded.

'Okay, I'll tell her.'

Debs realised she would have to face Carl herself with coffee in the lounge.

Back downstairs, the coffee was waiting for the guests in the kitchen, along with Doris' special butter shortbread on the tray.

Doris met her at the doorway. 'How's it going upstairs?'

'Nearly done: fifteen minutes at the most. By the time they've drunk the coffee, it will be ready.'

Doris gave her a smile and a nod. 'Hurry along then.'

'I'll go and find Barry and get the luggage up.'

Doris, looking at Debs rather intensely, didn't turn away. 'Are you alright? You look a little under the weather.'

'I told her that too,' said Nick earwigging in the background.

'No, I'm fine, just fine.'

'Well, I'll let you get on and serve that hot.'

Debs found her hands had a tremble about them, and her legs almost refused to obey her, but, somehow, she managed to push through the door into the lounge. The walk to his table nearly defeated her.

As Debs slipped the hot coffee onto the occasional table, the subdued woman raised her head to thank her.

She need not have worried about Carl; he didn't even raise his head from the newspaper he was reading. What a relief.

'Shall I pour, Madam?'

'Coffee, dear?'

A grunt of an answer passed as confirmation.

'Yes please,' said his wife. 'Black for me.'

'A shortbread biscuit, dear?' The wife seemed to be going through the motions; there was no affection in her voice, despite her calling him dear.

Carl dropped the newspaper just enough to stare at the woman.

'Yes, I'll have one. I wouldn't have one of those if I were you. You know how you balloon up if you overeat.'

The woman's hand gripped hard on the plate, but whatever she was feeling she kept under control. She replaced the biscuits on the serving tray.

Looking up at Debs, she responded, 'Why don't you take these away? Less temptation for me.'

Debs felt a kind of shame flush through her. How he could embarrass his wife like this, in front of her? But, yes, of course he could. She had tasted his selfishness seventeen years ago. It would appear he hadn't changed. He looked directly at her. There was no recognition in his eyes.

'Yes, take them away. One is quite sufficient for me.'

No 'please' or 'thank you'. He had looked straight through her. He hadn't remembered her at all.

Had she changed so much? She had grown from a child into a woman. She was taller, her gawkiness gone. Her fury was such that she felt her blood boiling inside and she wanted to vent her rage. He had taken her teen years away from her and made them hell. He left her with his child, who was also taken from her. How could she have imagined she had loved him? Was it possible she had been in love with the idea of love? Love had been in short supply in her home: there had been precious little coming from her mother. Amongst her anger was a moment of pity for her mother who had missed so much with her indifference. Well, better not to dwell. At least Debs had found a sort of family here at the Royal.

She was miles away when he tapped her arm, bringing her back to the moment.

'Well?'

He was waiting for her to go.

'Anything else I can get you?'

'No, just take the tray away.'

34

Julia and Barbara were taking a break now the bedroom was ready for the guests.

'How're my favourite two ladies?' Nick wrapped his arms around their shoulders. He kissed one and then the other on the cheek before releasing them and joined them sipping coffee in the kitchen.

'You got through making up that room in record time. It's been a bit of a morning out there.' He nodded towards the lounge. 'Debs looked a bit hassled when she brought the tray back. I think the guest was a bit rude to her. She was going on about him being a chauvinistic pig, by the way he treated the woman. She practically threw the plate in the sink. I managed to retrieve it, by the way, and the biscuits.' He smiled. 'Those you're eating now.' His eyes twinkled with amusement. 'Waste not, want not.'

'And they are delicious.' Barbara was on her second biscuit. 'Yours or Maureen's?'

'Mine, miss, if you don't mind.' Nick pulled a hurt face. 'Maureen only wants to do the fancy sweet stuff.' He tried to mimic Maureen's accent. 'She's such a fusspot.'

'But you, my friend,' he said, touching Barbara's knee in a familiar fashion (Julia noticed that Barbara didn't push his hand away), 'You know my worth, making good honest food for you and Doris.' He looked at Julia. 'You, too.' His hand moved to Julia, grabbing her hand and kissing it, looking into her eyes as he did. Her little moment of doubt about him melted away. Of course, he was good friends with both of them.

Nick had been faithful to Julia for over a year, the longest time ever for him to be faithful to one girl. Now he looked at her sitting next to Barbara. He did love Julia in his own way. But perhaps working with her day after day and seeing her all the time had just become a bit boring. He wanted and needed a little excitement in his life, and Julia was so predictable. He got angry with her from time to time because she was so passive and sensitive. Where was the fight in her? Was there any? Barbara, at least, gave back what she received.

Now he had to be careful, because earlier that year he had returned to his old ways of flirting. Two waitresses, who lived in the town, had been working for Doris. They were young and rather attractive. He was careful, flirting with them only when Julia wasn't around. It had been fun, a bit of a laugh until it went wrong.

Mandy and Di had been flattered, he was sure of it, but things had gone badly when he expressed his secret desire to them. It happened in the kitchen one coffee break. Thinking that these two modern girls were sexually adventurous, he took a chance. In undertones and whispers, he admitted, 'I've always fancied two birds together, in the back row of the flea pit, or, better still, in bed. We could find an empty one right here some time?' He cocked his head on one side, with a smile on his face and raised eyebrows, waiting for a response. He had thought they would be up for it – a bit of excitement in their dull lives – but Mandy was on him like a ton of bricks.

'You're forward, for an engaged person.' Her face pushed into his.

'It was just a bit of a joke, what's wrong with you?' he retorted, red faced and blustering. He had clearly not read the signs correctly. 'Can't you take a joke?'

'Some things are not funny,' she said in a sarcastic voice. What sort of girls do you think we are?'

As they turned to go, he had made another mistake by tapping Di's bottom as she moved out of the door.

'That's it, you poor excuse for a man. I'm telling Doris.'

Panic surged through him. 'You don't want to do that, Di. I'll lose my job.'

'You should have thought about that before you slapped my bottom.'

'It was a friendly tap.'

'To you, maybe.'

'Look, it was a mistake.'

'And how much is it worth, to keep me quiet?'

He knew she meant it, with that defiant look on her face. Mandy was rolling her eyes.

'Go on, Di, he's far too handy. Let's tell Doris.'

He was in big trouble, and he knew it could cost him more than his job.

It cost him a tenner to keep her mouth shut, half his wage for the week. Di didn't tell on him, but the two girls upped and left.

It had been a relief; but his fear was they may come back for more money. How would he explain that to his mum when he was short on the expected housekeeping? How would he manage? Weeks had passed and they hadn't returned; eventually, he had felt safe again.

He got on well with Doris and he could get away with most things, but making the Royal short-staffed was not one of them; if she ever found out he was finished. At least Doris would never know it was his fault that she had lost her staff.

He smiled to himself. Indirectly, he had brought Barbara on board, and then, to top it all, Debs had come to work with them too. So, it had all worked out just as it should… two for the ones that had bolted.

Barbara was looking prettier and prettier; he could hardly hold himself back sometimes when they met around the Royal. He could sense her interest in him and he was ready to rekindle that brief moment of history they had together, about which Julia knew nothing.

It had been a one-night stand, all accidental, nothing planned. He had passed her standing in the rain at the bus stop, and had pulled up and offered her a lift. He had had a row with Julia, and he was hopping mad. Funnily enough, when he had picked Barbara up in his car to take her back to her bedsit, his anger disappeared. Perhaps it was her easy manner, or perhaps he recognised that she liked him, liked him a lot. He only stopped for a cup of coffee, but there had been such an attraction between them, that when they ended up having sex, it seemed so very natural. Until afterwards. They had promised to keep it to themselves. It wasn't fair to hurt Julia for their foolishness; he was after all promised to Julia.

For a year, he had deliberately kept out of Barbara's way, when she visited Julia at the Royal. Then out of the blue, Barbara applied for a job there. Now she was working under the same roof, that feeling he had for her in her bedsit had come back with a bang. Strange, though: he didn't want to lose Julia. He trusted her love. But they did say a change was as good as a rest, and he was ready for a holiday.

A shout from Doris startled him.

'Julia, the room needs towels. Take some up at once, please.'

'Oh, my God, I forgot.' Her coffee was discarded, as she brushed crumbs of shortbread off her uniform.

Leaving her friends in the kitchen, Julia dashed up the stairs, grabbing fresh linen from the store and tapped on the oak door. She waited to be admitted. There was no answer, so she let herself in. The faint smell of tobacco hung in the air.

'So! You're here again, are you?' she whispered to the rocking chair, that held a faint outline of an old man with a clay pipe. She was used to seeing things that others didn't see now, and feeling extra sensitive to atmospheres in the Royal including hearing voices in this room. Sometimes, she even thought she recognised them.

Julia had become psychic the day that Nick had proposed to her. Something had happened then that she couldn't explain. It was like she became someone else, and the things that had come out of her mouth didn't come from her – but they had come, accusing him of cheating on her. She had been devastated when Nick admitted he had seen someone else, but he promised her it had been a huge mistake and it would never happen again, and she believed him.

Julia put the towels on the bed and went over to open the window. The old man had faded and disappeared. It was strange she never felt frightened when she sensed him with her in the room. It was always this room, and he always sat in the rocker. She could imagine him as a grandfather, enjoying a quiet moment. It hurt her that she had never known her parents or grandparents; the Catholic orphanage had been her home. Memories were not all pleasant. She had wanted a family so much. Some of the nuns were kind, but others never let her forget she was a bastard. On her own volition, she had left as soon as she was able and come here to work. This was her family now.

'What have we here?' A man's voice spoke from the doorway. He was quite handsome, well groomed. A woman stood behind him. 'I thought the room was ready?'

'Yes, Sir, it is. I've just brought clean towels.'

'Well, get on with it then, and shut the window. I don't want to catch my death of cold here.'

The towels were quickly put in the bathroom, and she moved towards the door.

'Sandra, get out of the way, and let the girl pass.' Sandra obeyed and moved into the room, pulling a case.

His hand went to the middle of Julia's back, as he ushered her to the door, dropping and touching her bottom as she moved through it. Was that accidental? She turned to look at his face. He was smiling. He seemed like a fox stalking a chicken. He would have to be watched. His wife seemed oblivious, but Julia made a mental note to warn Barbara.

35

Carl lay back and watched his wife fussing over her suitcase. Work had brought them together. Sandra had been working in the typing pool of a small free press paper. He was researching the area looking for good local stories. He was interested in architecture, and told her he wanted to become a writer, presenting the best in walks and historical buildings of England. Sometimes, because he lived in the same road, they travelled to work together. He had been different then, thoughtful and witty. He had made her laugh, and had said she was his soulmate. Now, here she was, his wife of ten years and an unpaid secretary, helping him research the castles, abbeys and many ruins of the North Yorkshire: all those that had been built on the rivers and hadn't survived Henry's reformation of the monasteries.

He had been so kind when her mother passed. Sandra was just eighteen and had lived a sheltered life. Her father had died just after the war; she didn't remember him at all. She had happy memories of school; her head was more often in a book than observing life or people. Studious and loving learning, she decided on a career as a secretary. She was naturally organised and could type at speed. With both her mum and herself working, they had a nice life together up to when her mother died.

Carl too lived with his mother, who owned the corner shop ten doors up from where Sandra lived. Sandra saw him most days. They left at the same time for work; what could be more natural than to bump into each other? Only they didn't really meet by accident, she watched for when he set off and she left her home accordingly, to walk with him. He lit up her life. He had the most engaging smile and intense blue eyes and she thought she loved him.

Then there was a fall-out with his mother, Nora. Sandra had never got to the bottom of the tale. His version was his mother had taken in a man friend, George, and they didn't get on. The new man had more or less told him to go, leaving him homeless. Nora had not come to his rescue and seemed to only care about herself and her new man.

Sandra was scandalised by his mother's attitude. She felt sorry for Carl and even persuaded her own mother to take him in for next-to-no rent. After her mother had died, Carl persuaded her to marry him – so that he could look after her, he said. He didn't want her burdened with bills and such; it was a man's job. He had fooled her, she knew that now, but she never understood how much until later. He took or rather stole from her slowly and she, like an idiot, was happy for him to look after her and her bank account. Once everything was in his name, the cruelty started.

All the money her mother had left her, including the proceeds from the house which he sold, had been spent, or so he said. There was no love left, only a yearning to be free of him.

Dinner, as usual, had been a one-sided conversation, with Carl choosing food for both of them. Control; she knew it was all about control. One day she would turn on him, but she wasn't ready yet.

The meal was accompanied by a red wine, and Carl had drunk most of it. That wasn't unusual. Perhaps he would be less rough with her tonight if he was filled with drink. He was never gentle, not now.

Sandra hated him and the thought of him touching her revolted her, but she couldn't leave him because she was totally dependent on him. She had no money – he saw to that – and she had nowhere to go. He had never actually hit her; she had no marks that could be seen, but he could kill her with his twisted and hurtful remarks. Oh yes, and the rape. She watched him down the last dregs of wine. With a bit of luck tonight, he would only want to sleep.

Carl slumped on the bed on return to their room. He was breathing heavily and near to sleep. Sandra looked at him with disdain, taking herself off to the bathroom to get ready for bed. The water was hot and the thought of a bath appealed to her. The longer she stayed away from the bedroom, the more likely he would be in a deep sleep when she returned. A soak in scented bubble bath, provided by the hotel, relaxed her body. It washed away his insults and she was able reset herself. By the time she had returned to the bedroom, Carl was already tucked up and appeared to be sleeping.

Trying not to disturb him, she slipped into bed, giving him space and lay with her back to him. She was about to turn off the night light in a lamp that sat on the bedside table when she felt a hand on her bottom. It tugged at her nightdress, teasing it up until she could feel his hands on her bare flesh. She held her breath, frozen and fearful. He was close now. His lips were next to her ear; the vapour of his intoxication caught her as she took in a new breath and the words he whispered made her feel sick.

'Good of you to take the trouble to have a bath.' She froze again as his fingers invaded and probed her between her legs. Then he rolled her onto her back, holding her fast at her neck with his arm. She knew better than to resist or talk.

Get it over with was her mantra now. She repeated it in her mind, while she felt his wet mouth on her breast. He nibbled at her over the cotton nightdress she was still wearing; the patch, wet with saliva, felt cold.

Get it over with. His fingers probed and hurt her. Keep your mouth shut. She held the scream in, like she always did. Finally, loosening his nightwear, he mounted her. His hands were now on each of her shoulders, holding her down while he thrust what he called 'his little man' into her, time and time again. He rode her hard until he spilled his seed, and, satisfied, he rolled off her in a sweat.

'You may not be good for much, love, but you are good for that.' Carl smiled, his handsome face beaming. He kissed her forehead and slapped her arm.

'Go clean yourself up, there's a good girl,' he advised, turning his back to her. 'We have a long day tomorrow. Let's get some sleep.'

She turned on the main light to go to the bathroom.

'God, are you trying to annoy me? Looking for a slap? Put it off.'

Sandra did as she was told and fumbled her way in the dim light back to the bathroom. Grateful of its light, she whipped off her nightdress, hating the sticky substance drying on it. She washed it out and wrung it part dry, before hanging it over a radiator to dry out completely for the next day.

She had washed him away once tonight; now he had soiled her again. She cleaned herself with a flannel, after which she wrapped herself in the towelling robe that hung behind the door. She leaned against it. The weight of the humiliation and disgrace robbed her of her strength. The smell of his breath and his body sweat were uninvited sores in her memory, and they made her heave.

Silent tears fell as she bit her lip to stop the sobs. Tears ran down her face until she was totally spent. Her knees gave way and she slipped to the floor, wiping away her shameful tears with her sleeve. Would it never stop?

She felt murderous towards him. Killing him was too good, though; he had to be punished. Tonight, she could taste the hatred that was lodged in her throat. It was choking her. She was sick and tired of being used. If only she could go back in time; she would change a few things.

36

The beautiful angel unfurled himself from his serpent form to his handsome persona, as he moved from the dividing rift that separated his world from that in the Royal Oak. It was a well-worn narrow path; Sophia, a very needy ghost, had welcomed him into the nether world she was occupying, although strictly speaking it wasn't in her gift to do so. But that was Sophia; she thought she had a right to all things. How he loved greedy, selfish people. The path between the worlds led to his hunting grounds in the human world, from the kingdom behind the wooden veil. He was a hunter and could smell out the souls ripe for his picking: damaged souls that were hanging about, not knowing they were waiting to be collected. Here were two more; he licked his lips.

He looked at the people in the bed. His forked tongue sniffed the air before it turned itself into a human, wet, pink tongue. And there it was, that smell that confirmed he was right: human arrogance, selfishness and, best of all, a cruel streak. This man was going the right way to be his. It would be worth visiting this room often to see how quickly this man slid down into the mire that he himself was making. All the dark angel had to do was wait, and perhaps encourage. What Malkira had was an appetite, and he fed well on anger and pain.

His soft, wet tongue dampened his lips; there was something else here too.

Lifting his nose in the air, Malkira took an extra-large sniff, taking the breath deep into his lungs. Yes, it was there, he could taste it. Humiliation, rejection, sadness and supressed anger. It was a serendipitous moment. He had one soul to feed off and one to join his army, but which was which?

Malkira called one of his children. A wisp of grey chiffon mist drifted through the rift and came to his side; her white skull with its hollow eye sockets and her wide toothy grin was veiled in the grey. Thoughts touched, directing her to the woman's side.

'Join with the woman. Find out who and what she is.'

He sidled up to the prone, sleeping man and touched Carl's crown with his stubby finger, connecting at once to the man's memories. It was a rich patchwork of events, clear and raw. This man was a disciple to Malkira's ways; he would be his in a short matter of time. The small morsels were tasty; it wasn't a meal, but satisfying, nevertheless. He would probe deeper. He wanted more.

'So, my man, tell me all.'

The beautiful angel licked his lips. The man opened up so easily. It was all so delicious.

He learned about a sulky boy called Carl, who could charm at will. He had had a way of manipulating his mother from an early age; he was so proud of that.

He had grown up a small corner shop that provided a broad selection of foods for the locals. The shop was vital in the working-class neighbourhood. He knew many customers lived on credit, that his mum called tick. They settled on pay day, whenever that was, and his mother was glad of it. It kept them coming back, she would say to him, when he grumbled that she was always busy. It paid for their food, she had told him, and kept a fire in the hearth. It was important that she talked to her customers. He hated it; she never had time to play with him.

Carl's grandfather had served in the war and always seemed cross. He lived with them too. Carl hated him. It was 'don't do that' and 'keep quiet', and he smelled. The old man had headaches all the time, and Carl had to creep around when Grandad was up and about. It was cancer that had taken him, and Carl was happy when he had died. Carl had thought he would have his mother to himself, not realising that Grandfather had babysat him while his mother worked, and they would lose his grandad's pension. He was four when it happened, too young for school, and instead of having his mum all to himself, he found that he had to be looked after by a neighbour, so his mother could work.

Mrs Marsh had her own children, and he could feel their resentment as soon as he was left there in the mornings to play. He didn't like it; he didn't like the boy and he hated the girl and her whining. The toys that got broken were never his fault; not really. The doll's head that somehow became separated from its body, when the girl hadn't shared the biscuit, wasn't his fault; he didn't like that she was rude. And the aeroplane with the bent wing that was laid somehow under the doll without the head; well, that wasn't him either. Malkira saw in those memories a wilful, scheming child that pleased him. Carl always made sure he was far enough away not to be blamed when the cry went up. Joe and Alice were in the frame, blaming each other. He learned to outwit these kids that were lucky enough to have two parents to dote on them. They were spoiled, his mother said so, but, regardless, he had to stay with them until he was five. What a relief it was when he could go to school.

Almost from the start, Carl attracted others and was a natural leader. A gang formed easily, and that trend followed all though his school years. As he grew into a teenager, he realised that the use of good manners helped him get his own way. He was popular with teachers and the girls in his class were bowled over by his charm and good looks. He liked girls, and they seemed to like the way he handled himself. Behind the bike shed, he learned how girls worked.

Malkira absorbed Carl's early life story like a starter before the main meal. He lay back and assessed it, deciding whether Carl would join his army and spread the ills to the world or become a luxury meal. It was a toss-up. It could go either way.

Carl's adventures carried on through his teens until he was twenty. A kiss and cuddle weren't satisfying; his urges and needs were much, much more. His first conquest was a little tease; she was young and fresh, and had never been touched: a virgin. She was unhappy at home. He remembered that her father had left, and her mother wasn't maternal. He liked young, pretty girls, and it helped his ego the way she hung on his every word. She was lonely and needy; it was easy to let her think he loved her. He arranged a very private meeting at his home when his mother was out. It was pretty good, and it made him a man.

Then she came back and accused him of fathering the child she was carrying. He was devastated. His mother heard, of course; he had a real job of convincing Nora it wasn't him. Hell, the silly bitch could have been with anyone. She was trying to ruin him; she just wanted a meal ticket, and he wasn't going to be it.

He was careful after that. What he needed was a steady girl, who was a bit prim and proper, or sheltered. That would show his mother he was a good sort.

Then George had arrived in his mother's life. Carl hadn't seen that coming and was really put out. What was she thinking about? She was old, and past dating, and surely, she didn't have sex anymore? Then she went a step too far, when she invited George to live with them. It turned his stomach to think what she got up to behind that closed bedroom door. Carl had laid down an ultimatum; it was George or him. The result didn't go his way. The crazy old cow had said George was staying. He was stunned. She told him that she didn't have many years in front of her and she was going to make the most of them with George; that Carl had all his life in front of him and he should be happy for them. She had been alone a long time.

Alone? Nora had never been alone; she had had him. Now, she was rejecting him for that interloper. In a fit of pique, he told her he would go. He was equally shocked, when Nora said 'When?' Lord, what had he done? His mother had looked after him, fed him; he paid very little to her for the roof over his head. Where was he to go now? His wage had mainly been his own pocket money. He had a bit of a thing with the horses and the dogs; he enjoyed a flutter. When the bet came in, it was better than sex and he did enjoy sex. If he needed a woman, well! He paid for it and would do so until he got married.

Sandra lived practically on his doorstep. He saw her every day, on the street or at the bus stop, and the way she looked at him, he knew he was onto a winner. She was ideal.

When he left home, Sandra's mother had taken him in. For a long time, he had to live as his alter ego. Watch his language, and have good manners. Smile a lot, and of course, be helpful to the poor ladies. He even had to give up betting for a while. It was all very boring but in the long run he knew it would pay dividends.

Sandra was malleable. He would be able to mould her into just what he wanted, and best of all, when she came, she came with income and property.

He had liked her at first, and he still did in a funny way. She met a lot of his needs, but she had lost her spark, and had become a lump with no personality. She didn't like adventurous sex – a bit of rough and hurt was exciting in the mix, he thought – but she didn't get it. Long-term he would control her. Control was the main thing.

The beautiful angel Malkira liked this man: narcissistic, full of his own importance. Even now, evil was growing within Carl. The memory he had read from the evening, between Carl and the woman, warmed his dark soul. Carl's total indifference to the woman was remarkable. It would be quite soon for Malkira to take him: quite soon. He would mark Carl through the next months, watch him, until he was ripe to pick.

37

Louis could feel a disturbance; there was a undercurrent in the kingdom. He hadn't wanted to admit to it, but it was there. Sitting in his favourite spot under the tree, he looked out at his creation, and had to admit it had grown more varied than when he had first discovered it, beyond his headboard. The red kite was back, making circles in the clear, azure sky, and he still didn't know where it had come from. Katie had brought birds and insects, even the breeze that they enjoyed. These had all been born through her thoughts. The grasses rustled and swayed in the meadow, and the breeze made them sing. It was a song he never tired of hearing. Positive change had crept in slowly and he had accepted each thing without a second notion.

Now, it was different. He worried that his kingdom had been tainted by Sophia. Her envy, jealousy and murderous nature had changed it, weaving strands that could bring evil into his world. He thought about the golden scales caught on the tree, that seemed to have been deliberately left there. He was sure that this small piece of skin had been the talisman that had allowed Katie to be kidnapped by the serpent.

He let his mind dwell on what Katie had told him of the trip out to St Mary's Church with that creature: the beautiful angel's guile, his silver tongue and the temptations of a dark world that offered a different life. He shuddered at the demon's insistence that their deaths, and Katie's in particular, were in reality all Louis' fault. It didn't help that deep in his own heart, he wondered if there was an element of truth in it. Katie, his own darling girl, had suffered because of him.

He should never have brought Katie to Ravensend. His guilt moved him to sorrow. He shook his head in disbelief, not quite believing his own folly. How could he imagine that, providing they stayed away from the Avondale Hotel, the home Sophia had haunted for over a century, they would be safe? He had had no idea that on their first visit north, Sophia had blended within Katie and had lived with – and heard and watched – them, for over a year. What a fool he had been.

His sigh was almost as loud as the breeze in the grasses. How had the 'angel-serpent' entered his kingdom? Katie had said he had come from behind the tree, but that was impossible. The entry point to his kingdom was by the veil. At least, that was the one they used to visit the bedroom and beyond.

There was a sound of a muffled sob, coming from beyond that entry point back in the bedroom. Katie and Champ were resting in a timeless sleep at the cottage, and were not privy to the sound. He listened intently. He was sure Lori and Joe had left the Royal. Indeed, when they had left his kingdom, their heavy hearts had been lifted, despite their grief, and filled with a new lightness. It couldn't be them, could it? His forehead crumpled into furrows when the next sob came clear and sharp into his world.

An emotional wave of pain was creeping through the doorway from the headboard. It was clawing. A fog of misery threatened to wrap itself around Louis and choke him. This couldn't be happening. His world was sealed from the mortal world. What was happening?

Sophia – it had to be her – had broken the seal somehow. It all made sense now.

Louis quickly dashed to the opening; he could smell it now. Evil always tainted the air. He pressed his head against the veil, listening, and heard the heavy breathing of a sleeper on the other side. Someone was using his bed.

The smell of evil was stronger here. He was unsure: should he take a look? One thing he did know was that it couldn't be Katie's parents on the other side. There was no evil in them. Still undecided, he was about to move when he heard that throaty sob again.

Someone was in pain.

As he moved through the veil, he became aware of a woman in distress nearby but not in the room. When Louis looked down, he saw a man who lay flat on his back, his mouth wide open, snoring. A man who was in a deep, alcoholic sleep, and, by the look of him, would remain so for many hours yet.

For a brief moment, the room lit up.

A door had opened, flooding light from the bathroom, and a shape stood still for a second before switching it off. The silhouette he saw was of a woman in her thirties, wrapped in a bath robe. She moved very slowly, making her way to the bed. She lifted the covers gently and slid in, still robed. She settled down, obviously trying to get comfortable, turning her back on the man. Louis could see her face was blotchy, red-eyed, and weary. Her pain oozed out of her pores, along with a deep-rooted anger.

Louis saw how she pulled the covers up to her ears; he had forgotten he brought cold into the mortal world. He should leave. He hoped she would find sleep and the strength to deal with whatever it was that caused her such distress.

Back in the silence of his kingdom, Louis was thinking about the woman.

Whatever had happened in that room earlier, the smell of evil was dispersing quickly. Perhaps the unconscious minds of the dreamers were letting go of the night. Had a lover's tiff got out of hand? He felt sympathy for her. He had seen how the dark side of people affected others and how evil could grow with it. Without wanting it, memories came flying back: the fights with Sophia his wife, their long, draining battles that nobody won. The hurt that was left hanging in the air cracked around them. Those hateful words that couldn't be taken back were still ringing in his ears. How was he to ignore them and make up? Once spoken, those words could never quite be forgotten.

Who was the protagonist, who the perpetrator, in this case?

He was still thinking about it when a fresh wave of darkness filtered through the veil to him. There were no raised voices. None. The smell that came with it was different, yet vaguely familiar, and then he realised. The beautiful angel that Sophia had called for was the connection. Hesitantly, Louis made his way back to the veil and pressed his face against it so that he could see into the room, as though he was looking though a mesh.

He saw two figures. The beautiful angel, Malkira, with the cloven hooves, was there with another figure who was covered in a shimmering mist of grey. Louis couldn't hear anything, but when they separated, the beautiful angel went to the sleeping man and the grey spectre moved to the woman.

The angel touched the man's head. Louis knew what that meant: Malkira was connecting to read the dreams of the man. Louis watched a smile grow wide on the tanned face of the dark angel; he was pleased with the connection. What had the angel seen? Nothing good; that was for sure. The spectre had moved away from the sleeping figure of the woman, slinking up to what Louis thought of as the demon master.

'She won't let me in. She has built a barrier around her unconsciousness. She is damaged, that's all I can say. Whether she will come over to us or not will only be proven with time.'

The demon raised his hand, dismissing his follower. Louis watched as the chiffon-like ghost, with Malkira close behind, crossed to the corner of the room alongside the bed. An unworldly glow cast light into the room, through a slit that stretched from the skirting board to the ceiling. Its opening was spitting molten fluid and the strong smell of sulphur came with it. The chink opened like a devil's doorway and, in less than a blink of the eye, the figures were gone.

Louis slipped immediately back into the Royal. He crossed the floor to touch the wall that was still lit up in a white glowing line that shouldn't be there. It showed clearly the breach between the worlds, and he flinched at the heat that almost burned his fingers. As he tested it again, it had instantly cooled, and it faded as he watched the wall return to its normal organic state again.

His thoughts went back to Sophia. She was certainly responsible for this. And now this devil seemed to be free to come and go, pestering and harming both this world and Louis' kingdom. This wouldn't do. He would have to be vigilant. He was left with a huge question: how was he to stop evil and the dark from coming into his world?

38

Louis was relieved to get back into the sunlight of his own world. He was met by a warm breeze and the hum of bees searching for pollen. It was a comforting sound after what he had witnessed. He shivered, despite the sun.

Katie and Champ were coming up the path from the cottage. He wondered how much he should tell her, knowing she would sense something wasn't right.

Champ bounded up to Louis, springing up onto him, pushing his master over and licking his cheek until a smile came back to Louis' face.

'Get off, down you daft dog.' Champ gave an excited yelp as Louis stood up and moved out of range of Champ's tongue.

'I thought I'd find you here.'

'Where else?' he replied.

'So, what have you been doing with yourself while we slept, darling?'

'I made a visit to Doris' world.'

'Why?'

'It was an uncomfortable visit, Katie, on two counts.'

'Tell me.' She sat down on the grassy knoll and waited for Louis to join her.

He recounted to her all that he had witnessed. To think that the demon could come and go unfettered disturbed her.

'Does it put our friends in danger?'

'I don't know. I believe the demon feeds on evil. I don't know what brought it here? Except that I think that the couple sharing our bed have something to do with it.'

39

She heard rushed footsteps coming up the stairs; someone was in a panic.

Debs was in the attic, enjoying a rest between shifts, when Julia came running in, out of breath and with tears streaming down her face. She was crying so hard that she couldn't form words to answer Debs' question.

'What's wrong? Come here.' Debs held her arms out for the poor girl to take comfort in them. Julia felt rigid, like a stone statue unable to take what was offered in kindness. Debs rather firmly took hold of Julia's shoulders and pressed her to sit on the bed.

'Stay there. I'll bring you a drink.'

Julia curled up on the bed and grabbed Debs' hand, begging her not to go.

The two women were locked in Julia's pain for what seemed like hours while the tears fell. When the last tear was wiped away, and the final sob was allowed to escape, Julia revealed the cause of her pain.

'I walked in on them. *On them,*' she repeated.

Debs didn't need to ask who she was talking about. She had seen the way Nick and Barbara looked at each other when they thought no-one was watching. No matter how sly they were, everyone seemed to know, except Julia. Debs had heard Barry more than once warning Julia about Nick not being good enough for her, without revealing his reasons, but love is blind.

'She was my best friend – how could she?' Then, with another sob, 'How could he?'

Debs understood the betrayal.

'Are you up to telling me what happened?'

Julia straightened up, twisting the small amethyst ring round and round on her engagement finger. The nervous action attracted attention every time she did it.

'He's been cheating on me, Debs. I caught him with Barbara. Oh! how could they do this to me?' A huge sigh expressed her pain. 'I was working in the new extension, but I finished my shift early and thought I'd go and give Nick a hand with the coffee for our break.' She breathed with a great gulp, trying to keep the tears at bay. 'I passed Barry in the bar and asked him if he wanted coffee. He said yes, and that Doris and Harry would be along in fifteen minutes.

'Nick wasn't in the kitchen. I thought it strange, but thought he may have gone on an errand for Roger. Barbara, I knew, was up on the Eden Room level, so I decided to make the coffee and then fetch her.

'I went through to the pantry. Oh God!'

She stiffened again, with the flash of memory and, in a whisper, said. 'He was touching her.' She clapped her hand over her offending lips as she said the word 'touching', as though the word burned her mouth. Wide-eyed, she looked at Debs. 'I love him.' It was a declaration of despair rather than sentiment.

Debs knew that feeling very well. She pushed her own thoughts of hurt away. This trusting girl needed all her sympathy.

More footsteps were climbing the stairs. Both women sat stone still when an urgent knocking rapped on the door. Neither spoke until Barry's Geordie twang travelled through the stout door.

'Are you alright? I know you're in there.'

Debs, with a sigh of relief that it wasn't Nick outside the door, leapt up and opened it a fraction. Barry's concerned face looked back at her.

'Good, I'm glad you're here with her. Did she tell you what happened?'

'She has, but I'm afraid she loves him.'

Barry's eyes went heavenwards. 'There's a bit of a commotion going on downstairs. Doris is on the warpath. Nick's trying to justify his actions. I think Julia should come down and hear it from him.'

Wide-eyed at what she had heard, Julia was shaking her head.

'Look, I'll come with you. It's better to sort it out while it's fresh.'

'I'm afraid, Debs.'

'I know, love, but you have me and Barry to support you. You'll have to face him sometime. You both work here, remember?'

What Debs couldn't know was that when Barry had seen Julia sprint from the kitchen and up the stairs with tears streaming down her face, he had decided to see for himself what had upset her.

Barbara and Nick were just emerging from the pantry, smoothing their clothes down, their hair in disarray and they both looked flushed.

'So, that's it, is it? You young beggar, can't you keep it in your pants? And you, Barbara – Julia is your best friend.'

'It's not what you think, Barry; we were going to tell her.'

'Tell her?'

'You don't have to answer to him, Babs.'

'Well, you young swine. You need to be taught some moral values.'

A very different Nick from the one the Royal knew turned on him. There was a snarl in his voice. 'What's it got to do with you, Grandad?'

Ringing with authority, a voice came from the hallway: Doris. 'Maybe nothing, but it's got a lot to do with me.'

40

Doris was pacing up and down, trouble written all over her face. She was waiting for Barry to reappear with Julia from upstairs, when she rounded on Nick.

'What have you been up to?'

'Look, Doris, I made a mistake.'

'You did that, lad. No mistake. Why round on Barry like that?'

'He was set to interfere and it's none of his business. He's always whispering to Julia about me. I know I've not always been fair or honest…'

'You can say that again,' Barry interjected, coming into the kitchen with Julia and Debs.

Nick bristled but held back.

Julia bravely came down to the ground floor with her two friends. She was shivering. Whether it was from fear or shock was undecided, but what was decided was that Debs was right. This was her home. And she would have to work with Nick and Barbara; she had nowhere else to go. She was over the age where the orphanage would find her a place to live or support her in any way and she wouldn't go back to them unless she was starving. At the magic age of sixteen, she had been considered an adult by the state. Now, she was on her own.

Nick had let her down before, but he had promised he would never do it again. She had trusted him, fooling herself even when she saw him take an interest in Barbara. Now, Julia faced them both in the kitchen, with everyone's eyes on her to witness her humiliation.

Nick stood, while Barbara sat, nervous, looking down and playing with her hands.

'As I said, I made a mistake. Not this morning.' He looked directly at Julia. 'Sorry, I should never have got engaged to you.'

'What?' Debs caught the girl as Julia's legs gave way from under her. Barry found a chair and helped her to it.

'Barbara and I have history. She was my one-night stand, Julia. I was full of guilt when you challenged me eighteen months ago. After I asked you to marry me, I did stay faithful until Barbara came here to work. Seeing her every day, I knew the passion we had was real. I even tried to get you to finish with me, to break off the engagement, but you were too good, too nice. I never wanted to hurt or reject you.'

'Well, this is a to-do and no mistake. Am I to lose three of my staff in one day? Am I?' Doris stopped in mid-sentence… 'On reflection, you three need to talk in private.' She waved Debs and Barry to follow her, but Julia stopped her. 'I need Debs. She said she would stay with me.'

'I'll be in my snug. Barry, let's have a small sherry; I need fortification.'

Debs was full of indignation. This man had some brass neck; he had almost managed to put the blame for his actions at Julia's feet.

Suddenly everyone was talking at once, with Barbara declaring that she hadn't thought her working with Nick would set their small indiscretion rolling again. Somehow, Debs didn't believe her. Nick claimed he needed this job, or his mother would put him out. Debs had trouble with that concept too. It seemed to her that the two of them were playing with Julia's good nature.

There was a business to run, and their coffee break had turned into a marathon of words that weren't going anywhere.

Julia was beside herself, hardly daring to look Nick or Barbara in the eye. Debs could see that Julia had given up any idea that Nick would want her back.

Her hands played with the ring on her engagement finger, until, with great effort of will, she pulled it off and in a very quiet voice said.

'You'd better have this, Barbara. It's no good to me, but every time you look at it on your finger, remember how he treated me, and wonder about yourself. Will you be the only one?' She spoke bravely. There was just a pause when a rogue tear filled her eye. She wiped it away, taking a deep breath and making a statement. Debs was so very proud of her.

'We should make a rota, to keep us out of each other's way for the time being. I will not be going; this is my home. You can leave if you want. I'll take the rota to Doris to approve. Debs, will you help?'

It was the strangest thing, cooperating with each other to make it work. The part-timers were slotted in to take Barbara's shifts when Julia was working, but Nick and Roger had strict hours and levels in their jobs. So, Julia declared she would not wait on in front of house so not to be near the kitchens. Julia would concentrate on housekeeping, which meant Debs would be waiting on, sometimes with Barry. No one wanted to let Doris down and they managed to put something together before they went back to work, making ready for lunch.

The test came for Julia that night. When work was no longer there to be a distraction, then the tears flowed. Debs lay under the eaves, listening to the muffled sounds coming from Julia's pillow, unable to help. Her own memories of this sort came back. How many nights, in the months leading up to giving birth, had been spent like that? That feeling of being used – of being worthless, unloved, and desperate – returned to torture Debs again.

At fifteen, she had easily been able to pass as an older teenager. When she had first met the twenty-year old Carl, he told her he was seventeen, and she pretended to be the same. It didn't seem to be such a big lie. Just two years' difference. He worked and had money in his pocket. He once asked what she did for a living and she pretended she was going to secretarial school. He didn't ask further questions.

He was so manly. At first, he took her walking in the local park. She felt so grown-up with him. Crazy as it seemed now, she remembered singing Elvis Presley ballads with him, and laughing when they both forgot the lyrics. He had kissed her, stroked her hair, and held her as though he could never let her go, but he had never gone beyond that. She felt secure in his company; he was her Sir Galahad. She absorbed his affection like a sponge in water; it was so scarce at home. They had strolled around the local shops. If she mentioned she liked something, he bought it for her. Not big things: a box of chocolates; a pair of fancy clip-on earrings, that she hid from her mother; and some marvellous popper beads, that were so fashionable. Six weeks after meeting him, he invited her back to his home. His mother would be there, so it would be alright. She was thrilled. It meant something, didn't it? The house behind the shop was more like a stock room. They lived, it seemed, upstairs. The shop had been closed, that surprised her. His mother had gone to the cash and carry with her friend George, and would be back later.

His bedroom was off the landing. Now, lying in her bed at the Royal, she remembered those dark-blue and cream floral curtains at his windows and shuddered. That was where he told her he loved her and wanted to show her how. She remembered his hands touching her, while his voice reassured her as he undressed her. And his excitement, when he touched her tiny bare breasts. She was bewildered but believed that this was love. By the time she was stripped, she was not sure what was happening. He told her to be a good girl and be still, and he would do what was needed. When he penetrated her, she wanted to scream, but he no longer seemed to be listening to her. He seemed to have lost sense of her. She clutched the bed clothes on either side of the bed and stared at the blue curtains until it was over. It hadn't been pleasant, but she trusted him.

'Go and get yourself cleaned up, there's a good girl. I'll make some tea before you go.' The words still rang in her ears. A cup of tea before he disappeared out of her life. Later, she had gone to the shop to see him, to tell him about the baby, and he had pretended he didn't know her. His mother had turned her out for trying to ruin her son's good reputation.

'Good reputation.' She cringed. And now he was here. The father of her child. A man who had not even recognised her, and she prayed it may stay that way.

Those last few weeks in the mother and baby home had been hell. The nuns had a peculiar idea of love and charity. There were so many girls there, just like her: lost, and betrayed, and many had been just as naïve as she was, believing that they were in love and loved.

Jessie, the girl in the next bed to her, still believed her man would come and marry her, and they would bring up the child together. It didn't happen for Jessie, and it didn't happen for Debs. Hope died a little more as each day passed towards the due date of delivery; fear replaced it, a fear that grew every hour.

The Sisters of Mercy misused them all. Calling them harlots and worse. They had sinned, and being with them was part of the punishment, though they called it atonement. Cleaning the cells and dormitories, working in the laundry, scrubbing floors – even the day before giving birth – was normal. There was no pity, no mercy. The sisters didn't care. They, the fallen women, had broken the rules, sin upon sin; their souls were blackened and damned. No amount of atonement would eradicate that.

Their sin, like Julia's, was no more than being foolish and loving badly.

But you didn't know that until you came out the other side.

The tears in the next bed were subsiding; perhaps sleep would overtake Julia. She needed to rest. These days that were set in front of her were going to be tough. Doris had been kind and assured her that she would always have a home at the Royal, but that would not be the ordeal. Facing facts was the problem.

Debs had been on duty that night. Once again, Carl and his wife had sat in the lounge before going into dinner. He had already had two rounds of gin before his wife joined him. Debs was serving them further gin and tonics when she noticed that the beer mat in front of the wife was being picked at and shredded while she sat. It was a simple sign of nerves – the pile of cardboard flakes had been pushed neatly to one side – but her body language seemed to be in defence mode, looking down and not taking note of what was around her. Did she know what she was doing?

'Do pull yourself together, Sandra. Do you want people to see your nerves?' He sneered the words, sharp and direct. Debs could see that

Sandra was under immense strain. Her hand was shaking when she took the drink that she was offered from the tray; by the time she had got it on the table, it had spilled over and had soaked the cardboard bits.

'You stupid woman. Can't you do anything without making a mess?'

Sandra groped in her handbag, bringing out a paper tissue and tried to mop it up.

'Don't do that, you'll get it on your clothes. The girl will do it. It's her job.'

'I'll be back in a minute with a cloth.'

His wife was paler than white.

This wasn't a love match, that was sure; twice she had served them and twice he had humiliated his wife in front of her. How could she ever have thought that she loved such a man?

There had been tension in the air all day long. Debs was pleased when Nick and Barbara went off shift and left the Royal together. Julia was already in her bedroom. Doris had insisted that she should rest, but Debs knew from her own experience that today would lie heavy on her heart. She would not be able to rest, but at least she was away from her deceiving former friends. In her heart, Debs hoped they wouldn't come back, but that wouldn't help the inn or Doris.

Tomorrow was another day; things would sort themselves out, wouldn't they?

At least Julia wasn't pregnant.

Oh Lord, she hadn't thought. Could Julia be…?

When Harry turned up that evening, he was mortified to hear Doris' account of the day. Something would have to be done.

41

It had been a disastrous day, and Nick would have to face Doris tomorrow. She probably would have Harry by her side. Not that she needed any help; she had a mind of her own and a tongue that she would use on him, no doubt. He knew in his gut she wouldn't leave it alone. He left the Royal with Barbara by his side.

What had he done? He had been caught and had had to think fast on his feet, but this had not been his true end game. This wasn't how he had envisioned his life would go. Well, he had made his bed, he had better lie in it. But he wasn't happy.

Barbara had grabbed his hand once they were outside.

'Oh, Nick. Isn't it marvellous? We don't have to hide our love anymore.'

It was dark. She held up her left hand to see the sparkle from the amethyst stone in the light from the shop windows they were passing.

He took her hand and pulled it down, smiling.

'I don't remember asking you.'

'Oh! You tease.'

She took his arm and snuggled up to him, like she hadn't heard him.

He had fancied her rotten, but he wasn't sure he wanted to be engaged to her.

He smiled again, as she patted his hand.

'We're going to be so happy,'

Nick's mind was elsewhere. Would Julia take him back if this didn't work out? He had always thought that one woman was pretty much the same as another; it was just that he, somehow, had managed to feel passion for both women. Well, he was a man, got to spread his seed. Now he was tied to Barbara. He had said he loved her; wasn't that what blokes said to have sex? She had put the ring on her finger as soon as Julia had left the kitchen; that wasn't supposed to happen.

He had had the best of both worlds before Julia had walked in on them. Barry was right; he couldn't help himself; he loved the ladies.

42

It bothered Louis. There was something in the air. It prickled like touching a holly leaf or a nettle; he was sure Katie could feel it too. Perhaps whatever it was had been seeping into his world bit by bit and for longer than he had thought.

Katie had left Louis under their tree and gone to the cottage. Champ, his faithful hound, had left him too. He was off sniffing out new smells and looking for new things to chase.

Rabbits had suddenly appeared from nowhere, their white tails flashing in the green of the meadow. They were new to the kingdom, and they had Champ pounding up and down the track. He had announced his presence with a playful bark, but as yet, they hadn't wanted to play his game. They, much like the red kite, had appeared out of the blue. Where had they come from?

Louis wondered if his meadow was safe from the pests, and what about the burrows they would make? He wondered if his thoughts be enough to stop them from breeding. He hoped so, as a twinge of fear rattled him; he was rather protective of his waving grasses.

A tobacco aroma announced the arrival of his father, visiting once again his rocking chair, next door.

Louis slipped through the headboard into the bedroom in somewhat of a rush to meet the old man. In doing so, he almost collided with the young woman who was busy making the bed.

Julia was shocked at the apparition that had flown out of the headboard, heading towards her at a rate of knots. A small cry left her throat in response to having witnessed yet another ghost, besides the old gentleman whom she knew quite well.

'Oh! My God. Where have you come from?' She was staring straight at him. 'Louis?'

'You can see me?'

'Yes, and feel you. It's like winter in here.' The girl took a second look at his face and stepped back. 'How can you be here?'

'More to the point, Julia, I didn't know you were psychic.'

'I keep it to myself; it's better that way. It came upon me the day Nick asked to marry me. I sense things now that I never did. This room is sometimes filled with a sort of anger, but most times it's just a bedroom. The old man comes every now and again.' She smiled at the vison that came to mind. 'He gets such enjoyment sitting by that window, pulling on his pipe. We don't speak much.'

'I didn't expect to find anyone here; Dad usually comes when the room's empty.'

'The old man's your dad? That's extraordinary.'

'What's extraordinary is that you can see and hear us.'

'I started seeing him over a year ago. It was a shock at first; I didn't know I had the gift, allthough I knew I had changed.' Julia had a faraway look on her face, remembering something from the past. 'He's a gentle soul. He doesn't bother me, and I don't bother him. But that doesn't explain you.'

'It's hard to explain, Julia. Believe me when I say that Katie and I are guests of the bed, that behind the bedhead is another place – my kingdom, where we live in spirit. Our love survived our deaths, and we are locked together there in a beautiful world. Where the bed goes, we go, and Doris brought us here when she bought the bed.'

For a moment Julia stood, trying to process how her friends, who had died in awful circumstances, could be ghosts in the Royal Oak. The bed, of course, was the key; it did make sense in a strange way. This mediumship was a lot to get used to, but she was calm. She had always been spiritual and had never been afraid of the thought of a spiritual life after death.

Ghosts, she thought, only reflected the nature of the soul of the departed. And Louis and Katie were good people.

Louis moved towards the faint outline that was his father, resting in the chair near the window.

'Dad, I need your help; I must ask you a few questions.' His father seemed to be fading as Louis spoke. The chair was visible through the apparition as he spoke, and it was getting stronger. The mist that was his father was shaking his head.

'I can't stay. Something malevolent stalks.'

'Dad.'

'Later, son. Later.' Massie was gone but left behind him his characteristic faint odour of tobacco.

A key could be heard in the door. It opened and Carl entered, looking surprised at seeing Julia with pillowslips in her arms.

'Not finished yet?' He smiled and looked on her with predatory eyes. 'God, it's cold in here.'

He sniffed the air.

'Having a crafty smoke, were we? It seems you have had the windows open to get rid of the smell. Who's a naughty girl? What else do you get up to?' The smile on his face was somehow threatening, like a fox who had found a stray chicken out of the pen.

Alarm bells were ringing in Julia's head. Debs had told her how he had treated his wife. She moved slowly towards the door; it was time to leave.

'I'll come back later, Sir.'

'No need for that.' His smile grew broader. 'I won't tell on your smoke, not for a little kiss.'

'You're mistaken.' Moving quicker now towards the door.

'Oh! I think not.' He placed himself in her path. 'No rush, my dear.'

She twisted to pass him.

He grinned. 'Easy girl, just you and me, let's make the most of it,' he said stepping towards her.

Carl was blocking Julia from the door and the safety beyond.

'What are you doing?'

'Don't worry, you'll enjoy it.'

Julia stepped back but Carl moved closer.

'You can't do this.'

Looking at Louis who stood behind Carl, she pleaded, 'Can't you do something?'

'Who are you talking to?' Following her eyes, he turned to the spot she was staring at. Julia used the moment of distraction and dashed for the door, slamming it behind her. Louis could see Carl's blue eyes were sparkling with excitement of the chase. His arrogance had filled the room.

The customer is always right, sang through Carl's brain. He was paying a tidy sum for this research trip or, at least, his wife was. And when he had finally written the book, and had become well-known, it would be time to move on. All he had to do was to get a publisher and an advance. God, he loved life. He had a woman who looked after him, who was a useful tool. He liked women to know their place; too many were challenging men nowadays. It wasn't to be tolerated.

His mother had been quite wrong chucking him out; she would see that eventually. George wouldn't stay forever; he was sure of that. Then she would want her son back. He might even go back, but not while he had Sandra and her money to play with. It was all a question of balance. He nodded, agreeing with himself. Yes, balance was the thing. With a small frown, he knew he mustn't spoil things. The young redhead was attractive, but not worth rocking the boat for, though she did have a nice bum. He stepped over to the window and sat heavily in the rocker, enjoying the movement. Feeling pleased with himself, he rocked back and forth looking out of the window at nothing in particular. This was the life.

He suddenly realised that in the temperature of the room had dropped dramatically and he shivered. It was probably time to go down to the lounge to join his wife. He put his foot out to stop the movement of the rocker, but for the life of him, he couldn't get up from the chair, which was still moving. He seemed to be stuck; a weight was on him that he couldn't explain, and the rocking, instead of stopping, had speeded up and was becoming frantic. What in the name of God was happening? Fear gripped him.

Louis was seething with loathing for this peacock, who thought he was superior on every level and who, by the smile on his face, had just enjoyed upsetting Julia.

Louis' temper was rising, and anger gave him power. With it, the temperature fell further, and a mist of ice particles began to form on the window. Louis sat on Carl's knee holding him in place, his hand pinning Carl's forearm against the wooden arm of the chair. With his free hand, he traced his fingertips over the skin on the man's face. Carl clawed at his face with the one arm that was free, trying to remove the invisible threads that felt like spiders crawling on his skin.

His breath was a white fog. One-handed, he tried to move what felt like cobwebs from his face, his solid hand passing through Louis' hand. Carl physically shivered, moving, turning, trying to free himself, but Louis didn't give up. Carl was getting more and more agitated, his hands scrabbling to claw away the invisible crawling sensations. He couldn't see anything in his hand, and he was getting colder and colder. He couldn't see out of the window; a light sheet of ice clung to it.

He couldn't even remember what he had come to the room for. All he knew was that he wanted to get out of it.

A quiet smile touched Louis' lips. The panic he saw on Carl's face was just what the man deserved. Thank goodness Louis had been there to help Julia. He hated bullies.

He recognised that the time had come to return to the kingdom, knowing that he had at least trimmed the peacock's tail feathers.

The room warmed immediately once Louis had left.

Carl was in a state of shock. He could move again and that creeping feeling on his skin had disappeared. He got up from the rocker and stretched out, touching his forehead. There was no temperature, but he did feel rather sick. In just a few minutes he had gone from enjoying the moment of teasing the redhead to – what? What had happened? Had he had a mini stroke? That would explain not being able to move and his skin crawling, also the loss of body heat. It all added up. He would have to rest, check his blood pressure. This was unexpected. Thank goodness, he had Sandra to rely on.

43

The coiled serpent stirred. A change in the air had woken him. A smug arrogance streamed towards the demon. He raised his head, peering with unseeing eyes at his surroundings, connecting much further afield. The vision he saw was the man, Carl, in that room, where he had first seen him in bed with his woman.

Malkira's forked tongue flicked back and forth in pleasure, tasting the air as he remembered the pain that emanated from Carl's woman. The secretion that was left behind had filled his already bloated belly. He took whatever he could, from wherever he could; that was the nature of the underworld. But this vision was different.

This image that he was seeing was sharp and clear. It was as though he was actually in the room, watching the events. He could see that this woman in the room with him was not Carl's woman.

Malkira congratulated himself; he had chosen well. Carl's nature was corrupted. He loved power. Carl was enjoying wielding his masculinity. He never questioned his instinct to take without giving of himself.

Vanity and pride were wonderful sins; Malkira really liked this man.

The redheaded girl was panicking, and Carl was in his element. Malkira approved. Carl had all the attributes the underworld wanted and appreciated.

Malkira had seen her before and, thinking back, he remembered her from his little trip to the kitchens some time ago, the morning he had played with a weak-minded chef. He allowed himself a little laugh; that silly man had been his own worst enemy.

The girl was a seer, and though she was young and inexperienced, her gift was strong, and he did not want to be known to her. There was fallibility in her; he could sense it even now. Yes, she wore her heart on her sleeve, and she needed love – that was a weakness – but she had the light from the angels; he would have to tread carefully. He moved to join Carl and dance with chaos around this girl, but something held him back.

Malkira wrinkled his nose, he could taste and smell something else. Carl moved to one side in the vision; he was trying to block the girl's path as she went for the door. In doing so, he cleared the demon's sightline, exposing a spirit. Malkira saw the outline of golden light that silhouetted a man's form, and he knew that this soul was full of God's light. This spirit belonged to the other place, not his. He could never be one of his disciples.

The invisible barrier that was keeping Malkira out of the room was this spirit, Louis. The demon shook himself, and his eyes returned to the reptilian orange and black. His breath had turned to a white fog. His scales felt as though they were covered in ice and an itching started from his tail until it reached his forked tongue. How dare this spirit block his path? As far as he was concerned the corporeal world and the netherworld were part of his territory to feed from. The fury grew inside him. The ice extended from his bodily scales, spreading like a virus over the rocks and growing up the walls and along the roof of his lair. It crawled throughout his cave until icicles were hanging from the rocks above his head and growing at an alarming rate.

The spirit next to Carl was Louis, the husband of Sophia. He remembered him fully, now.

Sophia, dear Sophia. She was a disciple to the chaos for a while, but she was far too needy. In the end, he had devoured her. It was for the best. She had made a better meal than she had a lover, but then, what did he know about love, except it made people weak? His dalliances were all about power or food.

Louis was the one who had followed him into Debs' dream, in that attic bedroom. He had tried to protect her. Louis was the creator of the kingdom that Sophia loved, behind the headboard – the kingdom that Malkira had been invited into. Because of that invitation from Sophia, it belonged to his territory now.

That's where he had found Katie, lost in thoughts and sadness under the tree. He should have known better than to take her to her place of death, but there was a chance, just a chance, she might have turned to him. Sadness and regret could be game-changers in the mortal world, and also in the nether world when a spirit had been unable to pass over. Malkira had invited many souls over, and he was always on the lookout for new disciples. He sighed. Perhaps he hadn't played his hand well; she had refused him. She, too, had the angels on her side. But no matter, she may yet be useful. He never gave up.

His cave was reverberating with heat and the cold was disappearing, slowly reversing the temperature of zero back to his normal, comforting, tropical one. His temper was subsiding now, allowing the ice to melt, but with it came the unpleasant damp.

The crevasse became wet and his skin touching the solid rock felt tender as his delicate scales rubbed on the damp, slippery surface. The roof, too, had started to drip, making pools of water in the many smaller crevasses that surrounded him. Wisps of steam rose from the cave floor that shimmered with water, and then the icicle over his head started to dissolve, melting with drops the size of conkers drumming down on his head. Damp, he hated damp. He should have known better than to get into a rage, but he hated to be outflanked by good spirits: his one and only failing.

He wriggled uncomfortably; his scales were sticking to the rock. It was no good. He would have to change into the human form until the cave stabilised again.

His hands pushed through his black wavy hair; his fingers wet at the touch. His clothes were clinging to him too. By the laws of the underworld and the power of his deity, he snapped his fingers; nature couldn't ignore him. He was a powerful agent of darkness. A wind swept through the cavern, hot and violent, and in seconds his home was dry as a bone and the scent of sulphur filled the air. A smile touched his lips. He loved that smell, and now he could return to his favourite form. He coiled himself back in the now dry hotbed of his choosing.

The girl's gift and Louis' selfless spirit had put up the barrier that was locking him out; Malkira was sure of it. His conclusion was that Louis received extra power by being near her. And that was troublesome. The angels were on their side. No matter. He had his own angels, his army of chaos, and he was ready to use them. When he visited their world – and he would, soon – he could deal with them one at a time. His eyes were without feeling or sentiments, empty as they looked into that bedroom. He would coil tightly and sleep. The picture was dimming and disappearing from the demon's mind's eye as Louis disappeared through the headboard and Carl rushed out of the door.

Malkira yawned. He would send a little support to Carl.

44

Julia had taken advantage of the diversion and was out of the door, along the passage off the landing and down the stairs, almost bumping headlong into Debs on the way.

'Hey, steady! What's the matter with you? You look as though you've seen a ghost.' Debs took the girl by her shoulder and felt her shaking.

'Debs, that man' – Julia was finding it hard to speak through her breathlessness but managed to say – 'tried to make a move on me.'

'That man?'

'That Carl bloke, the one you told me about, who treats his wife badly.'

'Are you alright?' Debs took Julia in her arms. This poor girl, was anything else going to go wrong for her? An unfaithful boyfriend and now Carl. That man, not content with ruining two women's lives, was trying his hand on her young friend. She felt she had to do something to help.

'Do you think we should tell Doris?'

'I'm fine, just a bit shook up. I'll stay away from him. No fear. And I think Doris has enough to cope with at the moment.'

Although Debs didn't argue with her, now she was worried for Julia. Perhaps she herself should have a word with Doris on the quiet? The man was here for another week. Anything could happen. Oh Lord, what should she do?

The flickering light danced on the walls in the lounge. The room was empty of guests. The high-backed chairs that screened people so well were all vacant and were being pushed back into position and the cushions fluffed up. The guests often moved the chairs around. Barry was helping her; Julia had gone for a break, one that was necessary after the advances of that monster, Debs thought. Late afternoon had brought a wind that was as restless outside as she was inside herself.

The clouds were slow-moving and were casting shadows. The dark and light chased each other across the cream paint on the walls, and, although it was still too early for dusk, the room was telling a different story.

It was like a forewarning, an announcement of doom, that came with the fear that Debs had locked in her heart. If she didn't speak out and Julia got hurt, she would never forgive herself. As if the sun was listening, it hid itself behind a large, purple-grey cloud, suddenly plunging the room into gloom. What should she do?

Barry was finished and called out to meet her in the kitchen as he left the room to make some tea. He was such a good man and treated her with respect and warmth. At times she saw love in his eyes, but he never voiced it. She loved him, she was sure of that, but she needed him to open up before she could tell him her own feelings.

A chair invited her to sit; she needed a couple of minutes. Secrets and stress were so emotionally draining. Sometimes, the secrets that she had pushed away, hidden in deep chasms inside of her, surfaced, screaming to be let out. She wanted so badly to unburden herself, but what would Barry or Doris think of her? As usual, her impulsive soul wanted to let it all out, but this time she heeded her common sense, knowing full well that once it had been spoken about it could never be taken back. Doris and Barry would never see or look at her in the same way again, would they? She would be naked, stripped of the protection she had here. This, her new start, would be soiled, and she would be judged.

This morning she had witnessed for herself the truly disgraceful character of Carl. The day had started well enough. Carl and his wife had come in for breakfast; he was holding on to Sandra, as though guiding her through the maze of tables, as though she was unable to make her own way and find their allotted table unaided. It could have been a loving gesture except that Debs could see his grip on Sandra's arm. Her sleeve was creased and crushed; his hold was noticeably tight. Sandra was looking distinctly uncomfortable. He, however, had a smile on his face, that said, 'See, what a good sort of bloke I am.' His eyes danced around the room. Was he looking for approval? Did he really think that these people had any interest in him?

The room was already quite full, with guests munching through their food and talking with a certain lightness, in holiday mood. Debs had just delivered hot plates to a table, when the couple was suddenly beside her.

'Got a table for us, have you?' The smile was there, but cold eyes told a different story.

She was unable to get out of his way. His eyes connected with Debs; they scared her for a moment before, with relief, she saw there was no sign of recognition in them.

Those penetrating blue eyes, that she, as a young girl, had trusted and loved, were bitingly hard. She knew better today and, with disdain, she saw no empathy there for her; nothing but a cold and haughty expression. His superiority and arrogance flooded from him, and his smile, so inviting, was only one of his lies: one of the many he used. How else, but to keep a check and control in his life and wife? she thought.

'Come this way, Sir.' Debs showed the couple to a table laid for two.

He let go of his wife's arm and she sat obediently opposite him. Her head was bowed. Her spirit seemed conquered and withered.

Revolted as Debs was, there was nothing she could do to help this woman.

She was suddenly aware that she had escaped an even greater ordeal than the one that had been forced on her by his betrayal. She wondered, at that moment, if he had stood by and married her and accepted his daughter, how he would have been as a father? Was he even capable of being a parent? Debs seriously doubted it. All those silly dreams she had spun as a teenager had turned into her worst nightmare, and yet she felt it might have been even worse as she looked at Sandra. For a moment, she had been lost in thoughts, but she was brought back to the present when his voice broke through her trance.

'Full breakfast for me. Sandra will have two poached eggs. Toast for two. One tea, one coffee.' He flapped his hand to dismiss her. What a fool she had been. Anger lurked in her breast as she retreated into the kitchen to get out of his way.

Debs' moment locked in the past that morning was concluded. She was left in the lounge, still looking at her hands, still uncertain as to what path to take. Tell all or stay quiet?

45

The utter despair she cradled in her heart was growing. The scream inside her head and reverberating around her body was trying to find a way out. Sandra had to escape; she had to find the strength, but it still eluded her. Each time she thought she was ready, he took her down and she found herself back in the bottom of a dark, deep pit.

Her humiliation was at its worst when he raped her. She was married to him, but it was still rape. He took her without love and used her like a sex toy: her body used and abused at his will, a chattel, as if she was without feelings and had no needs. The hate that grew towards him was minuscule, compared to the hate she felt for herself.

She was sitting on her own. Her husband had gone upstairs to find a tour book, a useful tool for his research. She could breathe at long last; it was good just have a few minutes to be free from his gaze. At the thought of him coming back down, her stomach knotted tightly. Acid reflux was burning the back of her mouth. What would her mother think of her if she was still alive? Would she be as ashamed of Sandra as Sandra was of herself?

Julia was passing through the lounge and saw her sitting alone. A red and black aura was draped over her like an outer cape. It showed Julia that anger and hatred were heavily entrenched in the crumpled figure of Sandra. A shadow was also standing near the woman: the shape of a woman coloured in a rose and gold mist. Although this figure was faint, and flicked in and out of her vision, Julia felt that it was a family member. It moved pulsating, and, at its strongest pulse, it moved as if it was trying to push though the red and black barrier. However, it only dented the aura and couldn't get through it to touch her. Sandra couldn't receive the touch of the angel that wanted to help heal her pain. Julia realised that Sandra's hatred was blinding her spiritual soul and blocking the gift of healing.

The heavy silence was broken by the sound of someone running. Carl rushed through the door to the lounge, making a bee line for Sandra. He was out of breath and his face was red, either from haste or anger. Whatever it was, it held his concentration. He didn't seem to notice Julia, but she watched as two images dematerialised and emerged out of the walls. Wisps of grey chiffon appeared to follow Carl, attaching themselves to him; thin skeleton-like arms and clawed hands reached out to touch him before dissolving into his body. She had seen the shape of eyeless skulls under the veils, and she was shocked to her core when she realised she was witnessing phantoms from the jaws of hell.

Carl felt his mood change. Just moments ago, he had been consumed with fear, but now he was suddenly filled with a stoic energy and his need for Sandra's help disappeared. He stopped in his tracks, four strides from her. Disdain poured from his breast as he saw his wife afresh. He slowed his pace and took deep breaths.

She looked up at him. Those hazel-coloured eyes took stock of him before finding something fascinating on her clasped hands on her lap. He could almost smell the fear she had for him, and he loved it. He towered over her and watched her shrink further into herself.

He felt a chuckling in his belly, though it seemed to be coming from some other place than from himself. He held it in.

He tapped her foot with his own, with more force than was necessary, and once again those fearful eyes looked up at him.

'Ready to go? Have you got all the notes, tour book and camera?'

'But. But you were going upstairs to get the tour book.'

'Yes, but it wasn't there, so I supposed you had it,' he said, grimly. Picking up Sandra's travel bag, he practically threw it on the chair next to her. With a great show, he unzipped the tartan holdall and started to rummage inside. A smile of triumph spread across his face when he drew out the lost book.

'See here!' He slapped her shoulder with the book. He stooped, putting his head down to hers, his lips almost touching her ear.

'You stupid woman, can't you do anything right?' he whispered.

Sandra didn't answer. She was grateful she was sitting in the lounge, in a public place, or the book might have been aimed at her head.

When he straightened up, he took her by her arm. 'Come on, my dear, let's go.'

Sandra didn't argue or fuss. She knew better. She had given up on finding her voice; she had learned the art of surrender. It could be less painful but she had never realised it was an art until then.

The weak, transparent image behind Sandra in rose and gold shuddered and splintered, disappearing in a wisp of light. The help Sandra might have got if she had opened up was gone with it.

Julia watched as Sandra was bundled forward with a little push, through into the hall that led to the world outside. What she had felt coming across the room from Carl was pure evil. She found she was shivering, and there was a heavy, lead-like pressure in her heart. She had to share what she knew with someone. Could she trust Debs? She had to make a decision.

46

Roger was pleased with himself. He felt safe; nobody had noticed a little money was missing from the takings, and Maureen couldn't be happier. She was pleased with him bringing her little extras home with his wages.

He was careful, and only took what he thought wouldn't be missed. He wasn't showy, and he worked hard. He was never complacent; he just wanted what he felt was his due.

It had been particularly busy that weekend: the end of the summer and the start of a glorious autumn. The weatherman had predicted an Indian summer, at least for the next ten days, and that seemed to bring out the ramblers, walkers and folk that wanted to catch the good weather before the real autumn settled in.

The bar that evening was bustling. Locals sat amongst the guests, sharing tables, such was the volume of customers. Barry had agreed to help out, and Roger was on duty too. Bar meals were coming out of the kitchen at a pace, as the restaurant had been fully booked and last orders served before it closed.

Carl Greaves had showed up and was annoyed that he and his wife couldn't eat in the dining room because he hadn't booked. He was rather unpleasant but, in the end, he and wife had eaten at the bar. After a few beers, Carl's voice rose in volume. His wife was looking uncomfortable, as he seemed to speak as though addressing an audience. She touched his arm to quiet him. With obvious disdain, and pushing her away, he told her to keep her hands and thoughts to herself. A few moments later, she had slipped off her stool, disappearing upstairs out of his way, so Barry thought.

Carl was telling a fellow who had taken Sandra's place beside him all about the book he was writing and how interesting the ruined churches and abbeys were in these parts. He had spent the day at Bolton Abbey, a 12th-century priory, and was charmed at the beautiful setting. The River Wharfe ran through its grounds, and Carl described the long walk on the riverbank. Miles and miles he and Sandra had tramped, until they had reached the Strid. That too was a famous landmark, where the river forced itself through a narrow channel of rocks. Carl remarked that it made a deafening sound doing so; it created thick white foam that bubbled like a witch's cauldron on its surface. The rocks were wet, slippery and dangerous, but more than one foolish person had attempted to jump across, misjudging the width, according to the warning notice. Once caught in the strong natural force, the water swept them under, locking them there under its weight and drowning them. Or, at least, that was the tale he was told by others who stood beside him looking down into the water. It was the noise of the gurgling water, pressing on the rocks near his feet that he remembered, and the odd spray of escaping water caught up in the air hitting his face as he peered down at it, over the edge.

He had looked at the gap. It didn't look that wide to him. At school he had been a long jumper, and he had jumped yards more than that width, he was sure of it. With his chest puffed out, he berated the fact that his woman was whingeing not to get too close. 'Honestly, women!'

He went on to boast, to those who were listening, that if he'd been on his own, he might have tried it.

Barry, behind the bar, shrugged his shoulders. He had heard it all before. Some people were just too stupid for their own good. Pride comes before a fall, and that man was full of it. Carl had been on the local brew while he ate with his missus, but now whiskey and dry gingers were slipping down rather easily. Roger was hovering behind the bar, and he raised his eyebrows in disbelief when he caught Barry's eye. Carl was in a spending mood, and Barry had changed two five-pound notes from the man over the course of the three hours Carl had sat there, buying drinks for the locals. Two, in particular, appeared to lap up his every word. Barry knew them well; they never missed a chance of free booze if it was going. The three of them hugged the bar. They were getting noisy; laughter and raised voices were typical of men that had had enough.

Doris appeared on cue about ten minutes later to ring the five-minute bell, and Barry, relieved, laid out the towel over the pumps. 'Time, gentlemen, please,' he called in his pleasant Geordie accent.

'Will you lock up, Barry, please? I've got Harry here.'

'Of course. We've been that busy, I never saw him come in.'

'Bring the takings through when you've finished and have a night cap with us.'

'Will do.'

Barry turned to Roger. 'Turn off the taps and start to clear while I see our guests out.'

'Right you are.'

Barry heard the ping of the till as he opened the doors; he looked back over his shoulder and saw Roger putting money into the drawer.

Louis watched with disbelief. Roger was up to his old tricks again. In a second, he was beside the thief, and seeing his hand inside the drawer of the till, Louis expelled his anger in a single breath.

The cold that danced on Roger's fingers was icy and his fingers instantly became stiff.

Roger was busy looking at Barry, while at the same time trying to purchase the corner of a note. He felt odd; it was all so peculiar, feeling this cold in the warm bar – but don't panic, he told himself, keep calm. He nodded at Barry at the doorway.

Roger had the towel over his arm and, under its cover, took the note. In the tension of that moment, he thought he heard words, but just one stood out, said with great force.

'Thief.' Louis was breathing on Roger's neck, making the hairs there stand on end. 'You ungrateful man.'

The bar emptied quickly as Barry stood with the door open, saying goodnight as the patrons left. The last remaining guest showed no sign of leaving and was banging the bar with the flat of his hand.

'Can I help, Sir?' Roger was engaging politely with a wide smile. He was feeling chuffed with himself, with a note in his pocket to share with Maureen; he would be away home in a matter of minutes.

Carl had lost his audience; his two new best friends, Joe and Sam, were being shown out the door. The autumn air rushed into the bar, and he was suddenly cold.

'I'll just have another one, a night cap.' His words were slurred, and his eyes looked a little glazed. No 'please' or 'thank you'; he didn't endear himself to Roger.

'Sorry, Sir, the bar's closed,' said Roger.

'But I'm a resident.'

'Sorry. That's the rule of the house.'

'No wonder the country's going to rack and ruin.' He spun rather too quickly off the barstool and landed in a heap on the cold flagged floor. He hurt his elbow and a great deal of pride.

'I could get you a coffee from the kitchen, if you like,' offered Roger, looking down at him.

'What are you implying?' confronted Carl, his face turning ruddy with drink and temper. He attempted to stand, grabbing at the stool he had left for support, but it rocked as he tried to purchase it. He thought better of it and sat for a moment, just staring at Roger.

'Nothing at all, Sir, just trying to be helpful.'

'Then get me a bloody drink.'

Barry, having locked up, came over to help.

'You get off home, Roger. I'll see to this gentleman.'

Roger didn't need to be told twice.

'Well, Sir, can I help you up to your room?'

'Not sure I'm ready to retire, thanks,' was the curt answer.

'Whatever you say. I'm making a coffee for myself to have in the lounge. Would you care for one? I'd love to hear more about your day.'

'Really?' Carl puffed out with pride but didn't want to drink with a waiter. 'Thanks, but no. And I can manage.' Barry gave him the support he needed to stand, though Carl winced when Barry touched his elbow as he eased him to his feet.

Barry watched the very unsteady man walk down the hall to the staircase and hoped he could make it to his bedroom without toppling over or vomiting. He really was difficult.

It was well over an hour later when Barry was finally straight and ready for the morning. Having counted the money at least twice, he took the takings into Doris with a puzzled look on his face.

Doris and Harry were looking through some official looking papers when he knocked and walked in on them. Doris, who knew her friend well, picked up on his mood and knew something wasn't right.

'Something wrong?'

'It's just, well' – he looked embarrassed – 'Doris, did you take a five-pound note from the till when you came to ring time?'

'I didn't. Why?'

'I took two five pounds tonight, but there is only one in the till. It couldn't have been changed, for there was no ten pound in it. And how many people would want to change pound notes into a fiver? None around here.'

'Are you sure, Barry?'

'I am. I'm sure it went in the last hour when there was only me and Roger serving.'

'Do you know what you're saying?'

'I hope I'm wrong, but if I am, where is the missing note?'

Doris jumped up. 'I'll go and have a look.'

'Doris, I've checked twice. It's not there.'

Doris went to check anyway. Barry understood totally. He was accusing Roger of theft.

Harry's fears about Roger appeared to be justified. Not that being right comforted him. He hadn't voiced his worries to Doris in order not to influence her opinion of Roger for the sake of Maureen. He now regretted not speaking about his fears. He had hoped Roger had changed from the boy he had known, and that he deserved a little help along the way. After Doris' kindness – giving them a job, helping them move on – he wanted this to be a mistake.

Roger had left the Royal in a state of panic. Things had not gone to plan. Two things had happened to knock him off his stride. First, when Doris had left Barry to lock up, Roger had opened the till, forgetting the ring of the bell. It was so normal he didn't hear it anymore. That was a mistake. It had alerted Barry.

Usually, Roger waited until Barry was busy elsewhere, but tonight it had been so busy that Barry had stayed behind the bar and near the till all night. Only when Barry went to the main doors, to usher the patrons out, did he have the chance to skim off the top.

The second mistake happened then, with Barry's eyes on him. He rushed the dip. His eye was on Barry, rather than on the drawer. He felt the paper of the note in his fingertips and whipped it out and, once hidden under the teacloth, he pocketed it quickly.

That sense of relief and smugness he felt had dissolved when he saw the cash properly. Barry was dealing with the drunken guest at the bar when Roger took the opportunity to look at his prize. At the shock at seeing not the familiar green pattern of the pound note, but the blue of the much more valuable fiver, his heart froze. It was not possible to put it back, not now. He was done for, that five-pound note would ruin him and his wife. Maureen, who had no part in this, would be blamed as well. Sick to his stomach, he knew he would have to tell her. All of it.

Hell; he had ruined both of their lives.

She was waiting up for him as she always did. A pan of milk was warming on the hob. The two china mugs that had come from the tearoom were all that was left from his own business. As per normal, two heaped dessert spoons of cocoa were waiting for the hot milk, and a shortbread biscuit, homemade from his wife's own hand, was laid in the saucer. It was usually heavenly bliss, but not tonight.

Maureen knew as soon as he walked in that something was wrong. He brought with him an air of despondency that filled the kitchen/living room.

Her smile of welcome was replaced with a frown, something he hardly ever saw on her pretty face.

She didn't tackle him straightaway, but let him get through the door and get a hot drink inside of him. He wouldn't be able to keep it to himself; of that she was sure. She turned up the tap on the gas, looking away from him, and watched as the milk bubbled slowly before it broke into a foam of energy. It steamed as she poured the magic of the soothing milk into their mugs, stirring briskly and handing one to him as he sat at the table.

There was silence for two or three minutes while the cocoa was sipped.

'Are you ready to share your thoughts yet?'

Her gentle blue eyes poured out caring and love to him. His shame was overwhelming as he absorbed her gaze. He felt small – very small and insignificant – sitting next to her, feeling the empathy that he didn't deserve.

She had been his salvation when, years ago, he had been in trouble. He had changed from a headstrong yob who didn't trust, who couldn't trust, having been let down throughout his life with parents who thought kindness and affection were a sign of weakness.

The only hand he felt was the back of one, usually across the head. Hugs were what you endured when you were wrestling in the park. He couldn't remember being thought of as a person until he met Maureen.

He had been working as a casual in the kitchen of the Avondale Hotel. She was learning a trade, a skill for life that would keep her fed and a roof over her head. He wanted that. It made him hungry to learn.

She was clever and had a natural talent in the kitchen, and, strangely, she took to him. She helped him, passing on what she could, and he became more than he could have ever realised under his own steam.

Not only had she taught him, but she had also loved him. She had hugged him and touched him with a gentleness and big heartedness that surrounded him when she was near.

He felt like a wicked child; how was he going to explain himself?

Her voice was patient. 'Start at the beginning and stop when you get to the end.' She smiled at her quote, but he knew she wouldn't be smiling when he had explained.

The smile faded when he didn't respond.

'Roger, you're scaring me. What's happened? What have you done?'

Roger coloured up. His gaze dropped to his mug of cocoa. He cleared his throat and his voice was gravelly with emotion when he answered.

'I'm so ashamed, Maureen. I've ruined our lives, been stupid beyond measure and there's no going back.'

Maureen's half-full nature was suddenly half-empty.

'What are you saying?'

'It started when I volunteered to help out in the bar. You were worried about money. We were finding life hard, and the extra money would help. I thought no one would miss the odd pound.'

It was hard to say just what he could see in Maureen's face. Shock, revulsion, disbelief, and pity: in one flash of emotion, he saw all four.

'Oh, Roger, you didn't?'

Her voice held no anger, but her eyes pleaded for an explanation. It would have been better if she had thrown the cocoa at him. But that wasn't her way. She seemed stunned, unable to speak to him. After what seemed like an age, she spoke in a whisper.

'But why?'

'I don't really know. It just sort of came over me, and it was so easy. It was never more than a pound or two until today. They were doing so well, and we had lost everything.'

'But Roger, they had given us a new start. Doris was kind, generous. It was a gift.'

'I know, I know. It was so easy, just for a little extra.'

She didn't raise her voice. 'What happened tonight?' Her stare was more than he could bear.

'I nearly got caught. In my panic, I took a five-pound note. It will be missed.'

His voice was no more than a croak. She had heard it before when he held back his emotions. This was time to face the truth.

'I see.' Maureen's voice was raised as though she was telling off a child.

She was the best. For a moment hope lifted him.

'Tell me what and how it happened.'

At the end of his tale, Maureen folded her ample arms over her equally ample breasts and leaned forward.

'This is what we'll do. We are both on morning shift tomorrow. We'll set off ten minutes earlier than usual and you will take the note and place it on the floor behind the bar. Tuck it, half-in/half-out of a low shelf or something. Visible, yet hidden.'

Maureen's face was stern. She was looking at him hard. 'It will be found, and questions will be asked. We won't mention anything; we know nothing. It will remain a mystery. Do you understand? And you must promise me that this is the last time you lead us down this road. I love you, but I don't need this.'

Roger's relief was written all over his face.

'You're right, love. If the note is found, that will be the end of it.'

'No, Roger, it won't. Yes, the money will be retrieved, but don't be a fool. You will be suspected. But they won't have any proof unless you give them some. And that won't happen, will it? Do you hear me?'

Roger knew he had no choice but to try and put things right.

'And another thing, you will repay all that you have stolen. Replace it bit by bit, as you stole it. I won't be married to a thief.'

Maureen's face softened; her blue eyes were encouraging. Roger nodded.

'Drink up and let's sleep on it. Tomorrow will take care of itself.' Roger was soothed by her words. She always knew what to do.

Roger didn't sleep well; he was up making tea at 4.30 am. This must work, he thought over and over: a thought that he couldn't turn off. He had worked out where he would plant the note, but he wasn't sure if he could bear waiting for someone to find it. An even worse thought overcame him: what if it was found and the person pocketed it? That thought left him in a sweat. That and the fear that Maureen would leave him, if this didn't work.

They left the house under a cloudy sky and in silence as they walked to the Royal's back door. The door was already ajar, though no one was in the passageway to be seen. Someone had opened up, and a crate of empty milk bottles had been put out, while another crate of milk was ready to be taken in. Roger stooped to pick it up.

Maureen stopped him as he stepped up to carry it in, by taking his arm, and in a low voice reminded him, 'Not a word about last night and choose your timing carefully. You have it safe?'

Roger patted his pocket over the stolen note and nodded.

'Be your natural self,' she warned. 'Now, let's get to work.'

Doris had had a restless night. Even with Harry beside her, she was not happy. He had not said anything but his silence was more powerful than words.

She had got up, desperate for a cup of tea, leaving Harry half asleep under the covers. Debs was on the landing already, as she was due to open up, but Doris sent her back to bed for an extra half hour. Doris needed to be alone; this business was pressing heavily on her. She would have to tackle Roger as soon as he came in to work. It had to be faced; she had hired him. But what about Maureen?

First things first, there was a crate of empties to go out and milk to come in. She would do that while the kettle boiled. The back door was as stout as the walls of her home and creaked, begging for oil, as she opened it. She mentally filed away that job for Barry to do later.

Two crates of fresh milk were waiting, one on top of the other. She put the used crate out and picked up one with newly delivered milk. She had forgotten how heavy it was, but managed to get it to the kitchen just as the kettle came to the boil. Dragging it into the cold room, she lifted out a pint; she was ready for a strong brew.

Forgetting the back door, she was sitting at a counter, sipping hot strong tea, when Roger and Maureen came in. Roger was carrying the crate she had left.

Maureen bustled in with a smile, wishing Doris a good morning, and adding, 'It's a bit dull out there just now, but it's due to clear and we'll have a sunny day.'

Doris responded with a slight nod and a curious smile. She hadn't noticed the sky that morning. Her mind was still on the missing fiver.

Roger went straight to the cool room and deposited the milk on top of the other before he took two pints from it and proceeded towards the bar.

'I'll just put these in the bar fridge – we ran out last night. It's done then for the teas and coffees for elevenses.'

Doris watched him go, following him with her eyes. She was not sure what to think or how to approach him about the missing money. But approach him she must and there was no time like the present. Her stomach churned. She didn't want to think ill of this couple, especially Maureen, who seemed as solid as they came.

She took a long draught, finishing the welcome drink. It was time.

Getting to her feet, she smoothed her dress down and took a deep breath. She was only a few steps behind him.

The glass door of the fridge was open and Roger was bending to place the milk in its usual spot on the bottom shelf. He stiffened at his name being spoken.

'Roger? A word, please.'

Doris came around the bar to where he stood. Her face was set in what one could only describe as ready to do battle. Doris couldn't know that the five-pound note was already in place to be found. His shoe pushed it a little further back under the ledge.

Roger remembered Maureen's counselling and he stood up, smiling at Doris.

That was a little out of character, Doris thought, but she felt she was already judging him and she must give him a chance to speak.

'Yes, Doris, is there something I can help with?'

He came to meet her, taking the glass towel from the beer pumps as he passed them. It seemed to act as though it had life of its own, jumping out of his hand and landing on the floor near his feet. He bent over to pick it up, hoping Doris would have a clear view of the area he had just vacated.

'Whoops, sorry about that. I'll just grab a clean one. Back in a mo.'

He was past Doris and back into the kitchen like a bullet from a gun. His eyes met Maureen's. No words, but a slight nod from him informed her that he had placed the note to be found.

Grabbing a clean towel from the linen drawer, he was relieved to hear, 'Well, I'll be blowed,' coming from the bar.

Roger walked back to the bar, carrying his alibi. Doris had a genuine smile on her face and was proudly holding the five-pound note like a prize.

'Would you believe it? It was here all the time. How I missed it last night I'll never know.' She paused for a minute. 'Barry, too.'

'What was that?' said Roger, his head inclined on one side, showing interest.

'Nothing, nothing at all. Just carry on.' She nodded to herself. 'A bit of a mix up, that's all.'

'You wanted to speak to me?'

'Ah, yes. Could you take toast and tea up to Harry and tell him I'll be up shortly?' The relief she felt was enormous. She was pleased to have found the money. She hadn't had to sack anyone, yet she had a hunch that something wasn't quite right.

For now, she pushed aside that niggle. The house was stirring. Breakfast should be prepared. She would think about it later.

47

The day had been filled with tension. It leached out of the walls like a bad smell.

Louis couldn't tell whether the mood was affecting the mortals around him, but that old saying 'by the pricking of my thumbs, something wicked this way comes,' rang in his head, and he wondered if Julia could sense it too.

The Royal Oak had been a haven for him, a place to come for solace right from the time when he was a carpenter in the nineteenth century, when he could escape for an hour or two from the demands of Sophia. The years of loneliness between then and now were forgotten, all because Katie had brought love to him, first in dreams and then in reality. It had been a kind of reincarnation and had given him a year as a mortal. He had had to relearn eating, breathing, sensations. Making love was beyond ecstasy. He had even worked with wood again, using his skills to create new carvings. Now, here in the twentieth century, he was a ghost once more, but not alone. He had his darling girl beside him, despite Sophia's best efforts.

Sophia had done her hardest to destroy their love. Her jealousy had not diminished after her death. It spanned though the centuries, surfacing when fate brought them together again by accident. She had caused as much pain as she could before her spirit was absorbed by the demon.

Louis assumed that her hatred had attracted the darkness he could sense now, and that she had invited that evil into the Royal. His worry now, despite his father telling him to trust the angels, was that there was a lot of disturbance that felt too big for him to resolve, even with angels.

Louis had positioned himself at his usual place in the bar. He had seen and heard Barry in the snug and, although despondent at the situation, he was pleased that Roger had been found out at last. Tomorrow was going to be an interesting day. He was on his way back to his kingdom; watching over the Royal was finished for the day, and he couldn't wait to have Katie in his arms and feel her love.

It had been perhaps an hour since he had watched the drunken Carl remove himself from the barstool. It had amused Louis to watch Carl make a fool of himself as he fell, like the arrogant drunk he was, onto the flagged stone floor. The wind was knocked out of him when he fell. Carl was certainly worst for wear as he staggered back to his room.

As Louis walked along the landing, he heard a muffled cry coming from behind the door that held his bed and his way to the kingdom. He passed through the door to see Katie standing by Sandra who was lying on the bedspread that was on the floor, in distress. She was holding a pillow to her face to muffle the sobs she could not hold back. Her nightdress had been torn and a red weal on her back would, in all probability, be a large bruise by the morning.

Carl was spread-eagled on the bed, wearing only his shirt. His eyelids were closed but whether he was asleep or not, Louis couldn't tell. What had Carl done? Louis asked himself, but it was rather obvious. The drunken self-serving man had abused his wife again.

A look of relief flooded Katie's face when she saw Louis pass through the door and into the room. An understanding passed from mind to mind. In the half-second that he stood looking at Katie, she was able to show him the scene she had witnessed.

From under her tree on her sunny knoll, she had heard Carl's voice, raised and angry. He seemed to be raving because Sandra had had the temerity not to have waited up for him and had gone to bed and was asleep. There was a squeal of pain, and she heard the words 'Please, no'. It was then that she passed through the veil and into the bedroom and saw the drunken man tearing at the nightdress of the frightened woman. Sandra was trying to roll away when he caught her back with a heavy fist that had been aimed at her head. Escaping him was impossible.

He had her by her arms and was pulling her back to the middle of the bed.

'Come to Daddy,' he said with a leer in his voice. The tone was threatening, but the volume soft. 'Don't be tiresome, I only want what is my right.'

Even from where Katie stood, she could smell the breath on him. She watched as he dribbled and licked his lips in gruesome anticipation of having his way.

Quickly he had wriggled out of his trousers, and struggled one-handed to relieve himself of his boxer shorts. It was grotesque watching; Katie could only imagine the fear and disgust Sandra was feeling. But fear did crazy things. Like a rabbit caught in a car's headlights, Sandra was still, submissive. Katie realised the poor woman had nowhere to run to.

'Sandra, show me some fight or something. Help the little chap to wake up and rise to the occasion.' He laughed, but it was sneering at its cruellest.

'Come on.' He had bared himself. Now free of underwear he was rubbing himself against her. His needs however came to nought; his manhood refused to rise. Sandra kept still and unyielding.

'Come on, you bitch, *help*. I need this,' he hissed. His anger had increased but his speech was very slurred as the booze finally hit his brain. 'Well, if you aren't going to play, I don't need you in bed with me.'

Katie, who was already shocked at the man's cruelty, was horrified as he raised his legs like battering rams and kicked Sandra off the bed. As she fell on the floor, he had thrown the gold bedspread at her. 'Don't come back.'

Katie felt as though Louis' bed had been desecrated. The bed that had known such wonderful love for them was now the fixture of lust.

Sandra had crawled to the foot of the bed, hiding herself from the view of her abusive husband. A pillow rained down on her; with a mighty throw, he lobbed the bulky white cushion after her. 'Cuddle that.' Then he was silent.

Louis had absorbed this information with a cringing stomach.

Another form slipped into the bedroom and, flitting in and out of visibility, moved towards Sandra. The rose and gold aura shimmered and flashed as though it was trying to gain a hold in the mortal space. Louis stared as the vision became stronger. An older female, her face glowing with an inner light, stood in their presence.

Louis wondered if this was the angel his father had told him about. Before he could satisfy his curiosity, he felt more movement in the room.

A black mist was starting to form around Sandra, and then Louis saw, in the corner of the room, a cold glow coming from the slit that led to the underworld. The rift had opened.

Grey chiffon half-beings slid along the floor and, on reaching the black mist, bonded with it. It was a mist Sandra couldn't see and it slowly covered her body in a dense fog hiding her from mortal eyes.

Carl was in a drunken sleep, oblivious to his surroundings.

The gold bedspread covering the woman was almost obliterated by the fluttering of black and grey movements. The sobbing stopped. Sandra straightened up. Throwing the pillow to one side, she started to get up. She moved stiffly as though in a trance. The glazed look in her eyes was unworldly and a terrible feeling of hatred filled the room.

Louis expected Sandra to be unsteady on her feet, seeing her in a wrung-out state from weeping. But she swept forward and looked calmly at the body that was sprawled out, undignified and gross, alone on the bed.

A rather sickening smile etched itself onto Sandra's face. She turned her empty eyes, searching for the discarded pillow. She held out her hands. The white body of the pillow rose from the floor and floated to her. She clasped it to the breast for a moment, as though she was making a decision. She moved with deliberate slowness to her husband's side, the smile widening as she looked down on the figure.

The rose and gold angel was trying to reach out to Sandra but the black protective mist became a moving barrier against the light of the angel and her touch. There was a manic look on Sandra's face. Her eyes were concentrating on the face of Carl, who was making small puffing noises as he slept. With great deliberation, Sandra raised the pillow, dropping it carelessly on his face before she fell on top of it.

The gold and rose angel looked towards Louis. Her face was appealing for help. He heard a woman's soft voice in his head.

'Help us, it's my daughter. We have to save her, before she loses her soul.'

Louis drew on his own power, and, with Katie, attempted to reach Sandra and stop her killing Carl, but the strength of the black mass also blocked them.

Katie connected with Louis. 'I need to blend with her.'

'Are you sure.'

'She'll never respond unless I do.'

'I'll be beside you.'

Louis joined the mother angel, pushing their hands through the mass to reach Sandra, but the mass responded and gathered, thickening, to protect their newest tool. Katie saw her opportunity and, at the weakest point, she squeezed through and reaching Sandra's flesh she blended immediately.

The darkness inside Sandra was thick and foul. The shadows of the serpent's agents were repelled at the light that Katie brought. They fled, leaving Sandra's body that now had the extra strength of two souls.

Katie sought to contact Sandra's mind, encouraging her to let go of the hatred that she held.

'Don't do this Sandra. You're better than this. We can help you if you let us. Listen to our words, your mother's words. She's here waiting to help you.'

The stiffness of the body relaxed as a great sigh left Sandra. Tension and anger were for a moment held at bay, as she connected with Katie.

'My mother?'

'Yes, she's here. If you listen, you will hear her.'

As Sandra's prone body rose from the suffocating body, Louis seized the pillow and threw it from the bed. The black mass scattered and fled.

The grey, chiffon-like harpies were defeated, and clambered over each other, returning to the hell from whence they had come.

Katie left Sandra and returned to the room, going at once to Louis, who simply put his arm around her and kissed her cheek. 'Well done,' he whispered. He loved her generosity of spirit.

Sandra, exhausted, had sunk to the floor. She was looking puzzled. What just had happened to her? she wondered.

Carl was coughing, spluttering and fighting for breath, but very much alive in his drunken state. Something had happened to him, he knew it, but he couldn't quite work out if he had just had a dream, or a nightmare or… could she really have tried to kill him?

48

Julia, thank the Lord, had not been touched this time, but Debs was worried. She knew what Carl was capable of and it filled her with fear. Perhaps she was thinking too much. Here in the hotel Julia would be safe, wouldn't she?

The day didn't get better: every few minutes the worry 'what if?' popped back into her head while she worked. And now, in her rest period, she couldn't let go. Julia thought she could handle herself; she reminded Debs of herself all those years ago: a stroppy teenager who thought she knew the world. Youth was overconfident and foolish. She knew nothing but fiercely thought she did. Hadn't she told her own mother, 'I can look after myself,' just before Carl had raped her.

Trust; it was all about trust.

Doris was a good sort, Barry too. Debs flushed up; the emotion was getting to her. Barry would have to know too, if they were to have a relationship, and what would he think of her? It nearly tore her heart in two thinking on it.

He often called her 'hinny,' an endearment. Would it all change? She shivered at the thought; she didn't want to lose that, it was too precious. But she shook her head; she couldn't allow Julia to be in potential danger. If she didn't speak up, she would be guilty of neglect and that was a garment she didn't want, nor would wear. That poor girl had lost her boyfriend and her best friend; what was coming next?

Trouble seemed to be floating in the air at the Royal. Looking back, it had started even before Carl had booked in. There was that uncomfortable feeling that prickled the back of the neck somehow. Her hand automatically moved to it to rub the feeling away; it was back again.

Those strange dreams were still vivid in her head. Carl, her abuser; a guardian angel, and a devil only supported her discomfort and distraction. She recoiled at the thought of them. Her vulnerability and exposure to the hurts of her past were all too clear.

And before that, Maurice had left in high dudgeon – then, weeks later, come back to the Royal and demanded his job back. In fact, according to Maureen, he had been quite threatening. Maureen was a star in the kitchen, a beacon of light given this mood of despondency that hung over Debs. Why had Maureen married that long string of misery? Debs couldn't understand it; his nature was the opposite of his wife's. Had she pitied him, or did she have a need to mother him? Roger wasn't exactly rude in the kitchen; it was more that he was a little surly, holding himself back from joining the staff totally. Was she being fair? Roger had lost his tearoom, the business he and Maureen had built together. In many ways, she understood loss, but that kind of loss? Perhaps he had not too much to talk about after all, and she was misjudging him. Maureen, thank goodness, had enough chatter and laughter for them both. And, Debs had to admit, when Roger looked at his wife, it was always with tenderness.

Debs was prevaricating. These thoughts were all very well, but she knew they were only a diversion. She had to face the walk to Doris' snug, for that conversation that she didn't want to have.

The twin bedroom, the room that was her space, was cosy and safe, but she couldn't stay in there forever. She stood up from the bed. It was time to find out whether this family she had at the Royal would be kinder to her than her own had been all those years ago.

Casually, she straightened the bedspread from the wrinkles she'd made sitting there. With a backward glance to make sure that everything neat and tidy, she turned with determination to the door. It was time to take that long walk to the room downstairs.

Each step she took, her tummy heaved and clenched. Thoughts poured into her head, repeating a script over and over. Would she get it word perfect? Which words described it best? If only she had had more time to practise her speech. She didn't want to leave this family; the sounds and the smells were home to her now. Could she turn back? Run to her room? But it wasn't about her anymore. Julia needed protection. Debs walked on, squaring her shoulders, but her feet were suddenly as heavy as lead.

The snug was tucked away off a hallway behind the bar. On her way there, she met Barry who was getting ready for the evening trade.

'Hello, bonny lass, and how are you this evening?' He was smiling broadly. It was so comforting to see him and hear his accent, she found herself smiling back. Her anxiety lessened for a brief moment.

'Hello yourself. I'll see you later.' She nodded, as if to encourage herself that everything would be alright, as she passed him by. 'I have to see Doris about something.' Debs could feel herself blushing under his gaze. At that moment, she made up her mind that if all went well, she would tell him how she felt about him. Life was too short to remain a coward. With fingers crossed and a knotted stomach, she melted into the hallway and knocked on the closed wooden door, almost praying that Doris wouldn't be there.

'Come in.'

Her heart pounding, Debs steeled herself as she pushed open the door.

The room reflected Doris perfectly. It was a cosy room, feminine, and yet, it was still, in part, an office. A pile of box files was stacked by a rolltop desk; its green leather tooled surface could just be seen under all the papers that lay there. A mock-Victorian lamp graced a corner of the desk; it looked very decorative if rather clumpy, perched on the edge in the busy room. Doris was seated on a pink, velvet, high-backed chair at the desk, a pen in her hand and her reading glasses perched on her nose.

'Come in, come in. Do you want me for something?' Doris enquired. A searching look crossed her face.

Debs was immediately tongue-tied; the script fled from her memory, and she had a lump in her throat. A sudden swell of tears tried to force themselves out of her eyes, as Debs was, equally, forcing them back down. She felt like a child that had been sent to the headmistress for some misdemeanour.

Debs brought an atmosphere in with her. She carried fear, anger and deep sadness, and Doris could taste all three in the air. What on earth was she going to hear?

Concern crossed Doris's face. Placing her glasses on her cluttered desk, she rose and in two strides was at Debs' side.

'Whatever is it? You look as though you've the world weighing on your shoulders.'

'I have to tell you!' The words tumbled out. Debs' voice was not much more than a whisper. 'I need to tell you,' she repeated, trembling.

'Sit yourself down, before you fall down.' Doris guided Debs to a two-seater sofa. And before Debs could say another word, Doris had taken charge. 'I'll get us a cup of tea.' She was at the doorway, calling down the hall.

'Barry, can we have a pot of tea, please?' She turned back to Debs. 'Come on now, get it out. Whatever it is, we'll sort it out.'

The sympathy was too much. Debs was overcome, and a tear trickled down her cheek. She could not respond to Doris; all she could offer was raw silence, a silence that was so heavy it pressed in on the two women.

'When you're ready. There's no rush.'

Doris put her arm around Debs' shoulder, and the dam of tears she was holding back was released.

'Oh! mercy. What in the world is…?' But Doris didn't finish the sentence. Instead, she took Debs' hand and held it tightly.

The tears eased just as Barry, armed with a tray of tea, pushed his way into the room. He stopped in his tracks, two steps in.

Barry's look of concern at seeing Debs in distress, was not lost on Doris. 'Aye, she's a bit upset. Best leave us.'

Debs looked up, red-eyed. 'No,' she said, directly to Doris and then to Barry. 'What I've got to say, I need you both to know. I can't keep the secret to myself anymore. I must think of Julia.'

A small occasional table bearing a People's Friend magazine was in front of the sofa. Putting the tray down on top of it, Barry, frowning, found a leather pouffe to perch on. His hands laced together on his knees, and he sat forward in anticipation of what he was about to hear.

The tea was forgotten.

'During my teens, I had difficulty in relating to my mother. I suppose like most teenagers, I thought I was grown up, but my mother had other ideas. We fell out so much, that I just wanted to get away from her.

'There was a boy who lived in the corner shop. I knew he was older than me but what did age matter? I thought him quite handsome. He was well-dressed and that impressed me. I knew from the local gossip that he had been to the grammar school. He had the success I failed to achieve, and I admired him.' Debs' face crumpled as the memories tumbled back. Her hands played at her mouth as she was searching for the sentence. She straightened herself on the sofa, wet her lips and looked over at the tea tray.

Doris saw the look. Releasing Debs, she leaned over and poured the cooling tea.

'Better have it while it's still hot. You too, Barry, but you'll need to get a cup,' she declared and handed Debs a cup. Barry shook his head, and muttered, 'Later.' Grateful for the warming drink, Debs took a minute to calm herself. She glanced at Barry, who sat pensively on the edge of his seat. His eyes alternated from his hands to her face. Was he embarrassed? Would he hate her once her tale was done? She knew there was no stopping now: she had set the ball running and she would have to see the run to the end; where it stopped, it stopped.

'I was fifteen but with a little make-up, I looked older. I would see him in the shop sometimes, when I ran an errand for Mum. He sometimes helped his mum out at weekends, you see. He liked me; I could tell. I was shy and I thought he was, too. I'd just left school and started my first job as a junior in the Co-op. It was by accident that I met him at the bus stop one morning. Everyone was going to work. It was rush hour, and the bus was busy – all the seats were taken, except one at the back. He had got on in front of me and headed to the free seat but instead of occupying it, he turned to me and spoke. 'For you, Madam.' I remember being flattered. I suddenly felt like a woman, and he was my gallant prince.

'The meetings at the bus stop became a regular thing and soon we were chatting like good friends. After a week or two, he asked me out, but I was to promise not to tell anyone because his mother wouldn't approve. It was like having a secret love; it was so romantic. We met in town after work, we walked the streets and did a lot of window shopping. For me, it didn't matter that we didn't go anywhere. It only mattered that we were together. He called me his princess. I loved him.' Debs was shaking her head, as though she couldn't quite believe her own story. With a frown and concentration, she continued. 'I was happy, I thought he was my future. A cottage and roses around the door. That kind of thing.'

With a great sigh and a faltering voice, she could see her next words shocked her listeners.

'Just one time it happened, when he invited me to his home. I thought he must have told his mother about us, but his mother wasn't there...'

Debs forced the next words out, with a mighty breath. 'I got pregnant. It was my fault.'

Doris and Barry looked stunned.

'I've always blamed him, but I was partly to blame. I did encourage him to think I was older, and I never did tell him my age until after... I thought he loved me. But there was never love on his part.'

Tears weren't far away again, but she swallowed hard and continued. 'Afterwards, when he'd finished with me, he told me to clean myself up while he put the kettle on. He was completely cold to me. I was in tears and felt worthless, sore, and degraded. He didn't seem to notice. I suddenly remembered my mother's words about getting into trouble. I had only heard whisperings of what sex was. I knew nothing, I hadn't had a little talk from my mum. People didn't speak openly about those things then. And that experience was not what I imagined making love would be. Oh God, when I think about it, I cringe at my stupidity.'

Silence reigned: so quiet, that each breath she took sounded noisy to her.

Doris was wriggling with embarrassment. 'Where's this going, Debs? Why are you telling us this?'

'I want you to know about me. I want to stay here without carrying a secret past. You see, my past has caught up with me.'

Still confused, Doris and Barry, like-minded, nodded as Doris said, 'Go on.'

'Nine months later, I had my Annie.'

Doris took in a deep breath, and Barry fidgeted, looking uncomfortable and strained, at what he was hearing.

'In a Catholic mothers and babies' home. They stole my baby.' Distress clutched Debs and she almost choked on the tears she was holding back.

'Dear God, what next?' Doris' calm exterior had cracked and there was anger in her voice.'

'Please, you need to know what sort of man he is.'

'What man?'

'The man who propositioned Julia. He tried to trap her in the Eden Room. He tried to blackmail her into kissing him. He's a predator, and she could be in danger.'

'What?'

'Your guest. Carl Greaves. He is my past. The man who… the father of my child. He didn't even recognise me when he booked in. I've grown, filled out, I know, changed even, but…'

She repeated in a voice of astonishment, 'He didn't know me. Can you believe it?'

Her story of an infatuated teenager and a self-serving young man was over. Debs looked unsteadily at Doris and Barry, trying to read their reaction to it. She was afraid they would judge her, like her mother had.

Both were silent.

What seemed like an age passed, until in a sympathetic voice, Doris broke the deafening quiet.

'You lost your baby? They took it?'

'Yes. They promised to find her a loving home and she would never know how she was conceived. As if, somehow, it was her sin.'

'How could it be?' Barry was on his feet. Angry with the story he had heard, his face was set in grim disgust. 'No lass, you were nowt but a bairn yourself. He should have protected you, not used you.'

'You paid an awful price for your love, pet.' Doris was shaking her head. 'Love can make a fool of you, but Barry's right; you were only a child yourself. It's shameful.'

Her friends hadn't judged her. It was a relief beyond all sense and emotion. She breathed deeply and allowed her body to relax. Tears came again, but these were ones of thankfulness, not fear. Her hands pressed against her mouth as though she was stopping any more words coming out that might condemn her.

Barry moved to be by her side. 'Come on, lass, you're safe here and you're loved.' Barry held out a hankie, offering it to her. 'It's clean, dry your eyes.'

Debs looked up through wet lids and saw a deep caring in the eyes that were looking back.

'I love you.'

A smile lit up Debs' face; she dabbed dry her eyes that were puffy and red, and responded in kind. 'I love you, too.'

'Well, thank goodness for that.' Doris was looking at Barry. 'It's taken you long enough. We've known for weeks how the two of you felt for each other.'

'We?'

'Harry and myself, who else?'

The mood in the room had become much lighter.

Doris adopted a practical stance, indicating for Barry to sit once again.

'Debs. This conversation never happened. Your past and its secrets are safe with us.' Barry was nodding in agreement. 'Not even Harry will hear of this. As to how we are going to deal with Mr Greaves, I can't say now, but it will come to me.'

Debs was holding Barry's hand as they left the snug. It had taken this to make them open up and admit the love they had for each other. The fear of rejection was a distant memory. Out of the pain of telling, good had come. As they passed down the hall to the bar, half an hour later, unconsciously Debs touched the back of her neck.

In a darkened corner of the ceiling, two orange and black reptilian eyes closed, before fading into nothingness. He was disappointed. He may have lost her, but there was always Carl.

49

It had been a busy day; Julia was torn between slipping into bed to sleep and waiting for Debs to come up from her shift. She paced the bedroom in anticipation of sharing her situation with Debs.

She thought that Debs might have a common-sense view on her special gift. It had come so unexpectedly two years ago, and she was still processing it. She had no reason to think that Debs would not, at least, listen to her, but would she understand something Julia hardly understood herself? Her friend had been so helpful and supportive when she split up with Nick. And she had to take the risk in revealing it to someone. Things were getting out of hand at the Royal.

Nick had been with her when she received her gift, but he thought she had lost her mind when she tried to tell him she heard voices. The voice had warned her about his fidelity, and he admitted he had had a one-night stand with someone; that had nearly split them up. They made up, but she carried on hearing things and because it had come so unexpectedly, it scared her. Nick didn't want to know and was so dismissive that eventually she had given up trying to talk to him about it. She was on her own.

She questioned sometimes whether it was a gift. And if it was, how was she to use it? It frightened her – especially given what she had seen today: harpies, no less. She felt danger in the Royal, something she had never felt before. She needed help. To be called a psychic, a person who saw and talked to the dead, made some people wary and suspicious. Yet, she had bonded with Debs and trusted her. As to whether Debs could advise her, who knew?

A glance at her watch coincided with the door squeaking as it opened and Debs, with a smile as wide as an ocean, entered. Her whole persona oozed happiness.

'What's happened? You look different.'

'It's a long story for another time.'

'It's a secret, then?'

'One day, Julia, I'll tell you everything, but for now all I can say is that tonight has changed my life. Barry loves me. I feel like a new woman.' And she did a little twirl.

Julia clapped her hands in excitement before throwing her arms around her friend and hugging her.

'That's so exciting, and about time too,' she said, laughing.

'Not you as well?' Debs was laughing now with her. 'Doris said the self-same thing.'

'Quite right.'

After the hug, the two were held in a moment of strange disquiet. Neither knew how to open the conversation until Debs spoke. 'Why are you still up? It's been a long day. I expected you to be fast asleep.'

'I wanted to talk to you.'

'That sounds serious?' The mood had changed subtly, and a frown appeared on Debs' forehead, her smile disappearing.

'You have to understand that this is going to be hard to talk about and you might not understand.' Julia voice dropped. 'You see, I see things.'

'You see things?' The frown deepened. 'What do you mean?'

'I see things, I have a gift. I see and hear… things. Ghosts.'

Debs was speechless and sat heavily on the end of her bed.

'I'm sorry, I didn't mean to shock you. It's just that things are happening in the Royal that have never happened before. There is a bad influence, a feeling of ill in the air, and the presence of spirits, both good and bad, occupying our home and I don't know what to do.'

The lightness that Debs had brought to the bedroom was dampened immediately, and Julia suddenly felt guilty.

'Sorry. Perhaps we should leave this for another time?' Julia was downcast. 'I didn't mean to spoil your evening.' She was aware that she had presented a difficult situation to Debs. Her word 'ghost' hung in the air. Would anyone have answers? she asked herself.

Debs hadn't moved. She was shocked, but not so much by what Julia had said, for she recognised that she, too, had had a feeling of foreboding in the Royal. It had been that way over the last few weeks.

She had to admit that she had thought it was just a low mood she was in, rather than an outside influence, but now she wasn't sure. There was that unease when she felt the prickling on the back of her neck, and that tingling of cold fear running down her spine that came with it. She had put it down to the nightmare that echoed the pain of her past and having to deal with Carl in the hotel. Now she shivered, as she acknowledged it was more than that.

She considered her recent dreams, or rather nightmares, and shivered again as she remembered the one who called himself a guardian angel, and the demon, so attractive yet evil. She had a flashback of the demon laughing at her from the ceiling, watching as she was taken by Carl, and raped. What were they doing in her dream?

Julia started pacing the carpet in the small space, and it brought Debs back from her dark thoughts to Julia's plight. Whatever next? She had never suspected that Julia had second sight. And Julia had only told her of the foreboding that she was already familiar with in her own subconscious self.

Debs roused herself and, patting the bed beside her, looked up at Julia's worried, young face and smiled.

'Come on and sit down and tell me all about it.'

For the next hour, Julia related the change in her perception of normality that had begun two years ago, and her confusion as to why it had happened to her.

She had always been sensitive and felt rather more than other people did, so said Nick, her ex. Where others could brush aside hurt and troubles, she lived with it for weeks and months after the event. Nick used to call her 'a proper little softy'; it was a good fit.

She started the story by telling Debs about the ghost of the old man that visited the Eden Room, who enjoyed a pipe while seated in the rocker, leaving the smell of tobacco in the room when he left.

Julia explained that she had smelled the tobacco often as she worked upstairs and then, one day, she saw him sitting there. It was a shock the first time, but there was no aggression in the ghost. Nevertheless, it had been a surprise.

Debs, wide-eyed, remembered the odour of tobacco in the single room the first night she had stayed at the Royal. She had put the smell down to a guest having a crafty smoke.

When Julia had mentioned the tobacco odour to Doris, Doris said she and her family knew about the soul that came with the chair; it was friendly, and not to worry about it. The ghost had come and gone over the years while Doris was growing up. He was part of the family, though Doris had never seen him. Her father had said the same and her grandfather before him. The ghost was like an heirloom and came with the rocking chair.

Julia hadn't let on that she could see him, though she rather suspected that Doris realised she could, especially when she had mentioned the white clay pipe he was smoking, at which Doris had looked sharply at her but had not said a word.

'It all changed the day Mr Greaves tried it on. That's when I saw a ghost I knew. Debs, I saw Louis.'

Debs' body stiffened and her hand flew to her mouth. A deep frown hooded her eyes, as she tried to take in what Julia was saying. She couldn't believe what she was hearing; after all, Louis' and Katie's deaths were what had led her to Ravensend. Now, Julia had seen his ghost and it sent ice through her as though she had stepped on a grave.

'Stop right there. You saw Louis, Katie's partner, here?'

'You must believe me, yes. It shocked me, and I think it shocked him too. It was strange to see someone you know as a spirit. Carl didn't see him or the old man. But I liked Louis and Katie. Fancy them still being here in that room somewhere.'

'Yes,' was all Debs could say, her mind in a whirl. She couldn't quite take it in. This was all too much, but Julia was still rattling on with an urgency to tell her everything.

'You see the old man was visiting, smoking his pipe, and rocking away, the tobacco smell hung in the room. I was busy making up the bed when out popped Louis from the headboard. He just sort of materialised. He surprised me, but I wondered if Louis wanted to see the old boy, them both being spirits. We exchanged a couple of words just before Carl came into the room. You know the rest, but what you don't know is that it was Louis who distracted him, so I could escape.'

'This is making me dizzy, Julia. Headboards? Louis?'

'I can only tell you what happened. I know it sounds like a tall tale, but it happened.' Julia stopped mid-sentence as a frown crossed her brow. 'It was the harpies that worried me. I watched as they emerged from nowhere; I saw them possess Carl today.' Her voice dropped and her hand came to support her chin as she recalled more detail. 'And there was a smell, though it was faint. It was like bad eggs.'

Debs was glad she was sitting down; her legs were turning to jelly at the story she was listening to. She knew nothing about the afterlife except what the nuns had taught her at school and none of that seemed helpful here.

Julia was still in full flow. 'I was downstairs, hiding if I'm truthful, in the lounge, when Carl stepped in. His arrogance had gone when he entered, as though not quite sure of himself, which was odd. He was making his way to Sandra when grey shapes appeared out of the walls: shapeless body forms with veiled white skulls and deep empty sockets under a transparent 'gossamer' grey cloak. Evil rippled through the room. I was so frightened. All these spirits from the underworld were following him as he made his way towards Sandra. I don't think he could sense them or feel them. He never turned, even when they attached themselves to him and disappeared, entering his body through his back. Then the swagger came back, Debs, I swear it: those harpies influenced him.'

Julia's face was quite pale, ashen with retelling the story, and there was a tremor in her voice. 'They frightened me more than I can tell. It was as though he was attracting evil, and evil responded to him. If that wasn't shocking enough, the way he treated his wife was dreadful. He was such a bully. She seems to be completely under his control and full of fear. But who controls him? It makes me shudder to think about it.'

Debs couldn't argue with that.

Where was this all going? Debs knew the girl wasn't deluded. Her own experience of the dream told her that; those two men who didn't belong, and that evil laughter from the handsome one. Reality and the spirit world were worlds apart, or so she had thought, but now it seemed they were crossing paths with only a thin veil dividing them. How could they deal with it? Was it possible to deal with it? She doubted it. Did they need the clergy involved? She remembered the church in Darlington, making a mental note to keep it in mind; you never knew when you might need that sort of help.

Julia was looking tired, and she herself was waning. The sad thing was that there was nothing they could do. It was time to bring the evening to a close. It was already after midnight, and a new day was beckoning, and they both needed sleep to meet it. She hoped that the night would gift them some answers. It was almost too much to absorb.

As she lay down, Debs didn't want to lose all the joy she had felt that evening. Barry loved her and she loved him in return. It would take an earthquake to destroy that bond they had just made to each other, but, by some strange pull, she didn't want to let Julia down either by rejecting her need. And besides, she now knew something in the Royal was definitely off-key.

Louis was concerned too; the Royal was being challenged by an evil force. Malkira and his fallen angels seemed far too powerful for Louis to go up against alone. Katie and his kingdom were vulnerable, and they had to be protected. When his father had said he must talk to the angels, he didn't say how to find them. Malkira, the interloper, had tainted his kingdom – Louis could feel that too – and there was a real possibility he would be back.

50

Louis was tooling the head of a waterlily when, out of the corner of his eye, the dark shape of wings in the sky brought him to a full stop. The red kite was back, circling lazily in dreamlike motions in the cobalt sky. The patterns grew wider and higher, soaring with all the freedoms that only birds knew.

Louis watched the creature, and a longing came over him. If only he could fly. His eyes followed the bird as it flew towards the blue hills that surrounded his home.

The hills, the words echoed in his mind. With the threat that came from Malkira, he had quite forgotten the walks he had with Champ. They had not found the deer or a way through the barrier onto the moors. His promise to himself to go back and find the path, find a way across to the light over the moor, had been pushed to one side. Perhaps a walk among the trees was overdue and would help him think. He was tired and he needed the restful tune of nature to interact with. The hills called him to refresh his spirit.

Champ gave a little yelp and was looking inquiringly at Louis from his position by Louis' side.

'Yes, I was thinking about a walk. You've read my mind.' Louis looked around him. 'But you'll have to wait a minute while I finish off.' The meadow, the hills and the babbling stream were singing in a voice that connected Louis to them.

His kingdom had distracted him from the carving that had kept him busy up until then. His gaze returned to it now. It was nearly finished. The babbling stream had inspired him. The structure on his workbench had what looked like a sandy bed under the tangle of river reeds, in fast running water. The relief was several inches deep on a flat base, three feet in length and one foot wide. Hidden in the reeds were fish, and a water vole or two peered out of a narrow bank on one side. Dragonflies were nibbling at long reeds, their wings spread wide, and they were delicately carved, almost like filigree.

Many pebbles in various shapes and sizes lay on the riverbed. They looked so real, with small, scavenger catfish nibbling at the algae that grew on them. He was happy with it. He had created a wonderful, peaceful world.

One last gentle tap on the wood with a fine tool and he was finished. The sound of it heralded the last petal to live on the bloom. It added its beauty to the others with their open heads that looked towards heaven's way.

Smiling, Louis gazed at the balance and rhythm that ran through his creation. He lay down his tools, smoothed his hands down his pants, and ran his fingers through his unruly hair. Stepped back, his eyes scanned the piece and liked what he saw. Walking around his work, he scrutinised his art from top to bottom on his workbench. It was interesting from every angle. The balance was seemingly perfect, and he was pleased.

He was about to call Katie, as he always did, for her opinion, when a small movement within the sculpture held his attention. The pebbles seemed to move, rise and then resettle, moving at such a minute pace that, at first, he thought his eyes were playing tricks. Frowning as he scrutinised the base, he screwed up his eyes and stepped forward for a better look. Unbelievably, the pebbles were reshaping themselves, slowly at first, until they represented the body of a small snake. A large, flattened, carved pebble rose slightly above the others, like a head stretching up to see better.

Louis was filled with trepidation. Something was playing tricks and he could only think of Malkira. He felt that wickedness was at play, but he was unsure what to do. The large pebble raised itself even further from the carved riverbed and seemed to grow, standing inches above the flat bed. Suddenly, a large eyelid flicked opened wide, revealing an orange and black pupil, like a mirror; Louis could see his reflection in it. Abruptly, the whole body swelled and grew, raising itself up with such speed that Louis was unprepared for it. The head had grown to the size of a dinner plate, and a cold and wicked glare looked out at Louis. A forked tongue leaped from its mouth, spitting out poisonous sulphur, aiming like an arrow, searching for Louis' eyes.

Louis instinctively closed his eyes and covered them with his hands, stepping back away from the menace. He had not moved a minute too soon but, in the act of protecting his eyes, he missed his footing, and fell backwards on the grass.

Louis saw from his new position a rut open up where he had been standing. The grass and earth seemed to fall in on each other. The smell of scorching came with it. Louis rolled away, jumping up and stepping back further as he watched the trench grow wider and deeper. Red embers glowed from at its base; distressed sighs rumbled from the pit with such abundance they seemed to attack Louis' senses. Wailing came next, the soft throbbing grew louder until he needed to clamp his hands over his ears to keep the cries out. At the same time, the snake was advancing, its body lengthening as it stretched out from the carving. Menace hung heavy in the air all around him; he had nowhere to run. All Louis could think about was Katie. Was this monster going to attack her? He had to protect her, shield her from this evil. He looked around. Champ had retreated some strides away, his hackles up as he watched the scene unfold. His body responded when he saw the assault on Louis. Suddenly, he went into action, leaping forward, barking at the serpent, as he put himself between Louis and Malkira. Champ warned of his attack by barking, before baring his canine teeth and snarling at the snake. With a growl deep in his throat, he settled on his haunches ready to spring and take the demon by the throat.

The snakehead flicked around, looking at the intruder that challenged him. His yellow eyes stared for a moment before looking back at Louis.

Then, like some master jack-in-a-box toy, it shrank, recoiling into the carving, and disappeared. The trench miraculously snapped shut, taking his heat and wailing with it. It coincided exactly with the moment that the snake disappeared.

Louis threw his arms around the dog's neck, grateful to have such a friend by his side. Cautiously, he moved back toward his newest creation and leaned over his work. The pebbles had returned to their original shapes and were back in the space where he had carved them.

Malkira and the danger had disappeared in the blink of an eye. The threat was over, gone for now, but Louis had felt the rage and evil that had visited him. He had been right to be worried. Malkira was getting bolder, and the kingdom was no longer safe. He cursed Sophia; she was the only person that could have invited the fallen angel into his kingdom. Her spite and selfishness were still affecting him. Would he never be rid of her legacy?

51

The door closed; Sandra stiffened under the sheets. She could smell the drink and the stale cologne from where she lay.

'Are you awake, sweetie?'

The words were slurred. There was no love in them. Her love had been killed years ago, and she despised playing his game. She was determined he would not use her tonight.

She felt her mother's nearness in spirit, and she no longer felt alone. It was after his last drunken assault on her, when he had kicked her out of bed, that she had resolved not to be the object of his scorn. A new strength had grown within her, and that meant she would fight him, no matter what. He had been missing since lunchtime; it had been a blessing not to have him near. Her only worry was how much he would have drunk before he came up to the room.

Earlier that afternoon, when the bell rang and the bar closed, Carl had sat at the bar with a superior look on his face. He had three glasses, full of amber liquid, lined up in front of him.

'Drink up, is it?' Carl inquired, looking at Barry as he laid the tea towel over the beer pumps.

'Not at all. But you might like to take them in the lounge, Sir, as I'm unable to serve more at the bar for now. I'll grab a tray.'

'No need.' Carl was smiling cockily and was obviously showing off to the few regulars who were getting ready to leave.

'Cheers.'

He downed one shot after the other, before abandoning his stool and staggering out of the bar. With the deliberate gait of a drunk trying to walk straight, he made his way to the stairs. He had seen the redheaded girl going that way a few minutes before, and he had some unfinished business with her, so decided to pursue her.

The stairs were almost too much for him. His feet didn't respond to his thoughts, twice missing the step and losing his balance. Stepping down two steps, before resetting himself to continuing up, he finally made it to the top.

'Yes,' he crowed, as though he had reached the summit of a mountain. His quarry was busy on the landing, cleaning the carpet. The noise of the carpet cleaner was loud and hid his footsteps. Tiptoeing, he moved towards her. She had escaped the other day, but she wouldn't today. He crept up behind her and grabbed her around her chest, taking her by surprise, but his surprise attack backfired. She twisted out of his clutches and slapped his face. He had not expected her response.

His rage was suddenly unquenchable. One hand covered the burning spot on his cheek, while the other curled up tight into a clenched fist. He was being tested; he really wanted to hit back. Grabbing her hips had stimulated him and he was feeling aroused. A little bit of uncomplicated sex was what he was after, but this bint had spurned him and his hand clenched even more. And then he thought of Sandra.

Sandra had gone to bed with a headache. It was their last day of their holiday, and she had said she wasn't feeling well. What was new? What was wrong with the woman? Hadn't they had had two splendid weeks roaming the county, seeing the ruins of the Benedictine churches and abbeys? Tramping the footpaths where pilgrims had trod. It had all been very exciting. He had gathered copious notes for his book; he just had to begin writing it now.

The door had closed noisily behind him in the bedroom. He looked over at the woman in the bed. Was she going to be reasonable and submit to him? He begrudgingly admitted to himself she was useful, and she hadn't done a bad job as his secretary. He felt a tingle and tightening in his loins. Sandra would enjoy a bit of attention; she'd soon forget her headache and he was ready to do the business. A couple of days ago he had dreamed she had tried to kill him. There was still a nagging memory that came to him as he looked at the bed; something had changed in her. He was still trying to work out whether it had been a nightmare or...?

From the hall landing, Julia watched the bedroom door close; it was barely four in the afternoon and the man was already drunk and unsteady on his feet.

She was scandalised. Not so much because of his drinking, but for the lack of respect he had for people, or did she mean only women? He had come up behind her and made a lunge for her, his huge hands cupping her breasts. What made him think he could fondle her and get away with it? Well, he hadn't this time. His cheek would still be stinging with the slap she had thrown at him. It had stopped him in his tracks.

He had been shocked; she could see that. His eyes narrowed as he held his cheek and for a moment, she thought he was going to retaliate and strike her, but Debs called out to her. She was climbing the stairs and her call startled him. Instead, he retreated, scuttling into the bedroom.

Julia recalled passing through the bar earlier; Carl had seemed to have lined up several whiskeys in front of him. She'd looked hard at Barry and then at the glasses; he had shrugged, as though to say Carl was a paying customer and guest, and he had to serve him. There were not many secrets that remained hidden in the small hotel, and she knew that Sandra had gone up to her bed after lunch with a headache.

Julia was worried. She and Debs were outside the bedroom door, listening. Julia was afraid that she had riled the drunken man up and he would take his pique out on his wife, but what could she do? Certainly, not give in to the lecherous bully. Still, it bothered her. From beyond the door a muffled conversation could just be caught, but it wasn't long before raised voices could clearly be heard. Her inner voice screamed out. She hoped her gift extended to contacting Louis in the next plane of existence, entreating him to come and help; she feared for Sandra.

Louis and Katie were dozing in the warmth of the sun under the tree of life, exhausted with talking that had taken them nowhere. Katie had frozen with anxiety when Louis had told her about the visit from Malkira and his attack on him. The idea that evil was walking in their special paradise chilled her. The breeze that blew through the meadow seemed colder, harsher, and the grasses moaned under its power. Even the sun seemed less warm. The kingdom had been violated by the incident with the serpent, and their souls were as unsettled has their kingdom seemed to be.

Malkira must somehow feel threatened by him, Louis thought, but why was that? He was a ghost in a netherworld with only some small powers. The demon, however, had all the powers of darkness at his disposal. He was still pondering the question, when he dozed off with Katie nestling in his arms.

It wasn't so much a sound, more like a radio wave cracking in his ear, and it woke him. For a moment, he wondered what it was that had disturbed him, before he realised that he was being called from the other side of the veil.

Blurry eyed, he sat up waking Katie as he gathered his thoughts.

'I'm being called. I must visit the Royal.'

'Who can be calling you?'

Louis put his arm around Katie, pulling her to him.

'It must be Julia; she's the only one who can. Something's wrong.' He looked into her eyes. 'Don't worry.'

'Too late. I'm coming with you.' Worry lines marked her forehead, and although she smiled at him, disquiet was in her eyes too.

As Louis passed through the carved headboard, he heard a slurred voice of a man, rising in volume as it chastised someone. The voice was sinister.

'Don't think I've forgotten you tried to kill me, you naughty girl. You need a little lesson from hubby.' He giggled as drunks do. The sound was awful in its intensity. Sandra felt a cold sweat sweep through her body. He was at his worst in this state and, deep in her heart, she knew she would be in for a rough time.

'Mother.' The word didn't escape from her lips, but the thought was sent up, like an arrow prayer, heavenwards. Her mother wouldn't let her down; she would strengthen her somehow. Sandra clutched the bed sheets and waited.

His footsteps came nearer. She lay still until his foul breath occupied her space and his lips touched her ear.

'Move over darling and come to Daddy.' His hand invaded the sheets, groping for her breasts. Sandra steeled herself. Moving like lightning, she turned and hit Carl, full force in the face. He was furious.

Suddenly, the strength she thought she had evaporated. She was petrified when she saw the shock and rage on his face and regretted her foolishness in striking him from the bed.

He was holding her arm tightly; a sneer sat on his lips, and she was unable to move from fear at that moment. He looked down at her, his eyes no more than slits. Under his stare, she turned her face away from him.

Carl's face was ebullient; he was confident that she was under his power. He let loose of her for a moment, freeing his shirt to pull it off.

Sandra was not slow to take advantage and took the initiative to make her getaway. Kicking off the bedclothes, she moved to the other side of the bed at speed, but she didn't have a chance. Carl's long, muscular arms reached out as he lunged at her, catching her by her hair, pulling her back towards him by it, ignoring her shrieks. The screams that left her lips were silenced quickly as his free hand closed over her mouth.

Julia's and Debs' eyes met. A startled cry had escaped from under the door. It was all the excuse they needed to investigate. Nodding acquiescence, it was an agreement that needed no words. In her pocket, Julia had the room key.

Stooping, she placed the key in the old lock and turned it. Unlocking the door, the two women rushed into the room to help Sandra. A cold gust of wind came from nowhere, catching their backs and pushing them further into the room, before the door behind them clashed shut, making them jump. Debs turned to it, wondering where the wind had come from.

They were no windows open upstairs. It prompted her to try and open it, but the heavy oak door wouldn't budge. It was their only way out. A tingle of fear pulsed through her.

Julia's eyes spun from the bed to the door, then from Debs' face back to the bed. The two women were trapped in the room and facing a scene that neither of them would ever forget, for very different reasons.

Carl was obviously enjoying the pain he was inflicting. A hideous smile was etched into his face; his wife was bent backwards in a backbreaking pose, unable to escape or speak. She was frantically trying to wrench his hand from her hair, without success.

Julia's senses were reeling; as well as the drama on the bed, she was seeing a completely different picture, one that Debs couldn't see. A heavy feeling of evil was pressing into the bedroom, coming from the location in the corner, over by the window. Dark shadows had formed a barrier, but beyond the darkness there was a bright red line. It ran from floor to ceiling, scoring the wall with a molten red liquid as it travelled the line. The opening was small, but a visible fissure exposed her world to what she could only think was some connection to the underworld and hell. The smell of rotting eggs was in the air, and it took her breath away. Her eyes widened when she saw movement. Slivers of grey were struggling to get through the slit trying to gain entry.

Noise of the assault in the bed brought Julia's attention back to Carl, but her jaw dropped as the headboard started to quiver behind the struggling couple. The tree moved, coming alive as a narrow piece of bark was filling out. The texture was evolving into scales which grew until a monstrous snake appeared. It unfurled itself from the tree-trunk and slithered out from the carving into the bedroom.

The 'Tree of Life' had hidden him well. Malkira was confident in his claim to this mortal domain. He eyed his prey that had so generously gathered in the room for him. His forked tongue was lively, flicking in and out in a frenzied rhythm, tasting the fear and the anguish that hung in the air.

The bedroom became darker despite the efforts of the sun shining through the window. Opaque shadows crept up the walls, moving, forming and reforming into the contours of humans that were empty of souls.

Julia's gift, in the blink of an eye, revealed a living nightmare to her. The mortal world and the spiritual world had somehow collided with each other, rupturing the barriers, and had merged.

It was difficult to pull her eyes away from the monster that was coiling itself on the bed close to the mortal degenerate. It sickened her. A loud rustling sound from the wall changed the direction of her gaze. The split had become a gaping wide hole, with a mass of black and grey shapes freely floating their way out of the beyond and into the mortal sphere.

'Harpies.' The word escaped loudly from her lips.

Debs frowned and looked at her young friend, confused. She couldn't understand what was taking Julia's attention, being unable to either see or hear the spirits, as they invaded the room; but Julia, staring at the corner, was mesmerised.

'Harpies,' Julia repeated. Hanging onto Debs' arm very tightly, she whispered, 'Here the repellent harpies make their nest… they have broad wings… a human neck and face.' She shuddered as she remembered part of a poem she had read. She looked again, closely, and saw that beneath the grey, there were white skulls.

A tight grip on her arm got tighter.

'Julia, what's going on?' Debs' voice brought Julia back to the moment.

'Louis, we need Louis.'

Malkira changed his identity into his handsome, bronzed angel, his face shining with an inner light. His cobalt eyes aborted the orange hue of the snake and, apart from his cloven hoofs, he looked angelic. He glanced with approval at Carl, enjoying the spectacle; Carl was really proving to be a good disciple.

Carl's hand was over Sandra's mouth as he towered over her. He put his lips to her ear and whispered, 'Is it as good for you, as it is for me, sweetie?' He gave her hair an extra twist. Even with his hand over Sandra's mouth, Debs could hear the muffled scream. Sandra's hands were still grappling at his with no joy; he didn't slacken his grip. Debs could see that Sandra was in agony in her contorted position.

Malkira moved to Carl and blended with him.

'Let me give you a helping hand.' Carl heard the voice in his head and felt the extra strength and resolve move into his body before his mind became foggy. His conscious self seemed separate from him. Malkira giggled and Carl did too.

Julia was still clinging onto Debs, frightened and shocked, but unable begin to describe what she was seeing.

Debs could feel Julia's fear, and her own body responded with goosebumps and chills that crept up her arms and down her spine.

A stifled moan came from the bed. It renewed her fear, and a desperate wish to be out of this room overcame her, but she couldn't leave Sandra in the hands of the man who had been her own abuser.

Carl had not noticed the door being opened, wrapped up as he was in his own warped pleasure. His total concentration was on controlling his wife, but Debs had heard that giggle that was pure evil. She wasn't going to stand by and watch Carl kill his wife. Enough was enough. If Debs got her way, she would be his Armageddon.

Debs moved quietly forward towards Sandra, totally oblivious of the underworld's darkness seeping into the room. All she could see was Carl abusing his wife.

The noise of rushing winds that was coming from the underworld was deafening overhead, so much so that Julia wanted to cover her ears with her hands.

The sound attracted Carl's attention and for a moment he lost his concentration, giving Sandra another slim, but much needed, opportunity for escape. She twisted from his grip and tried to leap off the bed, but her poor body had been in that position so long that cramp had set in. Her legs crumpled under her at the edge of the bed as blood suddenly pumped life back into her veins. Carl laughed; its eeriness had a double ring to it as it echoed through the room. He dragged her back by her arms from the edge and threw her effortlessly onto the mattress beneath him.

Taking her solidly in his arms and holding her hard to him, they faced each other eyeball to eyeball in his ferocious grip. In fear and pain, she breathed in his breath as she tried to concentrate on his face and read what he was planning to do to her. Shocked, she didn't know the liquid blue eyes that were staring down at her.

'You tried to kill me, you bitch. Now it's my turn. How would you like to go?' With one hand, he picked up a pillow. 'The way you tried on me or perhaps you would prefer my hands on your neck like a necklace? My hands circling your neck, slowly getting tighter and tighter?' The words were said so softly, they might have been endearments.

'Get off her, you monster.' Debs struck his back with balled fists, but it had no effect. She pulled at his arms, but he merely shrugged her off as though she was an irritating fly. He was pinning Sandra down on the bed, pillow still in his hand. Debs threw her arms around his neck, one hand on his forehead, pulling his head backwards, but with the strength of Malkira and his own, she was no more than an insect to swat. Dropping the pillow, one-handed he rounded on Debs, swinging his arm to give her a back hander, knocking her to the floor. She fell badly, slipping to one side, banging her head on the table and landing in a heap. Her head hurt as she tried to stand up, and a feeling she might vomit came over her, before her eyes closed as she fainted.

52

As if obeying Julia's summons, Louis and Katie appeared in the mist of the swirling grey army. In this dimension, these hideous creatures were as dangerous as eagles would have been to lambs.

The grey spectres were still spilling into the room from the rent in the wall. They swooped and dived at Louis and Katie, as if trying to drive them back into the kingdom behind the bedhead, but they stood their ground. Their arms were raised to protect their faces from the evil that attacked. They trusted in the goodness of spirit in angels and light. They would never be converted by fear, nor be driven away from help when it was needed.

Julia was trying to minister first aid to Debs who was prostrate on the floor. At that moment, her friend needed her. While she couldn't ignore what was happening to Sandra or the scene of bedlam in the room, she put Debs into the recovery position. On the side table, she had seen a glass of water and she was eager to reach it. Louis followed her gaze and understood her need to revive Debs with its contents. A lump the size of an egg had grown on the back of Debs' head, and she was clammy to touch. Julia couldn't quite reach the glass to put a splash of water on the clean handkerchief she was holding. Louis' verve was building; he could feel strength rising within him, as it always did in times of anger or stress. It gave him power to move objects and, sometimes, people. He knew he needed it now. More than ever he needed that power, as he sought to battle against the grey army. Without a second thought he reached over and, clasping the glass, lifted it and handed it to Julia.

Two harpies dived at him in full flight. His arms came up swinging at them. He knocked one sideways, ploughing it into a host that jostled behind it. The mass parted, allowing his attacker to retreat into the flock, but the threat was still there. Like waves, the throng surged forward, constantly moving and shifting around them. He and Katie moved closer together, protecting the women as best they could from the multitude of grey shapes.

The fear was palpable. Julia had seen the grey menace penetrate Carl previously and knew the evil they injected. She directed her thoughts to Louis, and he saw a replay of the harpies entering Carl, and her fear that they would enter Debs and herself.

Julia was grateful that Debs was unconscious, and although she knew Debs couldn't see the peril that she was struggling with, she was sure Debs felt the fear in the ether. A wave of dark grey spirits surrounded the bed, almost dancing in circular movements. They floated in the air, protecting Malkira, keeping help at bay, away from the bed.

Louis was in a dilemma. If he could get to Sandra, he could help her; he could blend with her and she could use his strength to fight Carl. But he couldn't leave Julia and Debs to the evil, and Katie wasn't strong enough to stand alone against the throng that hovered, threatening their friends.

The situation was dire. Never in all Louis' long existence had he felt such an evil presence; never had he been so torn. Was this the evil his father had warned him of? It seemed that Malkira was in total charge of spreading detestation and hatred. How were they to stop the demon?

It had been a long time since he had prayed, but this wasn't a fight they could win on their own. He implored the universal spirit to help. He was joined by Julia and Katie and, looking over at the bed, he saw Sandra's lips move; he saw her mouth 'Mother,' calling the gold and rose angel.

The smell of scorching was now alive in the room. Julia started coughing as it swept into her chest, choking her on the sulphur that filtered through the air. It came with the dark spirits, and still more darkness formed as more warriors of Malkira pushed into the room and joined the throng.

Sandra had lost her strength to fight. She was never going to get away from Carl. He was enjoying hurting her, and she just wanted it to be over. In her pain she called for her mother, which seemed to amuse Carl.

Possessed and drunk, Carl couldn't see the spirit world crowding in, all the evil figures that were gathered in the gloom and poisoning the room.

'She's dead, you crazy bitch.' It was Carl's voice, but with an extra edge to it.

Malkira heard the cry and was aware of the prayers coming from the group by the bed. He was feeding and enjoying the world he had brought to the Royal and didn't want to be deprived of his prey. Mortals, he thought, were weak-minded and easily influenced, and he was not about to have an angel appearing, summoned by Sandra. Especially not a guardian or relative angel; their strength could be almost as strong as his own.

Heavenly help was not to be allowed. Therefore, on his orders, Carl placed a well-aimed blow by his fist on Sandra's jaw. The brutal blow forcibly threw her head to one side, and she was suddenly limp in his arms. For a moment he looked puzzled, and a frown furrowed his brow, as though he had partly recognised his actions on Sandra. His eyes looked at her body before he dropped her on the bed, as though she was no more than a piece of baggage.

Julia saw how Carl had flung Debs aside with a strength beyond her own and she knew she couldn't help Sandra, so she sat holding Debs' hand on the carpet, encouraging her to stay where she was, until she felt better.

The room had been enveloped with sound of wailing, joining the roar of winds above her head. The noise was becoming unbearable to Julia's ears.

Sheltering under the protection of Louis and Katie, Debs slowly came out of her faint. And although she could neither see nor hear the commotion above her, the pressure of the grasp of Julia's hand told her there was danger. The presence of it was so powerful, she could feel it.

Julia shuddered; the noise was eating into her, making her feel sick. Debs had removed the damp handkerchief from her forehead and tried to sit up, looking at her friend in a rather bewildered way.

A new element entered the room moments later. In the darkness, and among the packed grey throng, Julia saw a beam of illumination cutting a line through the room.

Malkira, looking out through Carl's eyes into the gloom, was equally startled by the sudden brilliance; the lights were no more than pinpricks but they were many, emanating from the carved headboard. He stiffened within the borrowed body. Malkira, who rarely felt fear, quaked at this sort of spiritual light. Alarm bells rang in his head. Sandra had reached the angel; he had been too late.

Angels were bad news in Malkira's world. It was nearing the time to leave Carl, for even now the divine light was dispersing through all parts of the room. He saw with disdain that its powers were reaching his army and scattering his warriors. In the melee of their attack, the flock of lost grey souls suddenly stopped moving. What seemed like a hundred dark souls, bound together, were hanging in mid-air, blocking out any natural sunlight from the window. They had paused their attack as they became aware of these beams of light striking entry into their space.

The powerful angelic beams searched their targets like arrows shot from a heavenly bow. As the beams hit their marks, yelps and screams reverberated through the mass of evil. A smell of burning hung in the air, as the shafts from heaven seared the remains of these dammed souls, hidden as they were under the grey mantles.

The heavenly light burned its way through the darkness. Voices from the dead souls screamed out as they retreated, pushing and shoving towards the rift that they had come through. There were so many that were unable to flee. They sought refuge by cramming themselves into any remaining dark nook or cranny, in which they could hide.

Malkira paused, watching in silence as his army was routed, and in that moment he loosened his mental hold on Carl.

Carl's senses suddenly returned. The fog that had filled his brain disappeared, and his memories were filtering back as he recognised the room he was in. He couldn't quite put his finger on it, but he acknowledged to himself that he had lost time, that he had been in a trance of some sort and was not quite sure what he had been doing. He was kneeling on the bed, shaking his head and rubbing his eyes. Refocusing, he scanned his surroundings. His wife lay at his knees; she was sprawled out and looked senseless. Was she sleeping?

He remembered coming back from the bar.

Sandra had been there. She was already in bed when he closed the door on the landing. He was feeling raw, put out at his rejection from the redhead, and he had been furious.

Sandra would do, he remembered thinking; she was just where he wanted her, and he was still feeling 'in the mood'. He remembered it all up to that moment, but something had happened; he couldn't remember what.

He looked down at her spread-eagled body, her arms outstretched in sleep, and then he saw the mark of a colourful bruise developing on her jaw. His mouth dropped open. Had he done that? What had happened? It bothered him that he couldn't remember doing it, but who else could have? Had she refused him his marital rights? She sometimes needed some old-fashioned encouragement. Feeling little for her, he shrugged. His stupid wife had probably deserved it.

As his head cleared further, he scanned the dim room. There were two women sitting on the carpet. What were they doing in his bedroom? Looking closer, he saw that the redhead was tending the waitress. What had happened? Why were they here? Had he done that too? He suddenly felt panic rising in his belly. He had no recall; his memories were blank, and he could be in trouble.

Louis watched the confusing chaos. Darkness and flying souls, shadows of the harpies, hovered above his head. They were outlined by the glow that was coming from the headboard.

The pinpricks of brilliance were coming from behind Carl, who still knelt on the bed. They glowed, sparkling like stars behind the carved tree that had held the demon Malkira a few minutes earlier.

A glow of rose and gold twinkled between the leaves on the tree. Its brilliance grew in strength and shape, until Louis recognised the soul of Sandra's mother. She had arrived too late to fight the demon, but he saw the angel move to her daughter's side, scattering the few remaining harpies that lingered, her light scorching them as they fled towards the rift.

Still more radiant pinpricks were piercing the darkness, silhouetting the branches on the tree, one by one. More angels were on their way. The light had got stronger, spreading across the carved sky on his carved headboard. It spread further and further until it touched the edges of the headboard, giving life to the Garden of Eden. The sun, high in its sky, was, as ever a flame, its sphere flashing silver and gold. Help was coming; his prayer had been answered. Louis breathed a sigh of relief that the angels had heard them.

The angelic light was moving into all the nooks and crannies in the room, cleansing and rooting out the hiding grey army, sending them scuttling back through the molten slit. Louis saw the darkness of evil being driven away, and natural light returning to the room. 'The harpies', as Julia called them, were tangled, as they fought each other at the underworld's doorway to get to back their own domain.

Three heavenly angels came from the headboard. Had they come through his kingdom?

Louis thought about the hills and the moor, and the light beyond it. Was that the place of rest? Had they come from there? Was the barrier gone that kept him out of the moor? Heaven perhaps waited there: the place he had refused to go when he had died, almost two centuries ago, not understanding the implications of his actions.

Carl felt the urge to run flood through him. Panic was riding him and he needed to hide but wasn't sure why. He leapt from the bed, landing at the feet of the women. He ignored the redhead and stepped over the other woman, the waitress.

Stopping suddenly in mid-stride, he half turned to look down at the woman on the floor. He frowned. There was something familiar, something remembered. From this angle, it was a face he knew from another time, another place. What was it? There was something about her that rattled him. He turned to resume his retreat to the door. It would come to him but, right now, he wanted to get out of the room.

Two strides later, he had almost reached the door, when he backtracked one step, turning to stare at the waitress. He uttered just one word.

'Debs?'

He paused and repeated her name as his memory returned.

Debs heard him say her name again, as full recognition hit him. He glared at her prone body.

'You,' he said accusingly. 'What in the blazes are you doing here?'

The name 'Debs' was still hanging in the air when Malkira entered and took charge of Carl again. The demon puppeteer was hiding from the pure light in the man. Malkira turned Carl around, away from the women, and charged him forward to the door to safety.

Louis had realised Malkira's game and was standing like a sentry, blocking it. He was determined that this Carl – a poor excuse for a man – and the demon would not get away and escape the wrath of these heavenly beings.

Louis stood his ground as Carl, now seeing with reptilian eyes, moved towards him. Malkira recognised Louis. The demon assessed Louis. He was a weak obstacle to stop him. He almost laughed out loud but, as the thought passed through his mind, reinforcements arrived, in the shape of Katie and Julia. There were just too many good souls to deal with; it wasn't worth the effort for one defective male soul. Without another thought, Malkira left Carl's body again. Louis watched the demon slide towards his army, leaving Carl to deal with the trio. As Carl could only see Julia, it was understandable that Carl would not be bothered by a woman blocking in his way. Louis joined with Julia, with her permission, to give her strength, for there was little doubt that Carl would force his way past her, and probably with abuse.

Carl's momentum to the exit had slowed. Refocusing, he could only see the redhead standing in front of him.

'Get out of my way.'

'Not before I give you this.'

Throwing her arm with some considerable force, she landed a mighty blow on the man's nose, before kneeing him in the most vulnerable part of his anatomy.

Doubled up in pain, Carl, didn't know what hurt the most. His eyes were watering so much that it blurred his vison. His nose felt broken. Blood was streaming down his face, and he could also taste it in the back of his mouth. For a moment, he couldn't speak or straighten up. The door was near enough to reach out and open. Clutching his face with his free hand, with his other he pushed Julia to one side and stepped onto the landing.

'I'll be back with the police. You won't get away it. I'll say I found you robbing my wife, when I came up. And I stopped you. That you and that little tramp hurt my wife and attacked me.'

The door almost jumped off its hinges as Carl left the room. It rocked back in place with a thump, leaving the women shut in the room behind the solid door.

Louis left Julia's body. She was rubbing her hand; it hurt, and she might even have bruised or broken it. Using the strength that Louis had given her, along with her own, it had felt good to pay back the man who had shown such disrespect to her.

It was a short victory when she realised that now they could be in trouble. If he was serious, who would the police believe? Him or them? And what would Doris think? She turned back to see Debs and Sandra, and, suddenly, she regretted nothing in her actions; she had righted a wrong.

Carl was in the oldest part of the building. The landing, with dark wood banisters and beams, was original, making it relatively dark, despite the cream-coloured walls. The red carpet hid the trail of blood, as Carl staggered towards the stairs. He was sure she had broken his nose. Drips of red spotted his shirt. The whole of his face throbbed and his head was starting to join in the assault. Pain extended from his eyes into the back of his skull. His sight was blurry; tears were forcing themselves from corners of his eyes.

He never saw the cat who was huddled against the banister in the shadows. Mouser was spooked. He had been sensing the 'spirits' and their activity on the other side of the door, and was agitated. The sudden clash of the door, and the man charging into the landing, had Mouser spooked. He dashed out from the shadows to get downstairs to the safety of the kitchen.

Carl tried to avoid the slash of ginger-and-white that was moving like an express train. He failed. The pet collided with his ankles, and it was too late to save himself from the thirteen steps that were waiting for him.

53

Doris and Barry were having a well-earned rest, sipping tea, and chewing the fat, when they were startled into action... they heard the cry and a number of thuds repeatedly coming from the stairs into the hallway.

'God Almighty, what was that?'

Dashing out of the snug, they raced towards the stairs and were shocked to see a man's body crumpled at the base. Like a twisted rag doll, Carl lay bloodied and unconscious at the bottom of the flight.

'Oh my God!' Doris was biting her lips, kneeling by Carl and taking his wrist. She breathed with relief, feeling a faint pulse under her fingers.

'He's still alive, Barry. Go ring for an ambulance.'

'Better not move him, Doris. Not the way he's twisted.'

'I've no intention of touching him. If his back's broken…' There was no need to say more.

Barry was striding away, back to her sitting room, to use the phone.

'Tell them to hurry, he's losing all his colour.'

It was late afternoon, a quiet part of the day, and no guests were about. But for how long, she wondered. She needed to cover him and to get a flannel to clean up his face.

At that moment two figures appeared at the top of the flight.

Doris looked up and saw Julia and Debs poised ready to come to help. She put up her hand to stop them.

'No need to come down, no one can help him. We've called an ambulance. All we can do now is wait. Best get back to your work or whatever you were doing.'

The faint rise and fall of Carl's chest indicated his heart was still beating, but the pallor of his skin suggested how badly the fall had injured him.

'They're on their way,' Barry confirmed.

He was back minutes later with a throw from the snug and a cloth in a small dish of water from the kitchen. He covered Carl as gently as he could with the blanket, while Doris squeezed out the cloth and gently wiped the blood away from Carl's face.

'The steps weren't kind to him and that's a fact; it looks like a broken nose to me, among the other injuries.' Doris did what she could to clean him up. Normally, she was a person of charity, but today her feelings were mixed. When she looked down on that clean but battered face and remembered what he had done to Debs, she felt that perhaps this was Carl's comeuppance. What goes around comes around, eventually. She sighed. Life was so surprising.

By the time the ambulance arrived, twenty minutes later, Carl's breathing had become uncomfortably irregular. The ambulancemen tended him as best they could, but even to the kitchen staff who had joined the watching group in the hall, it was perfectly obvious that his life was slipping away.

The ambulancemen expertly moved him from the floor and onto a trolley. It was the knowing look that the men gave each other and that tiniest of a shake of the head to Doris that confirmed that he was gone. Nick and Harry had appeared on the scene and stood quietly in reverence with Doris and Barry, as they watched the men disappear out of the hotel to the waiting ambulance.

Julia saw the soul rise when it left the shell that once had been Carl.

'He's gone,' she whispered to Debs, who stood beside her.

'Are you sure?'

'I am. We had better go and see to Sandra; Doris is bound to come up to see her.'

Debs nodded in agreement, only partly listening. Her mind was evaluating what this meant to her. In the last moments of his life, Carl had recognised her. There had been no regret, no remorse or repentance from him. Even her name on his lips had somehow been dismissive of her as a person. But now he was dead. That part of the past had been wiped away by his last breath. That huge empty hole of disillusionment and bitterness and regret closed in her heart. She was ready to be whole again. At last, she could move on.

Malkira was on the move to return to his cavern. The angels were, at that moment, filtering into the bedroom; he mustn't be cut off from his exit. He shivered. It would seem he had lost the day, and a recruit.

It hadn't all been bad: he had fed off Sandra, and now felt rather full. And he was at liberty to return, once the guardians of light had gone. He was just about to slide through the rent when he heard the cry from a voice he knew, plus a buffeting of thuds that came from the landing. His head jerked back, eyes on the door. He spread his spirit wide and listened intently. Carl's breathing was shallow; his heart was weak. Malkira smiled. He might just have that recruit back in a few minutes.

No one saw Malkira invisibly move through the bedroom door and slide out across the landing. He hid in the ceiling among the beams, waiting for Carl's demise.

Malkira watched the white muslin-like spirit rise from the twisted remains and called it to him. Carl's spirit slowly gathered itself, resetting until the white aura disappeared into the air and a ghost, a second image of Carl, materialised.

A look of bewilderment crossed Carl's face as he hovered above his earthly remains. He looked up to where he had heard his name called, but saw only the women. Lost in his thoughts, he was trying to remember where he was and what he was doing. He vaguely recalled that he had been on his way to report a crime; the redhead had punched him. His fingers searched his face, feeling around the nose; there was no blood on his hand when he viewed it, and, strangely, he wasn't hurting anymore.

He licked his lips, but he couldn't taste any blood, then he remembered his tumble. He should be hurting. He looked down at the twisted body that lay there. The Doris woman was kneeling there beside it, and was looking shocked. Two other men were there too. They were each wearing a uniform, and one seemed to be taking a pulse, before the other took out a stethoscope and applied it to the chest. Carl peered at the injured man's face; the nose was swollen, he could see that, and, stranger still, the victim was wearing his clothes. He felt shaken, and sick. Was he really looking at his own corpse? Distrusting, he decided it couldn't be him and denied what his eyes were seeing.

What was he doing hanging about this accident? His earthly arrogance returned as he heard his name being called again. He looked up to find the caller and somehow, not knowing how, he was at the top of the stairs, looking over the banister. The waitresses were there but only the redhead's eyes followed him, and he knew it hadn't been her voice. Then he was beside them, though he had not registered his move, and behind the women he met a bronzed man with liquid blue eyes.

Malkira greeted his recruit. He still hadn't decided on Carl's final fate, but the soul had potential as a purveyor of evil for him around the world and that meant Malkira and his army would have a continuous feast.

The beautiful angel, Malkira, eyed Julia, and she stared back. Should she tell Debs what she was seeing? Debs was unaware that Carl was on the landing near her, and Carl, in his newfound state, ignored them both, apart from a glance of disdain when his eyes met Julia's. Louis and Katie had also heard the call of death and had joined the group of mortals to find out what was happening on the landing. Julia quickly established that the heavenly angels were clearing the harpies out of the bedroom, forcing them through the rift, and that calm was returning.

Carl was trying to accept that he had been called by a bronzed spirit, whom he thought he knew. He knew the redhead and waitress, as well, but these two other people – where had they come from?

Malkira was also eyeing up the four souls. He was very uncomfortable. These souls would never belong to him; there was altogether too much light in them, and it hurt his eyes. He had also seen the rose and gold angel attach herself to Sandra as soon as he left Carl. It was such a pity that she was lost to him too. Ah well! Carl had great promise. It was time to introduce him to his new life. There was nothing left for him on this side.

Directing Carl, Malkira moved quickly back into the bedroom. For Carl it was an unnerving experience to pass through a wall and even more unnerving to be met by a scene that seemed to be straight out of Dante's Inferno. The few grey shapes that fluttered were jostling each other to pass through a rent in the wall that was pulsing and spitting fumes.

Three – or was it four? – brilliant white spectres stood in front of them. The light they gave out bounced off the white walls, and they were blinding Carl. The only place to rest his eyes was where the grey shapes were cramming into the fissure. It was like looking at a living nightmare.

The angels in white grouped together and came towards them. The brilliance from them grew so bright that Malkira dropped to the floor to resist their radiance. Carl followed his lead and, head down, he followed the hoofed soles in the direction of the fissure.

Malkira's thinking that he could slink away from the angels' gazes came to an abrupt stop when he hit an invisible barrier. Rather than find a way around it, he changed his appearance. Taking his favourite shape of a snake, he had an idea he would slide under it or over it.

Carl's new world was suddenly very scary. He was connected to this magician who could change shape and walk through walls but he had no idea what was coming next. He followed the serpent on his hands and knees, but the snake was having trouble. Unable to move under the obstacle, he tried to slide over it only to find it reached up to the ceiling. Still overpowered by the light, Malkira coiled himself and hid his eyes from the glare. Carl could feel the power that came from the angelic group. But there was more. There was a mix of emotions: generosity, love, pity, and anger poured from them and filled the room, but the biggest emotion, by far, was that of sorrow.

Carl heard a voice in the thick of them. It surrounded him with what sounded like water cascading from a fall, but he heard the words plainly.

'You belong in the darkest of darkness. All darkness will be cleansed from this place, and you with it.'

The barrier that was keeping them from the rift disappeared.

Malkira was already on his belly, moving towards the sulphur-spitting rift. Carl followed his new master in trepidation, nervously moving to a gap in the wall, neither knowing nor understanding this spiritual world he had joined. As he was about to step through into his new world, a moan made him stop and turn to scan the bed.

His wife was moving. She was trying to sit up, holding her head. He looked at her without sympathy. It was probably her fault he had died; after all, if she had been more amenable when he came to bed, he wouldn't have been angry. What a stupid woman. She would be on her own now.

He was suddenly overcome by his body shape changing, altering to allow him through the gap. He lost volume, slimming down so that, sideways on, he could enter the rift and follow the demon. Another pang of fear flowed through him. Where was he being led? He turned, as if to return to the world he knew, but that way was blocked by an angel of light. A feeling of panic passed through him, seeing the slit being sealed by a burning flame that was coming from the end of the angel's finger. The outstretched hand followed the line of the rift from the floor to the ceiling, shutting off the underworld inch by inch, permanently closing the devil's doorway.

54

Sandra was dazed. Her head was aching, and her chin and neck were painful when she moved to sit up.

What had happened to her?

Then she remembered. Carl. It was always Carl. He had outdone himself this time. Striking her on her face would tell a tale or two. He had never done that before. The marks on her body from previous assaults had been hidden from the world under her clothes. Now the world would know what a brute he was.

Gingerly, she felt her jaw and jumped at the tenderness under her fingertips. It must be badly bruised. She tried moving her jaw from side to side, but the movement was excruciatingly painful. With a low moan she laid her head back down on the pillow and closed her eyes.

Moments later she stirred, when she heard the door open. Another involuntary moan left her as she forced herself up on one arm to see who had invaded the room. Had Carl returned? Her stomach clenched at the thought. It was a great relief when she saw the intruder was the upstairs maid, who had probably come to turn down the bed or bring new towels.

Following on behind, Debs pushed forward and made her way to the bed. It was then that Sandra remembered that Debs had tried to help rescue her from Carl's brutal hands. Debs had been there when he had tried to kill her. Sandra's hands shook as more memories flooded back, before her whole of her body joined in. She was cold, so very cold.

Debs picked up the crumpled gold bedspread from the bottom of the bed and wrapped it around the shoulders of the hurt woman.

'Where is he?' Sandra asked timidly. Still in fear, her tears erupted, until she was weeping uncontrollably. Debs held Sandra, giving her comfort, until her effort was rewarded when the sobbing eased, and Sandra whispered, 'Thank you'.

Julia stood by uncomfortably, watching the black aura of pain that cloaked Carl's wife and throbbed with each sob.

In the scene before Julia's eyes, a third figure sat on the other side of Sandra. The black was fading as the tears of pain eased. Sandra's mother's spirit glowed. Her hands were pushing through the black aura, breaking it up, and driving it away from her daughter. Louis and Katie watched with approval; the light in the bedroom was now filled with heavenly grace.

Sandra looked into Debs' eyes. 'Where is he?'

Debs, in a faltering voice, replied, 'I'm sorry Sandra, you'll need to be brave. He's had an accident. A fall. The ambulance has just left.'

'He's injured?' For a single moment, Sandra was relieved and ashamed of herself at the same time. The thought he might be hospitalised, and she would be free of him for a while, pleased her.

'Is he badly hurt?'

Debs bit her lip. Should she tell her Carl was dead, or let Doris, who would no doubt be coming up soon, do it?

There was pleading in Sandra's eyes for the truth. Debs decided not to make her wait.

'I'm afraid he fell down the stairs. The ambulance men couldn't help him. He's passed on.'

Sandra stared hard at Debs. A deep frown rested on her forehead as she tried to process the words she had just heard. After what seemed like an eternity she finally spoke. 'You mean he's dead?'

'I'm afraid so.'

Relief flowed through her body; her heart leapt with the news. He would never be able to touch her again. She wouldn't have to endure his taunts, his misogyny, and humiliation.

'He isn't coming back.' The words were said so softly that Debs only just heard her.

There was a strange faraway look in Sandra eyes.

'He isn't coming back.' The words were much louder.

The laughter, low at first, grew and gathered speed from her belly to her mouth. It soon became hysteria, and the sound reverberated around the room, bouncing off the walls before coming back to her. Debs still had her arms around Sandra, and she held her tight until the madness stopped, and the room became quiet again.

The black aura that Julia had seen around Sandra was gone. She was sitting upright and looked stronger. She no longer needed support and allowed Debs her arms back.

'Feeling better?'

'He's not coming back.' A hint of a smile hovered on Sandra's lips. 'Is he?'

'No.'

Sandra shook off the bedspread and grasped Debs hands.

'It's true?' Her eyes were bright with renewed hope. 'He can't hurt me anymore.' Her fingers touched her jaw. It hurt, but she would mend. A sigh came from deep within her. God was on her side after all.

This situation was not lost on Debs. In another life, it could have been hers.

It wouldn't change Debs' past or her pain from her teen years, but she too was free from his shadow, that had walked with her every day until now. She was glad he had recognised her before he died, that she had survived him despite him. She was a survivor and, as she looked at Sandra, she saw another. Sandra was reacting like a prisoner who had been let out of jail after serving a life sentence. The change that had taken place in that bedroom was like a butterfly that had been freed from the chrysalis. Her wings were being unfurled and ready to fly. And they were beautiful.

'Perhaps you would like some tea now?'

'Oh yes, that would be nice.'

'I'll bring you some up.'

'Yes, hot tea' – Sandra suddenly had a mischievous look on her face – 'and a large piece of cake, the largest you can find.' She chuckled. He couldn't control her now.

Debs was smiling too; this lady was finding her feet very quickly.

'If you don't mind – it's all been a shock for us too – I'll get a cuppa for myself and Julia and join you. Don't move, rest. I'll be back in a mo.'

Sandra nodded and smiled, despite the bruise that was coming out on her jaw making her jump. She looked happy, different. Snuggling down under the bedspread, she closed her eyes, as she said, 'Tea for three then.'

55

A rather subdued Doris sat in the kitchen, having tea with Barry. A guest falling down the stairs was not good for business. Barry was speaking in an indignant tone, as though some guilt was attached to him for the accident.

'He'd had at least two whiskeys and chasers after lunch; I don't know if he had wine when he ate. I didn't think he was drunk when I served him. But who knows? I reckon he tripped over his own feet.'

'Maybe, maybe. This is all very worrying; I expect we'll have the police up here soon. It will probably be Colin Ambler.'

'Who's Colin Ambler?'

'Oh, Colin? No, you don't know him? He's the desk sergeant down at the local nick.'

'How do you know him?'

'I went to school with him. He's a nice bloke. He was always very observant, a bit of a nosy parker in some ways – very helpful for his job. I expect the hospital will have been in touch with him and he'll be along shortly.'

'Who will be along shortly?' a deep voice asked from behind her. Doris was on her feet at once, turning to greet him.

'Oh, Harry, I'm so pleased to see you. It's been a terrible afternoon.' She wasn't crying but tears didn't seem very far away.

'You remember me telling you about that man Carl Greaves? He fell down the stairs, not an hour ago. He was all twisted and bloody.' She bit her lip before taking a deep breath and continued her monologue. 'He hurt himself so badly.' A sob was held in her throat. 'It killed him. The police will be around.'

Harry looked concerned. It was unlike Doris to show she was upset. She usually dealt with problems without a fuss. This accident had got to her tender heart.

'Don't worry, love. It will be okay.'

'No, it won't be okay; don't you understand? It could affect our business; it could affect all our lives.'

Harry looked crestfallen at the sharpness of her tongue; he had only been trying to reassure her. But she was right. All these years of work could be ruined.

Barry broke into the conversation.

'Look, Doris, I can vouch that the man had drunk too much and that I tried to persuade him to leave the bar. He was worse for wear and that's a fact. It was an accident.'

'It should be classed as an accidental death, obviously,' said Harry, trying to put a good spin on it. 'There will be an inquest, that goes without saying, but we have nothing to fear, do we?'

'There is no 'obviously', about it. The police will be looking for facts. A reason for his tumble. It's their job. We know he was under the influence and probably tripped over his own feet.' Her face was troubled, and her brows were knitted together. 'There was no one on the landing, at least none that we could see. No, nobody was there, I'm sure of it. By the time we got to him, he was on the edge of death. I tried to clean him up, we covered him with a throw and rang for help. The girls must have come out of a bedroom to see what the noise was all about. I heard the door shut, come to think of it. He certainly cried out as he fell.' She looked at Barry for confirmation.

He was nodding; it had shaken them both.

'Well, we can't prove it one way or the other. It's up to the police now.' Harry put his arms around Doris and held her tight. She allowed herself to slump against his shoulder, grateful for his strength. Harry realised then how vulnerable she was feeling – she was human after all, just like everyone else and enough was enough; right now, she needed his support. He chided himself for always being at work, making a mental note to make more time to be with his woman. He had to learn to delegate, he thought, kissing her hair, as she released herself from him with a tired smile.

'Well, this is a right to-do,' Doris muttered in muted tones. Finding her chair again, she sat, reaching for her cup of tea, seeking comfort in the cooling beverage. The kitchen was uncomfortably silent. No-one had anything to say as they mused on the events, drinking stewed tea.

The girls came into the kitchen, hoping to find it empty to make tea for Sandra. They almost tiptoed in when they saw the group drinking at the table. No one spoke, but their eyes followed them. It was quite unnerving. Julia was filling the kettle and Debs had gone into the pantry to find cake when Doris spoke.

'What exactly are you doing?' Her eyebrows were raised as she asked the question.

'We're making tea for Sandra,' answered Debs, carrying chocolate cake to the counter, and for the next few minutes she rattled forth, earnestly explaining what she had seen and bringing Doris up to date with the drama that had transpired upstairs, from Carl's interlude of groping Julia to the moment they, uninvited, burst into the room on hearing a cry from Sandra.

'We have told her Carl's dead and, if I'm honest with you, it's a great relief to her.'

Harry moved his chair and pulled it nearer to Doris. His hand reached out for hers, and she took the comfort from him willingly. She could hardly understand what she had heard.

'Is it true? My God, not in my hotel,' said Doris out loud, but, while not wanting to believe it, she knew it had happened. The distress showed on her pale face. If this news got out on top of the accident, she could be ruined.

'The constabulary may take a grim view of it all and think Sandra had helped push him down the stairs,' said Doris, nodding at Julia and Debs.

'Oh! That couldn't have happened,' said Julia. 'We were with her when we heard his cry.'

Before Doris could respond, the shrill sound of the telephone echoed from out of her office/sitting room, which brought Barry to his feet.

'I'll get that.' Relief showed on Barry's face. It was a welcome distraction; it had been a hell of a day and it wasn't over yet. He was pleased to leave Doris and Harry to consult with the girls.

'You do that, thanks.' Barry noticed Doris was still holding tightly on to Harry's hand, something in normal circumstances she would never do.

Barry was back in seconds, his face peering around the door.

'Sorry, Doris, it's Sergeant Ambler for you!' His eyes looked heavenward in silence, showing sympathy for his boss. She nodded.

'I'll be there right away.' Looking at Debs, she said, 'I'll be up later to see Mrs Greaves. You see to her for now, will you? Tell her we'll do all we can to help her. They were due to leave tomorrow, but the police might want her to stay around.' Talking more to herself than to the group, she added, 'I'll have to move her to the single.' She looked at Julia. 'I hope she won't mind.' It hadn't really been a request. 'We can do that, can't we?' It was more like a sensitive order. Barry smiled; that was more like Doris.

With a smile of acquiescence on Debs' lips and a nod from Julia, Doris and Harry disappeared to the den.

Barry had gone back to the bar to join Roger preparing for the evening's opening. His long day had just got longer. Guests would be turning up soon and the evening meal needed to be got under way. This was not going to be an easy evening; word would soon spread, once the police were involved. It was a small town and the patrons could be nosy.

Maureen and Roger had arrived just as the ambulance was leaving and Roger was full of questions. Barry told him just enough to satisfy his curiosity before he made his way to the kitchen to start his duty with Maureen. Dinner had to be served.

'All I can tell you is a guest died; he fell down the stairs,' said Barry. 'And he had been drinking whiskey after lunch. It was a tragic accident. You knew him; he was the one that insisted on being served after time, a couple of nights ago.'

'The guy that fancied himself?'

'That's right.'

'Tragic.' It was said without feeling.

Doris was at her desk on the phone, the receiver at her ear. Harry had made himself comfortable on the two-seater sofa, listening intently to the one-sided conversation.

'Hello, Colin, or should I call you Sergeant?' Harry couldn't hear the answer but the smile on Doris' face confirmed the connection of old friends.

'That's fine.' Doris was nodding as she replaced the receiver. 'We'll see you soon.' She directed her gaze at Harry. 'He's a good sort. He's going to come along personally to interview us.' Harry could see the relief that it gave her.

'Of course, he is,' Harry confirmed. 'How are you coping?'

'Me? As I always do, one foot in front of the other.'

'That's my girl.' Harry smiled, pleased that she had rallied and gathered herself.

Using the spare key, and having knocked at the door, Doris let herself into the room.

Sandra was wrapped up in the bedspread, sipping tea with Debs. A tea plate was on the side table, with a cake fork covered with the crumbs of the chocolate cake.

'How are you, Mrs Greaves?'

'Better now.' She looked at Debs with a grateful glance.

Debs got up to collect the cup from Sandra and made her way towards the door. Sandra seemed composed, but seeing Debs about to leave, she protested. 'No, please, stay. You're the nearest thing I have to a friend.'

Debs hesitated, looking at Doris. Doris nodded. Taking the cue, Debs found the end of the bed to perch on.

Doris saw that Sandra's jaw was puffy and bruised and felt a great deal of sympathy for her. From time to time, her hotel hosted undesirable guests, but most of the time the unpleasantness stayed in the bedroom.

Doris was kind. While assuring Sandra that she could stay until things got sorted out, police-wise, she explained that she had new guests booked into that room and Sandra would have to move to a single. Sandra nodded; that wasn't a problem and she was grateful for any help.

When Doris left the room, she had the picture of the two women, both of whom had suffered at Carl's cruelty, in her mind. That, she felt, was their bond.

56

He recognised me. Debs was still recovering from what had been an exhausting and frightening experience.

The two friends were lying in bed in the dark. Debs had heard Julia turning this way and that, the springs on the bed wheezing with each movement, for the last hour. There she goes again, thought Debs. Julia sighed deeply as she turned over.

'Are you awake?'

'Can't you sleep either?' Julia's young voice was full of anxiety.

This was all so unsettling, and too much for Debs. She hit the switch on the bedside table lamp and stared into Julia's face, just as Julia was about to do the same with her lamp.

'No. My mind will not let go of today. To be honest, I'm full of mixed emotions. Do you remember me telling you about a secret that I would share with you one day? Well, that day might well be here.'

'If you're ready, I am.' And Julia settled back on the bed.

'I'm in a kind of turmoil. Confusion and anger and relief all mixed up: one after the other, they spin in my head. I wonder if today actually happened or was it just a bad dream.'

'It was no dream. I can vouch for that.'

'I shut my eyes and see him at the bottom of those stairs. All tangled and twisted.' She paused mid-sentence, reliving the scene again. 'Blood on his face and the pallor of death.'

'It was awful, wasn't it? It might help if I tell you what you couldn't see or hear. There was quite a battle going on.'

'There was?' Debs looked at her friend's earnest face. 'To be honest I could feel tension all around me. And that monster.' Debs' face twisted at the thought.

'You could see the demon?' Julia sounded astonished.

'Demon? What demon? I was talking about Carl.' And a shiver flowed down her spine.

'Oh yes, Carl. I can't, nor would I, make excuses for him. He was a cruel man and a mean drunk. I know that. But Debs, let me tell you, he was not wholly himself this afternoon.' A much older Julia seemed to engage with Debs. 'What with the demon, the spirit of Sandra's mother, the harpies, plus the angels, it was terrible viewing heaven and hell colliding.'

'Heaven and hell colliding? Is that even possible? I was there… and saw nothing.' Her voice trailed away as she was trying to come to terms with Julia's second sight and her own blindness.

'Louis and Katie were there too. They shielded us from the attack of harpies when you were laid out on the floor.'

Debs looked mystified. 'What are you talking about?'

'This is going to be a lot to take in but, trust me, the Royal is totally safe now.' Julia carried on and described in detail the events, including the demon blending with Carl.

'That's hideous. Poor Sandra.' Debs was dumbfounded. Shock registered on her face, and she felt quite sick. Carl's character was bad enough, but combined with evil from hell, it was beyond her imagination.

Debs let her thoughts speak out loud.

'He recognised me. Called me by my name.' She had a distant look in her eyes and with a slight nodding motion, she shuddered, bringing herself back to the moment. 'I never told you, but in my past life, I knew him. He was a terrible person then and he hadn't developed into a better man. Worse, really.' She paused; a shocked look touched her face. 'Judging by what we saw, and the bruises on Sandra, he was evil.'

There was an uncomfortable silence. Julia swung her legs out of bed, looking at Debs' face, searching for a clue as to where this conversation was going.

Debs was lying on her side, raised up on her elbow. Facing her friend, she hesitated in sharing her secret. Did she really want Julia to know about her other self?

Making her decision, she patted her bed, inviting Julia to sit while she explained.

'That night when you shared your secret of being a psychic, you trusted me. Now it's time to return the favour. It's time I trusted you, and I hope I don't disappoint you too much.'

'Debs, you could never disappoint.'

Julia believed her own words; she knew how the past could hurt lives. She had a place in her heart that was constantly empty. She had no family, no blood relative to call her own. An unwanted thought crept into her mind when she was least able to deal with it. Why had her birth mother given her up?

Her path to adulthood had been challenging. Kindness had been lacking in the orphanage. She didn't remember being hugged, not then, not there. Debs, her friend sitting next to her, had shown her more caring in six months than the whole of her life in care. The main aim of the institution was to provide food and shelter; compassion and love didn't enter into it. Because of it, she had developed both single-mindedness and courage. She had wanted nothing more than to be free of her past and make a new life. She had cut all ties when she stepped out of their door.

If there was any way of helping her friend, she would. Over the months of sharing this room with Debs, a bond had grown between them: a bond that was more than friendship.

'He recognised me. Can you imagine that? I've served him for almost two weeks, and he never saw me: I was just the help. Someone to come and go at his bidding, his will. The arrogant beggar.' A deep frown rested on Debs' forehead. She had lowered her eyes, as if somehow meeting Julia's stare would stop her telling her story. Julia took her hand.

'You can tell me anything.'

Debs' mouth held a weak smile for a moment, but her eyes were wary.

'I was so afraid when he checked in. How could fate do this to me, bringing him north, here to the Royal? It was his voice that made me turn and my heart almost stopped when I recognised him.' Once again, her eyes became downcast, her fingers picking at her nails on her free hand.

'I have held my degradation and humiliation for eighteen years. He robbed me of my teens. Disgraced me. I lost my family, I was an outcast. But, worst of all, I lost my baby.' A smothered laugh had caught in her throat; her free hand flew to her mouth to stop the sound. 'He pretended he loved me and raped me… I loved him… Puppy love.' She grimaced and then sighed. 'I was convinced with the thought that I was adult. Romance and being in love were natural outcomes of that, but I was a child. I had no understanding about sex. It was never spoken about at school, except behind our hands in the girls' cloakrooms. Then it was mainly about kissing, and soppy love songs. We knew pregnancy happened, but didn't know how a baby was conceived or born. My mother was signally silent on the subject, until I came home pregnant. Then I was treated like a leper, because of my ignorance. I had trusted my emotions and had loved badly.' Debs face crumpled with a deep frown, that reflected her feeling her disgrace all over again.

'You lost your baby? How?'

Julia was getting upset; this part of the story was too close for comfort. It wasn't just empathy, it was a painful reminder of her own circumstances.

'I didn't lose my baby, Julia. She was taken from me six days after she was born. I begged my mother to take us in, but she said it was better that I start afresh. How could I? One day of instant love and six days of bonding with my lovely child. They tore her from my arms, promising that she would have a good life with loving parents. All of that may be true but I still grieve for her.'

'That must have been awful.' Julia's face revealed the truth of it. For her, this was a first-hand story of what might have happened to her own mother. Tears filled her eyes as she looked away, hiding her own pain.

Tears rolled down Debs' face and a large sob escaped with them. It was a sound of anguish, a cry from the heart. Her face was twisted in a mask of torment. She couldn't hold back the built-up emotions and she muttered a name through her tears.

'Annie, my sweet Annie.' Debs clutched the bedclothes to her face and smothered the noise of loss and grief into them.

Julia wanted to take Debs in her arms, much like Debs had done for her when she had broken up with Nick, but she held back. She could see Debs was heartbroken, but her own heart had leapt when Debs had called for her child.

'Annie? You called her Annie?'

Debs' knees had come up to her chest and she locked her arms around them. Her brow rested on her knees until she could respond. Her face was red and puffy when she finally looked up. Through the sobs, she nodded.

Julia was mentally grasping what she had heard, and an incomprehensible mix of feelings buzzed through her brain. Was she being fanciful? Perplexed, she asked herself, was she being stupid? Of course, she was. For years she had waited for divine mercy, for her wish to be granted. After such a day, did she really expect it? Perhaps?

She was compelled to reach out to Debs, and, touching her shoulder, said, 'Please don't cry. I have something to tell you.'

Julia was rewarded by Debs dropping her knees and mouthing 'sorry', over a rather damp cotton sheet. Taking a deep breath, Julia steadied herself until the painful tears dried up.

'There's nothing to be sorry about, but I need to share something.'

Debs, through puffy eyes, looked mystified at the forcefulness in Julia's voice and determination on her face. Finding a hankie under her pillow, she wiped her eyes and blew her nose. Whatever did she want to tell her? Sitting upright, she answered, 'Ready.'

'I have another secret, Debs, one I have never shared with anyone.' Julia was biting her lip, and she paused, emphasising how deep this went, before throwing back her shoulders and allowing its release.

'You see, my name is Annie.'

Incredulity registered on Debs' face. A frown crossed her forehead.

'What are you saying? You're Julia.' The frown seemed deeper when it found its way back to Debs' forehead.

'I'm not sure. It's just that when I left the orphanage, I left my old name behind with that life. I had changed it, to be a new person. Annie died on my sixteenth birthday, and Julia replaced her.'

Debs was shaking her head. 'I don't know what you're saying. Do you think for one minute that…?' her voice trailed; she couldn't say it.

'I don't know. It's a small world; sometimes the fate lines crisscross. That's all I'm saying.'

'But my Annie was adopted.'

'Are you sure?'

'No. I can't be sure.' Debs voice trailed, echoed a more thoughtful response. 'I wasn't allowed any information about her. Nothing about where she had been taken or who her new parents were. Hell, she could be in Australia for all I know.'

'Or…' Very quietly, Julia responded, 'She could be here?'

Debs looked into Julia's eyes, and saw the wanting there.

'That's wishful thinking. Isn't it?'

'Maybe. But don't we all want our wishes to come true?' A bold stare, directed at Debs, locked their eyes together.

'I was born in 1956. When did you have your Annie?'

'1956. December 6th.'

'St Nicholas' Day. That's the date on my birth certificate. December 6th. Annie White. Don't you think that's more than a coincidence? Perhaps our fate lines crossed years ago and have crossed again.' She looked earnestly at Debs. 'You could be my mother; we bear the same surname.' The pitch of her voice had risen with excitement. She wanted this to be true. 'I almost said something when Doris introduced us, but I couldn't because she didn't know me as Annie.'

Debs looked at this lovely young girl. It was true that their surnames were the same and Julia's face was now radiant with expectation. Debs didn't want to disillusion her. Julia's red hair suddenly reminded Debs of her own father, whose nickname had been Ginger. It wasn't original, but everyone with red hair had a nickname. Her father reckoned he could sing and dance just as well as Ginger Rogers with a name like that, and that thought made her smile.

Was this a strange trick of fate or was it a family trait that had her clutching to hope? She wanted Julia to be her daughter. And if she wasn't, Debs was determined she would adopt her, if that's what she wanted. Under the eaves, in that bedroom, Debs lost a friend and found a daughter.

Julia saw a flash of optimism pass over Debs' face and smiled. It was returned by wide open arms and a hug that left no doubt about the feelings of love they shared.

'Do you have a birth certificate for me? I have my copy; we should compare.'

'Yes, we should, and we will. But not now, my darling. Annie White, meet Debs White: your mother. We don't need to prove anything; at least not tonight.'

57

Doris lay in Harry's arms. It was past midnight. The tensions that still lingered were beyond the closed bedroom door and in the body of the Royal, her home and business, and she was glad to leave them there tonight.

The bed was cool, but she had the warmth of his body beside her. Harry had been so busy of late; he was away so often, but he had arrived back just at the right time today, to give her his support. It had also been a while since he'd been able to share the night with her, and she hungered for him.

The central light had been turned off, but she wasn't ready for the pitch-black darkness of the room, not yet. The comforting glow from the table lamps somehow softened her mood and lessened the memories of the realities that she had faced that day. She could feel the rise and fall of his chest and hear the rhythm of his heartbeat, a heart that he had promised to her, and she felt so fortunate to have him there. Together under the sheets, they felt so right as a couple. She was thinking about the future and wondered if he ever thought about them as a couple, in the same way she did. Or was it just feminine fancy?

Even in the safety of her bedroom, as hard as she tried, she couldn't quite shut out what had been a stark and rude lesson this afternoon. She shuddered inwardly. Life was unpredictable and could be cut short by a simple accident. How would she manage without Harry's love?

The image was back in her mind's eye: Carl's twisted, almost lifeless, body lying in her hall. She had done what she could; it was only what she would have done for anyone. Though she didn't care for the man, she had cleaned him up best she could, but his life had leached away.

The memory of that afternoon was back, and she shivered under the sheet.

'Are you alright, Doris?' Harry's concerned words made her sigh.

'Yes, I'm fine. It's just the thought of how precious life is. And I would hate anything happening to you.'

'Nothing is going to happen; you're still upset, darling. I'm not going anywhere; I'll promise you that.'

'I'll keep you to that promise. You see if I don't.'

Harry kissed her forehead. 'Turn off the light, let's sleep. Tomorrow is beckoning.'

Doris turned off the light, and tried to settle. Forty minutes later, she put it back on. The soft glow of light was reassuring, but now Harry stirred beside her.

'I guess it's going to be a restless night.'

'Sorry, love, but this afternoon is replaying over and over in my head.'

Harry didn't argue. He took her in his arms again, closing his eyes to the light, and told her to at least rest.

But the play of the day would not stop in her head.

Sergeant Ambler had come, with another officer, to take statements and see where the accident happened. Colin, her old school chum, was much changed in appearance, but his manner was pleasant. His crown of thick, dark brown hair was gone, exposing a shiny bald head, and he'd put on a few pounds. But when he spoke, Colin was there, and the schoolday memories filtered back.

He had been a straightforward talker, the no-nonsense type, and he hadn't changed. He had been affable during the interview, but left Doris in no doubt that the police were in charge and old friendships didn't count for anything.

It could have been worse, thought Doris, with another shudder. He hadn't accused them of a crime and, on the whole, had been quite helpful.

In her snug, she had explained to Colin about hearing a cry and a series of thuds, and how she and Barry had rushed to see what the noise was all about.

'Could you show us where it happened?' The smile was there, but it wasn't a request.

She walked the two officers to the spot where they had found Mr Greaves, injured and dying. The vison was all too clear in her memory. Barry had followed Doris and the police, and was staring at the spot where Carl had lain. Barry was the first to explain.

'We didn't dare move him, so I dashed to phone the ambulance, and brought something to clean him up. That's right, isn't it, Doris?'

'That's just how it happened. One leg that looked broken was still on the bottom step. He was twisted, with his arms flung out.'

'Right you are. Just stand back while we take a look, and if anything comes to mind, let us know.'

The police checked the landing, and every step down the flight to the hall, meticulously. They stopped every now and again, looking at a scuff or a streak of blood on the woodwork. They found nothing that might suggest an obstruction that could have tripped Carl.

Doris watched them inspect the scene from the hallway, believing there was nothing to find, but it was still worrying. The police were doing their job, and rightly so, she knew that, but this hotel was the heartbeat of her life.

After they had finished the inspection, Colin brushed his hands as though crumbs were sticking to his fingers, and indicated that he needed statements from everyone. Doris led the way to her snug. Harry was already there, waiting patiently for her return. He looked a little surprised when the police followed her in. Awkwardly rising, he asked, 'Would anyone like a drink?'

Colin smiled. 'That's very nice of you.'

'Tea?'

'Tea would be good. One with milk, no sugar; the other black. I'm on a bit of a diet.' He cleared his throat in embarrassment at having blurted out something personal. Then, suddenly he was back, all formal and business-like.

'We'll need your statement sir.'

'I wasn't here when it happened. I arrived not long after the event.'

'Nevertheless, I'll need it.'

Harry left them to it and sought Maureen in the kitchen to find biscuits to accompany the tea.

Same old Colin, thought Doris, friendly but at arm's length.

'It was a terrible accident that was waiting to happen.' Doris indicated with her hand the action of drinking. 'He liked a drop.'

'That would be the coroner's decision and possible verdict once he has looked over all the facts. They will be checking his bloods for alcohol levels and such at the hospital, as we speak. Would you say he was inebriated?' The officer, who was taking notes in a small black pad, had his pen poised, waiting for her answer.

'I can't say I ever saw him paralytic – he held it well – but Barry here will give you the facts of the afternoon.'

'I would still appreciate your opinion.'

'I can only tell you what Barry said, and that was that Mr Greaves had bought whiskey chasers and had them lined up on the bar.'

'How many?'

'Two or three.'

Barry interrupted. 'He was downing one and saving one. He ordered them two at a time. I would say he had six over a period of an hour. He was a big man and could take quite a bit, if previous nights were anything to go by.'

'Thank you, Sir. We'll get to you in a minute,' Colin said, a humourless smile on his face.

'I'll be back in the bar, then. You can catch me there.' Barry nodded an acknowledgment and left.

Colin turned back to Doris. 'And how long was he staying with you?'

'Oddly enough, this was his final day. He was due to check out in the morning after a two-week stay.'

'And where was Mrs Greaves when the accident happened?'

'In the Eden Room.'

'That would be…?'

'Upstairs, at the end of the landing.'

'I'll need to speak to her. Is she there now?'

'Yes, as far as I know.'

'Good. We'll get a statement from her before we speak to your staff.'

Doris had dithered. Should she mention that Mr Greaves had assaulted his wife, and that Sandra had been completely out of it, in a faint of some sort? And that two of her staff were helping Sandra come around in the bedroom?

Julia and Debs were witness to Sandra's non-involvement. It proved it was an accident. In the end, she left it to Colin to tease the facts out. Sandra could speak for herself, and her girls certainly could. Doris trusted it would all come out well in the wash, as they say.

An hour later the police had left. Sandra had been interviewed and Debs had confirmed that when Carl fell to his death, she had been in the room with Sandra.

Statements would have to be dated and signed down at the station, some time over the next two days. Doris, however, was warned not to clean the staircase until the police photographer had been over and he was due shortly.

It had been a trying evening, striving to keep the wheels turning with the police ferreting about. But, somehow, the bar had opened as normal, and all the guests who had booked had been served a good dinner. Of course, the place was buzzing with questions. What had happened? Had someone died? When did it happen? More questions than the police asked, in some cases.

Doris tried to play it down. It had been a freak accident; the hotel had never in all its history had anything happen like this before, and that was true. Doris kept it brief. The man had been taken to hospital, but unfortunately there had not been anything that could be done to save him.

Funnily enough, the bar seemed busier than normal. There was nothing like a bit of scandal or mystery to bring the neighbours in. Maureen and Roger had kept the wheels on in the kitchen, and even Nick had filled in where needed. It had all worked out.

Before Sergeant Ambler had left, he had had a quiet word with Doris, back in the snug.

'It looks like an open-and-shut case, Doris. No blame will be attached to you. It seems that this man was a bit of a Jekyll and Hyde character. Drink can do that to a man. I've seen it myself, many times over the years. There'll be an inquest, got to be, but I shouldn't worry about it. I would put money on it being an accidental death. As I said, no blame on you.'

Doris snuggled up to Harry. She wanted to put the day behind her, but it wasn't letting her go. She didn't dare put the light out. Her anxiety reared up again. She shivered; she felt so vulnerable.

Harry opened an eye.

'How are you feeling, love?' She was quiet and pressing closer to him. When she was subdued like this, which wasn't often, it was as though she had thrown in the towel and lost her fight. That worried him.

'I've been thinking, seriously, about us. Life can be so unpredictable, and fate can be cruel. Can't it?' She moved her head so she could look him in the face. 'I do love you; you know that, don't you?'

Harry felt his stomach turn over and his teeth clenched. What was coming next? His own insecurities were raising their heads. He hadn't been around enough lately; business was often pulling him away, sometimes for days. But she must know how he felt about her. What on earth was she about to say?

He blurted out, 'I love you too,' holding her even tighter to him. He kissed her hair and waited for a response.

'Well, I'll get straight to the point then, shall I?' She reached up and pulled his face down to hers, kissing him hard and long. All his misgivings suddenly melted away. She was back and he felt safe again, and then shocked.

'Let's get married, Harry. I want to be with you. Attached and legal, like. For richer or poorer and all that. I saw death today. It's so final. No second chances, no time to put things straight, no time to say goodbyes. I don't want that for us. I want you in my bed every night. I want to hear your key in the door, see your discarded socks on my carpet and your toothbrush in my bathroom. What do you think?'

Harry felt a leap in his heart and realised with the right answer, a new chapter in his life would be beginning.

'Come here, woman.'

He had propped himself up on a pillow and was urging Doris to do the same.

'I've wanted to ask you that for weeks now, but I was afraid you enjoyed your independence too much to share with me. I want to completely settle down. And,' he said, with all seriousness, 'It's my job to ask you. It's not a leap year, you know.' He laughed at the indignant face she pulled. 'But putting all that aside, the answer's *yes*.'

The room took on a new feel of emotion. The day had been awful; at least that was over and yet the situation had revealed a truth about life and death: a truth that would change their lives forever. They kissed and kissed until their passion stirred, and their souls hungered for more. It was late, yet the night was young and full of promise.

58

Katie and Louis had returned to their world. The Royal had been purged from the darkness of the underworld. It was great relief to know that their friends on the other side of the veil were safe and out of danger.

The angels had come when they were called. It was just as Massie had said: trust the angels; ask and they will help. They cannot interfere in the mortal world; they stand on the side-lines, waiting to be asked. Their gifts can only be accessed by prayer, and praying was not very fashionable in the twentieth century. In this age, these guardians were seldom thought of.

Louis himself had been something of a lost soul when he first became a spirit in his netherworld. He had cursed his predicament, but he had not thought to call on the higher orders to help him. With some shame, he remembered cursing them for his predicament. What a fool he had been.

Here, he was in the world of his vision. It wasn't paradise, but it was his sanctuary. And it was his heaven, with Katie sharing it with him.

Champ had been waiting for them, lying under the tree, dozing. He heard their footsteps coming up the track from the opening in the veil. He made a small sound deep in his throat, greeting the couple as they came closer.

Louis dropped to his knees, meeting his furry friend, who greeted him with a large and very wet tongue. The tongue found its mark, and Louis laughed as he pushed the eager head away from his cheek, patting his overzealous pet who immediately rolled over, exposing his belly to be scratched.

'Now, that's what I call a welcome.'

A reaction set in after the relief of coming home. Tiredness hit Katie from every angle. Her soul hurt from what she had seen. She could have never imagined the chaos of evil she had observed there, in the past hours. The darkness, the harpies, the serpent. Sandra suffering because of Malkira and Carl's dark souls. It had pained and wearied her. Louis was playing with Champ, he looked happy to be back, but strain registered in his face too.

Their connection and love was stronger than ever; there was no need for words. He looked up into her face and smiled. She heard 'You too,' though no words passed between them. She nodded, and a vague smile touched the edge of her lips. Louis patted the grasses alongside Champ, inviting her to join them. With his arm around her shoulders and her head resting in the nook of his neck, they both agreed that, after all the turmoil they had witnessed, they needed to find some peace.

Confident of their security in their kingdom, it was time for an undisturbed, and peaceful restoration of their spiritual souls. With the warmth on their faces from Louis' sun, they lay under the tree of life, closed their eyes, and drifted into that rest.

Something had touched his face – perhaps a butterfly on its way to the meadow. It brought him up from his light slumber. He opened his eyes to the blue sky and the sun. A longish wisp of a cloud was moving across his sky, and that was unusual.

Louis sat up, watching it make its way towards the hills. It glided towards the moors. He couldn't see them from where he was, but knew they were there, waiting for him to find a way to cross them. He smiled. Had Katie brought this addition to his kingdom, like some of the many other things her imagination had created?

He looked down at his lovely sleeping companion. How could he be so lucky as to have a partner like her?

Her chestnut-coloured bob was splayed out over the fresh green grass. What a wonderful contrast, the red brown against the emerald. Just one stray strand had remained straddled over her cheek. He moved it off her face and bent over and kissed her lightly on her cheek.

'Katie, love, are you awake?'

'I surely am now.' She raised her head, pouting and with mischief in her eyes.

'Is that the best you can do?'

Louis' smile widened before he kissed her passionately on the lips. It brought back a piece of their past.

'Do you remember when I first brought you here? We sat on this spot, and I asked if you liked my kingdom. Do you remember?'

Katie sat up and looked at the meadow as though it was that first time. She watched the grasses sway in the light breeze, and a thrill made its way down her back at the thought.

'How could I forget? I didn't quite understand who you were then.'

He put his arm around her, pulling her close. 'But you do now?' he whispered in her ear, before nibbling her earlobe.

'Oh, yes.' She laughed and pretended to push him away.

'So, you decided to put a cloud in my sky?' He raised an eyebrow, as though he didn't quite approve of it, but his smile hadn't left his mouth.

'No. Never. What made you think that?'

Louis pointed to the distant wisp of white that had almost disappeared on the horizon. 'You didn't do that?'

'No.'

'It's from the other place then, same as the red kite.' He frowned. This was a puzzle, something out of his control, but he promised himself he would try to resolve it. Katie snuggled up in his arms, changing the direction of his thoughts. The cloud and the butterfly were forgotten. He reached over and kissed her on her lips. They didn't measure time in the kingdom. Their world had no night and no seasons. Only by going through the veil and visiting the mortal world could they read how much time had passed. They had no need for that now; normality and balance had returned to the Royal, now the doorway to hell had been sealed.

Restored and reassured in that timeless space, they relished the promise of carefree days for them both. They enjoyed their love-making under the sun, living as one heart in perfect unity.

Champ, who lay next to them, opened an eye at the activity, wondering if perhaps a walk was on the cards. He decided it was not, and sighed, promptly closing his eye again.

Louis began to see a new piece of artistry in his head. He sat under the shade of his tree, watching nature; it inspired his imagination, as it always had. This time it was a little different; he saw a piece of sculpture that explored the four layers of the different existences. His thoughts were disturbed by the evil that had visited his kingdom. His memory turned back to the original carving he had made of Garden of Eden on his bed. Then, he had only seen a tree of plenty and a garden of abundance, that had been his template of love. The garden, his netherworld, was somehow in a middle place, sandwiched between kingdoms below and kingdoms above it.

Louis saw something like a plane tree, with tight roots in the ground that made the tree firm. In the dark tight twists of the roots, Louis saw the caverns of the underworld: caves that held the lost souls, skeletons, sleeping ghouls, harpies, and deities of evil.

Did God reside in any of it? He must be part of the roots. The roots held up the entire tree and were the foundation of it. God was surely without gender and was invisible. The spirit of God must start there and run through the trunk until, at last, the spiritual energy reaches the crown and gives out its light to the whole universe. That, at least, was how Louis saw it at that moment. It could all change once the journey in wood began. The more he thought about this venture, the more he realised how big the task was: so big that perhaps he should try to simplify the idea. A big idea needed a big piece, or the idea made the piece large, even if it was small in scale, but that was another thought. He brought the wood together with his tools at his workstation and started to explore the images that were hiding there. It was his job to find them and reveal them.

His favourite spot for his bench was near the tree. Lost in his work, he wondered how long he had been working on this piece. How many mortal days had passed since they returned to the kingdom?

Not that it really mattered. He was doing what he was called to do, and Katie occupied herself while he worked. When she wasn't playing or walking Champ, she spent her time singing, writing or reading. He teased her that she must be the most learned ghost on record, if there were any. And it was a shame that she couldn't share her knowledge with others.

He lifted his head from his work and stretched out his back. Oddly, he had never needed to do that before, at least not in spirit. Surely spirits don't have twinges of pain or stiffness. This was new.

A dark swirl moved into his sight from the horizon. In the distance, a murmuration of starlings was making patterns in his sky; it was marvellous to see, the patterns weaving in and out, like some wild polka and then gone. A puzzled look crossed his face. This wasn't right. He wondered for half a second if he had had a waking dream.

He felt a little cold. A shiver danced down his back. The breeze over his meadow seemed stronger and sharper. He looked back up at his sky. A large cloud had appeared from nowhere and was skimming the horizon, over his sun.

Now he was confused. These things belonged to the mortal world, not his. He was about to call Katie when he was surprised again as another sight caught his eye. A leaf on the tree of life appeared to be turning with autumn colours. This was impossible; his tree and its leaves never turned, couldn't turn; autumn didn't exist here.

Putting down his tools, he strolled up the grassy bank to take a closer look. The leaf in question was on a high branch next to a fruit of orange. It crossed his mind that it could be only a reflection of the orange colour in the light. He had never noticed anything like it before, in all the aeons he had spent in the kingdom. On tiptoe, he reached up to touch the strange leaf but, as he did, a gust of wind whipped up around his head, catching him off guard and blowing dust into his eyes. For half a second, he stopped moving and shut his eyes tight. The wind stopped and, rubbing his eye, the grit cleared. He was up close to the branch, and had to take a second look: the leaf he saw was a deep emerald green. It was obvious he had been mistaken and yet he had been so sure moments ago. Perhaps it was time to take a break from the panel he was working on. He went off down the track to the cottage to find Katie and tell her that he was overworking. He could already hear her laugh and say, 'What's new?'

The greyish-brown slowworm, half hidden in the part-exposed root, was feeling rather pleased. The eyelids blinked with special delight over the liquid blue eyes. He may have been locked out of the corporeal world by the angels, but there was always a way to find some sport if you really looked and wanted something. And he wanted to be here.

The angels hadn't said anything about the netherworld being closed off to him. And for that, Malkira was pleased. It was like asking him to enter. He joined the roots of Louis' tree and connected them to his dark world. He had that power and the will, both gifts that the angels couldn't stop him using. He chuckled; the tree of life had now been designated by him to become a tree of darkness.

He was contemptuous of the lovers, their half-lost souls that heaven had not taken; they were now in his sight. And a little revenge was in order. These ghosts had made him lose recruits and prey, all except Carl, but then Carl had always been his from the moment he was born; of that, there had been no doubt.

Malkira imagined he would play with them for a while and then, when he was ready, he would draw them into his kingdom and their light would be lost forever. Their pain would be a pleasant meal.

There was foreboding in the air. Louis was uncomfortable. He felt his kingdom might be at risk. Odd things and new sightings were visible almost every day, added to his world without his consent. At first, he thought these things were coming from the moor: the place he was yet to find a way through to; that heavenly place. He had thought that the new images were been directed from the golden light beyond the moorland. But now he wasn't sure. The calmness the kingdom once had was going. The birds, the clouds, a new and unaccountable blustering breeze all had a savageness to them. And the leaf, especially the leaf that had changed colour, bothered him. It reminded him of the snakeskin that Katie had found: that little piece of the demon she had shown him, and the piece he still had in his back pocket. He felt for it now, drawing it out onto the palm of his hand, and saw the gold, brown and orange glint in the sun. Could he sense a connection to it?

Was there a slight sensation on his skin? Was evil still within it?

He was arguing with himself, now. He had been there when the angels sealed the gateway in the bedroom to keep evil out. Was that enough to keep his kingdom free of evil too? Was his own lively imagination getting in the way of logic? Perhaps. But it didn't answer any of his questions as to where these new phantasmagorias had materialised from.

He put his uncertainties to one side. Work always helped; he needed to get back to his panel. That plane tree and its roots were now visible and were as tall as he was. Now he had to find the citizens that lived on and in it.

He had barely started when an unhappy Katie and Champ came marching up the track.

'You'll never guess what I've found on my roses,' said Katie, looking rather despondent.

'Do tell.'

'Black spot. The leaves are all marked with it.'

'No. That can't be.'

'I know, but it is.'

Louis put down his tools and, together, they returned to the cottage. The roses in the garden stood proud and tall, the yellow and red heads blooming under the sun, giving out their perfume.

'Over here.' Katie was showing the way, Champ at her heels. He suddenly whined, before charging into the meadow after a rabbit he saw.

'Ignore him,' said Katie. 'He's been doing that every two minutes. There do seem to be more rabbits than usual. Here, come look.' Katie had stopped in front of a large bush and was inspecting the lower leaves. Louis came up behind her, as she proceeded to peer at leaves mid-way up the plant.

'They were marked.' A look of disbelief crossed her face. 'Louis, they were there, honestly.'

Louis inspected the top layer. 'I can't see black spot, but I do see greenfly under these leaves.'

'No.'

Louis checked again. The blight was worse. On the underside of the leaf, the greenfly had been joined by blackfly. The bodies were still without wings and were trampling over each other to reach the leaf surface, to feed and suck the life out of the plant. Louis watched as the leaf withered under his gaze. The stem had been weakened too. The rose head was starting to droop, and the edges of the red petals were curling, turning brown and shrivelling back.

Louis stepped back to take in the whole picture and was saddened to see that all of them were affected.

An anxious yelp came from the middle of the field that Champ had entered. Suddenly, he charged out from the undergrowth and took refuge behind Louis.

Louis saw a large hawk gliding over the top of the grasses, coming towards them with the speed of a sports car. Its powerful wings supported its sleek body, while its deadly eye searched for its prey.

Oh, my God, thought Louis. Champ's under attack.

Katie was already batting at the bird, to divert its attention from their pet. A high-pitched shriek suddenly came from behind them. Another hawk was bearing down on them, with the same determination as the other. Danger was in the air. And fear returned. Hawks didn't hunt together; this was the work of an evil schemer.

With no time to think, Louis pushed Katie in front of him to the doorway. Champ was yapping and jumping up, trying to ward off the birds as they swooped at their backs. The door slammed shut behind them and the family was safe in the cottage.

'What's happening?' whispered Katie, looking pale and distressed.

Louis gathered her in his arms, holding her tight so she couldn't see the frown and furrowed lines on his forehead.

'I'm not sure. Something is influencing our kingdom.'

Louis kissed Katie's hair. Still holding her to him, he quietly told her not to worry, that, they would find a way through, whatever this was. Telling himself that he, too, had to believe that.

The things that had occurred in his kingdom were not of his world but that of the mortals. Louis was trying to make sense of what he had seen. Had the fabric that kept their worlds apart become so thin that the four worlds were sliding together and combining? Something like the equivalent of witchcraft was shaking up his little kingdom. There was only one answer: Malkira was involved.

A dreadful thought occurred to him. What if contact with the demon's scales had re-established Malkira in the netherworld? Was it a talisman that gave the demon access to his world? A feeling of panic stole over him. Louis had put the skin back in his pocket days ago. He hurriedly dipped his fingers into the deep pouch, probing to find the scales. He pulled the pocket inside out, shaking the fabric, but all he saw was a fine golden dust under his fingertips: it had disintegrated.

Champ was sitting patiently by the door; this was his usual position when he wanted to go outside. Time had moved on since they had rushed inside to seek the protection from the hawks. With no measure of time, Louis trusted Champ to know when it was safe to return to the garden.

'Are you sure?'

Champ was up on his feet, wagging his tail fifty to the dozen, his pink tongue and head flopped to one side. His mouth was open wide as if to smile confirmation, but to make his message even clearer, he stretched his neck upwards as if to enable his voice more power, and he barked a resounding 'Yes.'

A fresh breeze met Louis' face as he opened the door. His world looked calm and remarkably normal. The row of rose bushes looked pristine and were standing tall and fresh, their blooms robust and colourful in the bright light.

Intrigued, Louis went to inspect them. Whatever mischief had been at work was gone. No blight lingered, and the dying petals had been restored.

'Katie, come and look at these.'

She poked out her head from the doorway. An inquiring look filled her face.

'Is it really safe?'

'To that, I have no answer, but I do know the garden and your roses seem back to normal. No greenfly.'

Katie was wary, almost tiptoeing to reach Louis' side. Instinctively, he put his arm around her.

'See? They are all clear.'

As pleased as she was, she too felt a wariness.

'What do you think happened?'

'I honestly don't know. Unsettling as it is, this is where we live, and Champ is happy, so I think we can carry on as usual.'

Katie nodded; it did seem that the world was an oasis of peace again.

Despite telling Katie not to worry, there was a wariness in Louis as he walked to his workspace. With each step, he scanned his world and its horizon.

His sharp eyes locked on the tree. The health in the leaves and fruit was apparent. Satisfied, he picked up his tools and began to reshape the wood. A new thought was developing. How was he to portray this insight into how the worlds crisscrossed, connected by such thin barriers that spirits, good and bad, could cross and influence each other? The idea of the plane tree was discarded. Now he saw the four worlds, not necessarily in layers, but more as a collection of spaces connected rather like a rabbit warren, with tunnels that had exits and entrances and, perhaps, even a gatekeeper, at certain points. He thought about the birds, and the blight on the roses.

How had they entered his kingdom? It suggested that these doors might even move. He thought about the demon. Malkira had used the tree and the bedroom to enter and leave the different worlds. Why hadn't he realised that before? A new concept and a new challenge were born in his mind. It would be a multi-relief piece: tunnels that were fragile and paper thin that would include tree roots, clouds, planets. People, skeletons, ghosts, angels, cherubim. Animals and plants. The more he thought about the piece, the more complex it seemed to grow. Spirits of one kind or another were everywhere. It was just that for the most part, nobody saw them, expect for people like Julia. He was excited at the prospect of creating this piece.

Louis could hear Katie and Champ playing in the stream. The sound carried over the meadow, and it was lovely to hear. The sound of joy that came from them lifted his soul. In his blue sky, the red kite had put in an appearance. His kingdom for now, was back to normal.

Louis got down to reshaping the wood to invest in his new ideas. Working with blinkered concentration, he soon became so absorbed that he quite forgot about the attack of hawks and the demon. It was much later when he stopped to view his work and check himself. He had made good progress, and it was time to put down his tools; it had been a successful day and he had enjoyed the process. The wood had been kind and his idea was slowly materialising. He decided to sit for a while on the grassy knoll by his tree and watch the meadow. Louis found his eyes were closing as he watched the grasses waving hypnotically in the breeze. His eyelids became heavy; sleep was not far away. He shook himself awake. Was he being lured to the point of sleep? He was cross. It had been far too easy to think that Malkira would lose interest in them. Reason and logic told him to stay aware and alert.

He jumped with surprise and became fully awake when a dull thud sounded behind him. Turning quickly, he saw a small red object peering over a tree root. Louis' edginess was reawakened. He leaped to his feet and sprinted to find out what it was.

A large red apple had fallen from his tree and was wedged in between the risen roots. His fruit couldn't fall. This wasn't possible. Louis was in denial.

The apple lay on its side, offering Louis a view of rotting flesh. A circle of brown scarred the deep red on its skin. It was ugly, like a bruise, blemishing the beauty it had once held. Louis was in the process of picking it up when the skin split open and a dozen or so worms squirmed out of its centre.

Louis' face twisted in disgust. It appalled him.

What he didn't see was that one worm was less active than the others, and had stopped wiggling long enough to observe Louis' face. Its liquid blue eyes were focused on the downcast ghost and were full of guile and contempt for a second, before moving with the others. At lighting speed, they sped off in all directions, dropping into any holes or crevices they could find to disappear into. In seconds, all that was left in view was an eaten-out shell of the apple.

Louis could feel an ache at the base of his neck. His hand instantly rubbed the spot. Pain clawed at the back of his eyes. It was then he heard a silky, smooth voice in his head.

'So, you thought you were Adam? And she was your Eve? You are wrong, of course. I'll let you have a little guess who I am.' And an unearthly chuckle vibrated through Louis' body. 'I was there, in the beginning. But not by this name. Man was '*His*' experiment, not mine. We even had a wager which side man would turn to. That wager is still running.' The laugh grew louder. 'I am power: watch me.'

Immediately, the light in the kingdom faded. Louis looked up at his sky, which seemed to be losing its depth of blue. The sun had a grey haze around it and it was losing its heat.

He watched, powerless. The voice in his head was becoming louder and louder until Louis felt his skull might split. Both his hands were covering his ears as if he were trying to keep the voice out. He shut his eyes tight against the noise. He fell, because standing was no longer an option for him. He felt he might vomit, tightly curled in the grass, willing the voice to stop. When it did stop, it was so sudden, he hardly dared believe it had gone. Slowly he opened his eyes, gingerly looking at his world through slit eyelids. Bit by bit, he allowed his eyes to absorb the light. Very slowly he sat up, to test his own body, and saw more transformation.

The sky had changed again. Now it glowed in an orange and pink, announcing the coming of a storm. Louis didn't have to wait long; the atmosphere was becoming sultry and oppressive. From beyond the hills, a mass of purple and grey clouds was forming, growing like some monstrous mountain until the sky was completely obliterated.

A bitterly cold wind swept across the meadow, blowing ice shards at him that stung his eyes. The grasses were being forcibly flattered in front of him, and his thoughts turned to his family. Katie and Champ: where were they? It had been a long time since he had heard them playing in the stream. Louis was up onto his feet, running like he was being chased by bulls, down the track towards the cottage.

The first white ball hit him squarely on his head, the next on his shoulder, before a load discharged itself from the heavens. They physically hurt as he made his way to the sanctuary of the cottage. Hail the size of giant mothballs held his kingdom in its grasp. The ground was white with ice spheres, making his way more hazardous. He skidded and slipped over the ice until he reached the cottage door. It gave way at a tiny push, and he crashed though it into the living room, startling Katie and Champ. Louis was breathless, as he asked, 'Have you seen what's outside?' Katie looked nonplussed.

'Outside? No – should we?'

Going to the cottage window, she looked and shrugged her shoulders.

'What am I supposed to be seeing? It's a fine day out there.'

'What?' Louis scrambled to the window and then to the door. Only when he stood on the doorstep did he believe what he was seeing. His kingdom was pristine, not a leaf out of place. The meadow gracefully moved under a slight breeze; the sun was mellow and warm on his face.

Malkira was playing games with Louis' body and mind. There was no sign of a single hailstone and yet his back, shoulders and head told him a different story.

59

Malkira stretched out and yawned, as a pleasant thought came to his mind. Carl had crossed into Malkira's dark world as a child, a bullish teenager who wanted what he wanted and wanted it now. Darkness had been his friend. Selfishness was a such delicious sin.

Malkira enjoyed playing with souls; it was a bit like playing with your food and he did enjoy a tender heart.

Then he thought of her. He shuddered. Katie's tender heart fell into that category. He had nearly had her once. If only he hadn't mentioned Louis to her in the churchyard; that had been clumsy of him. He should have pressed and pursued the loss and separation she felt for her parents, then she might have been his. Had it not been for the love she had for Louis, he could have had her.

In fact, the more he thought about Louis, the more disgruntled he felt. He wanted to punish him for all his interference and the prey Louis had lost him. They had met before in a previous point in time. Their paths kept on crossing. Fate could be a bitch.

Louis seemed to get in the way a great deal. Debs was another victim he might have had, but Louis had protected her, even to the point of following Malkira into her dream and crashing in on Debs' rerun of her deepest fears. It had all been so delicious until he came strutting in.

He had interfered with Malkira's newest recruit, Carl, as well, when he was enjoying a little playfulness with the redhead Julia. She had escaped because of Louis and then he had frightened Carl rigid with a few tricks. It was a pity Carl was weak. Bullies didn't like being bullied. He sent his little grey helpers to come to Carl's aid, once Louis had left the scene. He always won in the end.

A shiver of irritation rattled down Malkira's back. If that wasn't enough, Louis had turned up again when Carl and he were feeding on Sandra's fear. He had broken the sport, the game and sent for reinforcements. Guardian angels no less.

His army had been burned and scattered. Louis would pay for that.

His tail flicked in anger, curling on a rock. He lifted it and flung it at no-one in particular. By some chance, the spectre of Carl was hiding in a corner, and it hit him squarely in his mid-section. There was no sound, no cry. It passed through him: he was fully a creature of the underworld.

A satisfied look and a deep sigh exited from the snake's mouth. Malkira buried himself even further into his rocky crevice bed. Settling down in thought, as his forked tongue licked his lips, he was satisfied with his first two sorties on the kingdom. Did Louis think he could get away with diverting his precious prey, those that were his by right? Not a chance in hell.

His one blip on the horizon was that cottage in the kingdom. He couldn't touch it nor anyone in it. Sophia had never invited him into it, and, without an invitation, it was off limits. Usually there was a way, but he had not found it yet.

He puffed up his cheeks. He would have Katie's soul, and the dog's too, and feed off them in his underworld kingdom, but first Louis must watch as he, Malkira, twisted the knife and destroyed Louis' sanctuary.

60

The kingdom was under threat, and he was too. Louis knew he was no match for an evil predator, especially a deity. There was a huge amount of mental pressure hanging over him, never knowing when Malkira was going to appear and send havoc into Louis' peaceful world.

Malkira was hunting for him and must be enjoying the pursuit. Twice now, Malkira had shown his power; twice he had sent and bent nature into a spiral of harm that was out of the character of his kingdom. Malkira's evil didn't belong in the shelter of his netherworld.

The kingdom was the only place to spend eternity with Katie, and it wasn't safe, not now. It seemed like they were on borrowed time here, but until he could find the way out, through the hills and over the moor, they were stuck. Louis was on tenterhooks waiting for the next visit.

The moor was calling to Louis; his daily walks were getting longer and longer, but no matter how many paths he took over the hills, he always ended being blocked by the invisible screen when he got to the edge of the moor. It was tantalising to stand looking at the brink of another world he couldn't get to. Twenty times he had stared at the golden light that glowed on the horizon. It was only a modest walk away if he could only find an opening to get through. Twenty times he had seen the stag and the red kite: this was their moor. On the first few sightings of the stag, the animal stayed way off, but on each consecutive visit, it was almost like the stag recognised him. In the last two of his hikes, though not finding that elusive gateway, the stag had actually come up close to the barrier and observed him. His antlers were at least two thirds of the beautiful beast's height; its long eyelashes framed eyes that were as black as obsidian, and seemed ponderous as the stag stared at him. Was there an inquiry within them? And was there a cryptic message that he didn't understand? Regardless, he felt he had a connection with the beast. If only it would show him the path to that gateway, or indeed its companion, the red kite, that was never far away from the beast.

Katie's face was full of hope when Louis returned from the hills, but she quickly read his face and recognised that, once again, his had been a fruitless trip.

'I'm beginning to think there is no way through. I saw the stag again today and the bird. He's magnificent, Katie, and is not afraid of me. He stood inches away from me today, almost measuring me up. It's like someone is tormenting me, teasing me, with a vision of hope telling me it's safe on that side, but locking me out.'

His constant disappointment affected her. How was she to help him? He mustn't give up, for she too feared Malkira.

'It will be alright. You'll find a way for us.' She smiled at him reassuringly, but her spirit and hope were crushed. It did seem that they were destined to remain here and be tested by the demon.

Katie didn't seem to want to admit that she was frightened. She put on a brave face each day, determined not to be a coward. She tended the garden with the same tenderness she always had and fed her roses with love. She walked with Champ, and still paddled in the stream with him. But there was a sense of sadness that had crept into the cottage when they were all together. This had been a place of love and sanctuary but not anymore.

She had never thought they would be separated from his kingdom. After all, they had both rejected the light, the doorway for the soul to rest, to be together. She knew that Louis was looking to escape his own world if he could find the way, but would they be accepted in another place? Not knowing what they would find on the moor and beyond was as frightening, in some ways, as the visits from the demon.

When Louis wasn't walking the hills, he spent time his time carving. It was the one task that allowed him to forget the pressure he was under. He was in the middle of a particularly fine and intricate wall that represented the thin fabric between the worlds, when a sudden scream jerked him back into the moment on the edge of the knoll, with his tools in his hands.

Champ had joined the cry of distress Louis could hear coming from the stream. His barking was of a nervous nature, quick yaps of a warning and then whining. Above all of that, Louis heard weeping.

Abandoning his tools, he ran towards the disturbance, covering the short distance quickly. What he saw when he arrived was beyond anything he could have imagined. Katie was barefoot and sitting on the bank with tears flowing, staring into the water. Champ greeted Louis with a howl before he bounded up to him and tried to herd him to Katie's side. She didn't move as he came up beside her; it was only when he dropped down beside her and took her hand, that she responded.

'Look.' Her face was pale, and her tearful eyes were registering deep, deep shock. His eyes followed hers. His bubbling stream was now still, with no movement in the water, and it had turned a garish green in colour, its rush of energy gone. A blanket of scum clung to the water's edge, while clumps of green algae grew and lay under its surface. Small silver flashes like precious treasure moved but couldn't escape the weeds' stranglehold, but most of the fish were already dead. The white bellies of dead, long-legged frogs floated on top of the devilish scum, along with water voles whose large eyes stared sightlessly out of their dead bodies, which were massing near their nests in the bank.

'It all happened so fast.' Katie could hardly take a breath, her sobs were so deep. 'We were playing like always. The water – normally so cold – started to warm up. At first, I thought it was the sun, but it became warmer and warmer, until it was uncomfortable to stand in. I got out. Champ followed. By the time I had scrambled onto the bank, the stream had stopped moving. As I watched, some evil magic took over and everything started to die.'

She crumpled then, falling gratefully into Louis' arms for comfort.

Louis was sickened at the sight before him. This tragedy was beyond any help he could give.

'Come on, my darling girl. Time to go home.'

Katie didn't argue. He helped her to her feet and, gathering up her shoes, together they walked to the cottage in silence.

It was much later when Louis slipped out of the cottage. Twice the demon had set a stage of disaster in the kingdom and then restored it back instantly. Katie was still upset at what she had seen. Louis was on his way to check the stream, hoping that it also would follow the same pattern.

His steps became heavier and slower the nearer he got to the stream. He couldn't hear any fast-flowing water; it was all too quiet. A thick, sickly smell greeted him as he got nearer to the stream, and with it, foul air. A new sound met his ears. He nosed forward over the green grasses and looked ahead: a black mass was moving up and down over the still water. He didn't need to go any further, the buzzing was loud from the hundreds of flies that were feeding on the carcasses that lay in the thick soup below them. It made him want to vomit. He couldn't be here; the vile poisoning of his stream distressed him intensely. His stomach churned as he walked quickly away from the smell of death and towards his tree of life.

Dizzily, he sat under the tree, thoughts cramming in his brain as he wondered if all his control had been usurped by Malkira. It was logical to put his own ability to create to the test and see if his imagination could still make things happen? He couldn't go back to the cottage with bad news…

He sat pondering the scene he had left. The first thing was to get rid of the flies. With a great deal of effort, he brought the scene back to mind, clear and sharp, and then erased the flies from it. Of course, the proof would be when he went back to the stream, but not yet. Now he set about cleansing the water, seeing it run from the hills, cold and fresh, bringing with it new life and energy. He closed his eyes. This was hard. He kept seeing the desecration in the water, and he had to clear his mind of that. Slowly, he started to envision the stream reverting back to its normal self. The green scum was wiped away first. Then he saw the water voles, peeking out from their hidden homes in the sandy bank, above the bubbling water. His creation was starting to come together. He concentrated on the next stage. He saw the frogs astride the larger pebbles, sunning themselves, and the small sticklebacks and tiddlers were playing hide and seek in the reeds. He closed his eyes and prayed.

A sound came to his ears from over the meadow. The water was playing its melody again as it swept down the stream.

Before congratulating himself, Louis was back on his feet. He needed to evaluate the scene before taking his findings back to Katie. With hope and fresh confidence, he followed the sound of its music until he was teetering on the bank edge, looking down into clear water. A beaming smile filled his face. It was as he hoped, and his smile somehow reflected the width of water that stretched out edge to edge in front of him with the sun playing on the ripples. He was filled with the beauty of it and was ready to laugh out loud, when the deep croak of a frog, sitting on a small rock, made him jump. It was just as he had imagined it. A water vole swam out of the reeds and disappeared into the bank under his feet. Everything was perfect, and he yelled with success.

Overjoyed, he walked to the cottage. The landscape – his landscape – had never looked better. It was possible that he might never be so happy again. The good news, the special news, was that he could tell Katie that it was possible he could reverse all the evil with his own gift of creation, and that the demon could be thwarted.

The great sigh of satisfaction that left Louis' lungs was heard in the deep recesses of the underworld. The demon, in reptilian guise, was sleeping in his favourite crevice when the sigh reverberated around the cavern, disturbing him. His eyes flicked open and Malkira's forked tongue tasted the air, guiding his senses to the point of disquiet. Something or someone had altered the order he had prescribed. His sixth sense and his third eye spied on the kingdom.

The ghost sat under the tree, his face was filled with light and happiness. It was disgusting; it turned Malkira's stomach. He couldn't feed on that. Why was his prey looking so pleased? And then Malkira heard it too. The stagnant water, the stillness of death was gone. His wonderful game of taunting them had been broken: the water was running clean again. How had Louis done it? And how dare he? But he knew, it was that dammed creative light that the ghost was filled with, a gift from his opposite number. So, the ghost had found power again, but it would be a hollow victory, that he was sure of.

Malkira focused on the ghost. He read every molecule, every hair. He breathed in the way Louis sat, how he was dressed from his shirt to his boots.

Malkira uncurled himself and, lying back against a rock, focusing on the ghost, he started bit by bit to transform himself into the image he saw. The dark hair that insisted on flopping over the brow. The right colour brown for the eyes. The hand size was important, too. Katie would see through his deception if he didn't get it perfect. He had heard Louis speak and could mimic any voice when he chose to. It was getting the words right; that was always the key to a good impersonation.

Keeping an eye on Louis, Malkira slid into the kingdom when Louis walked to check on the stream. Coming up through the roots was no problem for him. Now he had to get to the cottage before Louis arrived there.

This he knew would be the test. He called out Katie's name as he came through the garden, and she hurried to the door to let him in.

Invited, he burst into the cottage out of breath and, looking miserable, he gathered a scared-looking Katie into his arms. Champ whined and was clearly unhappy at him holding Katie. He used the warning that Champ was trying to give her for his own ends.

'We must go, and quickly, my darling girl. Malkira has blighted the kingdom. Death is all around us – birds and rabbits are lying in heaps on the tracks. See, even Champ is trying to tell you: we need to go.'

'Go where?' There was a strain in her voice. 'You didn't find a way to the moor – are we to go into the Royal?'

'No, no, I didn't tell you, but on my last walk I founds some caves, high in the hills. We can hide there while I continue to search for that gateway. I must have you safe.'

Malkira grabbed her hand and hurried her out and up the track towards the moor. She mustn't see his lie; she mustn't hear the water. Her sadness was delightful and he was already starting to feed on her.

Malkira was pleased with himself. He was quite ecstatic and preened himself, cloaked in Louis' disguise. He ran his fingers through his dark locks, pushing back the straggle of hair that fell loose over his forehead. He was having fun. His deception was so delicious: Katie hadn't made the connection that he wasn't Louis, and they had been walking for some time. She had even told the dog to stop whining when, in Champ's own way, he tried to tell her something was far from right. Malkira smiled broadly, before he remembered not to expose his mouth for fear that he might reveal his forked tongue. Katie mustn't see that; at least, not yet.

'Come on, my darling girl, we're almost there. He'll never find us in the caves.'

Katie was panting; it had been a long pull up the hill. Louis seemed to have a surfeit of stamina and energy that she longed for. Only Champ kept up to Louis' pace.

Staggering over undergrowth that was testing her balance, she asked, in between breaths, 'How much further?'

'Be patient, we are nearly there and then I will reveal all.'

'But how will it stop a demon from finding us?

'I'll tell you when we get there.' And he turned back to the climb.

Malkira felt her uneasiness and yet knew she trusted his guise as Louis.

She followed him, with Champ whimpering from time to time by her side, as if trying to slow her down, but she kept up the pace. After another one hundred and fifty yards or so, Malkira stopped in front of a large bush that was shielding two large rocks.

'Well, here we are.'

'Here we are? What do you mean?'

Malkira pushed past the tree and seemed to disappear.

'Louis, where are you?' Katie stood shocked and nervous.

A disconnected voice came from behind the rock. 'Just squeeze through the gap between the tree and rock. I tell you, he'll never find us here.'

Katie moved slowly, inching her way towards Louis' invitation. Champ had other ideas. He backed away, still whining, low in his throat.

'Come on, boy, it's alright,' she tried to reassure him, as she moved behind the tree. But instead of obeying, he barked twice, turned tail and ran back the way they had come.

'Louis, Champ's run off.'

'Not to worry. He'll be back.'

As she moved behind the rock, she encountered a hidden slope; stumbling, she fell into a narrow cave, rolling down another slope into its darkness.

Stomach-crunching vibrations ran though her body as she was pitched forward. She abruptly stopped rolling when she reached the flat and sat up. The cave was dark and claustrophobic, the jagged rock on its sides seemed to close in and then move out, threatening her slight body. She supposed it was all in her head and shut her eyes to keep the movement out. Then she thought of tons of rock surrounding her, above her and below, and she was suddenly overwhelmed and very frighted.

'Louis, where are you?' Her voice echoed, coming back eight times from deep within the cave. How far did the tunnel run? And where was he? Her eyes searched in the darkness. It would seem that being in spirit meant she could see in the dark, and Louis was nowhere in sight. Her head throbbed.

She felt she was inside a nightmare, and she wanted to get out back into the sun. Her legs were like jelly and didn't want to move and, even if they did, which way was out? From this flat space, both sides of the tunnel went uphill. Which should she choose? Fear had started small in a chink in her heart; it grew in the darkness until it filled the space.

Sitting miserably in the tunnel, not moving, was no good. She had to squash her fear and find a way out. Champ had run out on her, and

Louis seemed to have abandoned her – unless, of course, he had got lost in the caves too. Yes, that was it. She reassured herself that he must be somewhere further on in the tunnel. Turning onto her hands and knees, she pushed herself up. The ceiling was lower than she thought, and she brushed her head on the roof. Her fear of small places came rushing back.

Crawling on her hands and knees, she made her decision to make her way up the tunnel on her right, hoping she would find either Louis or daylight. It was strange that the rock under her hands and knees felt quite warm; she would have expected it to be cold with no light or sun. But, dismissing the sensation, she moved on; she had more pressing things to occupy her mind right then.

As she crawled uphill, the cave grew larger until she found she was walking upright, but she still felt panic. Although the cave had levelled off and her route was easier, she had no idea where she would end up. Was she going in the right direction? she wondered.

A warm summer breeze hit her face as she rounded a corner, and a glow of unnatural light, illumined the path in front of her. The walls had horizonal stripes running on either side of her. Some were inches deep; others were narrow slivers of colour: blue, ochre and gold. They glinted, winking at her, inviting her along. Above her head, intermittent small pockmarks grew into small shards hanging down. They looked like icicles, but they were rock. Silver particles shone in them, sparkling – it was almost like looking at stars in a blue-grey sky.

She was walking downhill now; the tunnel became a cave and then a cavern. Stalactites hung like huge chandeliers across the cathedral-like space. A voice carried over the void.

Malkira had abandoned his disguise back in the tunnels and melted into the rock. He had played a game of power with Katie, moving the walls to frighten her, and it had the desired effect. Katie was already vulnerable and shivering with fear in his lair, and that made her worthwhile prey to use or feed on, whichever came first. She had arrived on cue, and he changed his disguise back to Louis.

'There you are! I wondered when you would get here?'

Her heart leaped when she viewed the cavern. In the middle of the floor, Louis was sitting on a granite throne-like structure.

'Louis.'

You could hear the joy in her voice. Malkira held his laughter in; it was not yet the time to expose the farce. She ran, unafraid, to his arms, clinging to him, her fear quelled.

'Why didn't you wait for me?'

'I had to get ahead to see to him.'

A body moved in the shadows behind them. A thin, skeletal, emaciated wretch pushed up, until it was standing, and glared at her with a ghoulish grin.

'You remember Carl?'

It was as though she had been stung by a wasp. She flinched and tried to move, but Malkira had her tight in his grasp. He released the laughter he had been holding and, still holding her, he discarded his disguise. Katie watched in horror as the face of the man she loved turned into that of the demon.

Katie screamed.

61

The door was ajar when Louis reached it. It was odd that neither Katie nor Champ was waiting for him. Usually, Champ would greet him as he came up the path.

He had left them curled up together on the sofa, Katie cuddling Champ for comfort. He quickly passed from room to room, but there was no sight of them. Then he thought, what if Katie had been fretting about the stream and had gone to check it? But he dismissed the thought as quickly as it had come. Surely, he would have passed her on the way here. And where was Champ? Could they have gone for a walk in the hills? It was possible, but unlikely. She might be at their tree with Champ. That was altogether more feasible.

Louis hurried back through the meadow, following the track toward the knoll and his tree. No matter how he stretched his neck to see better, he couldn't see them at their special spot, but perhaps they were lying down. He was clutching at straws, and he knew it. His happiness had evaporated. Now, a queasy, unsettled feeling overcame him. Panic urged him to call their names. Champ would hear, even if they had gone in the direction of the hills. And shout he did, over and over, until he realised it was futile. When he finally reached the knoll, no one was sitting under the tree.

No one had answered his call. No sound came back from the surrounding landscape. His kingdom was eerily quiet. He remembered the time in his past when he had spent a century or more alone in his kingdom. No-one had been there to share his loneliness; a savage shiver drove though his body as he remembered the feeling of madness that ruled him, until he found he could connect with mortals. He found he was trembling; he couldn't envisage his existence without his family. They had to be somewhere nearby.

Distressed, Louis' legs gave way under him, and he sank to the grass.

His eyes searched his kingdom, desperate to spot something that would direct him to them. Suddenly a gut-wrenching tug pulled at his heart. Katie was in trouble. He knew it.

He hadn't heard anything, but he knew that Katie had connected with him somehow. It was hard to pinpoint where the sense of her might be, but, instinctively, he looked towards the hills. He saw the red kite circling above a wooded ridge, an area he still had to visit. It was back again. It seemed to visit often – was it a sign? His spirit reached out to her. He was relieved that he could sense her, until he felt her fear.

'Oh, my darling girl, where are you?' He heard his own words and wondered what had happened to her. He took himself to task: he should have been there for her, protected her; instead, he had left her at the cottage. He needed to get out into the landscape and continue his search. He had to start somewhere – why not where the red kite circled?

A small swirl of dust caught his eye down the track. Louis stood up to get a clearer view. More dust rose and an excited yap announced the incoming pet. Louis' heart took a leap. As he watched, his dog rushed up the track and practically sprang at him, bowling him over in greeting.

However, the greeting was brief, for, almost immediately, Champ was nuzzling him, butting his legs to move him down the track. Louis was being rounded up and led. Champ must have been with Katie, and he was going to take him to her.

Champ moved fast, running down the track, stopping now and then to check that Louis was following. Louis was moving fast, too, but had trouble keeping up.

Running through the trees, Louis was aware he had an onlooker above his head. The kite followed the same path that they were using, watching them from above the treetops. It struck Louis that the kite might be guiding them, perhaps in tune with Champ, and sharing information with him. Louis hoped so. Any help was gratefully received to get him to the right place.

It was quite a climb, and Louis was relieved when Champ suddenly stopped and lay down in front of a large bush. Louis heard the squeal from the kite from above.

'It would seem we've arrived, but where?'

Champ whimpered and stood, once Louis was beside him. Moving low to the ground, Champ moved stealthily forward between a bush and a outcrop of rocks behind it. Suddenly, he disappeared, before making a small yelp and reappearing. Louis assumed that there must be some sort of hidden opening behind the bush. Was Katie trapped there? With some urgency, he patted Champ on the head, stepping forward.

'Clever boy.' Louis moved eagerly, pushing low branches to one side, hearing them twang as they bounced back. The space was narrow, but Champ followed, crawling low. Taking several steps, he came to a rock that had a dark gap, close to the ground.

Eager to investigate, he was about to crawl into the space when the red kite, that had trailed them silently, swooped down and landed at Louis' feet. Frowning and surprised, Louis took a step backward. The bird's dark eyes were bright and intelligent; there was no fear in them. It opened its wings in front of the gap, barring his way. The eyes somehow bade a warning. It was as though the mind of the bird and his own connected.

'Think long. Danger is abroad in this place.'

'You don't understand. If Katie is in there, I have to go. She is my soulmate, my love. You must not stop me.' The bird shook its feathers and folded its wings.

'Take Champ with you.'

'Who are you?'

The bird put its head on one side. Its eyes suddenly became more animated and human, but there was no answer. Then it was gone. It was as though Champ, also, had been privy to the telepathy. He was back at Louis' heels.

62

Even with his spiritual eyes, he was partially blinded coming from the light into the dark tunnel. The space was cramped, with a low ceiling that threatened his head as he moved forward. Warily, Champ was at his heel.

He wasn't expecting the drop that opened up like a booby-trap. He fell headlong into a deepish hole. Lying on the bottom, on cold stone, he felt he was being enveloped in the evil, and, from the darkness, the vile atmosphere was seeping down and surrounding him.

Champ had jumped across the void and was now whimpering, looking down on his master, unsure for a moment what to do, mentally urging Louis to get out.

'It's okay, boy, I'll be with you in a moment.' Louis felt the smooth sides of the trap and he realised it was going to be an awkward climb to get out. He gripped the edge, grabbing on to a lip of rock, and started to pull himself up. His strength was tested but, with perseverance, he managed to get his knee high enough to crawl over its edge, much to the joy of Champ.

'Okay, we are going to have to be more careful, right, Champ?'

A tiny yelp confirmed the dog's agreement.

The tunnel seemed to be alive, and changed as he walked. The downward gradient was rough and stony underfoot, but the walls seemed to move, changing the shape of the tunnel as he moved forward. He knew the tunnel was under the influence of Malkira. He could sense the evil in the body of the rocks. The wall's surfaces started developing clefts and nodules, and there were sounds somewhere ahead that could have been the beating of wings,

Louis was nervous, but there was no way on this earth, or in hell, that his love for Katie would fall short. He was driven forward; he had to find her.

A vile voice entered his subconsciousness. 'You're so easy to read, Louis. For all your love and light, it is I who have the power.' He heard the laughter of madness loud in his head. 'I have her. Carl likes her, too. I do hope you'll join us soon. Perhaps even before Carl has had time to play with her.'

The next sound of laugher that entered his mind travelled through him, rocking him to one side. As Louis opened his mouth with pain, the laugh was set free from his body, escaping and bouncing off the walls. It was so loud that it knocked him to the floor. Scrabbling in the dirt and stones, with his hands pressing on his ears to stifle the noise, it took him a while before he could stand again once the sound had dissipated.

Louis reached out, steadying himself against the wall. He took a second to reassess the tunnel. A faint glow was inviting him forward and he realised that the height of the space had grown. He looked back to where he had come from and the trap that he had crawled out of had disappeared. The whole tunnel was constantly changing.

There was only one way to go and that was forward. The pebbly surface crunched with each step, and the glow at the end of the tunnel was growing and moving to meet him. The nodules on the walls were reshaping too. In the light, some seemed to be evolving into rough human facial images. Louis was shocked when, coming up to one, it projected itself in his way, stopping him in his tracks. It was the face of his murderous wife, Sophia. He heard her voice mocking him. The stone portrait opened its eyes and, although, he knew she was dead, her forget-me-not blue eyes were staring at him.

'You always were a fool, husband. You're walked straight into his trap because of love. I'm so pleased Malkira has robbed you of Katie. She will become his, just as I did.'

The eyes closed and the image resettled on the tunnel's wall. He moved on but was met by another face. Faces from his past, people he had loved, now dead and gone, were lined up on view. Multiple voices crowded into his subconscious: it was garbled, noisy and muddled. He was unable to decipher what they were telling him. His own thoughts took over, drowning them out. He repeated, over and over again, the same refrain and kept moving.

He's trying to delay you from finding Katie.

Louis rushed past the gallery of portraits from his past, and as he left the last image behind, a new glow moved towards him until he was within the glow. Hundreds of insects, fireflies, lighting bugs and glow-worms swarmed as he moved forward, trying to find a way through. He was blinded. Champ pushed his muzzle into Louis' leg. Feeling his pet, Louis reached down, catching hold of the dog at the scruff of the neck. Louis trusted him, and with his eyes closed tight, he allowed Champ to walk him further down the tunnel to the relative safety.

A few of the bugs and insects still clung to Louis' clothes. He brushed them off and ran his hands through his hair until he was free of bugs. As for Champ, his thick fur and long eyelashes had pretty much protected him, and a good shake got rid of the odd remaining stowaways.

The tunnel was becoming awkward to negotiate. Its downward gradient suddenly increased again, making Louis slip and slide. Champ, however, with his four feet squarely on the ground, was making headway without a missed step. Movement above Louis' head made him suddenly duck. A grey harpy slid from the cracks in the ceiling and shockingly aimed its threatening teeth at Louis' uncovered neck. Louis lost his footing again and slid downhill. More harpies dropped like bats from the roof. The menace chased him, but Champ, with a jaw of equally sharp teeth and strong hind legs, was leaping up and keeping them at bay from his downed master.

The floor suddenly levelled off, and Louis came to a stop just inches from the entrance to a huge cavern. He clenched his teeth and covered his head with his arms as he heard the mass of evil that travelled behind him. But, to his surprise, the harpies ignored him, their job presumably done by herding him to the cavern. They flew over his head and down into a deep basin. At the instruction of Malkira's waving arms, they flew once around his throne before flying over to the far side of the cavern and disappearing.

Louis was amazed at the scene they had brought him to. The cavern reminded him of a stage set in a theatre, or a huge art gallery, with splendid sculptures hanging from the roof. The walls with the horizonal stripes of blue quartz and gold were magnificent, but it contrasted with the atmosphere that was heavy with evil and the odour of something rotten.

Louis could see Malkira looking relaxed, sitting cross-legged on a stone throne. To the left of it, in an alcove, Katie was locked in the arms of the almost unrecognisable Carl. Both were sitting on the cavern floor. Katie looked frozen with fear, as Carl, seeing Louis looking on, extended his tongue from his grinning mouth and ran it up her cheek as through he was sampling something sweet. Louis could see her squirming as she was held fast. It turned his stomach.

'Come and join us.' The demon, in his beautiful angel's guise, looked genuinely welcoming as he taunted Louis. 'I think she likes him.' The smirk was wide, and his forked tongue licked his lips.

'Did you enjoy my little surprises? I did so want you to feel my warm invitation.' Malkira chuckled. It was as deep as a rumbling volcano, and the ground shook a little under Louis' feet, loosening a few pebbles that rolled before him down the incline.

A sudden change in the voice implied a real menace, showing his true nature, when, with a leer on his face and a raised eyebrow, he announced, 'I'm going to enjoy devouring Katie' – he paused to emphasise the last few words – 'while you watch. And before I give you to Carl. It's been a while since he ate.'

The creature in the alcove suddenly took notice, and a large smile crossed the skeleton-like face. Malkira's apprentice nodded, energetically.

'No,' cried Katie.

'Oh yes,' returned Malkira.

Champ had stayed back and low. His instinct warned him of the danger. He did not move when Louis started to make his way down into the body of the cavern. He was on his guard and listening intently. He crawled forward to the mouth of the cavern and watched. Nobody saw him. His nose was sniffing the air and his sharp eyes were looking for a way out as he viewed the landscape. His ears pricked up when he heard a familiar sound of the musical rhythm of water running over stones on the far side of the cavern. Was it an underground stream? He needed to investigate to see if there was a way out.

Louis stepped forward. A slope offered the only way down to the waiting deity. There was no way back and it seemed there was no way out. Malkira and Carl, who only seemed to know about pain and death, were waiting, and despite hating what he saw, he wondered how these creatures could never have known something as precious as love. As he walked down the slope towards he knew not what, it struck him that they probably thought him a simpleton and a fool. He didn't care. It was true he had walked into this trap because of love, but he knew that whatever happened, they couldn't take the love he held for Katie away. He looked at Katie, squirming in the arms of a monster, the horror and fear of it written over her face, and his blood ran cold.

Louis' father came into his mind. Massie had once told him of a journey he would take and warned him that Katie would be put in danger. Was this it? He rather thought it was. He remembered Massie's advice to ask the angels for help and they would come to his aid. An inner voice spoke to Louis: 'Trust the angels.' In a leap of faith that connected him to the true light, he stopped and called out, his voice echoing down into the vastness, as he repeated the phase.

'Please help us, Angel of light. Please help us.'

What Louis expected he wasn't sure. The echo brought his voice back to him, but nothing more happened, making him feel foolish. His hopes had started high, but then they dropped like a stone. He felt the crush of defeat, Katie would be sacrificed.

Malkira's voice rose from the cavern's floor.

'Don't take it too hard, Louis. I always win.' The smug look on the demon's face made Louis feel sick. In his heart, he had always believed that light would beat darkness, that good would overcome evil; in an act of defiance, he shouted at the gloating devil as he reached the caverns floor.

'You may take our souls, but you can never destroy our love.' Louis was nearing Katie and he turned to face her. 'I love you,' he shouted. 'Always.'

Malkira was grimacing at the declaration of love in his domain. Filled with anger, he rose to his full height. It was time to punish these lovers for their interference and the loss of his prey in the Royal. Dinner time was overdue, and he was beginning to lick his lips.

The red kite came from nowhere. It swooped down in front of Malkira, using its wings as a shield between Malkira and Louis. Carl, shocked at the winged interloper, jumped up to help his master, and, in the process, released Katie.

Carl came up behind the bird in a foolish attempt to grab the large, beating wings. Several feet of feather power knocked him to the ground by its strength, and Carl remained there, cowering in fear. His face was utterly confused, seeing the predicament that Malkira was in: one that he couldn't help.

Malkira was shouting instructions and obscenities at the bird in equal measure, and Carl was confused, not sure which instructions were for him.

'Get out of the way.'

'Come to this side, Carl.' Malkira was gesturing to him, while still shouting at the red kite. 'Away, you winged immortal – this is my world. Go back to your own.'

It was all to no avail; the bird guarded Louis while pecking at the demon.

The more Malkira tried to evade the bird, the more aggressive it became. The red kite beak targeted the demon's head and eyes, distracting Malkira all it could. Its wings were swirling, beating so hard it made a windstorm from them. That wind warped and caused small twisters, that turned into whirlwinds, to dance across the cavern floor. The rush of the wind and the beating of the wings had captured Malkira's and Carl's attention. Louis, seeing a possible moment to escape, grabbed Katie by the hand and guided her behind him.

Carl seemed still unsure as to what to do; should he help his master or recapture the woman? In the end, he did neither. Instead, he crawled under the beating wings to get out of its way, before getting on his feet and running to his alcove to hide. The dog watched and waited. The bird that he had connected with was holding the demon at bay; now it was his turn to help and he had run fleet-footed to their side, nudging Louis and Katie in the direction of the water he had heard on the other side of the cavern.

Without Malkira's power to protect him, the bird and the dog were more than Carl could manage. He sank into a heap and hid his face, covering his ears to block out the noise. He glanced only once to see Malkira take charge of the phenomenon before shutting his eyes.

Malkira eyed the twisters and, by his dark power, he ordered them to join as one. Obeying, one merged with another and then another, creating a cyclone that grew as large as the cavern. It rose in the air, crashing into the stalactites, causing them to fall and smash into thousands of pieces on the stony floor.

The rumble of collapse was heard behind the fleeing couple with their dog, and grew more ominous and loud as the three of them rushed towards the far side of the cavern led by Champ.

When they were halfway across the vast floor with the noise and rising dust seemingly gaining on them, they heard the muffled sound of wings. Louis turned and saw the bird gaining on them, it moved fast and straight until it was alongside; then, quickly and gracefully, it was moving in front of them, leading the way.

There was no time to stop but, looking back once more, Louis saw what he could only conceive as hell. Pure destruction was taking place behind them. The scale of it was enormous, and panic set in as the huge twister was gaining speed in their direction. And the bird that had been leading them had disappeared.

Beyond, and through a mist of grit, by some strange chance of fate Louis caught sight of the demon. He was disappearing into a tunnel. It could have been the alcove that held Carl, at this distance he couldn't know. There was no sign of Carl. Louis could only conclude that he had left the cavern first.

Louis pushed forward. The cavern that had looked so splendid in its blue and gold was nothing more than rocks and black soil Any gold and blue quartz must have been the demon's illusion, or dismantled by the demon as he left.

The noise and the dust had reached its peak, but the twister was losing its power and size, fizzling out through lack of energy. It dropped into the rocks and grit that were strewn on the cavern floor. Malkira most likely had taken its power when he left.

Louis didn't know if safety was ahead, though logic told him that the bird had found a way in, and if there was a way in, then there must be a way out.

As if answering his question, a shaft of sunlight suddenly lit the end of the cavern, shining on the underground stream. This must be what Champ had wanted to bring them to. The stream was narrow, running through the edge of the cavern, and didn't look deep. Slabs of stone edged the water as it bubbled up slowly from between the rocks in the wall. Louis wondered if this was the source of his stream. Champ was able to jump to the other side of it while Louis and Katie felt the full strength of the cold water as they waded across, hoping to find a way out to the sunlight there. Louis followed the line of the stream and saw, sadly, that it went underground. There was no exit to be found there but, once across, Louis walked the wall and could see a ledge running diagonally upwards. It was narrow but it looked climbable with care, and up above his head, near the ceiling, he saw an opening that was showing a blue, blue sky. His heart filled with gratitude at the sight: it was the way out, the way the bird used to escape.

Champ was already ahead of them, making his way to the sunlight, climbing the ledge with confidence. Louis nodded to himself; he, too, was eager to be free of the underground cavern and to see his kingdom in the sun.

With great relief, Louis remembered and thanked the angels. Far from not hearing him and doing nothing he felt they had sent the bird to help him. Then, taking Katie's face in his hands, he kissed her.

'Ready? My darling girl.'

'Oh yes.' And she kissed him back.

He took by her hand and he lifted his gaze to that blue that was his, and led her to safety.

63

As they climbed out into the sunlight, the red kite was waiting for them. He was sitting on a low branch, his bright eyes observing their joy at being free from the cavern and its dark master. He watched them collapse, breathless, on the ground some yards away from the cavity that they had just crawled through. The exit was at the topmost point of the blue hills; Louis' kingdom lay below them, looking splendid in the sun and before them, stretching out to the golden glow of its horizon, were the greens and purple heathers of the moors.

Relief showed in their faces, and Champ, encouraged by being in the sun again, was almost dancing as he leapt about. That quickly changed when they heard a crash underground, followed by a large dust cloud expelled in the shape of a mushroom, climbing into the air from the cavern. Exhausted, they moved further up the brow, further away from the hole, fearing a collapse under them.

The red kite lifted into the air, rising over the bushes and taking to the moors. Louis followed the flight and watched it land near the stag whom he had seen many times on his visits to the hills. The pair always seemed to be together.

The stag was standing proud, with his dark eyes studying their small group. Louis was excited. Perhaps this was the gateway? He jumped up and ran over the rough grasses to the edge of the moorland. The gateway had eluded him so many times before – surely this was the place? He was just a step away from the heather; he moved forward, palms up in a pushing movement. He tried to press through, but his hand met an invisible force. The barrier remained and held him back.

He slowly stepped back into his kingdom, his disappointment visible on his face. Shaking his head, his brows in a deep frown told the story. Katie came and stood by his side and together they looked to the horizon. The golden glow was just as tantalising as Louis had described it.

She took his hand. 'What are we going to do?'

'We'll carry on searching.'

'We have to leave. That devil is not going to let us be.' Katie's voice was low and stressed.

'I know.' Louis was resigned to losing his kingdom. 'Waiting for him to attack us, even if I can repair the damage he does, will make life here uncertain and miserable. We should ask the angels for help.'

'We should. They came to our help at the Royal. Do you think they will help us in this netherworld?'

'I believe they heard me in the cavern. We can but try and ask them again.'

Side by side they sat, their arms around each other, staring at the golden light as if viewing a sunset.

'Do you think that is the other place for souls?'

'I hope so; the light is so beautiful. I can only think it is.'

Katie aware that the stag and bird hadn't moved a muscle but seemed to be observing the three of them on the kingdom's side of this world.

'Why are those creatures still watching us?'

Louis' voice dropped so only Katie could hear. 'I'm thinking… they are not what we think they are. I'm sure the bird connected with me, warning me of the dangers in the tunnels. Warning or not, I couldn't leave you.' He squeezed her shoulder. 'I love you, Katie. And I hope the angels can hear my inner prayer for us.'

Katie laid her head on his shoulder. 'I love you too. For eternity. And I also pray that the angels will help us, with all my heart.'

Champ came alongside, flopping for a moment and nuzzling at Louis arm. 'Not to be left out, hey, boy? We love you too.'

Whether it was a trick of the light, Louis wasn't sure, but suddenly the moor looked sharper, brighter; the moss green was singing with purple-pink heather. The wildlife that lived on the moor were suddenly active. Rabbits were cheekily raising their heads from in the grass, before bouncing off with their white cottontails disappearing in the undergrowth.

Champ, of course, noticed the sudden movements and wanted to play. He was off like a greyhound out of the trap and was through the barrier and running on the moor, playing what looked like hide and seek with the rabbits.

Louis was open–mouthed and on his feet. How had that happened? How did Champ get through.

The voice of the red kite brought him back to a new vision where the stag and bird had stood. The bird had transformed into an angel, with a face of such light and brightness that Louis could hardly see.

'Well, are you coming?'

Louis tried to shield his eyes from the face by looking at the angel's feet. He saw what seemed like folded wings around the form; the tips of the feathers were tinted red.

'Let me help you. The light can seem overpowering until you get used to us.'

Without another word, there was a further transformation. The bird was back, nodding its head as if to confirm the message.

Louis helped Katie to her feet and very warily walked from the kingdom to the moor. Nothing held them back. Smiling at the rescue, the joy in their souls was exquisite. Their feet almost floated as they walked on the spongy heather, towards what could only be two immortals in the guise of animals, thought Louis.

'We have watched you for a long time; and we have helped where we could. You are children of the chosen, of light. Now you have come home.'

'Home?'

'You both refused it when you passed, but we know you have always longed for the place that some call heaven – which is only one of its many names that include Nirvana, Valhalla, Avalon. It was yours as soon as you asked for our help. Massie will be waiting for you. He's a good soul.'

'What will happen to Malkira and the kingdom?'

A different voice answered. The stag, striking the ground with his hoof, seemed irritated by the question.

'Why do you care about the kingdom? It has served its purpose. It allowed you both a place to share your love. As for Malkira, his world will carry on in its darkness. Some souls will never love or see the light: that is the sadness of man.'

'I care because I created the kingdom.'

'Ah! Not so. You were given a gift and you used it well. The carving was outstanding in all you did. But create a kingdom? I think not. We saw your fate, all of it, even this, now. We gave it to you, for your spell in the two worlds was to last many mortal years. The kingdom will stay behind the veil. It may even be used again, but for now it will only exist for the creatures that live there.'

Strangely, it was a great comfort to Louis to know that it would still exist.

'Come now, let us escort you to your ever after.'

The five of them turned to the horizon. The stag led the troupe; the bird was a speck in the sky and must have been already home when they were only halfway across the moor. Louis and Katie walked steadily, hand in hand, towards the golden light. Champ had returned to Louis' side having chased but not caught a rabbit and ran at his heels. Now, he behaved himself impeccably and ignored the few cottontails that presented themselves. Instead, he stayed with the steady stride of Louis, that was taking them home.

64

Julia opened the door of the Eden Room; it was her first job of her day to change the linen and clean the room after the last guest had checked out. She gathered up the dirty sheets and pillowcases and pushed them into the laundry bag before making up the bed. Ten minutes later, the bed was dressed, and a feeling of calm had settled over the room. After smoothing down the gold bedspread, Julia stretched her back out, stepped back to admire the bed. It was such a lovely touch and complemented the carving that Doris loved so much.

The bed had seen some strange things in that room: attacks, both mortal, and spiritual and she herself had witnessed Louis and Kate coming from their kingdom from behind the headboard to fight the evil. She had seen angels and demons at war with each other, and a husband abusing his wife before Debs stepped in. A chill went down her back as those memories from September, just three months ago, came back to life in her mind.

What a September it had been, with so many secrets given up and shared, some good, some bad. Would she ever get over finding out that the obnoxious womaniser Carl was her biological father? That had been a shocking revelation. She closed her eyes at the thought, and shivered, despite feeling the winter sun, coming through the window, blessing her face.

The rocking chair still stood by the window. It wouldn't hurt to sit for a minute and sort her thoughts out. The gentle rock the chair made, as she sat, reminded her of how she missed seeing the old man – her pipe-smoking ghost as she thought of him, who always left the smell of his tobacco behind. He hadn't been back since that fateful day when she had found Carl attacking his wife Sandra in that bed she had just made. Julia closed her eyes and remembered the scene.

This room knew light and dark, good and evil; they had danced their dance in it in a furious fight. In the end, good had won, and the angels had cleansed the room of evil. It had had two doors, besides the one she held the key to: two doorways to other planes, a gateway to the underworld, which she had seen closed and sealed by angels to keep the darkness out and one that led to Louis' kingdom and light behind the headboard.

Fate had brought Carl to the Royal and he had been a sort of catalyst in the whole sad business.

Carl was all the things she hated: egotistical, rude, and cruel, a taker, and a bully. With her gift of sight, she had watched as he was possessed by a devil and, through his arrogance, had died only to become one of the demon's slaves. What a comeuppance. Sandra, Julia was pleased to say, had recovered from her ordeal, and had a new lease of life. And because of Debs, Sandra had become a friend to both of them. Julia had learned that Carl had raped Debs when she was a child, misused her, just as he had Sandra, and of course she, Julia had been the product of his lust. He deserved all that had come to him. What goes around, comes around, so it is said. And she was glad he was no longer here. He had been evil and easily corrupted by Malkira. Peas in a pod.

In a way, the happenings of that fateful day had completed her. She shrugged at the memory. Imagine living and working, and sharing a bedroom with a woman who had become her best friend, who had accidently, in a late-night confession, told her about her baby, Annie. The thought caused goosebumps to flash up her arms and a smile touched her lips. Annie: the name she had discarded because it brought such bad memories. Julia was her name now, her choice, the name she chose to start afresh after leaving the orphanage. Debs understood that. The name

Annie belonged in the past, in the pain of her history. Julia was the name for her future, and she intended her future to be happy, and to share it with Debs and Barry. It finished off her story. Blessed with finding her mother, whom she finally knew had not given her up by choice, and had always loved her, Julia had the outcome, the family she had always wanted, at last.

Family. For a moment she felt downcast. Family was what she thought she would have with Nick. She couldn't stop a sigh escaping from her lips, as she opened her eyes to the room again. She nudged herself up out of the chair; it was altogether too comfortable, but work was waiting. Better get on with the cleaning or Doris would be after her. With dusters in her hands, she started on the rocker.

Memories muddled with her thoughts. She had worked with Barbara in the bedrooms, her best friend. A wistful smile crossed her face; best friend indeed. Barbara had stolen her boyfriend. She didn't mind about it anymore. Yes, it had been painful and there had been a lot of tears, until she realised that Nick would never stay true to Barbara. He would move on to fresh fields, as he had with her. Well, he and Barbara deserved each other. He had a roving eye and couldn't be trusted. For a moment, she felt sorry for Barbara, but only for a moment. She wondered if their friendship had ever meant anything more than enabling Barbara to get close to Nick. She didn't know, but she had moved on, away from that hurt and now she could see that the breakup had saved her from a very unhappy marriage.

Moving around the room with spray polish and the duster, another smile crossed her face. A week ago, she had bumped into the new delivery man from the brewery. Barry knew him, of course – didn't he know everybody? – and he introduced him to her. Paul was very attractive, tallish with brilliant blue eyes. His voice had the same twang to it as Barry's, lyrical and warm; she liked it. Their eyes had met without shyness and that contact said more than words ever could. Delivery day was tomorrow, and her heart leapt with a small thrill running through her. It was strange; that excitement was never as strong when she was with Nick, but now she fairly tingled with expectation.

Everything had worked out well at the Royal. Her mother Debs and Barry were going to tie the knot, and she was excited for them. Barry was a good man, and she could call him father with a true heart, because he had always treated her with the kindness a father would have done. She felt doubly blessed.

Thinking about marriage, the air in the Royal was full of wedding plans. Julia chuckled as she polished the chest of drawers. Only that morning, Doris had declared that this room was going to be her marriage quarters, and it wouldn't be open to guests ever again. It had been Doris' way of telling the staff that she and Harry were going to wed. She wasn't going to make a fuss in its announcement. She had never worn her heart on her sleeve, and was not sentimental, but Julia knew that Doris had a big heart and knew how to love. Harry was a lucky man, but then Doris was lucky too, for anyone who had the sight to see, could see he worshiped the ground she walked on.

Most of the dusting had been done, she gave herself another stretch and viewed the work she had already done. Pleased with the results, she turned to the headboard; it was the last on the list and her favourite task. Upsetting the pillows to get to the wood, Julia pulled out a clean duster from her apron and fumbled with the polish's lid that always seemed to get stuck when she was nearly finished. Finally, straightened, she began at the top of the headboard, enjoying the feel of the wood under her fingers and getting into the nooks and crannies that hid the dust. The sun, in the centre, started her journey, her fingers following the sunrays' path to edges of the wooden world. Next came the tree, with its widespread crown that was filled with different fruits, from different seasons. It thrilled her: if only there were such trees the world, she thought they would surely benefit mankind. She especially liked one apple that had a small stamp of a butterfly on it. She had noticed that the wooden sculptures in the dining room had the same mark when she cleaned them; no one else knew she had kept it to herself. She knew about ghosts, but how could she explain that the Louis, whom everyone knew and loved before he died, had somehow existed centuries ago and had carved the bed. Only she knew for sure. If anyone else noticed, she would say that Louis adopted the mark out of respect for the carver and leave it at that.

She was somewhat surprised when she finally got to the images of the lovers. She had thought so many times how lifelike the faces were, but today, although the portraits were good, something was lost in the expression. As the soft yellow fabric passed over the faces, they didn't seem to be quite the same images. She took a closer look; she had dusted them many times but there was a subtle difference, somehow. Why was it that she suddenly wanted to reach out to Louis? She remembered she hadn't seen the old man nor any sign of Louis or Katie for months. Julia concentrated, pushing her gift through the headboard into the kingdom.

'Louis, are you there?' Only an emptiness played back to her. She tried again, but there was nothing to connect to. Julia scanned the headboard again, and noticed another discrepancy: down at the man's feet, there appeared to be a gap. Surely a dog had laid there? She rubbed the place with her duster, as though trying to bring the small relief back to the surface of the wood, as if it had melted into the picture. She felt foolish but that carving of the dog was missing, disappeared.

The headboard had lost life from its wood. It was still a wonderful carving, but somehow a little soul was gone from it.

Julia puffed the pillows and straightened the gold bedspread for a second time that day. She didn't know whether to be happy or sad. Perhaps both. Sad because she would miss them being there, but happy, because it could only mean they had passed on to another plane for the rest of their souls' journey. Louis had been a sort of guardian angel that perhaps only she and Debs knew, but that was enough. He had filled the Royal with a special light. Kindness and love were never lost. He had been there for her and protected her from Carl; she had a lot to be grateful for. Happy won the day.

Would she ever see them again? Perhaps in her next life but that was still way off, God willing. Tomorrow was another day, and then she remembered Paul. Oh, yes, tomorrow was another day.

Nothing really ends or begins. We just move forward with time, doing the best we can with life and love.

Also by the author

Also by the author